The
ROAD
BACK

Also by Di Morrissey

The Winter Sea

Di MORRISSEY

The ROAD BACK

St. Martin's Griffin ☙ New York

THE ROAD BACK. Copyright © 2014 by Lady Byron Pty Ltd. All rights reserved. Printed in the United States of America. For information, address St. Martin's Press, 175 Fifth Avenue, New York, N.Y. 10010.

www.stmartins.com

Chapter One illustration courtesy of The Amazing People Club®

Other internal images from Shutterstock

Library of Congress Cataloging-in-Publication Data

Names: Morrissey, Di.
Title: The road back : a novel / Di Morrissey.
Description: First U.S. edition. l New York : St. Martin's Griffin, 2016. l "2014
Identifiers: LCCN 2015037878l ISBN 9781250051202 (trade paperback) l
    ISBN 9781466852068 (e-book)
Subjects: LCSH: Fathers and daughters—Fiction. l Teenage girls—Fiction. l
    Domestic fiction. l BISAC: FICTION / Contemporary Women. l FICTION /
    Family Life.
Classification: LCC PR9619.3.M67 R63 2016 l DDC 823/.914—dc23
LC record available at http://lccn.loc.gov/2015037878

Our books may be purchased in bulk for promotional, educational, or business use. Please contact your local bookseller or the Macmillan Corporate and Premium Sales Department at (800) 221-7945, extension 5442, or by e-mail at MacmillanSpecialMarkets@macmillan.com.

First published in Australia by Pan Macmillan Australia Pty Ltd

First U.S. Edition: January 2016

10 9 8 7 6 5 4 3 2 1

Dedication:

Peter B. Morrissey, US Peace Corps,
Sumatra, Indonesia, 1963–65.

And our beautiful new granddaughter,
Ulani Summer Devi Morrissey, who brings
joy and laughter to us all.

Acknowledgements

With love to Boris, who is always beside me, loving, staunch and caring.

My children, Gabrielle and Nick, and your beautiful children. I am so proud of you both.

Thanks are not enough to my friend and editor, Liz Adams, who is part of my life – 24/7!

To all at Pan Macmillan: Ross Gibb, Samantha Sainsbury, Katie Crawford, Jace Armstrong, Hayley Crandell and Danielle Walker.

Thanks to Ian Robertson, the lawyer with a sense of humour!

Also many thanks to:

Professor Tim Lindsey, Malcolm Smith, Professor of Asian Law and Director of the Centre for Indonesian Law, Islam and Society, at the University of Melbourne. My good friend, Kadek Adi. Also, George Negus and Kirsty Cockburn; Jim Sweeney, Bellingen Museum; Brett Iggulden and Patrick Cairns. My teen muses – Shak and Dana.

Beau Riley, computer whiz, who solves my technology glitches no matter where in the world I am.

Suggested viewing to learn about what happened in Indonesia during the 1965 coup – the Oscar-nominated documentary, *The Act of Killing* by Joshua Oppenheimer and Christine Cynn.

The
ROAD
BACK

I

CHRIS BAXTER STOOD IN line, holding his boarding pass and listening to the Australian accents of the other passengers as they made their way towards the Qantas flight that would take them from Los Angeles to Sydney. As he moved through the business class boarding entrance on this last leg of his journey home, he felt a sense of loss and sadness at leaving behind a country he was only just beginning to understand.

He'd arrived in Washington DC three years ago from his previous assignment in London. He'd enjoyed his time in the British capital, especially living near his sister, Kate. Arriving in the States, he had expected to find familiarity and egalitarianism, but instead he'd discovered a land of more complexity and contradiction than he could ever have imagined. From the silly and superficial to the talented and brilliant, from the liberal and tolerant to conservative fundamentalist, from the generous and open-hearted to the tight-lipped and mean-spirited, from the poor, marginalised and uneducated to the bigots, bureaucrats and brains, America was the ultimate jigsaw puzzle, a land seemingly made up of dozens of different countries. He'd loved every moment of his assignment as a foreign correspondent and was disappointed that the Australian newspaper he worked for had decided not to extend his term.

He smiled at the flight attendant standing at the door of the plane and showed him his boarding pass.

'Good evening, Mr Baxter. Upstairs on your right. I like the jacket,' the flight attendant said, indicating Chris's well-worn Schott leather jacket.

'A souvenir,' Chris replied.

'And the Harley? Is it in the hold?'

'Afraid not,' replied Chris with a rueful smile.

'Well, you have got the look if not the accent,' said the flight attendant before turning to greet the next passenger.

Chris settled his lanky frame into his seat, hoping no one would sit beside him. It had been a long while since he'd flown business class. Trinity Press didn't stretch to such extravagances these days, but he'd used his frequent flyer points to upgrade for the long-haul flight.

'A drink, Mr Baxter?' asked an attractive flight attendant, pausing in the aisle beside him.

'I'll take the champagne, thanks.'

'Have you enjoyed your time in the US?'

'Yes, I've been working there as a journalist for three years. I'm heading back home now for a bit of a break. Looking forward to spending time with my daughter. She's growing up so quickly.' The flight attendant nodded and smiled understandingly. She poured a glass of champagne and placed it neatly on a napkin in front of him.

'And then you'll be back?'

'Actually, I've finished up in America.'

'That's a pity. Are you going to stay in Australia?'

He shook his head. 'I'm not sure. I might end up somewhere in Asia.'

'Well, enjoy your drink. Champagne always feels like a celebration, doesn't it? I'll be back with the dinner menu shortly.'

It didn't feel like a celebration. Chris sighed and ran his hand through his thick hair. While he was looking forward to seeing his daughter and his mother, he still thought about all that he was leaving behind. As Washington DC was the political hub of the world he had relished his political assignments. But he'd also had a knack for finding off-beat stories and, whenever he'd had the chance, which was not as frequently as he would have liked, he'd headed out on the road in his five-year-old Lexus to track them down. Over time he had managed to cover conventions, rallies, quirky beauty pageants, agriculture events, rodeos, disasters, and life in city slums as well as rural and suburban small-town USA, which, for him, made up the fabric of modern America. He'd enjoyed the experiences, as they had given him a much deeper insight into the country and these stories had proved to be popular with Australian readers.

But even as he regretted leaving the States, Chris knew that no matter what sources he'd found and contacts he'd made there, he remained an outsider, for the foreign press corps never had the advantages of local media on home turf. And while he had made American friendships and socialised with his colleagues as well as members of the international press corps, his nomadic life had meant he hadn't fostered deep relationships. He guessed that some of the women in his circle had been attracted to him but his work had precluded his making any lasting connections.

And after a painful and expensive divorce some years ago, he had no intention of leaping into another commitment any time soon.

Chris finished his champagne and kicked off his shoes, glad the seat beside him remained empty. In the oasis of the upstairs cabin he pulled out his book, but when a flight attendant came by with magazines and newspapers he put it aside and asked for a copy of *The Economist* and *The Wall Street Journal*.

He quickly became absorbed in a lengthy article on the continuing Middle East negotiations as the plane began to taxi along the runway, then he leaned back and closed his eyes as the lights of Los Angeles airport shrank below him.

As the plane began to level out, Chris's thoughts turned to his fourteen-year-old daughter, Megan, and he realised how much he was looking forward to spending time with her. He hadn't seen her since his last trip home nearly twelve months ago. He followed Megan on her Facebook page – where he learned more about her than in the emails they exchanged – and they Skyped each other as often as they could. As far as he could tell, Megan seemed to be going through a phase in which she swung between behaving like a ten-year-old one minute and a twenty-year-old the next. As much as he loved his daughter, he had some sympathy for his ex-wife, Jill. Living with a teenager would not be a stroll in the park. Megan was coming to stay with him a few days after he got back. He made up his mind that he would take Megan somewhere special, just the two of them. Smiling to himself, he returned to his magazine and the eternal problems of the Middle East.

He had nearly finished reading the magazines when the flight attendant put a linen placemat on his tray table and offered to top up his champagne.

'I think I'd like to switch to a good red. What Australian wines do you have?' he asked.

She handed him the dinner menu. 'We have Coonawarra and Hunter Valley reds. The main course is lobster or duck.'

'Hard choices,' he said, smiling. 'Thank you. I'll go for the Hunter Shiraz, and the duck sounds good.'

After the delicious meal, he leaned back and closed his eyes, enjoying the luxury of stretching out his long legs along the extended seat. Enjoy the next few hours in limboland, he told himself.

Although he had some leave up his sleeve, Chris was curious as to what plans Trinity Press had for him. He knew that when he returned to work, he'd probably hit the ground running. The Bangkok office was up for grabs, and he was fairly sure that it would be offered to him. He thought he'd like that, but he also knew that he wasn't fussy; as long as the destination was abroad, he'd go anywhere.

He slept well on the flight, in as near to a horizontal position as he could achieve with his long limbs and, refreshed and enjoying a coffee after breakfast, he watched the sunrise as the plane made its approach into Sydney. The sight of the morning light gleaming on the sails of the Opera House, and the arms of the two headlands embracing the magnificent harbour with its bridge connecting the two sides of the city, reminded him again what a seductive city Sydney was.

Once he had cleared customs and immigration, he caught a taxi to his tiny apartment, which was in a three-storey building on a narrow street in Neutral Bay, within walking distance of the Neutral Bay Wharf. The tenant, whose rent had helped pay the mortgage on the one-bedroom unit, had vacated it some days before, and the place looked clean, if somewhat impersonal.

A couple of hours later, after he'd unpacked his suitcases, he walked up to Military Road. He was pleased to see that some of his favourite shops were still in business and he went into the supermarket for some basic provisions. Shopping finished, he sat at an outdoor table of a small coffee shop which served excellent espresso. With the sun warming his back and a fresh light breeze ruffling his hair, he admitted to himself that he was glad to be home.

*

The following Saturday, Chris grinned broadly as Megan walked towards him from the Neutral Bay bus stop. He saw how she'd grown taller and realised that her body was filling out. She was carrying a large backpack and wearing baggy floral shorts and a midriff top, earphones around her neck, black lace canvas sneakers minus the laces and, as she got closer, he could see daisies glued to her fingernails. Her brown hair with its natural coppery highlights was twisted into a side French braid. She was wearing pale lip gloss and eye shadow. Megan had a slightly quirky look which was fresh and appealing. He held out his arms and she gave him a big hug. Chris held her tight and affectionately kissed the top of her head.

'Hi, Dad,' said Megan, her bright eyes shining.

'How's my girl?'

'Good. Are we going to have something to eat? I'm starving.'

'If you like,' he said, taking her bag and guiding her down the street towards a café. 'Sorry that you had to get the bus to Neutral Bay. It's a bit of a long haul from Newport, but I haven't got a car yet. Once I get settled, maybe you could help me buy one.'

'That would be cool, Dad,' said Megan as they stopped in front of the café.

'This coffee shop is pretty good for food. Will it do?' Megan nodded and they went inside and ordered a coffee for Chris and some salmon sushi and a fruit smoothie for Megan. Taking a seat, Chris smiled again at his daughter. She had changed but she was still his little girl. Their orders arrived promptly and Megan tucked in with gusto.

'Have a piece of sushi, Dad, it's really good,' said Megan as her father sipped his coffee.

'Okay, thanks. I like your outfit. I'm a bit out of date with your taste in clothes these days. Does your mother buy things for you, or do you pick them out yourself?'

She wrinkled her nose. 'No, Mum hardly ever buys clothes for me. We have *veeery* different ideas. I shop with my girlfriends when I've saved enough pocket money. If Mum comes with me it usually ends up in an argument. I wouldn't be seen dead in some of the things she thinks are appropriate,' she said with an elaborate sigh.

Having put a toe in the water, Chris ventured in deeper. 'So how are you and your mum getting on? Have things calmed down since the wedding?'

Megan shrugged her shoulders and said wearily, 'No. Oscar and Ned drive me crazy. Mum is trying to be so nice to them, but I can tell they're driving her nuts, too. The boys are really messy, so Mum makes me keep my things tidy. She uses me as an example and makes a big show about how perfect my room is, but I hate them even looking in my space. The boys don't like me, and I feel the same about them. And I have to help clear up the kitchen and do other jobs to show them what they're supposed to do, but really they think cleaning is a girl thing. I don't think it's very fair.'

'Well, the twins are only, what? Eight? Ten? Doesn't their father insist they help? Put the rubbish out or something?' said Chris, frowning.

'No way!' said Megan, taking another bite of sushi. 'And would you believe Trevor has the cheek to ask me to fetch things for him? I'm not his servant. Dad, it's awful. I hate it.'

'Whoa, calm down,' said Chris, placing his hand on her arm. 'Look, this is a big adjustment for all of you. I know it's not easy, sweetie, but if your mother is happy and this is what she's chosen for her life, you have to try to be happy for her. Support her.'

Megan stared at him as if he had just spoken in Swahili. 'Dad. C'mon. Think about it. Trevor Franks is a sitcom joke of a stepfather with two spoiled, stupid brat sons. It's a teenager's worst nightmare. My own horror show. This is Mum's new life. Not mine. I didn't get any say in it.'

'Sweetie, your mother discussed marrying Trevor with you,' said Chris gently. 'She talked to me about it. She wants you all to be part of a proper family, especially as I'm away so much. And the boys are included in that. Maybe they're as unhappy about this adjustment as you are.'

'They're not unhappy. They have each other and they can make my life hell. Why would they be unhappy?' Megan gave him a thunderous look.

Chris was at a loss as to how to deal with this outburst but managed to say, 'Listen, Megan, sweetheart, give it a chance. Not everything can be bad. Now that I'm back, at least for a while, you can come and spend weekends with me. I know my place is very small and you'll have to sleep on the sofa, or I will. But it's only for a night or two at a time. And you still like school and you seem to have a busy social life, don't you?'

'I'd die without my girlfriends.'

Chris suppressed a smile. 'Well, it's great you have such good mates.'

'You have to meet Ruby. Can she come over to your place sometime, please?' said Megan, a more cheerful note entering her voice.

'Is she your bestie?'

Megan laughed. 'Are you trying to keep up with the lingo, Dad? Not easy, 'cause it changes every week. Some new word comes out.'

'It's all a foreign language to me, honey. I'm just going inside to get a glass of water. Can I get you one, too?'

When Chris returned with two glasses of water and put them on the table, Megan looked up from her phone.

'Texting a friend?' her father asked.

'Yes, Ruby.' She held up the phone. '*Chilling with my dad. Don't think he knows he's still got the looks. Some grey hairs starting. LOL. He wears bad American shirts. Wants to meet you.*'

'Cheeky possum. I like my Yank shirt.' Chris laughed, but he was pleased that Megan wanted to share her friends with him.

When they were finished they went back to Chris's flat for the afternoon. Chris checked his email on his laptop on the dining room table. He'd got in touch with his old friends and colleagues telling them he was back in Australia waiting for his next assignment and fishing around for news and gossip about the local media scene. Megan lolled on the sofa listening to the Thundamentals on her iPod while updating her four closest girlfriends with the details of what had happened so far that day on her smart phone.

A couple of hours later, Chris tapped her on the shoulder. 'Can you hear me? Where do you want to go for dinner? What sort of food would you like?'

Megan pulled the earphones from her ears. 'Dinner? I'm easy. What do you like?'

'I'd like some good Asian. How about we go to Chinatown?'

'That sounds really cool. I've never been there. Way too far from Newport. I'll go and change.'

Chris was pleasantly surprised when Megan emerged from the bedroom dressed in a short cotton floral dress. She'd paid a lot of attention to her hairdo and accessories. However, Chris was a bit startled that she had completed the outfit with a pair of multi-coloured basketball shoes.

'You look lovely, except perhaps for the shoes. What happened to sandals?'

'Dad, these are Converse! They call them Chuckies after the basketball player. Anyway, sandals are so, so . . . sixties.'

'Got it,' said Chris humbly. 'You look terrific.'

They trawled through Chinatown, deciding which restaurant looked good. The narrow streets were crowded, full of people enjoying themselves.

'I love the palace places with all the red and gold,' Megan commented.

'Okay. You choose.'

Chris followed his daughter up the stairs of one of the large restaurants and into an immense room already filled with families chattering in Cantonese. As they were shown to a table, they dodged teams of waiters carrying huge trays of dishes with appetising aromas. Taking their seats, Megan's eyes popped as she leafed through the lengthy menu.

'Dad, this menu is huge. There are pages and pages.'

'What would you like to do, Megan? Have a dish for yourself, or share dishes with me?'

'I'd like to share.'

She took her time choosing the dishes she wanted and when they ordered the food she asked for a Sprite, eschewing the jasmine tea.

Chris leaned his chin on his hand and studied her. 'So, Megan. What's next?'

'You mean at school? What do I want to do with my life? Boyfriends? Or Mum and Trevor?'

'Boyfriends? Do you have one? Someone special?' Chris asked, his eyebrows raised.

She smiled at him. 'Chill, Dad. I'm just tuning.'

'Translation, please.'

'Tuning is like a flirtationship. Sort of just having someone to flirt with. A bit more than a friend, but not a relationship.'

'So are you tuning with anyone special?'

'Not at the moment, no one that's serious.'

'And school is fine? I know from your reports that you're a hard worker. Have you given any thought to what you want to do in your final years? I don't expect you to have any clues about a career at this stage, unless there's something that really grabs you. Sometimes it's good to try different things.'

'I tell everyone who asks that I just want to be happy. They like to hear that. Sometimes I say that I want to be a lawyer, but I don't.'

Chris chuckled and shook his head. 'I hated being asked that, too. The other question I hated was, "What's your favourite subject?"'

'Easy. Commerce.'

'Really?' He was surprised.

Then Megan asked, 'Can you come to my next school parents' night? I hate Trevor coming along, even though Mum does all the talking.'

'Sure, honey. I'd like to meet your teachers. I'm glad that you like school. It's meant to be one of the best girls' schools in the area.'

'It's a great school. Everyone is fantastic. It's just a long trip each day from Newport, but I can hang out with my friends and talk about things on the bus.'

'And you like that it's only girls? You wouldn't

11

rather change to a co-ed school that's a bit closer to home?'

Megan shook her head. 'No way, Dad. One of my girlfriends goes to a mixed school and I can see the pros and cons, but I like where I am better.'

'Why is that?'

'She says the girls don't want to show that they're smart and be seen as geeky by getting high science marks or whatever. I think you can take more risks if it's just girls. Who wants to fail or look stupid in front of the boys in the class? And my friend says that if you date a boy from school and then it crashes, everyone knows and it's a big deal. It's good to learn to get along with guys as friends, which would be one good thing about co-ed, but I like all-girl classes. Anyway, we do things like dances at St Peter's, and we put on shows with the boys. We're going to do a combined musical this year as a fundraiser for a school in Myanmar.'

'Are you in this show?'

'Not out the front, but I'm doing backstage stuff, and helping out. I haven't found my true talent yet.' She smiled.

As their first dish arrived, Chris thought, and not for the first time, that Megan was a delight. He was pleased that she seemed so level-headed and he knew that she was very intelligent. Jill had done a good job in raising her. It was just a shame that Megan's life had become so complicated lately.

'Want some noodles?' he asked.

'Wow, all this food looks amazing. Nothing like our local Chinese.' After loading up her plate, Megan continued chatting.

'Dad, did you always want to be a foreign correspondent?'

Chris thought for a moment. 'Well, being a journalist came first, then my ambition was to become a foreign

12

correspondent but it took a process of elimination to get there. It goes back to my love of books and reading and being interested in communications, I think. I used to write and make up my own newspaper when I was six or seven and take it around the neighbourhood. Your grandparents were news fanatics, especially your grandfather. Had the radio on all the time, and when the TV news came on, not a word could be spoken. I guess their interest in what was going on in the world rubbed off on me.'

'Dad, I think it's really cool that you're a foreign correspondent. It's great when I see your name in the paper. I tell all my friends.'

'That's very nice to hear.'

'Yes, they all think you sound very cool. Dad, who were the most important people you met in America?'

'I didn't really get a chance to meet that many,' admitted Chris. 'Foreign correspondents are regarded by the local press as blow-ins and it's not easy to trespass on their patch, but when the Australian Prime Minister was in town, I could get a pass to attend any joint press conferences they had with the President at the White House.'

'Wow! Did you meet President Obama?'

'No, I'm not nearly important enough. I was just in the same room.' Chris smiled.

'That is amazing. He is such a cool dude.'

'I'm glad you think so. Another "cool dude" I did interview, one on one, was Hillary Clinton.'

Megan stared at him. 'No way. Wait till I tell everyone at school about that. How come?'

'She let me conduct an hour-long interview with her. It took months to set up and I didn't think that it would come off, but I did it just before I came back. The story will be in the paper's weekend magazine in a couple of weeks.'

'Fantastic.'

The next lot of dishes arrived and Chris picked up a piece of fried duck with his chopsticks.

'Tell me, have you spoken to Bunny recently?'

Megan tried to follow Chris's chopsticks style but with only partial success as she manoeuvred a piece of duck into her bowl. 'We talk on the phone all the time. And she's even learned to text and she follows me on Facebook. She came down for my birthday a few months ago. When are you going up to visit her? I bet she wants to see you.'

'Yes, the feeling's mutual. I'll go up to see your grandmother as soon as I can. What about Trevor's family, do you get on with them?'

Megan pulled a face. 'God, no! His mother is a dragon and his father's a bogan. Even Mum doesn't encourage family get-togethers.'

'I'm sure everything will work out. Just give it time.'

'That's easy for you to say. I'm under the same roof as them. I so hate it when Mum introduces those brats as my stepbrothers.'

'The school holidays can't be far off. What say we trundle up to Neverend and visit your grandmother then?'

'Yeah, that'd be pretty cool. I love visiting Bunny.'

'I'll raise it with your mother, but I can't see that a visit to your grandmother's would be an issue.'

'It's nice having you home, Dad,' said Megan after a pause.

Chris's heart twisted. He was glad to be home and to spend time with his daughter and he was looking forward to visiting his mother in the house where he'd grown up. These were the two people he loved most. But he felt a twinge of guilt, because he knew that what he wanted more than anything was another overseas posting. His job as a foreign correspondent was busy, fascinating and stimulating. It was the job that he had always dreamed of doing. He reached over and touched Megan's hand. 'It's nice to be with you, too,' he said.

*

The next afternoon, Chris and Megan walked up to the bus stop so that she could get the bus back home to Newport.

'Sorry about not being able to drive you. Do you think that you could come here next weekend and the two of us could go car shopping? You could give me your input as to which you think would be suitable.'

'Really? That would be great. I promise I'll get all my homework done before Saturday, so I can spend the whole weekend with you. See you, Dad.' She hugged him and stepped onto the bus.

As he waved to her and the bus moved along Military Road, Chris reflected on his weekend with Megan. It had been a lot of fun. He was interested in her thoughts, and he enjoyed the ease of her company. She wasn't demanding because she constantly entertained herself with Snapchat and Instagram and whatever other apps she had on her beloved purple phone. He was touched that she was interested in and proud of what he did, but he could also see that Megan's life had become difficult in his absence. Acquiring an instant family when she had been used to being an only child had not been easy for her, and Chris could empathise with her struggle to cope with these changes.

Walking back to his apartment, he thought of the years since his divorce and how he had come to treasure his own space. He liked just pleasing himself and not having to fit in with anyone else. He looked forward to a quiet drink in the evening to digest the hurly-burly of the day and appreciated not having to socialise if he didn't want to. He liked to return to the serenity of his

15

apartment and listen to music, or watch his favourite TV programmes. He suspected he had a reputation as a bit of a loner, but that didn't worry him. When he did seek company it was to feed his curiosity, to discuss current events, ideas and off-beat news, but generally he was content to be on his own. That said, next weekend he would enjoy taking Megan out to look for a new car. It would be fun to decide on one together.

*

A couple of days later, before he was due to report back to the office, Chris decided that he'd look up his old friend and mentor Sam McPhee, who had been his first news editor when he had started out. Even though he was now retired, Mac (as everyone called him) always knew what was going on in the newspaper business and it would be good to catch up.

In a quiet corner of the Black Swan, known to the journos who frequented it as the Mucky Duck, Chris put a schooner of beer in front of Mac and a light lager on the table for himself.

Mac lifted his glass. 'Cheers, Chris. Good to see you.'

'Cheers, Mac. Good to be back, for a while at least.'

The balding former news editor wiped his ginger moustache. 'Have you been into the office yet?' he asked.

Chris settled back in his chair. 'No. I've still got some leave and I wanted a little down time to get the feel of things again. I've spent a bit of one-on-one with my daughter. Do you remember Megan?'

'How old is she now?'

'She see-saws between fourteen and twenty. She looks her age, but sometimes comes across as so much older. Doesn't seem to have discovered boys too seriously at this stage, thank heavens. What were you doing when you were fourteen?'

16

'Trying out for the local cricket team. Didn't know girls existed.'

'Megan seems to be on her mobile phone all the time, mainly texting her friends. I suppose that's the norm these days for teenagers.'

'This generation is going to forget how to speak to each other, but I have to admit that mobile phones are bloody handy things if you're a journalist. So, what's your plan?' Mac raised an eyebrow.

'I've heard a few rumours, but I'm pretty sure I'll get another overseas post. Bangkok is coming up.'

Mac sipped his beer. 'Is that what you want? I suppose overseas postings are easier for you than for a family man. Not as many complications.'

'I want to cover stories that have some meat and for me that means being a foreign correspondent, but I know that newspapers are struggling. A lot have folded in the States. Hell, *The Washington Post* has been bought by Jeff Bezos, Amazon's CEO, for a song, just because he wants to keep the great paper going. So, Mac, I want to find out what you've heard about the local scene, and especially what's happening with Trinity Press. How's it really travelling?'

Mac rubbed his chin. 'Well, Chris, all the Australian papers are having a difficult time. The Murdoch press still carries on more or less as usual, because the papers are cross-subsidised from other News Limited enterprises. But, of course, working for Murdoch means having to toe the party line. Fairfax has been cutting back. As you know, they never recovered from the advent of online advertising. The "rivers of gold" that used to flow from their advertising department have now slowed to a trickle. I hear that the *Herald* is going to expand its online classifieds. Nowadays it's hard to tell what's real news and what a sponsored ad disguised as a story. If you don't get the revenue, you can't afford the staff,' said Mac emphatically.

'I know. I've heard that they let a lot of journos go,' said Chris, swirling his beer.

'It's bloody dreadful. Most of the best journos have gone. Decades of knowledge and experience out the door. 'Course, a lot of them got good redundancy packages and I guess that if you're close to retirement age, that's fine, but if you're not, then it's a worry. Too many journalists looking for too few jobs. Lot of them try freelancing, but it pays a pittance.' Mac's mouth twisted in a grimace. 'If you write a thousand words and they only use five hundred, that's all you get paid for, and if it's not used at all, no money, even if you've been working for days. Makes you sick. Even working fulltime you don't just file a story and that's it. You have to do an online version, and respond to tweets, comments and blogs. Fourteen-hour days and if you don't produce, out the door you go, and there are plenty of others waiting out there to take your place.'

Chris started to say something, but Mac, now wound up, barely paused for breath before he continued.

'Of course today technology has taken over. Where once a TV journalist travelled with a producer, cameraman and sound man, now they're a one-man band. They have to shoot digital footage, record the sound, do a piece to camera, edit it on a laptop then upload the story from wherever they can get a signal. Quite a job.'

Chris frowned. 'There are some journos who do well, though,' he said cautiously.

'Yeah, but that's usually when they have already made their name. Some well-known celeb journos can make big money, so they get a producer and a researcher plus a swank house up the coast. All for doing half an hour a week on the box. The rest are scratching. Even worse, media now relies on contributor's content. They get academics, business people or other specialists to write articles and the trouble is that readers don't know their agendas. We need committed journos like you to act as community watchdogs.'

'What about radio? Some big names there make a fortune.'

'No money in commercial radio, either,' Mac said, shaking his head. 'The bean counters that run the stations want to pay their personalities, their stars, the big bucks because they bring in the revenue, but the same can't be said for the journalists. They are seen as a liability that cost the station money.' Mac jabbed a finger at Chris. 'And so they are paid accordingly. Of course the ABC still does a great job, but it never has enough money and everyone there is expected to multi-task. Doesn't leave them much time to seek out the really interesting stories. Journalism is now reduced to the twenty-four-hour news cycle delivered in quick bites. God forbid that someone out there might want to know what is actually going on. Journos don't have time to do anything in-depth, so it comes down to "he said, she said" stories. Spin doctors. Gonzo journalism. And y'know what? The public is less informed. In fact, they're actually misled a lot of the time. I once thought I'd like to teach journalism. Get youngsters fired up to go and find the truth. But now I think, why bother? There are so few jobs out there for journalists, and as for finding the truth, they are way too time-poor for a luxury like that.'

Chris was taken aback by Mac's bitterness. 'Take it easy, Mac. You wouldn't have done anything else. I'll get us both another drink. Beer still okay with you?' Mac nodded and sat back in his chair.

Chris returned from the bar with the two drinks and placed a beer carefully in front of his former editor.

Mac smiled and thanked him. 'The business has changed,' he said, calmer now. 'Technology might be the means of delivery but it's still the mind and the intellect that gets to the source, analyses, and makes it all digestible to the readers. I like the challenge. You're younger than me. How old are you now?'

'I'll be forty-three this year,' said Chris.

Mac grinned. 'Still got a good career ahead of you. You did a great job in Washington, so I can't see that you'll have any trouble getting that Bangkok posting you're after. Might depend on how you get on with the new chief operating officer, the Pommy bloke. I hear he's a penny pincher like all the others. Cutting back on the Sydney staff in a big way. Still, there's only a staff of one in Bangkok, he can't cut that back,' Mac said with a wink. 'You'll be right.'

'I actually haven't met the new bloke. He's only had the job a few months and I've just got back to Oz,' said Chris.

'Heard he does it all by the book. Even records his interviews with the staff. And you have to make an appointment. None of this tapping on the door and walking into the office, so I'm told.'

'Sounds a bit draconian. I'd better ring the office this afternoon,' said Chris. They continued chatting for another hour, enjoying each other's company. It was great to reconnect with an old friend. Chris knew, however, that Mac was prone to melodrama. The industry had changed and he felt sorry for all the journos affected by the changes in the media. He was relieved that he probably had a plum position to go to. Nevertheless, Mac didn't make the office sound all that friendly and Chris hoped his meeting with his editor would go well.

*

'I asked Megan to come car shopping with me, so is it all right for her to come over again this weekend?' Chris asked his ex-wife on the phone that evening.

Jill was noncommittal. 'I'll ask her. So, if you're buying a car, does that mean you're staying here?' she said in clipped tones.

'I could be in Sydney for a few months, until my new posting is settled. I can use public transport but I suddenly feel the need for a car. I would also like to take Megan up to see Mum as soon as the holidays start,' he said.

Jill sniffed. 'Megan has a very busy social life. She may not want to go to the country to see her grandmother.'

'Well, we'll see what Megan says, shall we?' said Chris, rather tersely.

'So where are you going off to next time?'

'I'm hoping that it will be Bangkok.'

'Lucky you. Some of us just have to stay and raise a family,' said Jill, with some bitterness in her voice.

Chris ignored the comment. 'If you could ask Megan to let me know if she still wants to come and check out my shortlist of cars, that would be great. Thanks, Jill.'

Chris hung up. He didn't want to get into another argument with his ex-wife. Jill had wanted custody of Megan and since he travelled and worked overseas so much, Chris had never contested it. But Jill always liked to let Chris know that, in her opinion, she'd got the short end of the stick.

The next weekend Chris took a photo on Megan's phone of her sitting behind the wheel of an expensive European sports car so that she could send it to her friends.

'Now, let's try to narrow this down. It can't be too big because of the parking space at the apartment, but it needs to be comfortable enough for a long drive and not a huge gas guzzler.'

'So we're not getting the Maserati, Dad?' Megan laughed. 'Okay. Do we get to drive the new car home?'

'No, I can't get it until I take out a loan. I certainly don't have enough to pay cash. Maybe in a few days I'll be able to pick it up. You'll still have to get the bus home tomorrow, I'm afraid.'

He was glad to see her laugh. She'd been somewhat reserved since he'd met her earlier at the bus stop. He felt something was bothering her, but didn't like to probe. Leaving the dealership, he asked her, 'What do you fancy for lunch?'

'Fish and chips. But nice ones. Not just in paper,' Megan replied.

Chris grinned. 'Great idea. Haven't had any for ages. We could get the bus to Balmoral, or we can eat at the little fish place around the corner. You choose.'

'The corner place. It looks cute. Besides, I've had enough of bus rides.'

'Exactly what I was thinking,' said Chris. 'How about we see what the place around the corner has on offer.'

Megan chose a booth in the corner of the small funky eatery while Chris ordered at the counter. The food arrived quickly but Megan didn't look too enthusiastic about it.

'This was a good choice . . . flaky fish, crisp batter, yummy mayonnaise. Verjuice instead of vinegar,' Chris said brightly.

Megan nodded, eating slowly. He wondered if she was savouring the food or working up to something. He topped up her mineral water.

'Are things okay at school?' he ventured.

Megan sighed and pushed her food around her plate. 'Yeah. The same old, same old.'

'Well, that's good. So what's bothering you?'

She looked at him, then put down her fork, and he was shocked to see a tear roll down her cheek.

'Megan, honey. What is it? Are you all right?' He reached across and touched her hand.

She shook her head. 'It's Mum and Trevor.'

Chris's heart sank. 'What's happened?'

'It's Trevor's job,' Megan said, her voice shaking.

'He's quit? Been fired?'

'Worse. He's being transferred. To Perth.'

As Chris stared at her, the news sinking in, Megan burst into a flood of tears.

'I don't want to go to Perth! It's on the other side of the planet. I don't want to leave my friends, my school! Dad, please . . .'

'Hey, hey, slow down.' He handed her a paper napkin to dry her tears. 'Now, run this past me again slowly. Trevor is going to Perth and he's planning to move your mum and you kids over there, too. What does your mother say?'

Megan sniffed and dabbed her eyes. 'Not much. He says we're going. We all have to go. Sell the house and move to Perth! What am I going to do? I'll die over there.'

Chris was furious Jill hadn't mentioned this, given him some warning. 'When did all this come about? I can't believe he'd uproot you all, and sell up. I mean, it must be a huge job opportunity.'

'I heard them talking. It's a big deal, some supervisor thing. It's not fair that I have to go because of his stupid job!'

'Now calm down, it sounds like early days. It can't be all decided yet.'

'No, it's pretty certain. They won't leave me here, and I will not go over there. My whole life is here!' Megan's eyes filled with tears again.

'Megan, I don't think you have a choice, if that's what they want to do . . .'

'Why should I have to suffer for Trevor's dumb idea? Leave my life, my friends, my school? There's no way, Dad.' She shook her head and wiped her eyes with the backs of her hands. They sat in silence for a moment or two. Then she looked up at him. 'Hey, what about this? I stay here, with you.'

Chris hesitated. 'Megan, I don't think that's possible.'

Tears coursed down Megan's face again and Chris moved to her side of the booth and put his arm over her shoulders, glad there weren't any other diners near them.

'The problem is that my next posting is very likely going to be in Bangkok, sweetheart. I have a very demanding job, I'll be away a lot working on assignments in other parts of Asia, and I certainly don't want you living in Bangkok without me. Anyway, your mother would never let you come. It's impossible.'

'Can't you stay here, in Sydney? Do you have to go to Bangkok?' asked Megan, looking at him pleadingly.

'It's my job, darling,' said Chris weakly. He didn't like where this discussion was leading. 'You could board at your school,' he suggested, wondering as he said it from where all the extra money for that idea would come. When Megan didn't instantly shoot the suggestion down in flames, he added, 'Listen, it's not a decision we have to make immediately. Let's not spoil our day together.'

'Even though my whole life is about to be ruined,' she countered.

Later, after he'd put Megan on her bus back home, Chris decided to take a long walk to think about her news. He walked towards St Leonards Park, because he always enjoyed the relative peace of this North Sydney oasis. He especially loved its cricket ground, with its old Edwardian grandstands rescued from the Sydney Cricket Ground which had made the oval one of the most picturesque places to play cricket in the entire country. He was amused to see a lone bagpiper standing under one of the large palm trees, practising his instrument above the noise from the adjacent freeway. Chris sighed and kicked at a tuft of grass. He'd hated to see Megan so upset and he had to agree with her that she had good cause. He wouldn't want to be taken away from an enjoyable and secure life to move to the other side of the country with a stepfamily he didn't like. He felt very concerned about her future. How was she going to cope with it all?

Suddenly he felt gripped with anxiety. Years ago, when he was first starting out as a journalist, he had done a series of stories on the homeless kids that hung around Kings Cross. Runaways, kids with drug and alcohol problems, kids with nowhere else to go who relied on the soup kitchen, shelters and the Wayside Chapel as they drifted aimlessly, lolled in doorways, zipped up and down on skateboards or sat on the edge of the gutter, stunned and zombie-like, oblivious to passing cars. For a moment he feared this could happen to Megan, but then decided that such a thought was nonsense and he relaxed. Megan had two parents who loved her and cared for her welfare. As he walked to the edge of St Leonards Park and marvelled at the view of the magnificent harbour and the Sydney skyline, he pondered Megan's situation. She was really unhappy and he had to sort out some kind of solution. He decided he would call Jill as soon as he got home and discuss the situation with her.

*

'But Jill, she is dreadfully upset. I can understand how a teenager would hate to be uprooted,' said Chris, pacing around his living room.

Jill was nonplussed. 'Megan can be a frightful drama queen. It goes with being fourteen. And Perth is not exactly another planet.'

Chris tried again. 'I'm thinking of her schooling. She's happy there and doing well. Maybe we could see our way clear to pay for her to board. It's a crucial time.'

'Don't be ridiculous. Boarding would be way too expensive and besides, they have perfectly good schools in Perth,' Jill snapped.

'It won't be easy for me, Jill. It will be very hard to see her in Perth if I'm working between Bangkok and Sydney.'

'Chris, this is not about you. Trev has been offered a great job. Megan lives with us, so she's coming to Perth.'

Then Chris heard Megan in the background, shouting at her mother. 'I don't want to go to Perth! I hate Trevor and his evil little trolls!'

Their voices became raised as Jill responded. 'Do not speak about Trevor like that, or his sons. Trevor is very good to you and he's my husband. We're a family now. This is what is happening. Understand?'

'No! I want to stay with Dad. Here in Sydney.'

'Megan, don't be ridiculous. I can't see your father staying in one place, let alone Sydney. It's out of the question.'

'I'll run away!' Megan yelled.

Jill sighed. 'Don't be so dramatic, Megan.' She addressed Chris in a tight voice. 'Look, she'll just have to learn to live with us in Perth and be a bit more flexible. She'll have to adjust.'

Suddenly Chris heard himself saying, 'What if I offer to have Megan stay here with me? I'll turn down Bangkok if it's offered and stay in Sydney. Megan is clearly unhappy, so perhaps that's best.'

The idea had seemed to spring from nowhere, or was it the guilt he always buried that had finally cracked through the lid he kept firmly on top of family matters?

'No. Because, frankly, Chris, I'd worry about her being with you. Your place is way too small. Megan can't sleep on your lounge indefinitely and besides you have no idea what it's like to raise a child, let alone a teenager. You haven't had to weather the storm of puberty, which,

I have to say, is ongoing. Megan seems to expect to have things her way all the time. Whatever current fad there is, she'll expect to be part of it,' Jill warned, her voice sharp. 'Whatever new gadget appears on the market, she'll want one. It's all very well you swanning in here as Mr Nice Guy and making out that I'm the Wicked Witch of the West, but you won't be doing yourself any favours by taking Megan in. She'll wind you around her little finger. Even if you stay in Sydney, what happens if you suddenly have to race out of town to cover a story? No, Chris. It's simply not an option.'

Jill's response wasn't surprising, but Chris decided to press on. 'Jill, I'll talk to the editor, explain the situation to him. I won't be taking off out of town all the time. I'm sure he'll understand.'

Jill was unmoved. 'Chris, you'll never manage. You are far too bound up with your work. And you won't be able to put in all those extra hours you always do if you have to get home to Megan.'

'Okay, Jill, you've made your point. But can I ask when you're off to the west?'

'Towards the end of the Christmas holidays. I have to get there in time to settle the kids into school.'

Chris paused for a moment, his mind racing. 'Then how about this idea? What if I have Megan for the holidays. They're long enough for us to live with each other and see if we can fit in together. If it doesn't work, then there's no harm done.'

'Of course there's harm done,' said Jill shrilly. 'You can't raise her hopes then take off as you always do.'

'Jill, I promise you I will walk into the office and tell them I can't take Bangkok, and ask them to give me a job here in Sydney,' Chris said firmly.

'You're really serious about this, aren't you?' said Jill, her voice lowered. She paused a moment and Chris hoped it meant she was considering the idea. 'I can't say that I'm too pleased about this plan. I just think Megan's over-reacting. Still, I guess you'll both find out, one way or another, if you two can live together.' And with that, Jill said her goodbyes and hung up.

Almost immediately, Megan called. 'Hi, Dad. It's me. I can't believe you talked to Mum! I'll be so, so happy if you'll do this for me. I promise I won't be any trouble. You won't regret it. I'll work twice as hard at school, you'll see, and we'll find a bigger place to live in and I'll keep it clean and we'll get on really, really well. I promise.'

Chris was gratified by Megan's enthusiasm, but he knew it wouldn't be as easy as she obviously thought it would.

'Megs, nothing is settled yet,' he cautioned. 'This is just a trial and I still have to talk to my boss. He might not be any happier about this idea than your mother is.'

Megan was undeterred. 'Oh, Dad, yes he will. You just wait. Please go and see him. Please, please.'

After a few more exchanges, Chris rang off. He sat down heavily in a chair and stared at his phone. Megan sounded so excited, but Chris frowned. He wondered if he'd bitten off more than he could chew.

*

The following day, Chris phoned and made an appointment to speak to the newspaper's editor. With a few minutes to spare before the meeting, he called in to the newsroom to greet his colleagues, but while everyone acknowledged his arrival they all seemed too busy to stop what they were doing to chat. As he approached the editor's office, Rhonda, the editor's assistant, hurried towards him.

'Hello, Chris. Sorry, I've been trying to call you. There's a slight change to your appointment this morning.'

'Hi, Rhonda. Oh, sorry, I had my phone off. Forgot to turn it back on. A change of time? That's okay.'

Rhonda shook her head. 'No, your meeting's not with John. It's upstairs with the new chief operating officer, Mr Honeywell.' She turned to her desk and picked up the phone. 'Susie, could you please tell Mr Honeywell that Chris Baxter is on his way up.'

Chris nodded and peered over her shoulder to the shadowy figure behind her in the glass cubicle. 'Tell John I'll catch up with him later.'

'Certainly, I will.'

Chris walked through the open-plan floor with its rows of identical desks and computer screens, though only a third of them were occupied. He knew at this time of day the staff were generally out gathering material for the next deadline. When he got out of the lift on the next floor, he was ushered into Honeywell's office. The new head of Trinity Press was a large Englishman and he strode towards Chris with his hand outstretched.

'Chris, great to meet you,' he said, gripping Chris's hand in his large one. 'Shame we haven't had a chance to meet when I was passing through Washington DC. Please take a seat.'

Chris sat on rather an uncomfortable chair on the other side of Honeywell's desk. The man was a type familiar to him and his antennae pricked up. The charm, the patter, the smile that didn't reach his eyes and the very posh English accent all put Chris on the alert. What did this man want?

'You're a very talented writer, Mr Baxter, and I congratulate you on your excellent track record and solid reputation.'

'Thank you, and I'm looking forward to my next assignment, which is what I am here to discuss,' said Chris.

Honeywell nodded. 'As you are aware, the media landscape is changing throughout the world. Management has to be very careful where it spends its money. Have to be sure that it isn't wasteful and that whatever we spend will produce results and attract paying readers.'

'Yes, of course,' replied Chris, wondering where the conversation was headed.

'So it gives me great pleasure to offer you the position of South East Asian correspondent, based in Bangkok, because I think that you will be able to fulfil these objectives admirably,' said the Englishman, rather pompously.

Chris felt pleased to be offered the job, but he quickly came back to reality. 'Thank you very much, Mr Honeywell. If you had offered me this chance a few days ago I would have taken it with both hands, but unfortunately there has been a change in my circumstances. My teenage daughter, who previously lived with her mother, is now coming to live with me and I don't think that Bangkok is a particularly suitable environment for someone her age. She's only fourteen and her mother would never agree to her living there. So I'll have to turn down your offer and ask that I be reassigned to something based in Sydney.'

Honeywell looked at Chris with an expression that suggested he'd stepped in something unpleasant. He coughed slightly. 'I'm sorry. There is no other option, Chris. There is no job for you on the Sydney desk. Please consider your position carefully. This newspaper holds you in very high esteem and we would hate to lose you. But you must understand that a lot has gone into organising the Bangkok assignment for you and you must also realise that I can't just fire someone here in Sydney to allow for your personal requirements.'

'Yes,' replied Chris. 'I understand and I'm grateful for the Bangkok offer, but I simply can't take it at present.'

Honeywell glared at him as though personally insulted by Chris's refusal to take the position, and said in a very cool voice, 'Very well, then. You seem to be lacking in gratitude for the opportunities that Trinity Press has given you. I'm sorry, but if you won't accept what I consider to be a plum job, then it would appear that we have come to a parting of the ways. I will have to say goodbye to you.' With that the Englishman rose to his feet, an expression of icy fury on his face, walked to the office door and held it open.

Chris pushed back his chair and stood up, surprised to find that his knees were shaking. 'I see, I see,' he murmured, and he turned and walked from the office.

He went downstairs and straight to editor John Miller's office and tapped on the door. The editor waved him in, came around the desk and grasped his hand.

'I'm pleased to see you, mate. So you got the Bangkok office? Bet you're glad about that. You're the best person for that job, no doubt about it.' He took another look at Chris's now white face as he gestured for him to take a seat. 'Hey, you don't look that happy.'

Chris told him about Megan and then what had happened in Honeywell's office.

John stared at him. 'Oh, shit. I'm so sorry, Chris, really sorry to hear that. But it's your decision and I respect you for stepping up to take in your daughter.'

'I didn't expect that there would be no other position for me,' said Chris weakly. 'I'm in a bit of shock. Do you think he means it? What do you think the chances are of finding a berth?'

'Probably less than zero. Honeywell has the reins.' The editor got up and closed the door to his office. He sat back down and looked at Chris sympathetically. 'I don't know what's happening in this place. It's utter madness to get rid of you. There are some very odd decisions being made. Not a lot of happy campers here. You feel like you have to look over your shoulder all the time. But look, tell you what I'll do, I'll go and talk to Honeywell and see if he'll change his mind. I can find a spot for you on the city desk, if I put my mind to it. Just leave it with me.'

Chris looked at his friend with gratitude. 'I suppose Honeywell has every right to be angry. I made no secret of the fact that I wanted Bangkok and now suddenly I'm telling him no, he can give that job to someone else.'

'Have to put family first, Chris. I'll see what I can do and give you a ring.'

'Thanks, John.'

On the ferry ride back to Neutral Bay, Chris thought about what had happened. Unless John could pull something off, it seemed likely that Chris might now be unemployed. He couldn't believe the way the meeting had turned out. How would he be able to pay his mortgage, let alone pay off the loan he had just taken out on his new car? He knew he was a good journalist, but would he be able to get another position right away? Mac had warned him that there were a lot more journalists than there was work for them. And now the word would go out that he was the sort of person who would put his family, not the corporation, first. He would be known as being 'difficult'. Maybe he could survive as a freelancer until something turned up, but that was a hard row to hoe, too. Perhaps he would have to take the Bangkok post after all. He now seemed to have very limited options. Chris groaned inwardly with frustration. Should he speak to Jill about taking Megan to Bangkok? He dismissed the idea. No, she'd never stand for it. He wouldn't be happy for Megan to go to Bangkok either. He would only worry about her when he was away. It was all too impractical. No, if John couldn't wangle him a job in Sydney, there would be nothing else he could do but accept Honeywell's offer of Bangkok and leave Megan behind. He couldn't just throw his career away. He was sure that Megan would understand that, while he had had every intention of taking her to live with him, circumstances had changed and this was no longer a feasible option. She would just have to move to Perth.

But in spite of all these thoughts, the short ferry ride resolved nothing. He knew that when he told Megan he'd changed his mind about taking her to live with him she would be devastated, and this thought filled him with guilt. Jill was right. All Chris had done for Megan in the last few years was appear like a knight in shining armour every few months and spoil her and now, when she really needed him, he was about to let her down. He hoped that John would be able to come through for him. He would take any job to stay in Sydney.

About an hour after arriving home, he got his answer from his old friend and editor.

'Sorry, mate, it's a no go, I'm afraid. Honeywell is adamant. It's the Bangkok job, or nothing. I don't think he's too keen on any sort of compromise, even if I could find a position for you here. Thinks it would set a bad example. His way or the highway is his motto. So what are you going to do?'

'Bangkok, I suppose. What choice do I have? Look, I'll go and have a talk with Megan and I'll get back to you. You'll have my final answer today, John.'

Chris made himself a cup of tea and put on some music. His mind was still confused, but he knew that he had to make a decision, so he sat quietly in his favourite chair and went over all his options again. Finally, he looked at his watch and decided that it was getting towards the time when Megan would finish school. If he hurried he'd have time to pick her up and go somewhere quiet to tell her what had happened.

*

'Dad, this is so great, you picking me up. What a surprise!' Megan waved goodbye to her friends and jumped in Chris's car. She did up her seatbelt. 'Love the new car. We so made the right choice. Are you going to take me for a drive in it?'

'I'll drive you home, but first we need to have a little talk. How about we find a nice coffee shop.' Chris drove round the corner heading to a strip of nearby shops along the beach front.

'Okay, Dad, you sound serious. What's up?'

Chris parked the car close to a little café. They quickly found an empty table inside. He ordered a coffee for himself and a juice for his daughter.

'Honey, something's come up.' And he began to explain what had happened when he went into the office. As he got into his story, tears filled Megan's eyes.

'I knew it. I knew you didn't really want me to live with you. You were just saying it to make me think that you love me, but really you just want to have your life the way it suits you, just like Mum does. It's not fair. I didn't ask to be born and now neither of you want me in your lives. I just get in the way. All right, go to Bangkok without me. See if I care.' Her face crumpled and she sobbed in misery.

Chris tried to stroke her hair, but she brushed his hand away. He looked at her tear-stained face and suddenly felt overwhelmed by how much he loved his daughter. Megan was the most important person in his life and the acceptance of this gave him a sudden sense of calm. He took a deep breath.

'Megan, if you would just let me finish, I was about to tell you that I have turned down the Bangkok job. I wouldn't have enjoyed it knowing I'd let you down. So now I have no job and I'm not sure what I'll be doing, but whatever it is, I want to do it with you. I think I'm pretty lucky having a daughter who wants to live with her old man, so what say we give it a go?'

She looked at him warily. 'You mean it?'

Chris nodded. 'We're in this together, Megan. We'll manage. Something will turn up. It'll all be okay.'

As he saw a look of pure joy spread across her face, he hoped he was right.

2

THE WEATHER REFLECTED CHRIS'S mood; depressingly grey, hazy, cloudy. The kind of day when you wanted to hide under a doona, except that it was too hot and humid for that. Chris stood at the window looking at the small slice of view he could glimpse between buildings: a sludgy harbour, slanting rain, huddled passengers waiting for the ferry. He turned away. What an awful weekend to have Megan come and stay.

Chris paced around his flat feeling suffocated. The apartment was small, something he'd never minded before, but in the back of his mind he wondered how he could share this cramped space, and his life, with his daughter.

There was no question that he loved Megan and wanted the best for her, which was why he had agreed to step up and have her live with him. But now there was the crushing worry of how he was going to support both of them in this tiny flat, let alone find bigger, more suitable accommodation for them. Losing the job at Trinity Press – where he had been one of the stars in its newspaper firmament, albeit a modest one – had rocked him. He knew he had to look for another job right away. How hard could that be? he asked himself. He was reliable, a self-motivator and a good writer. Heavens, he'd won Australia's highest journalistic accolade, a Walkley Award, for his story on a school shooting in the USA. But he was realistic enough to know that since he'd been out of the country for years, he didn't have the network that the local journos did. So there was nothing else for it. He would have to start ringing around and see if any of Trinity's rival newspapers were interested in hiring him.

Staring at his phone, Chris had a sudden desire to ring his mother before he started the search. Talking to her always put him at ease. Susan Baxter would be calm and understanding as well as practical.

'A shock to the system, indeed. I know how much you were hoping to be assigned to Asia. Poor you. Poor Megan,' his mother sympathised. 'A good journalist like you shouldn't have a lot of trouble getting another job, though. There are other papers out there. Mind you, I mostly read them online these days but I shall certainly cancel my subscription to your former paper, forthwith.'

Chris relaxed at the sound of her voice. 'That's nice of you, Mum, but I'm really worried about being able to support Megan and a mortgage and car repayments,' he said.

'I can certainly understand that, but let's not panic just yet. What did Jill say about Megan moving in with you? Does she know the latest about your job? Is she going to insist that Megan goes to Perth with them?' his mother asked, pragmatic as ever.

'Yes, I had that conversation. Jill's not happy about me losing my job. She's prepared to let Megan live with me for the present because Megan has her heart set on it, but only long term if I can support her financially. So I hope I'm earning before they go to Perth. I can't bear to let Megan down. She will be incredibly upset if she has to go with them.' Chris frowned just thinking of the prospect.

'Look, the summer school holidays are coming up and you've already spoken about coming here for a visit. Why don't you and Megan still do that? Come here and stay, Chris. It won't stop you from looking for work,' Susan said reassuringly. 'We do have the internet and phone reception in Neverend. If you want to, you can use your father's office – I'm hardly ever in there. And you can easily zip down to Sydney when you have a job interview. It would be good for you and Megan to have time together and I'll adore having you both here for Christmas. Maybe you could rent your place out while you're here and that would take care of the mortgage for a while.'

Chris considered the offer for a moment and couldn't see a downside. For the first time since losing his job, he felt a wave of relief wash over him, as well as nostalgia for the place where he was born.

'Okay, Mum. Megan's already dying to visit. And you and I haven't spent much quality time together in a long while. I could do with a break, too. Get out of Sydney and look up some of my old school mates.'

'That's lovely, darling. I hope Megan doesn't get bored, though – it's a long holiday and she's used to the bright lights! Maybe one or two of her friends could come up and visit for a few days.'

'Perhaps. Let's see how things go,' replied Chris, who thought that one teenager would probably be more than enough for him to handle. 'Thanks so much for the offer,

Mum. Megan and I would love to spend the summer holidays with you.'

It seemed the perfect solution for the short term. His daughter got on well with her grandmother and had always loved visiting the town of Neverend, which was nestled in a beautiful river valley. Looking out of his misted window at the often chaotic life in the crowded city, Chris thought about the town where he had grown up, with its bustling main street, its well-preserved colonial buildings and its tiny side roads shaded by leafy camphor laurel trees. The town was divided by the wide, slow-moving Henry River, whose occasional floods marooned half the population. The river was always a picturesque spot for fishing, picnics or contemplative walks and, in summer, kids drifted along it in all manner of makeshift floats and boats. Dogs raced into the river to cool off, scrambling out to shake their coats in a sparkling spray. Lovers clung together in the shallows beneath the bridge, hiding from the world. Above the river sat a row of old homes, some converted into B&Bs, which all looked across to the green river flats, dotted with fat cows. Beyond the paddocks the dramatic Great Dividing Range rose towards the blue sky.

While Chris had loved his home at the end of View Street, where Susan's garden was a showpiece and his dad's shed was a boy's treasure house, he'd always itched to see the outside world. Although he had frequently visited his mother for two or three days when he had been on leave, this would be his first extended visit for years. Now, suddenly, he couldn't wait to go home and share with Megan all his favourite places around Neverend.

Buoyed by this thought, Chris decided that it was time to start putting out some feelers and seriously look for a new job. Megan wasn't due to arrive for another hour, so he had time to make a call or two. He was sure that he was unlikely to just walk into a new job, but there was no time like the present to make contact with people who might be able to help him. The first person he rang was Mac.

'So the bastard fired you. Couldn't put family before profits. Selfish sod,' Mac said sympathetically.

'Not really. I feel it was my decision. I'm going to see my mother for Christmas. Taking Megan with me. After that . . . who knows? Got any ideas?'

'Chris, after our drink the other day, I don't have to tell you that the newspaper game isn't in great shape,' replied Mac.

'I know. I'm wondering if you think it would be worthwhile contacting the other major Aussie rags,' said Chris, wondering how accurate Mac's gloomy assessment was.

'Get in touch with them, by all means. I've got a few contacts you could try. You're an excellent journo with a solid reputation, so at least let them know you're interested, but don't hold your breath. They've already let a lot of their best staff go,' Mac replied. 'Sorry I can't be more help, mate.'

Chris thanked Mac and promised to catch up with him after the Christmas holidays, then hung up. Mac had confirmed what Chris felt he had known all along, deep down: finding another job was going to be difficult. Still, he told himself, he had weeks to find something before the problem became critical.

*

The car was crammed full to bursting. Chris had picked Megan up that morning for the drive north. Jill had seemed quite happy to see her daughter off. No doubt, thought Chris, she'll enjoy a break from the constant hostilities between Megan and the twins.

'What is all this stuff?' asked Chris, eyeing the large overstuffed bag in Megan's lap as they drove away.

40

'Just my essentials, Dad,' said Megan and rattled off a list. 'Phone and charger, headphones, iPod, swimmers, my Peter Alexander pjs, skateboard, MinkPink sunglasses, Converse, Sukin face cleanser, a John Green novel, and a bag of snakes to eat on the road. Do you want one?' She waved the brightly coloured plastic bag in his direction.

'No thanks, sweetie,' said Chris, rather amused. 'I'm glad you brought those Converse.'

She moved her bag into the backseat and lifted her foot, displaying a well-worn sneaker. 'As if I would leave them at home, Dad.'

*

Neverend was more than six hours' drive north of Sydney, and at about the halfway mark they stopped for cold drinks and a hamburger from a store near a petrol station where Chris had stopped before.

'Don't get beetroot juice on you, it won't come out,' he said as Megan tucked into her burger with relish.

'Now you're sounding like a mum,' said Megan with her mouth full.

'Good,' said Chris. 'Just getting into practice.'

For most of the drive Megan sat back with her headphones on listening to music. Chris felt happy to have his daughter beside him. She seemed comfortable and at ease. He hoped this would be the pattern of their relationship.

*

It seemed as though the further north the car sped, the more relaxed Chris began to feel. As he passed the turn-off to Port Macquarie, he became quite excited about returning home and began to think again about Neverend.

He'd learned when he was in school how the timber-getters had first opened up the area in their search for red

41

cedar. The logs had been taken from the thick bush and floated down the Henry River to the coast. From there, the valuable timber was shipped all over the world. After the sources of timber had been depleted, the dairy farmers moved in, their herds fattening on the rich river flats, and the farmers' monthly pay cheques enabled the town to flourish. Land subdivisions in the town had quickly sold and substantial timber homes, reflecting the wealth of the area, were built. The town soon boasted a hospital, courthouse and police station as well as schools. The main street had been filled with pubs and busy shops, that stayed open as late as 10 pm on Saturday nights to cater for the affluent farmers.

Two entrepreneurial merchants, Webb and Mills, had built a two-storeyed department store which sold everything from shoes and china to bed linen and furniture. The store, now more than a hundred years old, still stood proudly in the main street and its wide iron awning continued to shelter Neverend residents from the weather, while its magnificent grand staircase, leading to a mezzanine floor, always produced admiring comments from visitors.

When Britain had entered the EU in the 1960s and Australian dairy products lost their major market, the town stalled, but gradually it began to adapt. New people moved in: hippies seeking a different way of life, retirees and tree changers, and then tourists looking for a quiet escape in an area renowned for its natural beauty. Chris had seen a lot of the world, but he had to admit that there were very few places that matched the loveliness of the valley in which he'd been born.

When he turned off the highway to wind through a landscape of farms and paddocks, Megan took off her headphones and watched the passing scenery.

'It's pretty, isn't it?' he said after a while, as large fields dotted with the occasional gum tree rolled past.

'Yes, it is. And empty.'

Chris chuckled. 'Amazing country we have. I'm bowled over every time I come back here. It's all so beautiful and, you're right, it does seem empty and isolated, but Neverend is only fifteen minutes from Coffs Harbour, and that's a big place.'

'Do you think Bunny ever gets bored living up here?'

'Heavens, no. She adores Neverend and loves the house she and your grandfather restored. I think she keeps pretty busy with golf, her friends, book club and various organisations. And you know how much work she puts into her garden. It takes up a lot of her time.'

'I always enjoy spending time with Bunny. Grandma Thomas is . . . tricky,' said Megan diplomatically.

'I think your mother would agree with that. Frankly, I always felt she didn't approve of me,' said Chris.

'Oh, no. She's like that with everybody. I don't think anyone's ever good enough in her eyes.'

Chris paused. He didn't want to be too critical of Jill's mother. 'Maybe we shouldn't talk about her behind her back – or your mother's.'

'Don't worry, Dad, Mum knows how I feel. I used to talk to her about everything. You know, girl talk?' She looked at him. 'I suppose it's different with fathers.'

'Maybe we'll have to learn to get along on a different level.'

'Dad, you're fun, I can joke and tease with you. You're interesting, we talk about grown-up things. You know, your work and politics and everything.'

Chris smiled. 'I'm starting to learn about your world, Megan, but it's still a bit of a mystery to me. Friends and brand names seem to be very important to you.'

'It's a popularity thing,' she explained, seriously. 'The kids at school are pretty harsh if you don't wear the brands they wear. I think that boys my age are probably even more obsessed than girls. They are all really judgemental. Bragging rights are a massive thing. I guess I play that game, too. I just got this new orange leather bag with a chain handle that I saved really hard for. It cost more than two hundred dollars and I made sure it was all over Tumblr, Snapchat, Instagram and Facebook. Everyone knew.'

Chris tried to keep a straight face. 'That's great for you, honey. But what about those kids whose parents aren't as well off? Does that put them on the outer?'

'Must be hard,' Megan said. She shrugged. 'Sometimes they try to fake it. The worst thing to do is wear a fake. You can always tell.'

Silence fell between them as they watched the scenery unfolding as the car approached the little township. Slightly disturbed by the turn their conversation had taken, Chris wondered to himself how a sweet girl like Megan could be so mercenary and status-conscious. But obviously all her friends were too, and peer pressure was a force to be reckoned with.

'Know where we are?' he asked as they crossed a wooden bridge spanning a fast-flowing river.

'Yes! There's the river and the park. I can't wait to get to the skate park place under the trees,' said Megan, happily. 'And we're coming up to that old butter factory that's got some pretty cool shops, like the one with those fossils. And there's the yellow shed building. There are some terrific things in there, too. Lots of really gorgeous crystals. I could buy my Christmas presents there.'

'And here we are, at last,' said Chris as they drove along the main street of Neverend.

'Wow, there are quite a few new places,' Megan exclaimed. 'Hey, there's a new vintage shop. Bet I can find something great in there. And more coffee shops. Can we come down here this afternoon?'

Chris grinned at her enthusiasm. 'Let's see what Bunny has planned. Personally, I'd like to put my feet up with a cold beer.'

Susan Baxter must have heard the car turning into the narrow gravel driveway beside the house, for she was waiting for them on the front verandah, standing beside her pots of hanging orchids. As they drove up to the house, Chris appreciated again the beautiful renovation that had seen original features like the wooden fretwork, the lead-light windows and the wide skirting boards all retained and restored. The wonderful pressed-metal ceilings had been meticulously repainted. Walls had been knocked out to provide four good-sized bedrooms, one with an ensuite and a walk-in robe. On the other side of the back patio, a shed had been converted into a guest cottage with the old laundry beside it replaced by a bathroom. All the old carpets in the house had been taken up and the solid wooden floorboards, which were made from magnificent local blackbutt timber, had been polished so they gleamed in the sunlight that filtered through several leadlight glass panels. The open fireplace in the living room still worked and was occasionally used in winter. Out the back of the house, the family could sit in privacy and admire Susan's magnificent garden.

Susan was in her late sixties, but she was slim and fit and had obviously looked after herself well. Her hair, cut fashionably short, was a warm brown, and its gold high-lights set off her hazel eyes. Her skin had been cared for, and her smile wrinkles and subtle make-up gave her a youthful look. She was wearing her favoured outfit of linen pants and a light shirt. She stretched out her arms in greeting.

Megan leaped out of the car and ran along the verandah, but before she reached her grandmother, a furry rocket streaked past her.

'Hi, Biddi.' She scooped the tabby cat into her arms.

'You remember me, you little darling. Hi, Bunny!' She put the cat down and wrapped her arms around her grandmother, who hugged her tightly.

Susan, or Bunny, as her family and friends called her, held her granddaughter at arm's length and studied her.

'So, what's the verdict, Bunny?' Megan asked as she tilted her head to show her braided hair and dangling frog earrings, and waggled her orange fingernails with gold trim in front of her face.

Susan looked her granddaughter up and down, her eyes twinkling. 'A-plus for the hair and the outfit. You're taller, lovely legs, but a B-minus for the nails. Orange isn't my favourite colour.'

Megan laughed. 'Oh, it's so great to be here. What's new?'

'Nothing much changes here,' said Susan. 'Go help your dad.' She watched her smiling son come along the verandah with an armful of bags as Biddi walked purposefully beside him. Megan took parcels and carry bags from her father, who put down the large suitcase he was carrying so that he could hug his mother.

'It's so good to have you home. It's been too long,' she said, her words muffled in his hug.

'I missed you, Mum. It's good to be here.'

She pulled away to study her handsome son, touching the small flecks of grey at his temples. 'You look tired.'

'Bit of a long drive. We'll talk later. I'm ready for a cold beer, if you've got one,' he said. 'I can always walk down to the bottle shop if you haven't.'

Megan reappeared, empty-handed. 'I've put my stuff inside. Are we going into town, Dad?'

'Let your dad have a rest first, Megan. Chris, there's a six-pack in the fridge. Was there anything else you wanted?'

'No thanks, Mum.'

'Megan, how about you help your father finish unloading the car and we can wander into town later. There's a new place that makes the best gelato. It's absolutely delicious homemade Italian ice-cream. I thought you could choose a tub for dessert.'

An hour later, the three of them walked the fifty metres or so from Susan's house to the main street, although their progress to the gelato shop was slow as everyone seemed to want to stop and chat to Susan, welcome Chris home and be introduced to Megan.

'You know so many people, Bunny,' said Megan as they strolled along the broad street.

'I've lived here even before your father was born. I worked in the Neverend High School for forty years, so I've taught generations of children in this area. It's little wonder that I know nearly everyone. Now, Megs, what flavour do you think you'd like?' Susan asked as they walked into the ice-cream shop.

Chris looked around. He remembered the old milk bar that had been there for years, and there were still a couple of old booths at the back of the place, but the front of the shop was now gleaming in new chrome and shiny laminex. 'A lot of gelato to choose from, Megan,' he said.

'You can taste a couple of them first, isn't that right, Travis?' Susan suggested.

'Sure is, Mrs Baxter,' replied the young man behind the counter. 'Take your time.'

Megan spent a long while considering the exotic combinations of fruit, coffee, chocolate, liqueur and nut flavours before settling on a macadamia, guava cream and mint combo to take home and a French vanilla honeycomb to eat straight away.

As they left the gelato bar and turned to hurry home before the ice-cream melted, the sounds of a brass band suddenly flooded the main street.

'What's that music, Bunny?' asked Megan.

'It's the local band practising. Your father used to belong to it, years ago.'

'Did you, Dad? You never told me.'

'I wasn't very good. I think they were pleased when I left,' said Chris with a smile.

'A lot of schoolchildren are in the band. Soon they'll be playing Christmas carols in the hospital and the two nursing homes. There's a big concert in the park on Christmas Eve performed by various groups and the band is one of those, too. We could come down if you like. It's lovely to sit by the river with a picnic tea and when it gets dark we light candles and sing carols.'

'I'd like to do that,' said Chris. 'We always used to go, you, Dad, Kate and me. It would be nice to do it again this year. I know you'd love it, Megan.'

'You said you wanted to show me places you've never taken me to before and I've never been to carols by candle-light. This is going to be fun,' said Megan, bubbling with enthusiasm.

'Let's do it, then,' said Chris.

Susan smiled at them both. 'It's so nice to have you two here. Your visits have always been too short, but now we can really plan things to do.'

They walked back into the house and as Susan put the ice-cream into the freezer, she turned to them both and said, 'Now, I was meaning to ask you, would you mind if I invited some other people to Christmas lunch? I always celebrate Christmas with a few friends.'

'Of course, Mum, you should do what you want, it's your house. What do you usually do?' said Chris, taking a seat in a cosy armchair in the living room.

'You'd be surprised. My friends and I have had some crazy Christmases! Sometimes we go to the aged care homes and put on a bit of a show, give the people there a jolly good laugh. Last year we asked a couple of refugee families from Sri Lanka and Afghanistan who have settled in town to join us and we had an international food fest. It was a combined Christian, Buddhist and Muslim Christmas lunch. It broke down a lot of barriers. Sometimes we've taken a picnic down to the river or simply had it on someone's verandah. I like to be a bit more formal and use the dining room, mainly because it's got air conditioning if we need it. Since I got my solar panels installed, I don't feel a bit guilty about using it.'

'Wow, sounds awesome,' said Megan.

'I'm not sure that "awesome" is the word I would use, but I do have some rather fun friends. Anyway, Christmas is still a little way off, and there are quite a few things I need to do before then. Speaking of which, Chris, if you have a few hours free tomorrow afternoon, I have to go up to the plateau for some foodie things. Perhaps you two could drive up there with me. Do you like to cook, Megan?'

'I like to eat! And I have to help Mum with meals, but that's not much fun. Ruby's parents have an outdoor pizza oven, and we get to make our own pizzas. I like doing that.'

That evening there was a lot of chatter and laughter at the dinner table. Megan insisted that she clear the table and stack the dishwasher by herself, so Chris and Susan went to the front verandah and sat in the cool evening air.

'I've missed Neverend. It's a warm feeling to come home and find everything's more or less the same. It gives me a sense of belonging.'

'This is Megan's place, too. Her roots are here as much as yours are. I hope she realises it.'

'Maybe staying here longer will make her appreciate that. I want to take her to some of my old haunts.'

'The famous waterhole?' laughed his mother.

'Yes. We could go there for a picnic one day. You up for that?'

'Always. So nice to have an excuse to visit it.'

Chris glanced around the garden. 'Everything looks wonderful. You sure this big house isn't too much for you to look after, Mum?'

Susan waved a hand at him. 'Not at all. George mows the grass when it needs it. Katrina comes in once a month to help me with the cleaning. The heavy things are a bit hard to lift when I want to vacuum. And if I keep on top of the gardening, which I enjoy doing anyway, the garden is not a problem.'

Megan came and joined them, curling into the old wicker rocking chair with Biddi purring on her lap.

'All finished with the dishes? Thank you very much. Not watching TV? I have Pay TV now,' said Susan.

'This is better than TV. What are we doing tomorrow, Bunny?'

'Well, I was thinking of going into Coffs to do a bit of Christmas shopping afterwards. Then we'll drive up to the plateau in the afternoon.'

'Christmas shopping. Could I come, please, Bunny?'

'Of course. I'd love that.'

Megan stroked the contented cat's ears. 'This is such a nice place. How long have you been here again, Bunny? Dad said he was born here.'

'Well, not in the house! In the Neverend hospital. Your grandfather and I came here as newly married teachers. We were really lucky to get a posting to the high school together. We rented a teeny old house on the other side of the river. It's now been beautifully renovated, I'll show you sometime, if you like. Anyway, we both loved Neverend so much we decided to stay. We were very stubborn and kept refusing transfers, so eventually everyone got the hint and left us alone. We bought this house and did it up and raised your father and your aunt Kate.'

'Yes, Neverend was a fabulous place to grow up.

I feel very lucky to have had such a charmed childhood,' acknowledged Chris.

'Bunny, I was looking around at some of the things in the house that I've never noticed before. Can you tell me the stories about them while I'm here? Old photos and ornaments that look ancient,' said Megan.

Susan smiled. 'Of course, Megan. Sometimes I think there's a bit too much clutter about the place, but every single thing I have means something special to me. I'd love you to know their stories, too. All in good time.' Susan turned to her son. 'Chris, in the next day or so, will you go and get the Christmas tree for me? Megan, you remember that I always have a big pine from Jim's Christmas tree farm and you can help me decorate it.'

'Not a problem, Mum. Are you using those same old ornaments? They must be getting pretty tatty by now. You don't still have the ones that you used when I was growing up, do you?'

'I do.'

'They'd be antiques. Have you made a pudding yet?' asked Chris. 'I love your grandmother's Christmas pudding, Megan. Do you still put sixpences and threepences in it, Mum?'

'Most certainly,' Susan nodded firmly. 'And if you find one, Megan, I'll buy it off you and recycle it for next year.'

'You really like sticking to traditions, Bunny, don't you? I like the way you do things. My mum isn't like that. Says she's modern. She's not sentimental. And she's a minimalist.'

'Less to dust, I expect,' said Susan briskly.

'But I like that everything is always the same in your house. I feel safe here. Is that a funny thing to say? I don't mean like safe from violence or anything, just well, warm,' said Megan.

'Cosy?'

'Maybe that's the word,' replied Megan.

Susan stood and leaned over to kiss the top of her granddaughter's head. 'My bedtime. Yours too?'

'I'm bushed,' said Chris. 'That drive is always longer than you think.'

'I might read a bit. G'night, Bunny, night, Dad.'

'Night, darling. Love you. I'm so happy you're here.' Susan hugged Megan.

'Me too.'

After kissing his daughter good night, Chris walked to the guest room, which had been his boyhood bedroom. His mother had left a few reminders of his time there and they made him smile. His cub scout shirt with his hard-earned badges was framed and hung beside a collage of boyhood photos. A tennis trophy and a certificate for winning first prize in a short story competition sat on the dressing table beside a clumsy ceramic vase he'd made in a much-loathed pottery class. *At least it doesn't leak*, thought Chris, admiring the fragrant rose-buds his mother had placed in it. He picked up a framed certificate. He must have been about Megan's age when he'd written that short story. He'd been pretty chuffed about winning. He had always loved writing, and journalism had been a way of earning money by doing what he loved. He put the certificate down. *Wouldn't make money out of short stories these days*, he reflected. *Still. It's nice to be home*, he thought and he smiled to himself.

*

Within a day of their arrival, it was known that Chris Baxter was home and his childhood friends began to contact him. Alex Starr rang and made arrangements to meet for a drink, as did Duncan Newman, while Shaun French walked straight in the Baxters' back door as he'd always done.

'G'day, Mrs B. I hear Chris is home. Is he staying through Christmas?'

'Hey, hey, Frenchy. I am indeed staying for the festive season.' Chris strode into the room and clapped his old friend on the shoulder. Frenchy was a short, compact man but his personality always made him seem bigger than he actually was. 'So what are you up to these days?' asked Chris.

'Helping Dad run the farm. He's a bit past getting up every morning to do the milking, but he's right into breeding. Artificial insemination and all that. Producing better milkers. Karen's up to her elbows experimenting in cheese making. You like haloumi, Mrs B? I'll bring you some next time.'

'Thanks very much, Shaun. And how are your children?'

'Going great guns, thanks, Mrs B. Both in high school now. Shame they don't have you teaching them. They're missing out on the best. How old's your girl now, mate?'

'Megan is fourteen. Interesting times,' remarked Chris. 'She's about somewhere.'

'I needed a couple of things from the supermarket, so I asked her to pop down there for me. She won't be long, and then we're off to Coffs Harbour,' said Susan.

'Is it too early for a beer? Fancy a stroll to the pub?' asked Chris.

'Sounds good to me. Bet you're glad to be out of the rat race in Sydney. Though I s'pose it's nothing compared to Yankee land.'

'I wouldn't say that,' said Chris. 'They both have their pluses and minuses.'

'I wouldn't live anywhere else but here. God's own country and we plan to keep it that way,' said Shaun as the two of them walked out the door.

*

Chris whistled as he helped unload the bags and parcels from his mother's car later that day.

'How many people is Santa catering for, Mum?'

'You have no idea what it was like, Chris. You were wise to stay home instead of coming into Coffs with us. The shopping mall was jam-packed. The carols over the PA were much too loud and the Christmas decorations were all starting to droop. It was festive mayhem,' said Susan.

'Bunny kept running into her friends and we lost each other, twice,' said Megan cheerfully.

'Thank goodness for mobile phones, or I'd never have found you and I'd have had to leave you there.'

'No, you wouldn't have,' laughed Megan.

'You've bought a stack of things, by the looks of it,' said Chris. 'Not all for yourself, Megan, I hope!'

'Only one or two, the rest are for my friends. I just see things I know they'll love. You're really hard to buy for, Dad,' said Megan, hastily changing the subject. 'But we found something perfect for you.'

'Oh, this all looks worse than it is. Megan found some crazy gift warehouse that had sprung up and bought a lot of silly fun things. She has a tribe of friends, it seems,' broke in Susan.

Megan took her parcels inside to inspect her merchandise while Chris and Susan walked slowly behind her.

'How did you go today? Did you get a chance to do any job hunting?' Susan asked.

'I rang the contacts that Mac gave me, but none of them could help. Told me that they'd get straight back to me if anything came up, but no one sounded very hopeful. Then I got on to my old editor, John, to ask him what the other journos who'd got the flick were doing. See if I could get some ideas. It wasn't very encouraging, either.'

'Can I ask what he said?'

'He told me that some of the old ex-Trinity staff were freelancing.'

'You could do that.'

'Mum, freelancing only pays about seventy cents a word,' said Chris.

'A thousand words and you've got seven hundred dollars,' countered Susan.

'Doesn't sound too bad, I know, but there are all sorts of conditions attached.' Chris explained how freelancers only got paid based on the number of words that actually went to print. And they got paid nothing at all if the paper decided not to go ahead with the story.

'That doesn't sound very fair to me.'

'Nor me, Mum, especially when you consider the costs of getting the story like phone calls and travel. I could do a bit, I suppose, but it would hardly support me, let alone a teenage daughter as well.'

'Well, it's early days yet. You know that new people rarely get hired over the holiday season. No one is looking for staff when they're busy planning their holiday,' said Susan.

'But on the other hand, this can sometimes be a good time of year to get a foot in the door because the regular staff are on leave. Your work has a better chance of being noticed, but I can't show anyone what I can do if I can't even get a short-term contract.'

'You're a well-known journalist, for goodness sake! I'm sure that something will turn up after Christmas. Come on, Chris, let's go inside. I need to set up Santa's workshop in my sewing room. And no one is allowed in to poke around,' she said in a warning voice.

*

Later that afternoon, the car wound up the narrow road that twisted around the mountainside. Megan gazed at the rainforest towering above them. At several places rivulets of water cascaded over well-worn rock faces beside the road in picturesque waterfalls. On the other side, the road fell away sharply towards a tangle of ferns and under-growth and a lush canopy of trees whose roots were grounded hundreds of metres below in the steep valley.

'Ooh, I can't look down there. It's too scary. Imagine what it's going to be like coming back down,' Megan exclaimed.

'Don't look down at the drop, look across the canopy. You can see the ocean in the distance, between the breaks in the trees,' said Susan.

Then Megan squealed as a B-double truck roared past their car on the winding road. Chris took evasive action by swerving close to the cliff face.

'Those trucks are damned dangerous,' he muttered. 'There seems to be no end to them. What are they doing here? This road is far too narrow for something that size.'

'They're taking rocks from the quarry for the highway bypass,' said Susan. 'But there have been a lot of near misses. And there was talk they are going to increase the number of trucks. According to the authorities, it's all about saving money.'

'A short cut to disaster. As far as I'm concerned, it's an accident waiting to happen.'

'*Daaaad*, stop that. It's scary.'

'It's okay, Megan. Your father is a very careful driver. Don't worry. It won't be long until we reach the top and get to the place where I like to buy something special for my Christmas guests. Then we can have a coffee and look around before we go back,' said Susan soothingly.

When they reached the plateau, Megan soon had her phone out, snapping pictures of the glorious scenery through the window. The road now weaved its way through flat, lush, green paddocks where lazy cows, too

56

fat and sleepy to move, dozed contentedly in the patches of shade cast by luxuriant trees.

'This is beautiful,' exclaimed Megan. 'It's all so green. It's sort of like how I imagine England to be.'

'It certainly is lovely. Quite idyllic,' said her grandmother in agreement.

In less than ten minutes Chris had parked the car in the main street of the town at the top of the plateau.

'I'm just popping into this shop,' explained Susan. 'I want to buy some of the local smoked trout. I use it for one of my special Christmas Day concoctions. There's a coffee shop a couple of doors down, but if you'd rather, Megan, there is a great junk shop on the corner. Of course, the owner doesn't call it that, but the number of things he has in there is amazing. I know you'll enjoy a poke around in it. How about we all meet there in ten minutes?'

With her fish safely stowed in the car, Chris and Susan walked into the very large warehouse, looking for Megan.

'Good grief,' exclaimed Chris. 'I've never seen so much junk in all my life.'

'Shhh. Keep your voice down,' whispered Susan. 'The owner is very proud of his collection of bric-a-brac. He would be very insulted if he heard it referred to as junk.'

Chris looked around him. There were so many collectibles that it was difficult to walk down the aisles to inspect them. The walls of the shop were hung with old commercial metal signs advertising things such as 'Keen's Mustard', 'Caltex' and 'GE Electrics'. On the crowded shelves stood cups and saucers, glasses, old vases and boxes of cutlery. Stacked one on top of another were cheap reproductions of artworks by the great masters, as well as ambitious but tasteless amateur paintings. Hundreds of books had been set out on shelves, although there appeared to be no particular order to them. In several glass-fronted cabinets stood dozens of ornaments, mostly poorly made, but Chris suspected that if he had time to hunt seriously, he might find some good pieces.

'Dad, this is so amazing,' said Megan as she manoeuvred her way down a crowded aisle towards Chris and Susan. 'Look what I've found.' Megan held out a set of salt and pepper shakers in the shape of two pandas hugging each other. 'Aren't they too cute? And they cost hardly anything. I'm going to get them.'

Chris shook his head. 'Your money,' he said.

'Bunny said that she keeps things that mean something to her, so I'm getting these to remind me of this day,' Megan explained.

Chris looked at his mother, but didn't say a word.

'Do we have to race back home, Chris?' his mother asked. 'If we have time, we should take Megan to see the waterfall. We've had quite a bit of rain lately, so it should have plenty of water going over it.'

As the waterfall was only a few minutes' drive away, Chris agreed that it was worth taking a detour. They parked the car in the small car park and walked to the edge of the well-fenced observation platform. They could see the waterfall and the river flowing far below. There was certainly a lot of water coming over the falls, which plunged about thirty metres into a large pool beneath.

'Dad, this is gorgeous,' said Megan. 'I just love it.'

'It certainly is lovely. It's not one of the world's great waterfalls, not like Niagara, but you're right, it's very pretty.'

'There's a path right down to the base of the falls,' said Susan. 'You can walk down and swim in the pool, but the water is very cold.'

'Dad, can we do that?'

'No time today, but maybe after Christmas.'

'I'd like to come back here,' said Megan. She smiled at Chris. As they climbed back in the car, Chris felt relaxed and happy. Showing Megan around Neverend was proving to be just the bonding experience he had hoped for.

*

On Christmas morning the house was filled with people, as neighbours and friends dropped in to share good wishes and exchange small gifts.

On Christmas Eve, Susan had shown Megan how to flake the smoked trout they had bought up on the plateau and make a dip from it by putting it into the food processor with herbs, crème fraîche, shallots, parsley and lime juice. Now Megan served it to the visitors with tiny toasted triangles of bread.

'Mmm,' said one guest. 'Bunny's famous smoked trout dip.'

'Megan made it this year,' replied Susan.

'Well, all I can say is that she's done a great job.'

Megan beamed with pleasure.

Later, as those who were staying for lunch congregated on the front verandah while Susan's organic turkey finished cooking, there was the roar of a motorbike rumbling up the driveway.

A figure in leathers dismounted, took off a black helmet and, pulling out a large red handkerchief, mopped a perspiring face.

Chris put down his drink and exclaimed, 'Well, Carla! What a fabulous surprise! I haven't seen you for ages.' He walked over to embrace the large, smiling woman before calling to Megan. 'Carla, you haven't met my daughter. This is Megan.'

Carla held out her hand and Megan shook it. 'I feel I know you already. Bunny talks about you such a lot. Lovely to meet you at last.'

'Pleased to meet you,' said Megan. 'Wow, that's some bike. Do you live around here?'

'I rode into town a few years ago and liked the place, so I often come for a visit,' said Carla. 'I met Bunny, who offered to let me stay here for a while. She's a great woman, your grandmother.'

'I know,' said Megan, smiling. 'Would you like a glass of water?'

'I would, thank you, dear, but then I'll ask your father for a beer. I'll go inside and get out of some of this clobber. It's too damned hot to socialise in it.' She picked up her small backpack and headed indoors.

Chris's old friend Duncan, who'd popped in to see the Baxters before going to his family celebrations, looked at Carla heading indoors and then at the bike.

'Your mother is very hospitable and certainly has a varied group of friends,' said Duncan. 'Well, I'd better be off. Going to the out-laws for dinner this year. How about we catch up after Christmas? Go fishing or play a round of golf?'

'Sounds good to me. I'll be in touch. It was good to see you, Duncan, and please say Merry Christmas to the family from all of us.'

After Duncan left, Chris wandered out to the kitchen to see if he could give Susan a hand with lunch. Megan joined them from the dining room, where she'd been put in charge of the floral decorations for the table.

'Are you ready for lunch, Megan? Well, a rather late lunch, I'm afraid. How sweet you look. I love seeing you in that dress,' said Susan, gesturing at the white A-line lace dress Megan had on.

'Well, it *is* Christmas. And I wasn't sure how proper or formal your friends might be, Bunny,' said Megan. 'Carla surprised me. Didn't know you had a biker friend. Not that I mean she's bad or anything.'

'She's mean, she's bad, she's wicked,' laughed Susan. 'A tamed wild woman, and she rides her bike in rallies for charities all over the place. You'll soon see why I enjoy her company. She's smart and quick and funny.'

'Does she have kids?'

'No. She never married. But she supports kids from all over the place. I know she's helping educate an Aboriginal brother and sister out west.'

'How come you two are friends?' Megan asked.

'Mum first met Carla years ago when she came to town to check up on some old hippie friend she had. He ended up being put in the nursing home in town where Mum used to volunteer. Carla visited the old chap every day and that's how the two of them met,' explained Chris.

'Dear Carla,' said Susan, checking on the potatoes cooking in the oven. 'She was looking for a place to stay while she was in town, so I suggested she come here. The old chap only lasted two more months, but it was certainly fun to have Carla here for that time. She likes to take off on long road trips rather than settle down in one place, so she is a sporadic visitor to Neverend, but a welcome one.'

'It was nice of you to ask her to come for Christmas, Bunny.'

Susan smiled. 'And it was nice that you came to church with me for the midnight service last night.'

'It was different,' said Megan thoughtfully. 'I enjoyed the singing. I liked going to the carols in the park, too. It's great that you can just walk everywhere. You don't have to get the car out and then look for a parking spot. Mum says looking for parking is the worst thing.'

'I'm not sure that it's the worst thing, but it can be very frustrating.'

Suddenly Megan hugged her father and her grandmother. 'Thank you for my presents. This is the best Christmas ever.'

'I think so, too,' said Chris. 'And I love my new swimmers. I'll look really flash when we go out to the waterhole.' Megan rolled her eyes at his comment, but smiled broadly at him.

Susan held Megan for a moment. 'It's so lovely to have you here. You're growing up so quickly now.'

Some twenty minutes later, Susan announced to everyone, 'The food is served.' With Megan's help, Susan set out the various dishes as Chris carved the turkey. Friends and family came together around the table sharing food, laughter, friendship and stories. Time was of no consequence.

Susan was a traditionalist on Christmas Day. There were crackers to pull. Everyone looked festive wearing their paper hats, and they all took turns reading out the silly Christmas cracker jokes, which produced more loud groans than laughter.

Chris smiled at Megan from time to time, hoping that she wasn't finding such a grown-up Christmas a bit boring, but the look on her face suggested that she was absorbed by the interesting conversations that flowed around her.

The guests were Susan's friends, some of whom were recent friends while some she'd known since she'd first moved to Neverend.

Charles and Shelby were originally from America but had emigrated during the seventies as flower children escapees looking for nirvana, which they hadn't found in India. Shelby laughed. 'We felt right at home when we got to Neverend, though.'

'Yes, the locals always give a warm welcome,' said Carla.

'Oh, yes, they've heard about your special cookies, Carla,' said Charles, laughing and refilling Carla's glass.

'Oh, I gave up growing dope years ago. Very old hat. I'm into dahlias now,' she said matter-of-factly, and Megan glanced at her father, not sure if Carla was joking or not.

'Don't stir the pot, so to speak,' said Susan. 'The hippie wars are over. It's all love and lattes now.' She spooned out another helping of cauliflower cheese onto her plate.

'So, what were the hippie wars exactly?' asked Megan.

Everyone started talking at once, as it was a subject familiar to them all. Eventually Susan made herself heard above the din.

'Megan, back in the dark ages of the 1970s a lot of people wanted to escape the city. They wanted to live a more fulfilled lifestyle, practise self-sufficiency. They thought that if they banded together and lived in harmony with each other and their environment in a non-materialistic way, they could encourage everyone else to change for the better, too. They were generally well-educated professionals, and very idealistic,' she explained.

'Some of them moved here from Nimbin when that region got too political, crowded and expensive,' put in Valerie, a teaching friend of Susan's. 'A lot were radicalised by the Vietnam War debacle and wanted to bring up their kids differently from the traditional way children were raised.'

'Yeah, multiple occupancy had started. This meant that a group of people could purchase large acreage and everyone could build their own house on it without having to formally subdivide the block. This made the individual plots of land very cheap, which suited artists and musicians who wanted to do their own thing,' added Stephen, Valerie's husband.

'They weren't well received here by the locals, though,' said Chris, shaking his head.

Charles leaned his elbows on the table. 'They certainly weren't. The newcomers behaved quite differently from the conservative locals. They dressed in hippie clothes, had long hair, the women breastfed in public and advocated home births. They were perceived as being dole bludgers and drug takers. Yet the newcomers had a very strong community spirit.'

Tony, who had done a lot of the renovations on Susan's house, nodded emphatically. 'When we came up here from Melbourne in '74 to start our building business, this place was going backwards economically. We were rather disillusioned at the time. I was called a hippie lover because I hired a few long-hairs from the bush,' he recalled. 'Damned good craftsmen they were. Appreciated the old wood in those timber places we renovated.'

'And sold to other tree changers at city prices,' added Stephen, with a smile.

'I'm very glad you were part of the trend to save the beautiful old homes we have in Neverend,' said Susan.

'And I love the work. Gradually, too, the locals began to wake up to the fact that the town now had a population of hip city slickers who might have looked a bit different, but who had open minds and smart business initiatives.'

'And look where we are today,' said Judy, Susan's favourite golfing partner. 'We've evolved into an artistic town with a tremendous community spirit.'

'Yes, the so-called hippie wars finished years ago,' said Susan. 'I think that the problems were always peripheral really. It's funny when I run into someone who came here forty years ago to change the world, who tells me that they are just off to have a game of golf, or are going to Sydney to see a show. People change and mellow over time. I wouldn't live anywhere else.'

'Best place in the world to live,' roared Carla.

'But you don't live here,' said Chris.

'So? I've been all around Australia, and trust me when I tell you that this little town is the best place to live.'

Carla glared at everyone around the table, as if daring them to say otherwise. No one did.

'Here's to Neverend!' Charles raised his glass, and they all followed suit and joined in the toast.

'I'd get another bottle of wine, but someone's on my feet,' Carla suddenly announced.

'Who's under the table? It's far too early,' said Charles in mock alarm.

'It's Biddi the cat,' giggled Megan. 'I'll get the wine.'

'And some ice and the other bottle of champagne while you're at it, Megan. Thanks,' added Tony. 'We must toast our hostess. As always, Bunny, you put on a magnificent spread.'

'I had two very lovely helpers this year,' said Susan with a smile.

'Oh, that's all right, Bunny,' said Megan, coming back in and putting the bottles on the table. 'I like helping your friends. I think you guys are funny.'

'Funny outrageous,' added Chris. He lifted his glass. 'Merry Christmas, everyone.'

*

After the guests had gone home and twilight had begun to make long shadows across the lush fields on the other side of the river, Susan, Carla, Chris and Megan sat on the front verandah enjoying the cool breeze. They sipped their drinks and picked lazily at the remainder of a fruit platter.

'I didn't bother making a pavlova this year. The fruit has been so heavenly that I didn't think it needed anything more than a bit of local cream.'

'Mum, I'm not sure it even needed that. Not after that wonderful plum pudding,' said Chris.

'And thank you, Megan and Carla, for all your efforts in cleaning up the kitchen,' said Susan.

'Least I could do to repay you for such a glorious meal,' replied Carla. 'Loved your trout dish, Megan.' Carla got to her feet. 'Listen, folks, I think I might turn in now, if you don't mind. Have to get an early start in the morning. Places to go, people to see, but like I said, Neverend is always the best.' With that, Carla nodded her good nights and lumbered out towards the guest cottage.

'How was your mother when you rang her?' Susan asked Megan.

Megan shrugged. 'Okay, I guess. I feel a bit mean not being with her and I could tell that the two little brats were getting on her nerves.'

'I can understand that,' said Susan, nodding. 'But it was lovely to have you and your father here to share Christmas with me. Time passes very quickly, especially when you get to my age, so it's nice to be able to share important events with the people you love. Megan, do you remember when you came to stay with Poppy and me when you were younger? Do you still remember your grandfather?'

Megan looked at her in surprise. 'Of course I do! You know what some of my favourite memories ever are? Being here years ago, when I was, like, seven, and I used to come into your room and get in your bed . . .'

'At five thirty in the morning . . .' Susan smiled.

'And we used to cuddle and talk and then Poppy would go and make us cups of tea and bring in little bear bickies.' Megan paused. 'You were my favourite people in the whole wide world. Do you miss him?'

'Of course I do, sweetie. I think of him every day for one reason or another. He'd be so proud of you. And your dad.'

'Yeah, Dad's pretty great.' Megan nodded in agreement.

'Enough, you two,' laughed Chris. 'A man can only

66

take so much flattery. But this Christmas has been very special. It's meant a lot to me.'

'Me too. I have plenty of friends and I never feel lonely, but having you and Megan here has been wonderful. It reminds me of how important families are. Our little family was wonderful. We had some fun times when you and Kate were growing up, didn't we? All those holidays in the caravan.'

'You and Dad were good parents. You gave us lots of your time. I'm sorry I haven't done that sort of thing with you, Megan.' He reached across and squeezed her hand.

'It was easier for us. You have a more complicated life, but it's not too late for you to do things with Megan now.'

'Dad, I would so love to go away in a caravan,' Megan said in a delighted voice.

'Well, I can't see that happening these holidays,' said Chris hastily. 'But I was thinking. Mum, I know that Megan loves your friends, but they are hardly her demographic. Perhaps you wouldn't mind if we asked Megan's bestie, Ruby, to visit for a while. The girls might like to see in the New Year together.'

'That'd be awesome, Dad! Can you speak to her mum? She would have to fly up, wouldn't she?' Megan sounded elated.

'I think that's a terrific idea. We can ring her mother first thing in the morning and make the arrangements,' said Susan, smiling at her granddaughter. 'Tell me, why is Ruby your best friend?'

'Because we like a lot of the same things, and we can be ourselves around each other. I don't feel like I have to be someone I'm not, just to be her friend. She is a free spirit, doesn't care what anyone thinks of her, doesn't act differently when she is around other people. And we have the same taste in almost everything – clothes, bikinis, shoes, earrings,' Megan answered with gusto.

'In that case,' said Susan. 'I can't wait to meet her.'

*

After Susan and Megan had gone to bed, Chris stood in the cool shadows on the verandah, gazing at the rising moon and the familiar silhouette of the distant mountain range. It had certainly been a happy day.

Quietly he walked down the hallway. His mother's bedside light glowed under her door, and he knew she was reading before going to sleep, as she always did. Further along he paused, gently turned the door handle of Megan's room and peeped in. His daughter was fast asleep with Biddi curled against her.

He felt a catch in his throat.

Things would work out for Megan and him. They had to.

3

MEGAN WAS BOUNCING EXCITEDLY on her toes at the arrivals gate as the disembarking passengers began to file into Coffs Harbour airport terminal.

'There she is! Ruby!'

The two girls squealed and ran to each other, hugging and both talking at once as though they'd had no contact for years.

Chris joined them. 'Hi, Ruby, how was the flight?'

'Really good, Mr Baxter. We flew along the coast and there were so many beaches and they all looked terrific.'

'We have great beaches near us and at Coffs, too. Can we go to the beach, please, Dad?' said Megan, taking Ruby's arm as they walked out of the airport. 'Ruby and I love surfing and I haven't had a surf in ages. Ruby, you want to go to the beach, don't you? We have so much to catch up on.'

'Well, it's not like you haven't spoken to each other,' said Chris with amusement. 'There've been a lot of long phone calls. But I think we can fit a bit of surfing into the programme.'

'My mum says there's a fantastic rainforest up here somewhere, but it would be cool to go to the beach too,' said Ruby.

'There's an amazing waterfall my dad can show you, if you want,' said Megan.

Chris walked behind the two girls as they made their way back to the car, chattering like a couple of magpies. Ruby's honey-blonde hair, blow-dried into a straight, shoulder-length bob, was a contrast to Megan's bouncing chestnut curls. They were both dressed in an eclectic style of denim shorts and cropped tops. Megan had spent time accessorising her outfit with a jumble of colourful necklaces, bangles and a long silky scarf knotted around her hips. Ruby's look was more restrained, except for a pair of very elaborate hair clips. Both wore Converse on their feet.

The girls sat in the back seat of the car, talking non-stop as Chris drove the thirty minutes from the airport back to Neverend. His ears pricked up when Megan said, 'I've met some okay boys at the park. Some skate, some just hang around. But they're friendly. Not mint enough to have a fling with, though.'

'Are we going to do anything on New Year's Eve?' asked Ruby.

Megan leaned forward to speak to Chris. 'Dad, what are we doing for New Year's Eve?'

'I have nothing specific in mind. There's always fireworks by the river. People take picnics down there to watch them. Some stay on to see in the New Year and others go to parties. There used to be a dance at the hall. I'll check with Bunny and see if that's still on.'

'We could take a picnic and watch the fireworks,' said Megan, turning back to Ruby. 'It's really neat by the river. I went down there with Bunny on Christmas Eve.'

'Do you know any local kids who would go, Mr Baxter?' said Ruby.

'I'm afraid I don't have my finger on the pulse of the Neverend teenage scene, but I could ask my old friends. Some of them have kids your age,' Chris replied.

'Don't commit us to anything, Dad!' said Megan in alarm. 'Ruby and I don't want to get stuck with any boring guys.'

'How can you tell if they are going to be boring? Do you have a checklist or something?' asked Chris.

Ruby laughed. 'That's a cool idea. When you meet someone you could say, "Wait a sec while I check my list. What's your favourite band? What sort of music do you like best? What movies do you like? What's your idea of a hot date? Okay, you pass, let's go."'

'Or, "No way, José, I'm outta here!"' laughed Megan.

'This is a pretty town,' said Ruby as they headed up Neverend's main street and then turned into View Street and pulled into Susan's driveway. 'Oh, what a cute house! Look, it's even got a name.' She craned her neck forwards to see the plaque beside the front door. 'Why is it called *Selamat*?'

'It means "welcome" in Indonesian and this house has always been a welcoming place,' replied Chris.

'That's sweet,' said Ruby. 'Where's your grandmother, Megan?'

'In the garden out the back, probably. Her name is Susan, but everyone calls her Bunny. My grandfather gave her that nickname,' said Megan as they went indoors. 'You can call her Bunny, too.'

After dinner that night, when the sun had set, Susan suggested that the four of them go for a walk in the cool of the evening. Turning left onto View Street and away from the main street, they strolled slowly, taking in the vista across the paddocks to the nearby ranges, until they reached a large reserve. A track from the reserve led down the hillside to the open grassland below, where a small stream flowed.

'Chris and his sister, Kate, used to collect tadpoles down there when they were little,' Susan told the girls. 'There are mozzies there, so let's walk around the block instead. There are some lovely gardens along here,' she added as they turned into a quiet street lined with aged jacaranda and golden rain trees. 'Years ago a local doctor was horrified by the lack of trees in the town – which is a bit ironic considering the area started as a timber-getting region – so he planted lots of them. When the trees are in bloom it's raining either yellow or purple petals and the ground beneath is like a carpet.'

'Wow, look at the houses,' Ruby exclaimed at a row of timber houses.

'I thought you might like them. Some of them are more than a hundred years old. It's one of the things that makes this town so special.'

'But these are painted in modern colours,' said Ruby. 'I like them. They're sort of trendy-looking.'

'Megan's grandfather and I did our place up years ago,' said Susan. 'Many of the old houses have been done up by newcomers with taste and style. A lot of people go out to old farms and buy authentic items such as old fretwork and fireplaces, or even rescue things from places that have been demolished. Of course, the more people look for treasures for their houses, the more the prices go up.'

'The locals think the new folk have more money than sense,' said Chris, chuckling.

'Well, that might have been true for some, but the newcomers did save a lot of these old places. Ruby, there's a lovely old church down near the cafés that would have been pulled down if someone hadn't come along and turned it into a very smart shop,' said Susan. She leaned down to smell a rose on a vine cascading over a white picket fence. The house behind the fence was lavender blue and it had white iron lace trim along its wide fronted verandah, making it look like a picture in a calendar.

They walked to the end of the block and then turned back towards the main street on a road similarly lined with lovely old homes.

'Are there any old places left that haven't been restored?' Chris asked.

'Yes, a few in town as well as out in the hills and the valley,' said Susan. 'It's surprising what's tucked away on farmland.'

'Why is the town called Neverend?' asked Ruby. 'It's a funny name.'

'There's a creek not far out of town that has never dried up, so the first settlers round here called it the Neverending Creek. The town is named for the creek.'

'Makes sense,' said Ruby, nodding her head.

'Better than calling it Henryville, or something boring like that. The Henry is the river that runs through the town,' Megan explained to Ruby.

'Speaking of the creek,' Chris said to the girls, 'I want to take you out to my secret swimming hole. Maybe we could go tomorrow.'

'And the beach,' said Megan. 'But we don't want to put you to any trouble, Dad.'

Chris grinned, reading between the lines. 'I understand that. I'll keep out of your way. But there isn't a lot of public transport around here and I don't want you to hitchhike. And I've been meaning to show you some of my childhood haunts that you haven't seen yet.'

'Actually, the swimming hole is part of a string of waterholes along the creek,' said Susan. 'But I'm sure your father will stay somewhere out of the way where he won't embarrass you.'

Chris grinned at Susan.

'Do you mind, Ruby?' Megan asked.

'It's cool. A waterhole sounds kinda different. Will you come too, Bunny?'

'I might, if you're sure I won't get in the way. We could have a picnic lunch. I haven't been out there for years.'

*

The next morning the girls, Chris and Susan walked into town to pick up some things for the picnic and to show Ruby around.

Under the trees at the end of River Street, where the patisserie and coffee bars were, they decided to order cold drinks. While they waited for their order, they went to the viewing rail that looked down onto the large park beside the river. The park had a skateboarding area where some of the local boys were showing off their skills.

'There's Dylan and Matt in the red and green T-shirts. And that's Hayden, he's kind of cute,' Megan pointed out.

'Do you know the one in the striped boardies?' asked Ruby.

Megan shook her head, but Susan chimed in, 'Oh, that's Taylor Frost. I know him. He's a nice boy. Wants to be a vet. I know his mum.' Susan smiled at the girls. 'I know most of the young people in town if you want an introduction.'

'How do you know them?' asked Ruby.

'Bunny taught at the high school for years and years.

74

She knows practically everyone,' replied Megan. 'Bunny, we don't want you to introduce us outright. We wouldn't want to seem interested. But thanks.'

'Maybe after the New Year's Eve fireworks you could go to the dance at the hall. That's where you'll meet everyone.'

'Thanks, Bunny, but Megan and I are okay on our own. We have a lot to talk about,' said Ruby hastily.

When they'd finished their drinks and picked up a few groceries, they dropped the parcels at home and then headed out for the waterhole. In minutes they were out of Neverend.

It was a pretty drive following the river, passing several old farmhouses. Further along, tucked into the fold of a hillside, they spotted a modern home with tinted windows, white sculptured walls and the glint of a swimming pool.

After they had driven over a rattling wooden bridge, Chris pulled off the road and bumped across the grass till they pulled up beside several other vehicles parked in the shade. They got out and stretched.

'There's a picnic table down there near the bridge,' said Chris as he picked up the food hamper.

'What a funny old bridge,' said Ruby.

'That's how you get to the waterhole. You go under the bridge and wade upstream along the creek, though the rocks can be slippery, so be careful. I'll set up our picnic while you're gone,' said Susan.

'As long as we can cool off. The sun is hot,' said Ruby, taking a towel from one of the bags.

The girls followed Chris down the bank of the creek and began to wade through the glassy water. In familiar territory, Chris soon disappeared around a bend up ahead, leaving the girls alone. A hundred metres or so further along they found themselves in a hidden green alley. Trees leaned over the waterway, reaching for their partners on the opposite bank, their tangled roots forming dark caverns in the water which sheltered small fish and other creatures. Strands of reeds waved lazily on the surface of the water, now so clear that it was almost transparent. Instinctively the girls lowered their voices.

'It's, like, prehistoric,' whispered Megan.

'Yeah. Jurassic Park,' answered Ruby.

'Some of those trees must be hundreds of years old. It feels like we're the only people left in the world,' said Megan.

'It's not creepy, though. Really magic.'

'What's that? Hey, listen.'

'Is that shouting?' whispered Ruby.

'Yes. And laughing. There are people up ahead.'

They pushed on through the water until, rounding a corner, they saw a large swimming hole. Chris was already on the far bank, where he dropped his towel and made his way over to a fat rope hanging from a tree. Grabbing it, he swung out over the creek and let go, falling into the water and disappearing. His head bobbed up and he roared with delighted laughter.

Fat old trees lined the creek, their sturdy branches suspended above the deep swimming hole. Amidst much laughter and squeals, a group of boys and girls were taking turns to drop feet first from the branches, plunging into the water with loud splashes.

'Come on, girls, have a go!' Chris shouted.

There were four boys and three girls all about the girls' age, and the fun they were having was infectious. Megan and Ruby didn't need a second invitation to grab the rope and swing out over the water.

'Do you think there'd be fish in here, Dad?' asked Megan as she bobbed up beside her father.

'Not any more,' he laughed. 'This mob would frighten away an elephant!'

Finally, arms tiring from hanging on to the rope, they all floated in the pool and began to chat lazily with the local teenagers.

'How'd you find this place?' asked one of the boys. 'You're new. Not that it's a problem,' he added, after eyeing the two girls.

'I brought them. I've been coming here since I was a kid,' said Chris. 'In fact I might go upstream a bit further, I remember another spot I used to like.'

'It gets a bit overgrown further on,' said another of the boys.

'Yeah. I remember. If I'm not back in half an hour or so, send out a search party.' He winked at Megan. 'I'll be fine. You stay here.'

Chris swam confidently through the water and thought back to the times he had spent in this creek, years ago. Often he and his mates had come out here adventuring, exploring, swimming and fishing. Memories flooded back to him. Even the trees looked familiar. There was one tree he remembered particularly well. He'd always loved its wide branches that were flat enough to lie on. Once he and Shaun French had dragged an old plywood sheet up onto one of them to make a platform they could both fit on. One winter in the freezing rain they'd settled themselves on the precarious platform above the river, to watch the swirling creek. Shaun had suddenly seen something floating downstream.

'Hey, is that somebody's fishing rod? Let's grab it,' he'd yelled.

'No, it can't be,' shouted Chris. 'No one would be fishing when the weather's like this.'

But Shaun had ignored him. He'd leaned forwards and tried to grab the long pole as it swirled past. Suddenly, without warning, he'd lost his balance and had fallen into the river. The creek had raced furiously, carrying the boy with it, and Shaun had been swept from sight in seconds.

Chris had scrambled down the tree and, quickly slashing one of the ropes holding the platform in place with his pocket knife, he'd raced back along the bank, carrying the rope and shouting Shaun's name. As he'd rounded a bend in the creek, he'd seen Shaun on the opposite side, clinging to the root of a eucalyptus tree.

Chris had tied one end of the rope to a sturdy tree and, with the other end tied around his waist, he'd made his way across the creek, fighting against the current. But the rope had held, and he hadn't been swept away. Even now, Chris wondered how he'd managed to haul Shaun back across the creek to the safety of the bank.

By the time they'd ridden their bikes home that day, they'd decided not to tell anyone what had happened. They hadn't wanted to be forbidden from going back to the creek. It would just be their secret, and they'd never mentioned it again. Chris wondered if Shaun still remembered the incident.

He gazed around at the tranquil scene, remembering how different it had been that grey afternoon. So much water had gone under the proverbial bridge since then, he thought. Good times, bad times, exciting times and now . . . well, things weren't going quite as he'd planned. He turned and went back to the main pool where the girls were laughing with the other young people.

'I'm hungry,' he told them. 'I'm going back to Bunny. See you when you want to eat,' he called.

The girls arrived back shortly afterwards with two of the boys and a girl who was about their age. Susan offered them some sandwiches and fruit as Chris sat quietly in a folding chair.

'They've asked us to join them and their friends on New Year's Eve,' he heard Megan tell Susan.

'Lovely. Where are you going?' she asked.

'There's a group of us going to the river to see the

fireworks. We're taking music and stuff,' said one of the boys.

'You're Jake Timmons's boy, aren't you?' Susan said, peering at him. 'That sounds like a good idea, girls. You two could walk home when it's over, if need be. Speak to your dad, Megan. I'm sure it will be fine.'

*

Chris found himself feeling just a little concerned on New Year's Eve as midnight came and went. He and Susan had celebrated the New Year quietly together. Then his mother had gone to bed but he had stayed up, sitting on the verandah with a drink and his book, his phone beside him in case Megan called him to fetch her and Ruby. The girls had insisted on being independent and walking home the short distance from the river by themselves, but Chris knew he would not relax until they arrived safely.

Just before 1 am, he heard muffled giggles as the girls came tiptoeing down the driveway.

'Hey, Dad, you still up? Happy New Year!' called Megan, and went over and kissed him.

'You too. And you, Ruby. How was it, have a good time?'

'Yeah, we did. Met some nice people, some stupid guys. Got a few kisses,' said Megan.

'One serious one,' laughed Ruby.

'Ah, it was just fun.'

'A couple of people came along who sang and they were pretty good,' said Ruby. 'It wasn't a wild night. But that's a good thing,' she added as an afterthought.

'We met the son of your friend Shaun French. Troy. He's nice,' said Megan. 'He might call us to go somewhere tomorrow. I mean later today.'

'Great. Well, you girls had better get to bed.' Chris

stood up and put his arm around Megan's shoulders. 'Did you wish your mother a Happy New Year?'

'Yep. Ages ago. She was at a party. Thanks for waiting up, Dad.'

'No problem. Sleep tight, you two.'

Chris took his glass to the kitchen and turned off the lights, but suddenly there was a piercing scream from the family bathroom at the back of the house. Chris raced down the hall.

'What is it? Ruby?'

'In here! Quick!' squealed Ruby.

Chris pushed the door open to find Ruby in her pyjamas in a corner of the bathroom, pointing at the toilet seat.

There, perched on the edge, sat a large green tree frog.

'It's okay, Ruby. It's only a frog. It's harmless,' Chris said, suppressing a laugh.

'What is going on?' called out Susan from her bedroom.

'Nothing, Mum. It's only a frog,' replied Chris.

'It's hideous! Take it away! Don't put it down the toilet! I'll never go again!'

'Oh, yuck! How horrible! How did it get in the house?' said Megan, who had joined them. 'Oh, this is so embarrassing.'

'Rubbish. Frogs are part of the rich tapestry of country life,' said Chris as he grabbed a hand towel, scooped up the fat little creature and marched outside.

'Don't let it go in the garden, Dad. Or we'll never go out there either!'

Chris rolled his eyes. 'Megan, don't be so squeamish. You used to play with frogs when you were little.'

'I did not,' said Megan indignantly.

'Yes, you did. Ask Bunny. You scooped them out of her fishpond.'

'Well, they were little ones. Not huge like this.'

'God, Megan, how can you bear all these creepy-crawly

jumpy slithery beasts?' shuddered Ruby. 'I couldn't stand to live with them.'

'We don't actually live with them,' said Chris. 'Our lives just overlap occasionally. Who knows, if you'd kissed him Happy New Year he might have turned into a prince.'

'Dad, that's not funny. We don't have frogs in the house in Newport.'

'No, you have funnel web spiders instead,' said Chris. 'Now, no more fuss. Off to bed.'

'You don't think there are any more, do you?' Ruby asked in a shaky voice. 'This is a bit too close to nature for me.'

'Very unlikely,' said Chris. Then he added mischievously, 'And look on the bright side, at least you didn't sit on it!'

'Arrrgh!' cried the two girls, but then they both laughed.

*

Since Megan and Ruby were fully occupied between the boys they'd met, the beach and Susan shepherding them off to Coffs Harbour to shop, Chris decided to accept an invitation to go fishing with some of his old school friends.

'Just like the old days,' Alex enthused. 'Remember our fishing trips?'

'Do I ever! We were mad, looking back. Shooting the rapids by moonlight in those rubbish old canoes. What were we thinking of?' laughed Chris.

'If we're going fishing, let's do it properly. Get serious,' said Duncan.

'I caught a serious fish under the town bridge the other day,' said Shaun.

'You were just lucky, Frenchy. I'll get my tinnie out. We can all fit into it and the river has a decent flow,' said Duncan.

They made a day of it, with food and beer and bait and gear.

Duncan insisted they launch the boat at his special spot, which entailed them dragging the light aluminium vessel across a paddock that belonged to one of his friends.

The paddock was full of cows who viewed the men and their boat with great suspicion. Chris was sent to keep an eye on them while the others hauled the tinnie to the water's edge. After a great deal of grunting, they managed to lower it into the river and they all settled themselves in.

'Don't think much of your magic spot, Duncan,' said Shaun. 'I reckon the town boat ramp would have been a whole lot easier. I think I worked up a thirst after all that work.'

'There's an idea,' said Duncan, reaching for the beer cooler. He passed a can to Shaun. 'Want one, Alex? You too, Chris?'

'Save it. I just had breakfast. It's not even eight o'clock! My rule is, no grog till after the first fish.'

'Bugger that, we could die of thirst,' said Alex.

Chris laughed as the little open boat puttered slowly down the Henry River, while insects buzzed across its surface and a bird circled high above them. Alex and Duncan trolled their lines in the hope of a strike.

The day was starting to heat up. Chris leaned back, his hat pulled over his eyes, enjoying the warmth of the sun as well as the company. This was how it used to be, he reflected, the four of them fishing, hunting, messing around, telling silly jokes and stories, sometimes getting into a spot of bother, but completely carefree. Some days had been more successful than others, but always the day had ended with their being tired and relaxed. Not that they had any real worries or commitments in those days, Chris thought. Looking back, he knew that they had led a pretty idyllic life. They'd all lived in an oasis of lush abundance, surrounded by family, friends and a close-knit community. Was it any wonder that Shaun, Alex and Duncan had never left such a perfect environment? And now his three friends were happily married, raising children, leading comfortable lives. They'd been away on holidays to Hawaii, Bali, New Zealand and Disneyland but maintained that, while these were great places to visit, they had never considered living anywhere else but this beautiful place.

Over the years, Chris had sometimes thought himself superior to these small-town friends with their narrow horizons, content to live quietly and protect what was familiar. But now he realised that although he had been challenged and enriched by the life he had chosen, here he was, back to square one with not a lot to show for it, while they seemed content with their lot. He felt so discouraged. The media contacts he was in touch with were sympathetic, but not helpful, or even hopeful. He wondered if his luck on the job front was ever going to change.

He drew a deep breath. Still, it was pleasant, even for a short while, to be back where he came from, to know he had a place where he belonged, with friends that he'd known all his life who did not judge but simply accepted him because he was one of them.

The day turned out to be much like those he remembered, full of silly jokes and mateship, light-hearted debates about football and cricket. The men recalled, with much laughter, old teachers who had made school life difficult and the triumphs and failures of the encounters they'd had with girls they'd been sweet on. Today Chris revisited those halcyon days and for an instant wondered if he had done the right thing when he turned his back on Neverend.

*

Ruby stayed nearly two weeks and the two girls crammed a lot into each day. But once Ruby had gone home, time dragged for Megan, and nothing Susan or Chris suggested seemed to interest her.

'Dad, I'm bored. It's no fun without Ruby,' she said, lounging on the couch in the living room.

Chris looked up from his book. 'Maybe it's time you started to like your own company, entertain yourself, or you could always help Bunny in the garden. I'm happy to do something with you – go back to the waterfall or the swimming hole, or go for a hike. I have taken you to the beach a few times.'

'Dad, I like going to the beach, but not with you watching over me all the time,' Megan said, and with a dramatic shrug of her shoulders, she marched to her room.

Chris watched her go, feeling badly not only for his daughter but for himself as well.

Susan joined him. 'I heard that exchange. She's missing Ruby. And Jill too, I expect. It's unfortunate that she doesn't have a special friend in Neverend, although I have heard her talking on her mobile to a couple of the boys she met on New Year's Eve. The Christmas holidays are rather long and most kids get bored towards the end of them. She'll be all right, I'm sure.'

'I expect things will be fine when we get back to Sydney.'

After the pause that followed, Susan said tentatively, 'Chris, dear, can I ask how you're going with your job hunt?' When he didn't answer she pressed on. 'It's nearly the middle of January and a decision is going to have to be made about Megan's schooling. You've told me that Jill isn't interested in paying boarding fees for Megan to stay in her Sydney school and you can't afford to do that by yourself at this time, so have you thought through what your next move might be if the right job doesn't eventuate pretty quickly?'

Chris sighed. 'All I can do is keep trying. But yes, you're right, if something doesn't turn up soon, I'm going to have to make some hard choices, and that will have to involve Megan.'

'I hate to suggest this, because I know that you only want to be a journalist, but while you're waiting for a media job, you could perhaps do something else to earn some money?'

'You know, Mum, you're being really wonderful. I don't know where I'd be without you, but what can I do? Walk into the supermarket and stack shelves, for goodness sake?' Suddenly Chris's frustration and fear boiled over.

'You shouldn't be too proud to do any kind of work to earn a living,' Susan said pointedly.

'Sorry, Mum. It's just that I have to keep banging away at doors. If I stop, I could miss an opening somewhere.'

'Chris, it's up to you, but crunch time is coming. Are you going to stick to your word and keep Megan with you? And if so, how are you going to manage?'

Chris knew his mother's blunt assessment was right, but at that moment, it didn't seem to be helping. 'Mum, I don't bloody know!' He got up and walked to the front door. 'Let me think about it.'

Later that afternoon, Megan trudged up the driveway chewing the last of her gelato cone, her skateboard under her arm. Chris watched her from his father's office. From her slumped shoulders to her dragging feet, Megan radiated sulky boredom. Chris understood how she felt, and didn't want to be too hard on her when being in Neverend was so different from her life in Sydney. He wished he could get her motivated and interested in something. *Mum's right*, he thought. Eight weeks of holidays was too long.

But when Chris was her age holidays had never seemed long enough. The car trip towing their old caravan, the long summer days camping, swimming, fishing, hiking and meeting other kids had seemed to go by in a flash. The card games at night by lantern light, cooking meals over the open fire in the old camp oven or frying pan, reading in the shade and even the sunburn, oyster cuts, sprains and embedded fish hooks were fond memories. Chris and Kate had never been bored with the games of cricket, swimming races in the lagoon, exploring the caves up on the hill and taking the old rowboat to a secret fishing hole. It would have been enjoyable to have done that sort of thing with Megan. Now it all seemed too late, the opportunity gone.

He turned to his computer screen to type out yet another email to a contact asking about work.

He came out of the office a little later feeling tense.

'You look down in the mouth, sweetie,' said Susan, looking up from a magazine.

'That's one way of putting it,' he said, his mouth twisting in a grimace.

'No luck?'

'More knock-backs. You know, Mum, I even tried the local media – the ABC and regional TV as well. I mean, I'm here, I could whip up a story or two for them.'

'They'd be thrilled to have you, too. "Local boy made good" and all that.'

'You might think so, but they just weren't interested.' He began to pace around the room. 'I know that some big-name journos can make good money in TV, but not in the sticks, and not if the journo has to be retrained like I would have to be. The ABC does a great job, especially in the regions, but there aren't any vacancies.' Chris rubbed his face with his hands. 'Mind you, they were kind enough to accept my resume and told me that if a position came up they'd let me know, but I got the impression that's highly unlikely.'

'But Chris, you're a print journalist. Surely you went and saw the local *Star*?'

'Mum, when I approached them to write a piece or two, it was assumed that I was going to write for free. When I asked what I'd be paid, there was a shocked silence. Then I was told the pay rate and it was a pittance, so I said I'd changed my mind.'

Susan frowned. 'Was that wise? Even a pittance is better than nothing. I mean, just to get yourself out there.'

'Mum, I earned more when I was seventeen.'

'I see,' she said quietly. 'Have you thought about what I said? Considered any other kind of work, just in the interim?'

'I have, but Mum, I just don't know that I have many other skills,' said Chris ruefully. 'You remember what a disaster it was when I tried to mow the neighbours' lawns.'

'You weren't that bad,' said Susan. 'You managed to save up enough from that job to put down a deposit on your first car. Your dad and I were very proud of you. And what about Megan? Does she have to work for her pocket money?'

'I'm not sure. Gosh, I haven't even discussed that with Megan. Is that another thing I'll need to pay for?'

'Let's make a cup of coffee.' Susan went into the kitchen, flicked on the kettle and got out a couple of mugs. Chris followed her.

'Where's Megan?'

'I caught her moping, so I sent her down to the supermarket for a few things for dinner.'

'She's still missing Ruby,' said Chris. 'She had her bestie with her and now she's alone again.'

'I would scarcely say she's alone! She's milled around with the kids at the skateboard park. She thinks Carla is kind of cool and she's visited some of my friends. Stephen and Val have asked her out to their farm, as they have new kid goats which are adorable. Her life can't be all shopping malls and trips to the beach,' said Susan briskly.

'Maybe you're right, Mum, although I can understand how Megan feels. Her friends are getting on with their lives without her. I guess she feels left out.'

Susan poured their coffee and they walked back into the living room. 'Chris, sorry to bang on about this, but you have to decide what you are going to do about Megan's schooling. You can't keep putting off the decision.'

'I don't know what to do,' said Chris, slouching in his chair. 'I have no idea where I'll be.'

'You have to decide,' said Susan firmly, taking a seat beside him. 'Do you think you should sell your flat and rent for a while in Sydney? You could use the sale money to pay Megan's school fees and live off your savings until you find another well-paying job. Could you use your savings and money from selling the flat to send Megan as a boarder? How much is it for her to board?'

Chris told her the amount and Susan looked shocked. 'That's even more expensive than I thought,' she said. 'No wonder Jill's baulked at wanting to pay for that.'

Chris shook his head sadly. 'Being realistic, Mum, I know the flat wouldn't bring me that much. I haven't had it long enough to have much equity in it. Besides, have you any idea what rent is like in the area near Megan's school? I'd run out of money in no time.' He ran his fingers through his hair. 'And I don't have much saved up either. I just never expected this situation. Maybe Jill was right after all when she said that an expensive school wasn't a very good idea, but I didn't know when Megan enrolled that I'd lose my job.'

Susan put her hand on his arm. 'Then what? Shall I loan you the money so you can stay in Sydney and Megan can keep attending her school? I have more than I need and everything I have goes to you and Kate anyway, so you could take part of your inheritance now.'

'No! Thank you, Mum, that's very generous of you, but I wouldn't hear of it. I wouldn't know when I could pay it back.' Chris was horrified. How could he take money from her? Even for something as important as Megan's education, taking money from his mother just didn't seem right. He rubbed his eyes. 'I appreciate your offer, Mum. I'll think about it. I just can't believe I'm in this nightmare.'

'It's called Life, sweetheart. Ups and downs. The good and the bad, but nothing lasts forever.' She sipped her coffee. 'May I make a suggestion?'

'Anything. I feel helpless and at a loss. My career might be over. I'm worried about whether I'll be able to pay my mortgage and my car loan. And worst of all, I'm scared I'm going to let Megan down. I've finally had the chance for real time with my daughter and now everything is a total mess.' Chris put his head in his hands. He didn't want to say it out loud, but he recognised that this was one of the lowest points in his life.

'Well, I think you and Megan should stay here, with me, until you get back on your feet,' said Susan. 'Hopefully it will only be for a short time, maybe no more than one school term. I'm sure arrangements could be made between her current school and the perfectly good high school here.'

Chris stared at her. 'She'd hate that! What about all her friends? And it would really disrupt her schooling.'

Susan shook her head. 'Not necessarily. She's not at the stage of having to sit any big exams yet. It's the beginning of the school year, which is the best time to change schools. Quite frankly, as a former teacher, I think it would be easier for Megan to start a new school now rather than having to change later in the year. Besides, if you get a job quickly, you can always return to Sydney and really nothing will be lost. She can pick up where she left off. Kids are really more adaptable than we give them credit for.'

'I suppose her other option is Perth,' Chris said. 'I don't think she would like that either, although she might prefer it when faced with such a choice. But you're right, Mum. I've known it all along, really. The expensive school is out for the time being.' Chris paused and then drained his coffee. 'But what about me? We can't stay here forever. What should I do?'

'Keep doing whatever you have to do to get a job back in your world,' said Susan. 'But if you lived here, it would be a lot cheaper, no rent. If you feel the need to share household expenses, that's fine with me, although as far as I'm concerned there is no need. But I do think that you should get some sort of work to put some cash in your pocket. Do anything, work as a tradie's helper, farm worker, see what's going in Coffs Harbour. Look online or in the local papers. Ask your mates.'

Chris frowned. 'That'll be awkward.'

'For goodness sake, Chris, no it won't!' exclaimed Susan. 'These are your friends, people you've known all your life! And it's the country, where real people live, not the city where everyone feels they have to keep up a super-successful façade!'

Chris managed a smile. 'Okay. I hear what you're saying. The boys and I are playing golf tomorrow. I'll sound them out about finding work.'

'Good,' said Susan, looking mollified. She took their empty cups to the sink and washed them out. 'It seems dire now, Chris, but it will all work out. You'll see.'

Chris watched as she padded down the hallway to her bedroom. He felt better having talked over his problems with his mother. Some of the weight he had been carrying had lifted. Staying at Neverend wasn't a perfect solution, but it was the best thing for the time being. But how was Megan going to take it?

*

Megan chose the next morning to have a long sleep-in, so Chris postponed his conversation with her until the afternoon. Chris decided to revisit the *Coastal Star*, the newspaper that serviced the local area around Coffs Harbour. He asked at reception to speak to Oliver Brand, the editor, and gave his name.

'Not sure if Ollie'll see you without an appointment, but it's a bit of a slow day,' said the girl at the desk with a smile.

Chris was ushered into the editor's small office, which was separated from other cubicles and a larger room where an older man and a young girl were working at computers. Along one wall Chris could see storage cabinets so over-stuffed that their drawers were unable to close properly, sitting beside files of old newspapers attached to wooden frames.

Oliver Brand was in his early thirties, if that, Chris thought. He was wearing a club football jumper.

'Sorry to just drop in,' said Chris. 'I was in town.'

'Very pleased to meet you,' said Oliver, shaking Chris's hand. 'It's a privilege. I believe you were in the office a few days ago. I'm sorry I missed you. I'm a new boy here and I didn't realise you came from the area.'

'Are you from down south?'

'Wagga Wagga via Mildura. You gotta go where the work and the promotions are, right?'

Chris nodded. He'd been keen like this once, ready to go anywhere, write whatever stories he was given. This job was a stepping stone for this young bloke. But would he continue to hop around the chessboard of new journalism or find the pool of papers drying up and have to move sideways into digital and online work like so many others?

'I think I mentioned when I was in here before that I've just come back from the US. I was about to be posted to Asia but my family situation has changed and now I have my fourteen-year-old daughter living with me. I know I said I couldn't take that column that was offered, but I was wondering if you might allow me to reconsider. I like to keep my hand in, and as I'm staying in the area . . .'

Oliver held up his hand. 'Don't tell me. You're doing some research up here! Anything to do with that highway upgrade? That's a nightmare. No, look, sure, Chris. We'd be honoured to have your by-line in the paper. Can't pay over the going rate, you understand . . .'

Chris made a gesture. 'Of course. I understand budget constraints. But it would also help me get a feel for what's happening in not only this part of Australia, but the general mood of the country. I want to stay in touch with the grass roots of Australia.'

'Well, that's great, it'll be fantastic to have you on board. Look, feel free to write what you want. Seven to nine hundred words max, say?' They shook on it. 'I still reckon this is a cover for something big you're doing. G'luck with it.' He winked and grinned. 'Tuesday for Wednesday's paper, okay?'

'Fine. Appreciate it. Cheers, Oliver.'

'Ollie. Can't stand Oliver, dunno what possessed my mother. Leave your number with Gina out the front. Just in case.'

Chris left the office feeling like a fraud. Ollie clearly didn't believe that Chris needed a real paying job. But Chris knew that his mother had been right; for the time being, he was going to have to be flexible until something better came up in Sydney.

*

'Haven't played here in years,' said Chris as the four friends walked beside the flowing river to the first tee. 'Such a mighty view. Not too many courses overlook a river *and* the ocean.'

'Playing beside the river is relaxing but in the summer the mozzies feast on you. I've brought plenty of insect repellent, if anyone needs it,' said Duncan, spraying himself liberally from a can and then offering it round the group. 'We'll get eighteen holes in, it's not a comp day. Do you remember the course, Chris? You get to tee off first. Watch the dogleg to the right and those pine trees. Par four for this hole.'

'Can't say I remember this course in much detail, but I do recall the time I was attacked by a magpie in the breeding season,' said Chris, laughing.

They played the first nine holes and paused for cold drinks at the clubhouse before going round a second time. Alex and Duncan, always strong competitors, compared score sheets and analysed every hole, deciding where they could have improved, while Chris and Shaun relaxed in the shade with their drinks.

'You're doing pretty well, considering you haven't played for a long time,' said Shaun. 'I thought everybody played golf in the States.'

'Business execs do, Frenchy. Lots of deals done on the golf course, apparently. I didn't have a coterie of golfing buddies, just people on the paper in the same position as me.'

'Do you miss the States? Where're you off to next? This has been a nice long break for you here. First time in ages we've all had a chance to really catch up.'

Chris paused. Up till now he'd been vague and tried not to reveal his true situation. But he knew these childhood friends were good people and there was no need to keep up any pretence in front of them any longer. 'Actually, Frenchy, I don't have any definite plans,' Chris said quietly.

'Spoiled for choice, eh?' Shaun grinned, not picking up on Chris's tone.

'Not quite. You mightn't realise it, but the media business is in a bit of strife. Some of the best journos in the business are being let go. They've become expendable due to financial constraints, that sort of thing.'

'But not you, surely? I mean, you're big time.'

Chris gave a weak smile. 'Unfortunately that's sort of what's happened to me. I was offered a posting to Bangkok, but I turned it down because Megan wanted to live with me in Sydney. It turned out that as far as my former employer was concerned it was Bangkok or nothing. So at the moment, I have nothing.'

'Ah, I'm getting the picture,' said Shaun, shaking his head. 'You and Megan are very close, I noticed. Guess she hasn't seen as much of you as she'd like. It's a pretty big call to make, your daughter or your job.'

'I figured this was my last chance to spend time with her before she grows up.' Chris shrugged. 'But the job situation is looking a bit grim and I've got so many financial commitments: Megan's school fees, the mortgage on my flat and now a car to pay off. Without a job, things are quickly getting out of hand.'

'I would've thought with your name a door would open. And you've exhausted every avenue?'

'Seems like it, but school goes back in two weeks, so I have to make a decision soon.'

'I can see why. So what've you decided?'

'Bunny suggested I stay here with her for the time being and put Megan into the local high school.'

Shaun nodded. 'Makes sense. My kids go there, it's a good school. Some really excellent teachers and everyone is capable. Megan would fit in, and, well, your parents taught there for years.'

'She'll be really upset to leave her friends and school in Sydney.'

'If she wants to be with you, she's gotta take the rough with the smooth. She does have a choice. She can always go back to Jill.'

'I don't think that would suit her. I've spoken to Jill about what's happening. She doesn't have any objections to Megan going to the local school. She also said Megan could come to Perth if she doesn't want to go to Neverend High, but I'm hoping Megan will accept the idea of staying here once I explain what's happening. But the crux of the issue, Frenchy, is that I need to make some money. I can't just sponge off Mum. The *Star* offered me a column and I initially turned it down because the money was a pittance. But I went back later and ate a bit of humble pie. Funny thing was, while the editor took me on, he's convinced I'm researching some big story.'

Shaun laughed. 'You're not, are you?'

'I wish,' replied Chris ruefully. 'No, I just need the cash.'

'C'mon, you blokes, let's get going or we'll have other players up our bums,' called out Alex. 'Anyone want to lay some money on the outcome?'

'Winners stand the first round at the nineteenth hole,' said Shaun. He added quietly to Chris, 'Let's talk later.'

*

Shaun walked with Chris to their cars after the round was over and they'd had a couple of drinks. 'Listen, Chris, Dad and I have started a second business, a courier service, and we're desperate for drivers,' Shaun said. 'We're paying reasonable money. Would you be interested? I mean, just till you get back on your feet,' he added, hurriedly. 'I know it's not what you're used to, but the money is okay, and it'd help Dad and me out.' When Chris didn't immediately answer, Shaun shrugged and said, 'Well, anyway, think about it.'

'Frenchy, thank you. I'm grateful for the offer,' said Chris slowly. 'But I don't want you to feel sorry for me, and feel you have to . . .'

'Mate, you'd be doing us a favour,' Shaun cut in. 'Dad and I have been taking turns running all over the joint and frankly Dad's a bit past it. Mind you, we might have to pay danger money. There's often a trip up to the plateau on that bloody road with those B-double trucks from the quarry.'

'Yeah, I noticed them. I'll be okay. Frenchy, I can't thank you enough. You're a real life saver.'

'Hey, listen. I owe you one. Remember the day we went up the creek at the swimming hole after the storm and I fell in and got swept away?'

Chris nodded. 'Funny you mention it, I was thinking of that just the other day, when I took Megan and her friend up to Neverending Creek.'

'My kids like to go up there, too. But I'd have given you the job anyway, even if you hadn't saved my life. That's what mates are for.' He held out his hand. 'Let's shake on it. Dad'll be real pleased.'

It was done. Suddenly Chris felt the decision had been taken out of his hands. Without really thinking, he had accepted a mundane job in Neverend. How was he going to tell all this to Megan? It wasn't just an option; they were staying. In his head he knew this choice was the right one, but in his heart he felt he was letting her down.

*

Chris knew he needed his mother's support to help him explain to Megan that accepting Shaun's offer was the best possible plan, at least for the time being. After forty years as a teacher at the high school, Susan would be able to convince Megan that Neverend High had a solid and respected reputation. And he hoped that Megan would understand that in spite of everything that was happening to them both, he loved her and only wanted the best for her.

Megan knew something was up as soon as she saw her father's expression as he ushered her into the sitting room where Susan sat on the sofa, scratching the cat's ears.

'What's happened? Is everything all right? You're not changing your mind about me, are you, Dad? You're not going to make me go to Perth, right?' demanded Megan.

'Of course not, not if you don't want to,' said Susan. 'Please sit down. Your dad has something he wants to discuss with you.'

Megan looked suspiciously at Chris as she sat beside her grandmother.

Chris dropped into his father's old armchair. 'Sweetheart, as you know, everything is rather complicated with my job situation, so we need to discuss what I propose to do.'

Megan's mouth tightened. 'Have you got a job somewhere else and we're moving?'

'Hear your dad out, sweetie,' said Susan calmly.

'Yes, I've got a job, and no, we're not moving.' He took a deep breath. 'We're staying here in Neverend for the time being. Staying here with Bunny.'

Megan stared at Chris and then at Susan, looking confused. Then she frowned. 'Staying here?' When Chris nodded, she shouted, 'Dad, I can't stay here. I have to go to school!'

'Megs, let me explain the whole situation . . .'

Megan stiffened and sat rigid, her hands tightly clasped, as Chris calmly outlined the job offers he'd had from the *Star* and from Shaun, and how they were the only viable work he'd been able to find.

'Darling, I can't afford to live in Sydney, support us both and pay your school fees without a well-paying job. At present I can't find one, but now I have work here, so I think the only practical solution is to stay here and hope that it won't be long until something suitable turns up in Sydney and we can move back there.'

'I don't want to go to school here! Couldn't I become a boarder at my school?'

'Megan, that would be far too expensive. I simply couldn't afford it.'

'Now, I do have to step in here, Megan, and say that Neverend High School has a high standard of education and is well respected,' said Susan. 'Remember, your grandfather and I taught there for many, many years. I am very proud of our school here.'

'But it's the country, Bunny! The kids, they're all from here. I have nothing in common with them! What about my friends?' Megan's voice cracked.

'They can come and visit any time,' cut in Susan. 'Anyway, you already seem to be getting on well with some of the kids here.'

'But having to put up with them all the time, that's different.' Megan looked at Chris and tears trickled down her cheeks. 'I guess you must hate me for asking to move in with you and making you give up the job in Bangkok. This is all my fault.'

'No! Not at all, honey,' protested Chris. 'That's not the case at all!' He leapt up and went to sit beside her on the sofa, the three of them dislodging Biddi, who scrambled onto Megan's lap. 'Megan, having you live with me is wonderful. I know that life has become more complicated, but I wouldn't change anything. I now realise that being with you is the best. I don't for one nanosecond blame you in any way for my losing my job. You come ahead of everything else in my life. I'm just sorry that things haven't worked out exactly as we planned. I've spoken to your mother, and if you don't want to stay here with me and would prefer to go back to her and live in Perth, I would understand that too, but I hope that you'll stay.'

He took her hand as she looked down, gently stroking the cat with her free hand. Chris glanced over her head at Susan, whose expression was serious. He knew she didn't want to interrupt.

Finally Megan said, 'I'll have to talk to Mum.'

'Of course you will,' said Chris. 'Megan, this is one of the times in life when you'll find things don't work out the way you'd like them to. It's how you handle these hurdles and hiccups that makes you stronger. And better. It's not going to be easy all the time, but we can make the best of it for the short time we're here. Okay?'

'I guess so.' She sighed and shrugged her shoulders. 'I don't have much choice, do I?'

'You do have a choice. Perth or here,' said Susan firmly.

'Bunny, I don't want to go to Perth. And I understand what Dad's saying. But I'm not sure I'll manage. My friends are going to wear black armbands when they hear this news,' said Megan dramatically.

Susan rolled her eyes. 'Megs, you're not dead, for heaven's sake. When you're ready we can go and meet Mrs Hardwick, the school principal. Sally is a lovely woman. She'll sort things out and get you enrolled, and your father can let your old school know that you won't be back for a while.'

'I promise, darling, I'll try my very best to get back on my feet as quickly as I can,' said Chris. 'We might not even have to stay in Neverend very long. Whatever happens, I won't let you down.'

'I'm very proud of you both,' said Susan. 'You're strong people and you'll fit in, Megan, even if that seems a daunting prospect at the moment.' She stood up and kissed them. 'Cup of tea time.'

Megan went to her room to call Jill and her friends. Chris headed to the verandah and sat down, drawing a deep breath and gazing across the valley to the beautiful ranges in the distance. The rattle of cups in the kitchen was comforting. He watched as the mist drifted down from the plateau, heralding a rain shower.

Megan had taken the news pretty well, considering, he thought. He'd even surprised himself with his little speech. He realised that it was quite true that he didn't want to relinquish her. Megan was now entirely his responsibility. He just had to prove himself worthy of his daughter's love and respect, and his mother's kindness and generosity.

But it wasn't going to be easy.

4

A TINY SHINING WATERFALL dribbled down the rock face beside the road like a silver snake.

In the month or so he'd been driving for Shaun, Chris always looked for this particular fern-fringed cliff which abutted the roadside. He had learned that the little cascade marked the halfway point on the precipitous road between Neverend and the plateau. But while the road was narrow and treacherous, especially when sharing it with the overloaded B-double trucks that barrelled along, he never tired of the dramatic scenery around him. The longer he spent in Neverend and the more he saw of the town and its surrounds, the more he was reminded of how unique it was.

Rather than hurrying into the landscape, Chris preferred to tread softly, letting nature come to him.

Sometimes, sitting quietly as he ate his lunch by the side of a seldom-used road, a large goanna or a dozy rock wallaby would come close while the birds fluttered in the branches above him. All ignored his presence as they passed casually by. He could now better appreciate this place, where the rainforests were as dense and impenetrable as they had been when white people had first arrived in Australia, and the nearby beaches still as pristine.

Chris felt relieved that between driving the courier van for Shaun and writing his newspaper column, he was able to help his mother financially, as well as keeping up with his car repayments. Thankfully, the rent from the flat in Sydney just about covered the mortgage. But while he had grudgingly become used to what he hoped was a temporary pause in his career, he knew that Megan was finding the adjustment to the new school difficult.

Every evening he and Susan were regaled over dinner with some new problem, issue or complaint about Neverend High. Chris tried not to overreact to Megan's incessant negativity and he let his mother take the lead in handling these matters. But it seemed to him that Megan was deliberately finding fault with everything. Susan had spoken to Sally Hardwick, the school principal, who'd said that while Megan was doing fine academically, she was having trouble fitting in with classmates who had known each other for years. She was still the outsider.

'Give it time,' Mrs Hardwick had said. 'It's only been a few weeks.'

Nonetheless, Chris felt guilty that he had caused the upheaval in Megan's life and he hoped he'd quickly land a job back in the city. But no matter whom he asked, it just seemed that there weren't any well-paid journalistic jobs around.

One morning in early March, as she packed her things for school, Megan radiated unhappiness. It was becoming the norm for her.

'You all set to leave? Got your lunch?' Susan asked her.

'Yes. I made a Japanese bento box today,' said Megan quietly. 'Some sushi, carrot sticks, radish roses and miso soup in the mini thermos.'

'That sounds great,' said her grandmother.

'Yeah, I think it is, but all the other kids think it's weird when I bring things like this. They have sandwiches and pies and boring stuff. I hate that sort of food.'

'That's odd,' said Chris. 'The cafés in town have some very adventurous food. I would have thought that those ideas would have rubbed off.'

'Well, they haven't,' said Megan sulkily. 'No one has any idea about decent food. The whole school is so dull. And I hate being in classes with boys, too. They're loud and they smell sweaty. And they always think they're right and don't give you a proper go at saying things. I don't think I'll learn anything with them around.'

'Nonsense,' replied Susan. 'I was only talking to Mrs Hardwick the other day and she said that you're doing well academically.'

'Only because I've done the work already at my old school,' Megan shot back. 'I'll never learn anything new at Neverend. I won't get the chance.'

Before the argument could escalate, Chris changed the subject.

'I don't have to start till ten. Want to walk part of the way to school with me?' he suggested. 'I'm going to get the morning paper.'

'Fine,' said Megan, sighing and slowly picking up her backpack. Chris and Susan shared a look as she trudged to the front door.

After dinner that evening, they moved into the sitting room to watch the one TV set in the house. Watching TV provided a welcome mental break for Chris from his fruitless search for a job back in the world of journalism and some peace from Megan's refrain of how little she was enjoying school. Megan was about to go to her room to watch her own programmes on her laptop when she looked at the mantelpiece.

'What's that card leaning against the clock, Bunny?' she asked.

'It came in the mail today. An invitation. Nothing very important,' said Susan, shrugging.

'What kind of invitation?' Chris asked. 'Or is it private?'

Susan offhandedly told him to look himself. Chris reached for the embossed card. 'Looks fancy.' He read it quickly and looked at his mother. 'Bit of a blast from the past, isn't it?'

'Is it a party, Bunny?' asked Megan.

'Sort of, it's an invitation to a reunion,' said Chris.

'It's just a luncheon. I get these invitations every five or so years. I've never bothered to go, although it is nice to be remembered.'

'Who? What's it about?' asked Megan curiously.

'It was a long time ago, sweetie,' said Susan, waving her hand. 'Ancient history. All to do with the Neighbourhood Aid project I worked on.'

'I sort of remember you telling me about that. Never quite got off the ground, did it?' Chris said.

'No, not really. A bit of a shame, though; we had such high hopes when it started.' Susan pulled Biddi into her lap and began stroking her fur.

'Can I see the invitation, please?' asked Megan. Chris handed her the card and Megan read it aloud: '"The participants in the Indonesian Neighbourhood Aid project, 1968, are invited to a Luncheon Reunion to reminisce, recall and reflect. 11 am, 2 April, Croydon House, Sydney."' Megan looked up. 'You should go along, Bunny. It sounds great,' she said. 'What's it all about?'

'I'm not sure that I want to reminisce or reflect,' said Susan quietly. 'It was all such a long time ago that it feels like someone else's life.'

Megan pressed on, not noticing Susan's reticence. 'Bunny, did you go to Indonesia? Like, Bali, for a holiday?'

'No, it wasn't a holiday, and it wasn't Bali, Megan. I went to work in Indonesia, on Java, for a short time in my life, and I certainly haven't forgotten what happened there.' Susan's face darkened. 'It left me with some rather searing memories.'

'I thought you always lived in Neverend. Did Poppy go with you?' asked Megan, now thoroughly intrigued.

'No, it was before I met Poppy. It's rather a long story, sweetheart.' Susan moved Biddi off her lap, got up and straightened a picture on the mantel.

Chris studied her. 'Why don't you want to go to this reunion, Mum? Aren't you even a little bit keen to catch up with the other people you went away with after all these years?'

'Chris, I've had very little to do with them for years, except for the occasional Christmas card,' said Susan. 'We all moved on with our lives. I know that some of them have been very successful in the business world. I wasn't interested in pursuing that sort of career. I loved teaching. Anyway, I think the life I've had, here in Neverend with your father, has been extremely happy, but because that's all I've done, I don't think I have anything to contribute at a reunion like this.'

'Mum, don't be so modest. You know you have been really important to this town. Besides, weren't these people your friends during an extraordinarily dangerous time?' said Chris quietly.

'What do you mean, dangerous?' asked Megan, her eyebrows raised. Susan looked at Chris.

'Mum, why don't you tell Megan what you were doing in Indonesia? She might like to know that you weren't always a high school teacher in this little part of the world.'

'Chris, it was such a long time ago, Megan wouldn't be interested.' Susan walked across the room towards the kitchen.

'Yes, I would, Bunny.'

Susan paused in the doorway and turned to face them.

'Remind me how you got involved in the project in the first place, Mum,' said Chris.

'Please, Bunny,' said Megan beseechingly. Susan was quiet a moment as she studied Megan's face.

'All right, if you insist,' she said finally. 'But I'm getting a fresh cuppa first.'

A short time later she returned to the sitting room, mug in hand, and settled herself on the couch between Megan and Biddi.

'Tell me when you both get bored and I'll stop. I had just finished my university degree,' she began. 'First class honours in cultural anthropology. Not a very practical choice of subject,' Susan laughed. 'But anthropology was very popular in those days. I was rather idealistic and thought that if you could understand what were thought then to be simpler cultures worked, then that knowledge could be transferred to our seemingly more complex society to make it a better place.'

'And did it, Bunny?' Megan asked, snuggling down on the couch.

'I don't think so, Megan, but I enjoyed finding out how different societies worked. It was fascinating and I began to put other cultures into perspective. Anyway, when the results of my thesis came out, I was approached by someone from the government in Canberra. At that time, relations with Indonesia were rather difficult. There had been a lot of unrest there and many western countries, like the USA, the Netherlands and the UK, had disengaged from it. But Australia didn't want to do that because Indonesia was our next-door neighbour and so was very important to us, politically.'

'I believe it still is,' Chris commented.

'But even more so then, for you have to remember that we shared a common border with Indonesia on the island of New Guinea. They had the western side of the island, while we controlled the Australian territories of Papua and New Guinea to the east. I'm sure the Australian government was worried that the Indonesian army could cross over to our side if we didn't stay friendly.'

'You're right. I'd forgotten about that.'

'Dad, don't interrupt,' said Megan crossly. 'Take no notice of him and go on with your story, please, Bunny.'

'As I was saying, when I was approached, it was explained to me that a government agency was setting up a pilot scheme to trial a programme where young Australian graduates would live and work in Indonesia to assist with its growth and progress and to foster friendship between the two countries. It was similar to the American Peace Corps programme which was no longer operational in Indonesia. The idea was that we would fill the vacuum it had left. Anyway, that was the brief. In reality it was all, quite frankly, somewhat disorganised.

'There were six of us. Evan was a medical doctor, Alan was a civil engineer, David was an agronomist, Mark had graduated with honours in economics and Norma, the only other woman in the group, was a qualified midwife. We were sent to Canberra for a week to be briefed on what was expected of us and then we were flown to Jakarta.'

'Doesn't sound as though there was a lot of training, Mum?'

'Dad, you're interrupting again! Bunny, please don't stop. This is so, like, the best story. I want to know all about it,' said Megan, settling closer to Susan. Her grandmother smiled at her and continued her story.

JAKARTA, 1968

As I stepped from the plane onto the tarmac at Jakarta airport, the first thing I noticed was the smell. It was sweet, almost sickly. I found out later that it was the local *kretek* – clove cigarettes – that everyone seemed to smoke. So right from the beginning I was on a sensory overload that never really went away. No matter where I went in Indonesia, there was something new and different to see, smell, hear and taste.

For the first few days the six of us were put up in the grand new Hotel Indonesia. That first night I looked from my high-rise hotel room window down at a huge traffic roundabout. In the middle, surrounded by a pool of water, was a monument: a tall column topped with the statue of a waving boy and girl. I stood watching old American cars, bicycles and the three-wheeled rickshaws the locals called *betjak*s drive around it. I almost pinched myself to make sure that I was actually there, in Indonesia. I felt optimistic, excited and rather privileged to be part of this small group tasked with bringing some positive change to this nation that was such a close neighbour of ours yet so unknown.

The hotel was filled with Indonesian paintings, murals, statues and mosaics. It had a huge pool, a supper club and a fancy restaurant where everyone dressed up and ate things like Beef Wellington and used masses of cutlery for each course and different wineglasses for the various wines that were available. All very proper and impressive, I thought. There was a fancy Asian-style restaurant in the hotel too, but that first evening we all decided to eat somewhere more adventurous. In any case we had very little money, as we were expected to live much as the locals did, so we had to be frugal.

I asked the others if they knew what the monument I had seen from my window was all about.

'It's called the Selamat Datang, the Welcome Monument. It was erected to welcome people to the Emerging Nations Games organised by President Sukarno, and the statue on the top is nicknamed Hansel and Gretel,' said Mark with a grin.

'Very appropriate welcome for us, too,' I replied.

'It's just another example of conspicuous nationalism,' said David. 'I expect that we shall see a lot of these sorts of statues and monuments. They're usually large and generally tasteless.'

David, our agronomist, was of medium height and quite gregarious. He'd told us that he came from a large family and that if he'd remained silent he would have been totally overlooked by his older brothers. But he was easy to get along with and had a great sense of humour.

'Well, I for one am looking forward to seeing the more ancient examples of Indonesian monuments,' I told the others. 'If we get a chance to travel.'

'There's so much to see that's really interesting,' said Mark. 'I'm sure we'll be able to explore the country a bit.'

Mark, an economist, was, to put it bluntly, drop dead gorgeous. His even features were complemented by a charming smile. He obviously came from a well-to-do family and had been given an expensive private school education. We found out later that his father was the managing director of a very large Australian company. Mark was assured and confident, and the rest of us could not help but wonder why he had become involved in this project in a third-world country when a much more glamorous future would certainly have beckoned.

We got our first chance to explore the city later the following day. In contrast to the grandiose government buildings and heroic statues, what we saw on our walk was a scrambled congestion of marketplaces, slums and dilapidated buildings. In the crowded lanes squatters lived under sheets of tin or plastic, and there were people everywhere, selling food, cooking, eating or begging. Lining the busy roads were stalls, small shops and sellers crouched beside their goods that were spread out on small mats in front of them. A smelly open canal served as a sewer but also as a bathing and washing stream for the poor and small children frolicked in its brown water.

'Susan, it's all so disgusting. How can they bathe in those dirty canals? It's putrid. Disease must be rife in these slums,' said Norma, pursing her lips.

Norma had spent some years as a midwife and was a bit older than the rest of us. She hadn't been to university, but had trained in one of the best hospitals in Sydney. She was critical, judgemental and argumentative. Everything was black or white to Norma and it soon became apparent that she would not be easy to get on with. Yet I sensed that she was sincere in wanting to help the Indonesians, and she certainly had the skills to do so. Whether her inflexible nature would enable her to be successful remained to be seen.

Beside the canal, I could see an old, rather substantial house. It had certainly seen better days, but it still retained a rather faded grandeur.

'That old place must have been gorgeous, once upon a time,' I commented.

'Probably belonged to a Dutch merchant,' said Mark. 'The Dutch ruled these islands for more than three hundred years and many Dutchmen made their fortunes from the spice trade.'

'I'd love to have the money to be able to restore it,' I said wistfully.

'Can't imagine why you would want to spend money on a place that overlooks a sewer like that house does,' said Norma.

'I suppose you're right. But doing up an old place appeals to me.'

As afternoon melted into evening the locals all appeared to be out and about too; it seemed no one ate at home. People walked in groups, stopping to chat with friends or examining the merchandise on sale. There were lots of families eating together. Food of every description was being prepared over small charcoal fires, sold from baskets on bicycles, from small boxes on stands and carts, or from portable kitchens from which appetising spicy aromas wafted. So many seemed to have something to sell: small gifts, children's toys, cigarettes, coconut and rice sweets, garishly coloured cakes and biscuits.

All around us there was noise. It came from the crowds, the jangle of bicycle bells and car and truck horns, the rumble of buses belching fumes, the *click-clack* of hawkers' sticks vying for customers, the skittering and shrieking of small children, laughing, clinging, occasionally crying.

Every tiny thing I saw interested me. When I told Norma how fascinating I found all this nightlife to be, she looked at me in amazement and said, 'I will never get used to this chaos.'

'It's not so bad, Norma. Local colour,' said Mark.

'I hope the hospital and clinics are not so crazy,' said Norma.

111

'I guess we'll find out soon enough,' said Evan, our medico, who'd recently finished his residency at a large Melbourne hospital.

'I love the women's traditional dress. How pretty they are in their batik sarongs,' I said.

'*Sarong kebaya*. It's quite an art form,' said Evan, then he blushed and added sheepishly, 'I read about it.'

Evan had grown up in a coastal Victorian town where his father had been the local GP for years, but we soon found out he was no country bumpkin. Evan read voraciously and appeared to know something about almost everything. At times he seemed embarrassed to display his breadth of knowledge.

'Yes, I read about them, too. I'd like to ask if it's acceptable for a western girl to wear an outfit like that. They look so graceful,' I said. I'd noticed the beautiful and intricate batik patterns that most Indonesians wore and I was determined to buy some of the fabric. 'Come on, let's try one of those satay sticks. They smell heavenly.'

The boys bought the tasty skewers of barbecued chicken drenched in peanut sauce and I loved them. But Norma refused even to try one.

'You're going to get diarrhoea and a stomach-ache from that sort of germ-laden, unhealthy rubbish,' she said, shaking her head.

'Worth it,' said Evan. 'Let's sit at that place with the laminex tables and order something to drink. They've got Bintang beer, which I'm told is quite palatable.'

That night marked the beginning of my love affair with Indonesian food. Cereal and toast quickly seemed a dull breakfast after I discovered tasty *nasi goreng*; fried spicy rice with a small portion of shredded omelette on top. I quickly grew to love fried bananas, or rice steamed in a banana leaf and put into a bowl with coconut milk and all kinds of additions: nuts and bean sprouts and green onions. Eventually I even braved adding *sambal*, the chilli condiment that goes with every sort of food.

'I'm never going to get used to the hot spices,' David said, tears running down his cheeks after he'd tried it for the first time, but he was wrong. The boys and I all came to love the tang of lime and chilli and the spicy pastes used in many Indonesian dishes. But I don't think Norma ever tried a single local dish. If she couldn't get European food, she ate plain cooked rice, fruit she could peel, or boiled noodles topped with a fried egg.

We sampled several other foods that night and then, despite the calls from hawkers and roadside stallholders, we turned and headed back towards the hotel. It was dark and the dust from the street rose in a sort of mist, backlit by a few dim streetlights. We passed a night market set up under strings of coloured lights and oil lamps which looked very festive.

'We must come back here sometime,' I said, and the boys agreed while Norma sniffed.

'Full of pickpockets, and we'd be the target.'

'Damned right,' agreed David cheerfully. 'Put your money in your shoe. That place looks fun.'

The following day we went to the embassy, where we met Andrew Robinson, a former Australian diplomat who had been one of the driving forces behind the project and who would now oversee it. He introduced us to Mr Putra, who would be our Indonesian liaison officer. Over the coming weeks, Mr Putra was to give us a crash course in Bahasa Indonesia, the official language of Indonesia, as well as outlining the history and political situation of the country. We would no longer live in the luxurious hotel, but would stay with local families in Jakarta so that we could practise our Bahasa. After that, we would head out to where there were hardly any English speakers.

'Mr Putra will be your contact in Indonesia, so if you have a problem or a query you can seek his advice. I travel in and out of Jakarta frequently, so I'll arrange for us to have regular briefings so that we can gauge the progress you're all making,' explained Mr Robinson.

I nodded nervously at the thought of being out of my comfort zone. I wanted to be able to understand what people were telling me and for them to understand me. Suddenly the adventure was starting to look rather daunting.

So, for the next few weeks, we had an intensive course in all things Indonesian. We worked long hours in a small room in a building near the embassy, cooled only by ceiling fans. In that time we did manage to learn quite a lot, not only about Indonesia, but about each other.

Mr Putra explained that Indonesia was made up of thousands of islands. We would be living on the most populated island, Java, but I hoped that at some stage I would be able to visit other islands, such as Sumatra or even Bali, which seemed so romantic. Some of the islands were out of bounds to foreigners, and the Mentawai group off the west coast of Sumatra was apparently rife with Indian and Arab smugglers, so that was a no-go area, too.

Before the war, Mr Putra had explained, the Dutch had been severe rulers, but when the Japanese invaded the Indonesian islands in the Second World War, most of the Dutch left. After the war, when they attempted to return, they found themselves opposed by a strong independence movement led by the man who became the first president, Sukarno, often called Bung Karno. Big brother.

As soon as Mr Putra began to talk about Sukarno, the boys all began to ask him questions.

'Please, let me explain first,' he said. 'And then if you wish to know anything else, please ask me.' Mr Putra continued, 'From the time he was a young man, Sukarno spoke out against the Dutch occupation. He was imprisoned as a subversive and then when he continued working against the Dutch, he and his family were exiled to a remote island. When the Japanese invaded Indonesia in 1942, he saw this as a great chance and he decided to work with them. So, in exchange for organising food and fuel for the Japanese war effort, the Japanese military allowed him to spread his anti-imperialist propaganda. He always said that he regretted collaborating with the Japanese, but argued that the end justified the means.

'As soon as the Japanese surrendered, Sukarno immediately declared Indonesian independence and was appointed the country's first president. He used his diplomatic skills to persuade other countries that Indonesia should be allowed to rule itself, and so pressure was put on the Dutch to give up their claims to our country, which they eventually did,' finished Mr Putra.

'Well that seemed easy enough,' said Alan, somewhat smugly. Alan, an engineer, had come to help the locals construct roads and bridges. He seemed rather abrupt at times and was always ready to give us his opinion on everything, even when it was not sought. But I soon saw that he was enthusiastic about the projects he embarked on, and worked hard to make sure they succeeded.

'Yes, Alan, that may seem so,' replied Mr Putra darkly. 'But creating a democracy in a country with many different regions, cultures, religions and languages and no experience in self-rule was to prove very difficult. Sukarno did very well in the early years, as his charisma helped him balance the competing interests, but this could not last.'

'Mr Putra, did you ever see Sukarno?' asked David.

Mr Putra's eyes flashed. 'Oh, yes, I heard him speak at the opening of the huge games he organised for so-called emerging countries. He spoke for so long that the rest of the ceremony had to be cut short. He could talk for hours. Audiences had to stay there; no one would have dared leave. But his passion was hypnotic, and there was such mystique about him. World leaders seemed to find him mesmerising. He always carried a short stick, and many people believed it had magic powers. But that is nonsense. It was his oratory that snared people.'

'I've seen pictures of him. He was very good looking, always wearing his safari-style suit and that black brimless hat,' I said.

'It is called a *peci*,' said Mr Putra.

'What did Sukarno do about his competing problems?' I asked.

Mr Putra resumed his story. 'Sukarno decided that western-style democracy was unsuitable for Indonesia, so he started to become very authoritarian and he instituted what he called "guided democracy". But this actually inflamed tensions and there was an attempt to assassinate him.'

'A guided democracy is no democracy at all,' snorted Alan.

'Nevertheless, he became increasingly autocratic. To make himself more popular he nationalised all the Dutch companies, including Shell Petroleum and confiscated all Dutch property. He also banned the commercial activities of all foreigners, not just the Dutch but also ethnic Chinese who dominated commercial life in the rural areas. Many of them returned to China.'

'I bet they weren't happy about that,' said Mark.

Mr Putra acknowledged Mark's comment and continued, 'He also used the army to curb the Islamists, but in doing this he found that he had given the military too much power.'

'Not an easy thing to do, playing one group off against another,' agreed David. 'Obviously something was going to go wrong.'

'Is that when he became involved with other communist countries?' asked Alan.

116

'Yes,' said Mr Putra. 'He visited China and the Soviet Union and both gave him financial aid. The Americans became concerned by this and so they also gave him aid.'

David whistled softly. 'Nice trick,' he said. 'Should have set Indonesia up. Money coming in from all directions.'

'By now it had become clear that Sukarno wanted to be seen as a world player and so he began to raise Indonesian prestige by using aggressive tactics,' said Mr Putra. 'Firstly, he claimed Dutch New Guinea as part of Indonesia, and then he started the Konfrontasi movement.'

'I think that Australia was somehow involved in that,' said Evan.

'Really?' I said. 'I didn't know.'

'I don't think it was reported much,' said Evan quietly.

'You lot might know all about this,' said Norma coolly. 'But I don't, so could you please let Mr Putra explain it to someone who didn't go to university?'

Mark and Evan exchanged glances. Mr Putra took his cue. 'When the Malay states became federated in 1963 and established themselves as the country of Malaysia, Sukarno wanted to destabilise the new state, so he sent raiding parties across its borders. These border raids were quite easily repelled, but when the skirmishes continued the British became concerned that they might escalate, so they asked for help from other members of the British Commonwealth to protect Malaysia from disintegration. Australia agreed to help and a small force was sent to the former British colony.'

'I've heard from a friend of mine in the Australian army that several Australian soldiers were killed, but it's all been kept very quiet,' said Evan in his understated way.

All of us looked around in shock. Here was an undeclared war being fought on our doorstep by Australian soldiers and yet we knew next to nothing about it.

117

'Governments can keep secrets very quiet if they don't want their people to know what they are up to,' said Mr Putra, softly. 'It is quite usual.'

'So was Konfrontasi what brought Sukarno down?' I asked.

'No, no. It was the domestic situation,' replied Mr Putra. 'As Sukarno became closer to the communist countries, relations with America deteriorated. Sukarno retaliated by becoming very anti-American. Hollywood movies were banned, as were rock and roll records, and he condoned communist-led attacks on American interests in Indonesia. Americans began to be fearful and most left the country and all American aid was withdrawn.'

'So I'm guessing that Sukarno went to the communist bloc countries for more money to make up the shortfall,' David said.

Mr Putra nodded. 'Yes, but as he became more and more dependent on aid from communist China, the power of the local communist party also grew, while the economy began to deteriorate.'

'I know that there was terrible hyperinflation in Indonesia not so long ago,' said Mark.

'Indeed,' said Mr Putra. 'That is true. Too much was spent trying to make Indonesia a major power, but there was not enough income to cover the cost. Sukarno thought this problem could be solved by printing money.'

'At one stage inflation was running at a thousand per cent,' said Mark. 'As an economist, that's hard to comprehend.'

Evan frowned. 'How can people live with such a huge rise in their cost of living? Where do they find money to cover their expenses if the price of goods is continually rising?' he asked.

'That was precisely the problem,' said Mr Putra, inclining his head. 'People found it very difficult to live from day to day and there was terrible poverty amongst ordinary people and great discontentment.'

'So how did it all end?' asked Norma.

'Towards the end of 1965 there was an attempted coup and six senior generals were murdered. The plotters tried to take over the government radio station, but the coup was poorly organised and it failed.

'General Suharto, now the most senior military officer, acted swiftly, and the next day it was obvious that the fragile alliance on which Sukarno had based his power had collapsed. Suharto was now in charge and military propaganda began to sweep the country. The communists were blamed for everything that had happened and there was terrible retribution. Communist leaders were rounded up and executed, especially in Java and Bali . . .' Mr Putra paused, then continued slowly. 'Many, many innocent people were killed. The Chinese in particular were targeted because people thought that they had connections with Red China. Sukarno was stripped of his presidential title and put under house arrest in Bogor Palace, and that is where he remains. I believe that he is in very poor health.'

When Mr Putra finished, there was silence as we all thought about those momentous events. Eventually Norma spoke.

'Mr Putra, that coup was only about eighteen months ago. Where were you when all this was happening?' she asked.

'At the time I was working in an isolated part of Sumatra, so I was not much affected.' He smiled and changed the subject. 'Now we have a new president, President Suharto, and western countries welcome his presence, including your Prime Minister, Mr Holt. This is why your government is eager to build closer ties with my country. So you are all here to be part of that. It will be a new beginning.' Mr Putra beamed at us.

We quickly realised that Mr Putra was not going to say anything more about the terrible events of 1965, but his talk had left us all rather stunned.

'I hope you're right, Mr Putra, and the country has settled down and wants a new beginning. I would not like to be involved in the sort of violence that you have described,' said Mark.

'No, of course. I can assure you that things in Indonesia are now very peaceful. You will all enjoy your stay here very much,' said Mr Putra with polite smile. He moved on to introduce us to the language we would be studying intensely over the next few weeks. I tried to pay attention but my mind wandered back to his story. It had struck a deep chord with me. Although I hadn't been ignorant about Indonesian politics, I hadn't appreciated how politically volatile the country had been such a short time ago. I applied myself to the studies with a new understanding.

*

While we were staying in Jakarta, Norma and I shared a room in the small three-bedroom house of the Wijaya family. I became very fond of the mother and father, Pak and Ibu Wijawa, and felt very guilty that their five children were crammed into the second bedroom to make space for us. They didn't appear to mind this, though, and we all got along famously.

At first we found the living conditions rather primitive, but I adapted quickly. In the room I shared with Norma there was no window glass or screen, just a grate to keep thieves out, though it let insects in. Lying in bed, we could watch the little chuk-chuk geckoes, with their splayed feet and almost translucent skin, scurry across the ceiling. At night we slept inside a mosquito net, pushing it in tightly under our thin mattresses. We burned foul-smelling coils to deter the mozzies. The elderly maid who lived at the back of the house left a few candles burning at night to keep away bad spirits. She also did some of the cooking and cleaning, as even relatively poor families tended to have a servant to help in the house.

I learned to take a *mandi*, or wash, by standing next to a cement tub of water and tipping a tin bucketful of water over myself. It was really refreshing in the humidity of Jakarta, even though the water never got really cold! The toilet was more challenging. It consisted of two bricks used as foot markers on either side of a drain hole. We were quickly told that the left hand was never used for eating or passing anything to anyone as it was the dirty toilet hand!

Norma was horrified by this lack of hygiene. She had gone with Evan to one of the city's hospitals and came away disillusioned by its lack of facilities. She was appalled to see families camped by the patient's bed, sharing home-cooked food and helping care for their relative.

'I cannot believe how primitive it all is. The nurses do try to keep things clean,' she admitted. 'But the wards are full of non-patients all the time. There is no privacy. Susan, I was so shocked. I thought that at least the city hospitals would be something like the ones at home, but they're not. They only have basic facilities and I'm sure that at night the wards will be crawling with cockroaches, and it wouldn't surprise me if there was even an occasional rat.'

'It can't be that bad, surely?'

'Well, it is. I shudder to think what conditions will be like when we get out into the more remote areas.'

*

After our three weeks in Jakarta we were told we were being sent to the provincial town of Bogor, which was a sleepy place of about one hundred thousand people, approximately two hours away from the capital. It lay beneath the shadow of Mount Salak, an active volcano, and because its altitude was higher than Jakarta's, its climate was cooler and a lot more pleasant. But before we went, we were invited to an informal reception in our honour in one of the rooms at the Australian Embassy.

It was a modest function hosted by the Second Secretary, but Mr Robinson had flown in from Canberra for the occasion. Mr Putra hovered over us like a mother hen. It was wonderful to talk to other friendly Australians and meet some people from the international community. I was especially charmed by an American, Jimmy Anderson, who had been in Indonesia since 1961. Jimmy was very tall and lanky, handsome in a clean-cut way, wearing a button-down shirt, loafers and crisp cotton pants.

'What brought you to Indonesia?' I asked him, sipping a sweet cocktail.

'I originally came out as part of the American Peace Corps movement. Have you heard of it?'

'We're all familiar with the Peace Corps. Actually the programme we're implementing incorporates some of President Kennedy's ideas,' I said, very impressed that this American had been part of that famous organisation. I thought that was probably why he had been invited to meet us.

'The Peace Corps was a wonderful idea. Kennedy was a remarkable man,' Jimmy said. 'I was swept up by his vision. "Ask not what your country can do for you, but what you can do for your country."' He placed his hand over his heart. 'So I decided that I wanted to be part of that, and I joined the Peace Corps right at its inception. I was lucky enough to meet the President in the Rose Garden at the White House before I left to come to Indonesia. I was in a village in Medan when I heard he'd been assassinated. I still can't believe it happened. What a waste.' He shook his head.

I nodded in agreement. 'What did you do in Medan?'

'I was there as a sports coach, although I think a lot of Indonesians thought I was actually a spy for the US government,' said Jimmy with a smile. 'I've loved Indonesia since the moment I arrived, and so when the Peace Corps personnel were withdrawn after Sukarno started his anti-American campaign, I decided that I wanted to stay on. An Indonesian businessman thought I would be useful in his import/export business, so he hired me. My family has always been involved in that sort of thing. My brother has started his own business at home. At first it was difficult, but now that relations between the States and Indonesia have improved, my boss's business has become very successful.'

Jimmy and I talked for a while and I found him charming and witty. He seemed to be the textbook all-American guy. He gave me his business card and suggested we meet when I next came back to the city.

*

Provincial life was very different from life in crowded Jakarta. While the others in our team lived in Bogor itself, I was living just outside the town in a small village known as a *kampong*. I grew to enjoy living in the small community, where one could grow food to eat or sell, and savour the more leisurely pace of life. To enable me to study the dynamics of village politics, I lived with the family of one of the elders, Darma, and his wife, Utari. Darma was often called upon to help the paramount village chief settle disputes.

The days there followed a similar pattern, although rituals and festivals were welcome diversions. Each morning began with the local mosque calling the faithful to prayer. My day started with a *mandi* behind the house, screened by a small section of thatch, with the tantalising smell of breakfast fried noodles for company.

I spent my days asking questions. Sometimes I would be with the women as they worked in their gardens or carried home bundles of sticks for the cooking fire or as they helped their men in the rice paddies. It was such hard work bending over to plant the seedlings. Often a baby was tied onto a woman's back in a batik sling, snuggling close. At other times the women would walk along the curving narrow dirt paths between the paddies carrying their husbands' lunches to them, the food cleverly wrapped in a folded banana leaf.

I sat with the women as they prepared food and I made notes as we talked. They showed me how to husk the rice by throwing the grains into the air from a large flat bamboo tray and allowing the wind to blow away the lighter husks. They talked about their courtship traditions, birth and childrearing customs. I was impressed by the great respect they had for the older members of the family.

I went with them to market. I played with the children in the muddy lanes and watched the boys kick around the hard rattan balls with great skill in the game of *sepak takraw*. The girls, and some boys, preferred to fly paper kites. The older children were very good at it, making their kites soar and dive with great dexterity. I noticed that a lot of the boys liked to play football, a game that was becoming increasingly popular, at least around Bogor.

Slowly, too, the men also came to accept my presence, and would answer my questions about farming, the care of the water buffalo they used to plough their fields, and how their system of payment for the use of the land operated, which, of course, favoured the land owners. But what

I really wanted to know from them was how the political dynamics of the village worked. It was not always easy to get details about this, but this was essentially what I had been sent to find out, for unless there was understanding about the way the village operated, it would be hard to institute workable reforms and improvements.

It wasn't long before I saw that, although the village looked to be a harmonious place, there was a permanent power struggle going on.

The village was run by two paramount chiefs, one of whom looked after civil affairs, while the another dealt with religious issues. These men were helped by village elders whose judgement was held in esteem, and one of these was Darma, with whom I lived. But I also learned that other men, who were assumed to have expertise in other areas, especially magic, might also be consulted by the villagers. This undermined the authority of the paramount leaders and often led to tensions.

Situated where we were on the equator, Bogor, although not as warm as Jakarta, was still always hot, and late one afternoon when I took off my cotton slacks to wash them, I wrapped a length of batik around myself. Utari saw me, pulled me into the little room she shared with her husband and opened a box. She took out a sarong and *kebaya* top and insisted that I put it on. She wound a long sash around my midriff and then added the sheer top edged in cotton lace, fastening it with tiny press studs. She called to the other women, who crowded around and admired me. They pulled back my hair with pretty plastic combs, smoothing it with oil that smelled of vanilla and coconut. That evening we walked with the little children through the *kampong* to the water pump, giggling and singing.

I felt very feminine and comfortable, and decided that when I went into Bogor I'd try to persuade Norma to come with me to the big market and buy a *sarong kebaya* to keep as a souvenir. My blouses and skirts were difficult to press because the irons were heavy charcoal-burning ones that were tricky to use, so I was very tempted to wear sarongs all the time.

However, I pressed my clothes with more care than usual when I arranged to meet Jimmy Anderson in Jakarta. David, Mark and I had decided that we would travel to the capital for a weekend's break and I would stay with the Wijayas again. Both David and Mark teased me when they knew I was having dinner with Jimmy.

'You're a bit of a dark horse, contacting that Yank, aren't you, Susan?' said David.

I blushed. 'Communication is so difficult from the *kampong* that I just had to take the bull by the horns and I sent Jimmy a note. It's something I probably wouldn't do at home,' I explained.

'I think it's a good idea and I hope you have a lovely night,' said Mark kindly. 'David and I shall just have to put up with each other for the evening.'

Jimmy gave me the choice of eating a western meal in a hotel or venturing to a local restaurant. Of course I chose the latter. It turned out to be a rather romantic place with a small courtyard with candles on the table and lanterns overhead. Jimmy did most of the talking as I was keen to hear about his time in Indonesia, especially during the overthrow of Sukarno. I found some of his experiences unsettling and quite scary. I was saddened when he told me how the libraries set up by the US Information Service had been targeted and the books burned.

'The libraries were established so that Indonesian students could borrow books for their studies. It was such a stupid anti-American gesture. So pointless.'

'Mr Putra spoke to us about President Sukarno. There seemed to have been a lot of irrational actions under his rule, but Mr Putra seemed very reluctant to talk about the violence that occurred in the military coup,' I said.

'That's not surprising,' said Jimmy, sipping his drink. 'After the army deposed Sukarno, it took the view that anyone who was not on the side of the military was an enemy. So much anti-communist propaganda was put out there that just knowing someone who might be considered a communist sympathiser, or worse, being suspected of belonging to the communist party, could be signing your own death warrant. No one questioned the military. People were killed for a perceived association or merely a slip of the tongue. Even now most Indonesians are suspicious and fearful, even though they appear to be friendly and go about life as normal. So I can understand why Mr Putra does not want to say too much. It could cause him problems.'

'So do you have any idea how many people were killed in this period?'

'Not really. Possibly hundreds of thousands, maybe as many as a million people, but the government isn't going to inquire too closely about what happened, since they were the beneficiaries of the purge.'

I was shocked. 'It all sounds so terrible. Did you get involved?'

'No, I was very careful to stay out of things and my employer had enough influence to stay on the right side of the military, but some of my Indonesian friends disappeared and I can only think the worst.'

Even after everything I'd learned, I still found it difficult to believe that such things could happen. 'Jimmy, that's awful. Do you think it's still dangerous in Indonesia now?'

'I suppose there is still some unrest about – I guess that is to be expected – but in the *kampong* where you are staying, you would be quite safe. The villagers would look on you as an honoured guest,' Jimmy said gently, reassuring me.

'It seems to be a big task, getting this country back on track.'

'Suharto has made it clear that he is aligned with the west, so more help will come from countries like Australia and America. Just look at you and your friends. You are the start of this increased cooperation. And Indonesians will work hard to improve their country. There's a group here, in Jakarta, nicknamed the Berkeley Mafia. They're smart Indonesian students who were sent to study at the University of California at Berkeley. After they graduated they didn't look for lucrative jobs overseas, but came back here to work in finance and economics and are now being given positions in the new Suharto government. These are the sort of people who will help this country prosper.'

'Well, I hope they find a way to help the village people prosper too,' I said.

'You're right. When the economy starts to pick up, it's imperative that everybody benefits. Now, enough of this serious talk. I need to ask you a really important question. How spicy can you take your beef rendang? Or would you like to try the frogs' legs?'

I laughed. But I did try the frogs' legs and I loved them! They tasted like chicken. The time flew by with Jimmy and I couldn't believe how late it was when we left, so he bargained with a *betjak* driver and we squeezed in together as the driver pedalled to the Wijayas' house.

The city was quiet around the sleeping streets, except for the distant chug of the odd car and stray dogs snuffling amongst rubbish. Jimmy's leg was warm against mine and I had to admit I found him very attractive. Jimmy waited out the front of the dim house, where everyone was asleep, until I was inside.

This was to be the pattern of our friendship. On the occasions I returned to the city, we met and went out somewhere different and I was glad to explore Jakarta in the company of the tall American.

Back in Bogor, we had all more or less settled into our jobs. Alan was helping the Bogor council construct a bridge over a nearby river, Mark was organising meetings with the local small business owners to help them develop their various concerns, David was in his element discussing ways for farmers to improve their crop yields and Evan was enjoying the challenge of working in the local hospital. Norma, however, was finding her job at the hospital very depressing.

'I know that the nurses know what they are supposed to do, but they don't always do it. They don't seem to understand that they must look after all of their patients. They will neglect a mother in great need in order to help one of their relatives who doesn't really need much attention at all.' Evan reassured her that her work was important and necessary and she would be able to bring about those changes in attitude.

Then Norma suddenly got sick. She didn't want to leave her room in the hostel where she and Evan boarded and lay on the small hard bed, sweating feverishly, throwing up everything, even a mouthful of boiled water. I left the *kampong* to visit her and became really worried.

'Do you know what's wrong with her, Evan?' I asked him as I held Norma's clammy hand.

'Dysentery, but it's pretty severe,' Evan replied, frowning. 'Funny that it should happen to Norma, since she is the one who is so fussy about what she eats. And the problem is that she won't go into the hospital. Absolutely shrieked when I suggested it. But I don't blame her. Can you imagine Norma in a twenty-four-bed ward, complete with masses of relatives? It wouldn't work. But if she stays in her room there is no one who can look after her properly and feed her the right things.'

I looked at Norma's sweaty face. Her eyes were squeezed shut and she moaned softly. 'I could take her back with me to the village, but I don't think that would work either. Evan, could we get her to Jakarta? I am sure that the Wijayas would be happy to put both of us up. I can leave the *kampong* for a few days and, besides, I've got a lot of notes that I need to write up, so I could stay with Norma and nurse her while I do that.'

So Norma and I went to stay in Jakarta. Norma was a very difficult patient, but Ibu Wijaya was very kind and made sure that she bought the food that Norma was able to eat. I cooked it for her and gradually Norma began to improve.

While I was staying in Jakarta, I saw a lot more of Jimmy and we become close. He was the first man I'd known whose company I loved and with whom I could sit and talk for hours and hours. We came to share our family stories, our life back at home, our university days, and spent time trying to solve the problems of the world. Like me, he was deeply concerned about the Vietnam War and both of us were uneasy about its escalation.

'The Tet Offensive early this year was quite a shock. It's the first time that the Viet Cong has attacked South Vietnamese cities,' said Jimmy.

I nodded. 'A lot of my friends are questioning Australian involvement in Vietnam. They don't like the idea that conscripted soldiers have to go there and fight.'

Home seemed very far away when I was sharing a beer with Jimmy in a crowded downtown bar. People lived cheek by jowl in the city, but even in the rural paddy fields and farmlands one had the sense of never being alone. Jimmy told me that he had the same feeling even when he ventured into Indonesia's large forests where wild tigers and other dangerous animals lived. 'You're never by yourself in this country,' he said.

For the first time I realised what a homogeneous society I'd grown up in. At university there had been some Singhalese and Malaysian students and there were Chinese people running businesses in some of the suburbs, but I'd never met an Aborigine. Here, however, I was the odd one out. But I liked it! Each day I tried to learn new words to improve my Bahasa. I loved the food, the customs, and I was slowly grasping the complex levels of traditional society. The religions in Indonesia were still something of a mystery I was trying to unravel. Back in the village I had begun to learn the fundamentals of Islam, and Buddhism also interested me very much. The Chinese family next door to the Wijayas were Theravada Buddhists who made daily offerings to the monks at the small shrine nearby. When I mentioned this to Jimmy, he made a suggestion.

'Would you like to go to see Borobudur, in central Java? It's the biggest Buddhist temple in the world. It's not in the best of repair, although I've heard that UNESCO is interested in restoring it properly. It will be a major task and will probably take decades to complete.'

'Heavens, it must be big! It sounds fascinating. How does one get to central Java?' I asked. As much as I wanted to see this amazing-sounding temple, I thought the idea of travelling somewhere with Jimmy was even more appealing!

'We'd need a few days to really see it, but it's not hard to plan. That is, if you're comfortable with the idea?'

'Of course, we'll share expenses. Norma's a lot better now so she won't mind if I leave her in Ibu Wijaya's care for a few days. Ibu will cook Norma's food the way she likes it if I show her how.'

I had no qualms about travelling with Jimmy. He was so easygoing, interesting, and to use the word my mother

131

might have said, gentlemanly. And he cared deeply about the Indonesian people. I thought he was a bit on the old-fashioned side in some ways as he also sported an all-American crew cut.

He laughed when I mentioned it. 'Don't worry, long hair is catching on at home, but crew cuts are still in, especially here in the tropics because they're cool and comfortable.'

We got a train to Yogyakarta and then caught a local bus, which took hours of uncomfortable driving to reach Borobudur. We booked into a guesthouse where we each had a small, clean room, if simply furnished, and shared an Indonesian-style bathroom.

The next day we went to see the temple, and I was stunned at its stupendous size spread out over an enormous area.

'Just think of the millions of stones that were dragged here to build it, all of them sitting perfectly together with no cement or mortar,' said Jimmy. 'Some say that it was built to represent a lotus floating above a now dried-up lake, but I don't know how true that is.'

We slowly ascended from terrace to terrace. The lower levels were ringed by a high balustrade that blocked out the view of the landscape below, instead drawing us into the life and teachings of Buddha as depicted by carvings and sculptures on the walls. We wandered amongst the statues for hours. The temple seemed to go on forever.

'No wonder it was a place of prayer and pilgrimage,' I said. 'But it's heartbreaking to see how much has been broken off and taken away.'

'It was built about twelve hundred years ago, but over the years fell into disrepair. Sir Thomas Stamford Raffles heard about this fabled place when he was briefly Governor of Java in the early nineteenth century.'

'You mean the Raffles of the hotel in Singapore?' I asked.

'The very one. He heard about the temple and encouraged the Dutch to take an interest in it. They did, and gradually throughout the nineteenth century they developed the site. Unfortunately, looting was rife and happened on a large scale. The Dutch allowed many of the statues to be taken away. In the early part of the twentieth century, they began to look seriously at restoring Borobudur, but it all stopped with independence as it was not a priority. Still, hopefully UNESCO will step in now. It will be a tragedy if this place is not properly preserved.'

'It is amazing that such an incredible place could be built long before the cathedrals of Europe were even thought of,' I said.

'Europeans don't have the monopoly on extraordinary and impressive buildings.'

It was a long hot day. Sometimes we stopped and sat to simply try and digest the richness of all that surrounded us in the magnificent temple. We passed several local people praying and making offerings. At sunset we made our way back to the guesthouse.

After the cooling *mandi*, I changed into a sarong and a loose top, and picked some small frangipani flowers from a tree in the garden to pin in my hair. Their perfume was heady and that, along with the slim-fitting sarong, made me feel as though I was gliding rather than walking.

Jimmy jumped to his feet when he saw me and kissed my cheek.

'You look so beautiful, Susan. Just lovely.'

We sat in the garden at a small table while the staff lit candles and burned small kerosene flame torches. They brought us cold drinks and plates of peanuts as well as crispy *krupuk*, a deep-fried prawn cracker. We still had a lot to talk about after our exploration of the ancient temple.

'There are so many extraordinary places to see in Indonesia. Every island has something different and special,' said Jimmy.

'Where else do you think is a really brilliant place to visit?'

'My favourite place is Lake Toba, on the island of Sumatra, the biggest volcanic lake in the world. It's more than fifty miles long and like a clear deep blue ocean. In the lake is a massive island called Samosir, which is attached to the mainland by a tiny isthmus. There are a few little guesthouses scattered around the steep hillsides as well as an old Dutch colonial hotel, which I like. Swimming in the lake in the calm morning or in the melting sunset is like being lost in the mists of time. And the other amazing thing is that it's full of goldfish!'

'Sounds incredible. How romantic.'

'It is. Very.' Jimmy smiled at me.

Our meal was served: noodles, a delicious fried fish and a salad with my favourite *gado gado*, or peanut, dressing. We drank two Bintang beers and talked more and laughed a lot. I was tired, my legs aching from all the climbing and walking, but I felt exhilarated.

And then, when we went to our rooms, Jimmy kissed me at my door. But this time it was a very passionate kiss and we were both breathless. He pulled away and opened my door, saying, 'You'd better go inside, right now, or I won't be able to stop kissing you.'

I knew then that he felt as I did. And it was a warm and wonderful feeling. I knew that I was in love for the first time in my life.

5

WHILE I CONTINUED TO research life in the *kampong*, my thoughts turned constantly to Jimmy. I couldn't stop thinking about him. We were seeing each other regularly, and while the boys teased me about him, they agreed he was a nice bloke.

'Not too much of a Yank,' laughed David.

'What does that mean?' I asked.

'Doesn't go on about how great America is, I suppose.'

As a group, we had become very close since moving to Bogor. Even though I spent most of my time in the *kampong*, I saw the others regularly in town. Evan and Norma had rooms at a hostel beside the hospital where they worked, while the others were housed with local families. Norma was happy for me to share her room when I stayed in Bogor overnight. Mark was billeted with an ethnic Chinese family, the Tans. The family had been born in Bogor, but clung to its cultural heritage. If Jimmy came for a weekend visit, he would stay with them as well. He could have afforded one of the small hotels, but he knew that the Tans appreciated the money he paid them and he enjoyed their friendly hospitality. It was more fun than staying in a soulless hotel.

Much as we liked getting to know the local people, we were a band of Aussies glad of each other's company. Every Friday night we would meet at a local eating house and talk about our work as well as simply let our hair down. We soon learned that Norma would never leave a mother in labour, but she joined us when she could, picking carefully at what she ate and saying she came for the company, not the food. She was not the most joyous companion. She was one of those people who lacked a sense of subtlety, taking everything at face value and looking annoyed when she realised a comment had been made as a joke.

Alan could also be a bit taciturn at times. I quickly realised that if things were going well for him then he could be good fun, but if the project he was working on was experiencing difficulties, he was not really interested in anything we had to say, and instead would brood over his own problems. Generally, though, on these nights out we had a lot of laughs and it was always good to exchange notes.

'One of my problems is that the villagers, especially the farmers, are all so conservative,' David complained one warm evening as we sat together enjoying the fading light.

'That is certainly true of my *kampong*,' I said in agreement. 'Although, to be fair, the younger ones see the need for progress. But the older ones, especially those in authority, don't want to change anything.'

'How true,' said David. 'But sometimes not wanting to implement radical change can be for the best.'

'How so?' asked Alan. 'I think that any progress is good for the villagers.'

'Recently the Javanese officials wanted to modernise the rice industry, by bringing in massive rice-processing mills from overseas and pushing the locals into more intensive planting, that sort of thing. But it didn't happen,' said David.

'Sounds like a good idea to me. Produce rice more efficiently more food and more profit. Good for everyone,' said Alan.

'Not for the women in my *kampong*,' I replied, swatting an insect. 'A big mill would mean that the money the women earn through grinding their own rice would dry up.'

'I think that the main reason the idea didn't take off was that people don't trust the government to be able to provide them with rice at affordable prices. They think that whoever controls rice production controls the local economy,' David explained.

'I think they are probably right there. So, what have you done for your local farmers?' asked Mark.

'I've managed to get them working together, doing simple things like cleaning out the irrigation drains. I've also organised some agricultural students to come along and introduce some new ideas, like planting high-yield rice varieties, and we're supplying them with fertilisers,' said David.

'That sounds pretty good,' said Evan. 'It's unrealistic to expect us to be able to implement big changes, but if we are able to make people's lives better, even in a small way, then I think we can count ourselves a success.'

Jimmy, who'd come from Jakarta for the weekend, nodded and said, 'That's exactly how I felt about the Peace Corps. We couldn't make a lot of big changes, but the ideas we introduced, even if they were small ones, did have a positive effect. You guys are all doing a great job.'

'Thank you, sir. Round of applause for our Yank mate,' David responded, and we all laughed and clapped.

The more I saw of Jimmy, the more I fell in love with him. I had never been able to talk so deeply with anyone else before. I loved how courteous and thoughtful he was with other people, whoever they were, Indonesian or foreign. He was perceptive and intelligent and popular with my Australian colleagues.

Later that same weekend, as we walked through the beautiful Botanic Gardens that made Bogor famous, I told him that I wondered what he saw in me. I said that I felt so provincial and unsophisticated.

Jimmy put his arm around my shoulder and gave me a squeeze.

'Susan, I love your sincerity, your unpretentiousness and the fact that you have volunteered to help the Indonesians. You are genuinely interested in other people, especially me. And I'm really glad that you like it here. Maybe you could stay on after your contract is up. You would have no trouble getting a job.'

Then he again raised the subject of Lake Toba.

'Look, can you get away for a few days? How would you feel about taking a little trip with me? Going away to Lake Toba on Sumatra, where no one knows us, means we can have some wonderful time together.'

There was no mistaking the look in his eyes. I felt the same, a bit shaky, excited and nervous. I certainly had never been away with a man before, but I didn't want him to know how inexperienced I was, so of course I said, 'I'd love to. You know how interested I am in Sumatra. And Lake Toba sounds wonderful.'

'Count on it.' He gave me a huge smile. 'It will be really special to take you there.'

A week later, we flew to the large and bustling town

of Medan on Sumatra. Once we left Medan, we headed through *kampongs* and padi fields in a wheezing 1950s Chevy, driven by Suhaimi, a pal of Jimmy's he'd known from his Peace Corps days. We passed large rubber plantations that gradually gave way to tea and coffee plantations as we started to climb the high winding road up to the lake. The car began shuddering on the steeper inclines and was overtaken by rickety buses coughing oily fumes, even on the dangerous bends. Jimmy and I exchanged glances and I clutched his hand.

The higher we got, the more spectacular the scenery became. Eventually we reached the steep approach to the lake and the car drove along the thickly forested ridge of the ancient volcano until we finally rattled into the courtyard of the Parapat Hotel.

The hotel was an old Dutch place still showing bits of fading colonial glory. Painted scenes of Lake Toba and murals of stylised *wayang kulit* puppets adorned the walls. Batik cushions sat on heavy leather lounges and dusty plastic flower arrangements decorated the cavernous lobby. Jimmy checked in for both of us, but I felt embarrassed when I handed over my passport, revealing we were not married.

We were given a warm, overly sweet juice to drink before being shown to our room. As we stepped outside the reception area I caught my breath. Below us stretched a huge aquamarine lake, surrounded and almost hidden by steep forested hills. The water glittered in the afternoon sun like a polished jewel. I'd never seen anything so beautiful and I was speechless.

There was a giant brass gong at the top of a flight of stone steps which Jimmy told me was to summon us to meals. The steps led down to the gardens below. As we followed a young boy in his batik sarong and batik *peci*, I couldn't help wondering where the other guests were.

I was excited to find that our room was actually one of the small bungalows scattered around the lake's edge. They had been built as traditional *batak*-style houses with twin peaked roofs and rattan shutters. Our bungalow was comprised of one large room containing a bed that faced the window with a magnificent view of the lake and, joy of joys, a western-style bathroom. On a tiny porch, a table and chairs also faced the lake and on the table was a printed menu anchored by a heavy glass ashtray.

'Do you bring food and drinks down here?' I asked the young man who had brought down our luggage. He nodded and pointed to the menu and asked if we wanted to order *krupuk* and beer. We did, though Jimmy had his doubts about how cold the beer might be.

'We should celebrate. This place is spectacular,' I said.

That evening I put on a batik print dress a tailor in Bogor had made me and we headed up to the top terrace to have a drink and watch the sunset. Apart from us, the hotel still seemed deserted, so Jimmy suggested we take a *betjak* into Parapat.

The little town of Parapat was almost as quiet as the hotel. Families seemed to have retreated into their houses, although in the watery glow of a few sagging streetlights we could see several young men loitering about.

There were few restaurants to choose from, some local stalls and hawkers, a small place called the Satay Shack and a larger place simply called *Rumah Makan*, the eating house, or restaurant, which we decided looked the best.

The town was certainly a sleepy place and off the beaten track. I felt I was far away from the rest of the world. As though he had read my thoughts, Jimmy mused, 'I wonder what this area will be like in, say, twenty years' time. Will it be packed with tourists, or entirely forgotten?'

We sat in the small, walled garden of the restaurant, which contained four tables and a splashing fountain, but the flying insects quickly drove us inside under the rattling fans. We ordered frogs' legs, which had become one of our favourites, and several spicy side dishes, and drank the local beer in preference to the sweet fruit juices that were on offer. The meal was surprisingly tasty, but afterwards, since there seemed to be little to do in Parapat at night, we decided to find a *betjak* and return to the hotel.

We sat in the neglected bar of the hotel and Jimmy ordered a gin and tonic while I had the barman make me a lime and soda.

'This is so refreshing. It's become my favourite,' I said.

After we finished our drinks, we prowled through the foyer, past a sitting room designated 'Ladies Only', and peered into a shop filled with dusty souvenirs. Hanging on the walls were sepia photographs of the hotel guests taken about forty years before.

'This was a favourite place of the Dutch planters. Doesn't seem to have changed much!' said Jimmy.

'Look, President Sukarno was here with his wife Dewi. How exquisite she is!' I pointed out a photo.

'He likes marrying pretty women; Muslim men are allowed more than one wife.'

'Well, I wouldn't like that!'

'You wouldn't get a choice,' said Jimmy with a smile.

Taking me behind a pillar, he kissed me, took my hand and we walked quietly down the steps to our bungalow beside the now silver lake, awash in moonlight.

*

As the sunrise gently melted through the shutters in golden lines which spread across the sheets and the whitewashed walls, we lay enfolded together until Jimmy jumped up and flung open the shutters and from our bed we watched the lake awaken. Eventually, hunger pangs drove us from the bed and we ordered breakfast. We sat outside and waited for an age for it to be delivered.

'Susan, I'm sorry. This place doesn't seem to be very efficient. Do you want me to chase it up?' said Jimmy, agitated.

I wasn't concerned. 'No, it's all right. I'd never get tired of this view. It's such a mysterious lake. Could your friend take us out on the water?' I asked.

'We can ask. Suhaimi's bringing around a motor scooter for us to use. If you're brave enough, we can zip around and do some sightseeing.'

'Sounds great.'

'We could have a swim in the lake if you like, but the water can be chilly. Refreshing, though. There're lots of places Suhaimi knows, old stone tombs and burial sites that are hundreds of years old, and there're a couple of local artists who are good and some women weave cloth particular to this area that you might like to see.'

'I could buy something if it's not too expensive. I haven't got much money after paying that airfare, not that I'm complaining. I would not have missed this for anything. I'll ask Suhaimi to bargain for me.' I sighed as I gazed again at the beautiful view. 'I like the idea of a painting of the lake. I could roll it up and pack it. This is such a different place; I feel as though time has stopped.'

'Well, it is special. There was a super volcanic eruption seventy something thousand years ago which left a crater a hundred miles long. Lake Toba is the remains of that crater. Look, I'm getting crabby without coffee. Maybe I should bang the gong outside our door and see what happens,' said Jimmy.

But before he could do that, we saw two boys approaching with large trays and they proceeded carefully to set out our breakfast at a leisurely pace until Jimmy, frustrated and coffee-less, snapped at them in Bahasa and said we'd manage it ourselves.

I had to laugh at the meal. The hotel had attempted an English breakfast. The eggs were stone cold, as was the toast, and Jimmy wondered if they'd cooked it the night before. But the coffee was in a thermos jug and still hot. So we ate the cold toast and eggs and decided to have a slap-up Indonesian lunch later on.

While Jimmy finished his coffee and sat with a cigarette, I headed to the bathroom. It was basically a large cement box with a shower head and a gap of eight inches or so under the roof so the steam could get out. The water was barely warm, but it was refreshing. I had my eyes closed as I was washing my hair, when I suddenly felt something touching the back of my head. I immediately thought it was a large frog or, worse still, a snake, and spun around. I shook my head, trying to get rid of whatever it was. In a swift movement a sinewy arm pulled away from my head and I saw a face staring at me through the gap under the roof. I screamed and the man dropped from sight before Jimmy got to the bathroom.

'What is it? Are you okay?'

I started to sob and shake, and pointing towards the roof I managed to say, 'A man, there was a man looking at me. He tried to grab me, he touched my hair . . .'

Before I had even finished telling Jimmy what had happened, he was already out the door, although by the time he was around the back of the bungalow all he could see was a figure disappearing through the gardens. One of the staff, who had heard Jimmy's shouts, took up the chase.

I was trembling as I dressed. The invasion of privacy, of my personal space, the feeling of being threatened, had rocked me profoundly. Jimmy held me and calmed me. He poured me another cup of coffee and sat quietly, trying to let the peaceful surroundings act as balm to my shaken spirit.

A man from reception appeared at our bungalow and had a conversation with Jimmy in a lowered voice.

After he left, Jimmy said, 'The hotel manager wants to see us. I think he wants to give us an apology.'

'You go. I don't want to be reminded of what happened. I'd rather just forget it,' I said.

'No. That's not the Indonesian way, you know that. Honour must be addressed and faces saved. Besides, news of this episode might be bad for business. Don't worry, darling, I'll handle things. You won't have to say a word.'

'You won't leave me?'

'Of course not. Come on, let's get it over with, then we can meet Suhaimi and go touring and maybe do some shopping.'

To our surprise, when we reached the hotel lobby we were greeted not only by the manager, a plump man who looked more nervous than apologetic, but by a number of the staff, who clustered around, staring at us and making me feel even more uncomfortable. However, instead of apologising, the manager took us to his car and got in beside the driver, while we were ushered into the back seat.

'Where are we going? What is all this about?' I asked Jimmy.

'He says we're going to the local police station. Maybe they want a description or something.'

'Oh, no. This is awful. I couldn't give a definite description, it all happened so quickly!'

My legs were shaking when we arrived at the police station, a grim-looking cement building. The manager,

Jimmy and I were then shown into the office of the Chief of Police.

He was a middle-aged man who greeted us warmly. Indeed, he looked extremely happy to see us, which surprised me. He rubbed his hands and addressed Jimmy, referring to me as his wife, and announced that they had found the culprit. Suddenly, a side door opened and a policeman entered, dragging with him a frightened young man who had his hands tied behind his back.

'Here is the man,' said the police chief, and whipped out his hand to force the fellow to look up so I could see his face. I didn't know if I was supposed to identify him, but to be truthful I couldn't be sure if it was the peeping tom. Then, to my horror, the police chief picked up a nightstick from his desk and began to hit the young man about the head and shoulders and shout curses at him.

Jimmy made a move to protest as I screamed, 'Stop it! Please, stop beating him!'

The young man was now bleeding profusely from what I guessed was a broken nose. Then he groaned and sagged to his knees. Angrily, Jimmy turned to the hotel manager and asked if the boy was an employee at the hotel.

The manager shrugged and shook his head. 'I do not know every person who works at my hotel.'

'I'm not sure this is the man. Please, stop it!' I pleaded.

Jimmy put his arm around me and I pushed my face into his shoulder and began to cry.

'Please, stop this immediately. Take the boy away,' protested Jimmy.

I heard a few more whacks and groans and then the sound of the boy being dragged away. I looked up and saw the Chief of Police shaking the hand of the hotel manager before extending it to us.

'Are you satisfied that your intruder has been punished?' he asked.

But Jimmy simply turned to the hotel manager and asked him to bring his car around, before firmly ushering me out of the horrible little office and away from the brutal police chief.

My mind swirled. I couldn't believe what had just happened. 'I don't want to go back to the hotel yet,' I said trembling as we stepped outside. 'Let's just walk around somewhere.'

Jimmy told the hotel manager that we would find our own way back to the hotel and the two of us linked arms and walked around the little town until we found a stall selling *kopi susu*, the strong local coffee sweetened with condensed milk. We sipped the coffee and Jimmy lit a cigarette. He didn't smoke much but I could tell he needed one now.

'Are you okay?' he asked.

'A bit shaky still. The police chief upset me just as much as the peeping tom. And I'm not sure that was the right fellow, I had such a fleeting look.'

'I don't think they care all that much if he was. This was a face-saving exercise, so anyone vaguely matching your description served their purpose. It made it look as though the authorities were taking action.'

'It was the brutality that got to me. Scary.'

'Yes, Indonesian justice is very arbitrary.'

'It's all so horrible,' I said with a shudder.

Jimmy nodded. 'Let's not talk about it. It's too upsetting. Hey, look who's here . . .' Jimmy jumped up and raced down the street to where Suhaimi had stopped on his scooter.

We told Suhaimi what had happened and he didn't seem at all surprised by the quick response of the police. As far as he was concerned, I had made a complaint and it had been dealt with swiftly. As if to assure me that it really was over, he then put me on the back of his scooter and ferried me down a street to a small art shop before heading back to fetch Jimmy.

By the time the two of them joined me, I had found a wonderful oil painting of Lake Toba in the moonlight. Suhaimi and Jimmy laughingly bargained with the owner and for a reasonable price the painting was taken from its frame and rolled up for me. We spent the rest of that day on Suhaimi's motor scooter, enjoying the lake and boating on its crystal water.

In spite of the incident with the intruder, the trip was a wonderful interlude. When I got back and went out with the boys and Norma, I tried to explain how magical Lake Toba was, but they were far more intrigued by the story of the peeping tom. Norma was horrified and declared she was going to be much more careful about personal privacy from then on.

A couple of days later, I quietly admitted to David that the episode had removed some of the scales from my eyes.

'I've lost some of my innocence about Indonesia. While people are warm and friendly to us, I guess we've been somewhat cosseted. Now I feel that I have to look over my shoulder and that I can't trust some people, and I hate that feeling.'

David nodded understandingly. 'I think you are just being realistic. This isn't our country, so of course things are different, and if the incident at Lake Toba has made you more cautious then that's a good thing.'

'The expectations people have in Indonesia are quite different from those at home, and I suppose I have been a bit naïve to expect them to be the same. I'll just have to be a bit more careful, won't I?'

'That's the right attitude, and I'm sure nothing so unpleasant will happen to you again,' said David. He was kind and he made me feel better.

Jimmy was back in Jakarta and we were busy in Bogor. I had shown Norma my Lake Toba painting and she thought it looked too beautiful to be a real place.

'You know, I haven't bought any souvenirs since I've been here. I think it would be nice to go home with something to remember this place by, although, in all honesty, we are hardly likely to forget it. Next time you go to the big markets I might tag along, if you don't mind,' she said.

So the following week, Norma, Mark and I headed to the popular evening *pasar*. In those markets you could buy just about anything you could think of, from food and household goods to live animals, clothes, jewellery, gold and local artefacts. Mark headed in one direction and Norma and I went to the fabric section to look at the batiks. It was rather overwhelming to see so many varieties of beautiful batik all in one place. The predominant colours there were brown and indigo, and they had been made in the traditional way with the designs either hand-drawn with wax pens or applied with delicate copper stamps which were dipped in wax and imprinted on the fabric before the whole cloth was dyed.

Norma picked through the lengths of material on display, as well as the neatly folded sarongs. 'I think I prefer these older fabrics which have faded. The colours are muted and the fabric softer,' said Norma. 'Did you know that different parts of the country favour different patterns and they all have interesting meanings? The designs might tell a story or indicate royal rank so that only certain people can wear them.'

I looked at her in astonishment. Norma had previously shown little interest in Indonesian culture.

'You could write books about batik, you know,' she said. Then she gave a little laugh. 'I've been talking to Evan. He knows a lot about it,' she added.

Norma picked up a rusty-looking copper stamp that had been used to make batik designs. 'Look, it's in the shape of a stylised lotus. See, the thin copper outline is a bit broken in places so they don't use it any more. And it's old. I think this would be worth buying. It would make an unusual gift.'

'What a great idea. There's another one over there. Let's get them.'

Pleased with our purchases, we headed down an aisle towards the Chinese gold shops, which were just little stalls consisting of a small display case with drawers beneath. We spotted Mark, as he was so tall, and we were just about to catch up when we were distracted by some laughter and loud voices. Then we saw several young men, as well as a large older man, all wearing colourful shirts, pushing their way through the narrow aisles of the marketplace. They shoved past people who didn't quickly leap out of their way. They stopped in front of a gold stall. The owner, a Chinese man in a singlet and sarong, clearly knew who they were. Ignoring their bluster and performance, which was evidently for the benefit of the crowd, he reached into his money drawer and pulled out an envelope which he pushed across the counter. The older man grabbed the envelope and shook it in the shopkeeper's face.

He pushed the envelope back, shaking his head, and the Chinese man, who was now trembling, slipped his hand beneath the counter where he grabbed some money and stuffed it into the envelope.

Satisfied, the men, smiling broadly and laughing and shaking their fists in the air, moved on, and to our surprise stopped at the next jewellery stall and rapped on the small glass-topped display case, demanding payment from its stallholder.

'They must do this regularly,' muttered Mark as he came over to us. 'Move away quietly. We don't want to be a target or spark some sort of scene.'

As we inched through the silent crowd, there seemed to be quite an altercation between the men and this shopkeeper who must have objected to the extortionists' demands. Suddenly one of the men smashed a heavy iron bar down on the display case, shattering it and sending several pieces of gold jewellery scattering into the crowd. In the confusion, everyone leaped on the pieces, either to rescue or steal them. Then the laughing gang became surly and hit the shopkeeper across the head with a stick.

We hurried away.

'How often would that sort of thing go on? It's extortion,' said Norma. 'Who are those men and where are the police?'

'Those actions were so brazen. Those men must assume that the police won't intervene,' I said.

'I agree,' said Mark. 'The police would almost certainly keep well clear.'

The following Friday night, we all gathered for dinner as usual. Jimmy had come up from Jakarta, but Norma had sent a message to say that she couldn't leave an expectant mother and we would just have to manage without her. Alan had also begged off joining us, as he said he was working on his bridge plans. Mark and I immediately told the others what we had witnessed in the markets.

'Do you know what all that was about?' Mark asked Jimmy.

'I have a fair idea. As you all know, the attempted coup of 1965 gave free rein to the military. Attacks began on anyone thought to be a communist or in any way opposed to the new military regime. Hundreds of thousands of families have been scarred by these actions. Then the army encouraged local militias to carry on with the purge with brutal force. These militias became fearless because they were never punished. Indeed, many of their members are treated as heroes. But they are little more than thugs and gangsters and the police will do nothing about them because they have the support of the military. So it is easy for them to persecute any one who is perceived to be opposing the army, even if they aren't.'

'So who is the perceived opposition?' asked David.

'It's often the Chinese,' replied Jimmy.

'Is that because they are thought to be communists or because they have money?' asked Evan.

'Both, I suspect. There is a huge amount of anti-Chinese propaganda under this government. Chinese families can't go to the schools, speak their own language, or practise their customs because of their supposed affiliation with the communists, and they have little protection against violence. But those youth gangs are also going after those they think have money, and it is always assumed that the Chinese have it. There is a lot of jealousy about the success of the Chinese traders,' replied Jimmy.

'No wonder I can't get people to talk about political matters,' I said. 'It seems that anyone who protests or disagrees with the Suharto government could be locked up.' I shook my head at the realisation. 'There is certainly a dark cloud hanging over this country. I'm not sure that I want to go to the markets again. It's unsafe.'

'You know, Susan, most Indonesians are law-abiding, and have had a long system of dealing with miscreants through village headmen and religious tribunals, as well as the courts. But this is still a very poor country and you can't really blame most people for turning a blind eye to the recent upheavals. Their first duty is towards their families and being able to survive the chaos. I'm sure that you'll be safe in the markets. These youth gangs have no quarrel with us. They will only prey on the weak and helpless,' said Mark kindly.

I thought what a good man Mark was. He came from a privileged background, yet he was here roughing it in Indonesia with the rest of us because he thought it was worthwhile helping our closest neighbour rather than pursuing a more materialistic career at this time. He was so very idealistic.

*

But I particularly loved being able to share what I was experiencing with Jimmy. In my letters home I tried to explain my life in Indonesia, but I knew my family would have a hard time imagining it. I realised what a pretty cloud they lived on in Australia. They had a home that was comfortable. They were economically secure in a politically stable country, with no concerns about where their next meal was coming from. Yet Indonesia, while exotic and beautiful, and with its warm and friendly people, fascinating culture and dramatic history, had an uncertain future full of political threats and fears and was far removed from anything I'd known. But talking to Jimmy about it had made me realise that for all its faults Indonesia had cast its spell over me; it had opened my eyes and made me see things from a new perspective. And this was another link in the sweet ties which bound us together.

So I was pleased when Mr Robinson sent us all an invitation to a reception at the residence of the Australian ambassador with an attached note suggesting that I could bring Jimmy along if I liked. The function was to be formal, and since neither Norma nor I had anything appropriate to wear for the occasion, we had dresses made for us.

At the markets I found a lovely piece of black Chinese silk, embroidered with golden chrysanthemums, which I had made into a cocktail dress. Norma chose some yellow silk with a fine silver thread, woven in Solo, in central Java. Luckily we had been told that, because of the climate, we didn't have to wear gloves.

I arranged to meet Jimmy in Jakarta a couple of hours before the evening started, and he looked at me in my new outfit and simply said, 'Wow.'

'I'll take that as a compliment,' I said, linking my arm through his. 'I'm looking forward to tonight.'

'Me, too. The guest of honour is a British woman who lived in Indonesia before the war. She's quite well known,' said Jimmy with a smile. 'And she's had quite a chequered career. When the Japanese invaded Indonesia, she stayed on and while it was thought that she was working for them, she was in fact working for the resistance. It was very dangerous for her.'

'How intriguing. Why do you think she's here?'

'I don't know, but I expect it will be fascinating to meet her.'

While we had been to the small welcome function at the Australian Embassy when we arrived, this was by far the most important event I attended in Indonesia. The ambassador's residence was a lovely colonial home and as we were waiting in the vestibule before being ushered into the function room, I spied Mr Robinson.

'Is it all right if I pop over to speak to my boss?' I asked Jimmy.

'Of course. I can see a couple of people I'd like to have a talk with, so I'll catch you on the way in.'

'The cultural attaché must be hard up for events,' surmised David, who, along with Alan, was already talking to Mr Robinson when I joined them.

'I suspect that this is really an intelligence-gathering exercise. A reception like this is a good way to get a lot of people that Australia is interested in together in the one place,' confided Mr Robinson.

153

'That makes sense,' said Mark. 'Australia is the eyes and ears of the world in reporting about this new regime, and a big reception gives us the chance to bring a lot of useful people together, not only political leaders, but business ones as well. There are a lot of untapped riches in these islands.'

'You're well informed,' commented Mr Robinson.

'I'm not sure about that,' replied Mark. 'But I am beginning to learn how things work in this country.'

'How is Mr Putra?' I asked.

'He's very well.'

'He worked very hard to teach us Bahasa and we learned a lot about Indonesia from him as well,' said Alan.

'Yes, but I was sorry that he didn't tell us more about the events of 1965. I would have liked to talk to him about it, since it affected nearly everyone's lives. We've had to fill in a lot of details for ourselves,' I said.

Mr Robinson lowered his voice. 'Susan, there is a very good reason why Mr Putra avoided discussion of those events.' He hesitated before he continued. 'His family is from Bali, and they were amongst the thousands who were killed on that island. They were all murdered, including his pregnant sister.'

I was taken aback. 'But Mr Putra is such a nice and friendly person. You would never know that such a terrible tragedy had happened to him.'

The others were equally surprised. 'I guess many Indonesians can't express their sorrow or outrage because it's just too dangerous for them,' said David.

'Yes,' replied Mr Robinson, looking over his shoulder. 'There are still militias out there who look for any excuse to take action against so-called communists and Sukarno sympathisers.'

'That's Indonesia. Perfect on the surface, but rotten at the core,' said Alan, shrugging. 'Anyway, I intend to enjoy myself tonight. How about you, Susan?'

As I saw Jimmy walking over towards me to escort me inside, I was sure I would.

We were greeted by an official reception line, starting with the Australian ambassador and his wife and then the rest of the Australian embassy staff who were present.

When we were introduced to other guests after going down the reception line, I was surprised to find there was a very large Indonesian contingent, comprising high-ranking generals and politicians as well as members of the cultural community. Jimmy pointed out some of the more famous people present, including artists, an elderly and respected filmmaker, and the most famous *dalang* in Java.

'The *dalang* is the man behind all the shadow puppet plays. The puppet master. He does all the voices and conducts the orchestra, manipulates the *wayang*, that's the puppets, narrates the performance and sets the scene. This man is famous and highly respected,' said Jimmy. 'I'd love to take you to a performance, but I have to warn you that they are very long. It might start at nine in the evening but could go on until six in the morning. Do you think you'd enjoy it?'

'Good heavens, but I suppose we don't have to stay for the whole performance. Are these the plays that tell the stories of the Indian Mahabharata and the Ramayana, good versus evil?'

'Yes, but over the centuries the great deeds of Indonesian princes have been woven into them. More recently they've become quite political and poke a bit of fun at politicians and famous people,' said Jimmy.

It was easy to spot the guest of honour, who was seated on a lounge chair at one end of the long reception room. Guests had queued in front of her and were slowly being ushered forward to meet her. She was such a tiny woman that she was swamped by her armchair. She was wearing an elaborate *sarong kebaya* and had short, dyed bright red hair. Her large round glasses gave her an owlish look, but her eyes seemed to miss nothing. She was speaking perfect Bahasa to an Indonesian official and as we were introduced she gave a smile and held out her hand. Her accent was clipped English with a faint burr that I couldn't place. When the six of us, along with Jimmy, moved to the top of the line, the ambassador's wife introduced us.

'May I present Miss K'tut Tantri. These are the young people on the Neighbourhood Aid programme I mentioned,' she said.

Miss Tantri smiled warmly at us. 'Wonderful. It is good of Australia to help this country. I live in Australia now, although I lived here, in Indonesia, for many years, you know.'

An official-looking Indonesian standing behind the armchair spoke in reverent tones. 'K'tut Tantri is our Joan of Arc, the White Rose of Java. She stayed to fight for us when everyone else fled.'

Miss Tantri accepted this flowery sentiment as her due then gave Jimmy a smile which was quite flirty. So I introduced him, saying, 'This is Jimmy Anderson, Miss Tantri. He came here with the American Peace Corps and has stayed on to work with an Indonesian company.'

'That's smart. This country has a tremendous future. I have great hopes for its progress. I foresaw its potential many years ago, but unfortunately the arrival of the Japanese interrupted my plans.'

'And you are settled in Australia now?' I asked.

'Oh, indeed, for many years. This is my first visit back here since I escaped the Dutch.'

'This must be very nostalgic for you,' commented Jimmy.

'I am an adopted Balinese. My home was Bali. I built the first hotel there in 1930, though few tourists came. But some very important people visited Surara Segara – The

156

Sound of Sea, as I called my hotel. It was a mystical rajah's palace, a dream as though from the *Arabian Nights*, hidden amongst jungle and at the edge of the world's most beautiful beach.'

'How romantic. I would love to see it,' I said.

She shook her head. 'It is all gone. The Japanese destroyed it. But they could not destroy the beauty of Bali. One day it will be the most famous island in the world and people will flock to Kuta Beach. But I cannot go back, it is too sad.'

'Can I ask why you are back here in Indonesia?' Mark ventured.

'This is a business trip,' she said importantly. 'There is a proposal to make a motion picture of my life story. I wrote my autobiography several years ago and General – now President – Suharto is giving it his support.'

We all looked suitably impressed.

'What is the book called?' I asked to be polite.

'It's a wonderful book,' said the ambassador's wife. 'It's called *Revolt in Paradise* and I found it an absolutely riveting read. Now if you'll excuse me, K'tut Tantri, it's speech time.'

We gathered in the centre of the reception room to listen to the glowing speeches that were made about K'tut Tantri and how she had come from the Isle of Man to make Bali her home and had refused to leave when the Japanese invaded, working against them in the resistance movement. They had captured her and tortured her, but her inner strength had enabled her to survive. Then, after the war she had joined the independence movement and worked to free Indonesia from the Dutch. But before independence was declared, she had decided to leave Indonesia for reasons that were 'complicated'.

'Can all this be true? It sounds like a rip-roaring story to me!' said Evan. 'I must see if I can find a copy of her book.'

'Well, if her story is as interesting as we are led to believe, I hope she gets the film made. It would be good to show the world how beautiful and fascinating Indonesia is,' said Mark. We had to agree with him.

For the rest of the evening we mingled with the other guests. After our Indonesian diet it was lovely to enjoy some great Australian wines and delicious canapés which were constantly offered to us by smiling waiters.

'This is a pretty privileged sort of affair,' said Norma to Alan and me quietly. 'I'm not sure that as volunteers we should be at this sort of do.'

'Nonsense,' said Alan. 'We work very hard for practically nothing, so when a chance like this comes along, I say we should enjoy it.'

'Well, since this is being paid for by the Australian taxpayer, the least we can do is to mingle with the guests,' I told them.

Later in the evening the ambassador's wife came and talked to us and asked how we were enjoying Indonesia. We were all enthusiastic.

'It's an intriguing country and we have been through interesting times here,' she said, smiling.

'You were here through the riots?' asked Mark.

'Several of them. First were the Konfrontasi riots. There was a lot of anti-British feeling and we were caught up in that. We had to be evacuated to Singapore for three weeks. Then we were here for the '65 coup. It was awful. There were continual demonstrations, so we really couldn't go out much. Our life was significantly curtailed. Qantas stopped flying into Jakarta and we couldn't leave the city except to get away for short periods in the hills, where things weren't quite so volatile. Food was drastically short, so we all lost masses of weight. In our street, we had four private armies and our children used to play with the young men and their guns.

Through it all, however, many Indonesian students still came to apply for study visas. They had an eye to the future.'

'How frightening,' said Norma.

'It's been a very interesting experience, but also a time for making great friendships, as you too will also discover,' she said.

That evening I met some very interesting people; an Indonesian general, a couple of politicians, including the governor of our province, who had no idea about our existence, and the master puppeteer Jimmy had told me about. They were all very keen to tell us what a wonderful and rich country Indonesia would be to invest in. I think they were disappointed when they found that we were only poor volunteers, but they were very polite and said they were grateful for our efforts. Overall, I found the whole high-powered evening a very heady experience. Indonesia had presented me with some exotic experiences I would never have encountered at home.

But in spite of my growing acceptance of the Indonesian way of life, I found that it still had the capacity to surprise and upset me.

Jimmy and I loved to wander through Bogor's magnificent Botanic Gardens which the Dutch had created centuries before. The gardens contained fabulous banyan trees, enormous palms and serene ponds filled with fish. We could stroll close to the presidential summer palace, built by the Dutch and now housing the deposed president, Sukarno. Walking hand in hand past the magnificent old building, I couldn't help but wonder about the former president sequestered so close by.

'Do you think he still harbours dreams of returning to power? Is he bitter? What does he think of how the country is now being run?' I asked Jimmy.

'I don't think we'll ever know. He isn't in good health,

so I doubt he's writing his memoirs. Maybe his wives will tell stories about him one day.'

'Hmm. Now that could be interesting.'

We were alone, walking through a grove of giant bamboo, when Jimmy leaned over to kiss me. We paused, holding each other, and I was feeling a little overwhelmed by a rush of emotion, when there was a horrible screech and something flung itself towards us from behind the bamboo.

I screamed and clutched Jimmy. Both of us leaped back. I initially had no idea what had launched itself at us, but as Jimmy held me, I saw that it was a woman. Her skin was very dark and her long tangled black hair streamed over her scrawny shoulders. Her clothes were tattered, but it was her wild eyes, flailing arms and her shrieking mouth that unnerved me.

She advanced, stabbing a finger towards Jimmy and jabbering at him. He took a step forward, trying to speak calmly in the face of this tirade as I shrank back. I couldn't understand what she was saying. It made no sense, but it seemed almost evil. Then the woman fell down, writhing and twitching on the ground.

'Jimmy, don't touch her!' I shouted as Jimmy bent over her. I felt gripped by some unfathomable fear.

Just then a gardener holding a bamboo rake came running along the pathway, followed by several curious locals. He began shaking the rake at the woman as if to protect himself from a rabid dog.

'What's wrong with her?' I asked, and started to cry.

The woman lifted her head and for a moment her eyes focused on Jimmy and she howled at him again before collapsing, her eyes rolling back in her head. By now there were more people and a security guard had arrived. He gathered up the woman as though she was weightless and carried her away.

The gardener looked at us and tapped his head. 'Bad spirits. You need to see the *dukun*.'

I was shocked. The *dukun* were the traditional medicine men, the men whose authority came from their ability to use magic. The villagers had told me about witchcraft and they all accepted without question the power of those who had this special knowledge.

The gardener was telling us that the poor woman had said something to us that was so potent that it could only be removed by a *dukun*. Here in the beautiful Botanic Gardens of Bogor, on a bright sunny day, I was being confronted by witchcraft. It seemed completely bizarre.

'What was she saying?' I asked Jimmy, bewildered.

'It was nonsense. I couldn't understand it.'

The gardener, however, reiterated his opinion that we should see a *dukun*.

'That was so scary. Why would she attack us like that?' I asked, still shaking.

'Forget it, Susan. Don't let it trouble you. These things happen.' He thanked the gardener and gave him some money and we walked away, but I could tell Jimmy was unnerved.

That night, we were all able to meet for dinner at a small restaurant down the road from the comfortable hostel where Evan and Norma lived and where I would be bunking in with Norma for the night. The accommodation was clean and spacious, if bare, but I was beginning to like the simplicity of the furniture in Indonesia and I didn't at all mind sitting on mats on the floor, or even sharing the big wooden platform that served as a bed. Outside the door, an elderly lady, bent over her short-handled whisk broom, always wished us '*Selamat jalan*' as we set out.

At the restaurant, smiling, barefoot boys in crisp white drill suits and black caps served us an array of local dishes with a cheerful chorus of '*Selamat makan*'. We had a view of the river and somewhere behind the rain clouds Mount Salak towered over the town.

I shared the story of the wild woman and her curse with the others over dinner.

'That's so creepy,' said Norma. 'Do you believe in that magic stuff? I certainly don't.'

'It seems the more you learn, the more real it appears. I've seen people brought in to hospital convinced they will die because someone has performed magic on them,' said Evan.

'And do they die?' asked David.

Evan nodded. 'Sometimes, although one could put the death down to any number of health issues besides superstitious beliefs.'

Norma agreed. 'The health problems here are endless; no wonder their life expectancy is so short.'

'We do what we can to change things, and can do little more,' said Mark pragmatically. 'How's your bridge coming, Alan?'

'I think it will be a long time coming. The access road is creating problems. *Korupsi*, corruption, has reared its head. It's Rafferty's rules around here.'

'Maybe the Chinese should be allowed to run things,' said Mark lightly. 'They seem to have a much better head for business. Certainly that's true of the ones I've come in contact with.'

Alan shrugged. 'You have to be joking, Mark. In my opinion they are the root of all that is wrong with this country. Communists, every last one of them, all working for the Reds in China. As far as I'm concerned, mate, this country will never progress while there are still Chinese in it.'

Mark looked at Alan and replied, quite calmly, 'Yes, I appreciate that your view about the evil Red Chinese is shared by a lot of other Australians, but all I can say is that when you get to know individual Chinese, like the Tans, then you know that not all the Chinese in Indonesia have communist sympathies.'

After we'd eaten, Jimmy asked me if I'd like to see a puppet show that he had heard was performing on the other side of town. He asked if any of the others wanted to come along, but they all politely declined.

I quite enjoyed the performance of the puppet show, but after a couple of hours we decided that we'd had enough and decided to return to our respective beds for the night. It was late when we headed back towards Norma's hostel, and we were surprised to see a lot of people still about on the streets. When we asked the *betjak* driver what was going on, he muttered something about it being a festival.

Jimmy, who was staying with Mark at the Tans' place as usual, kissed me good night at the entrance to the hostel and left. Norma was asleep when I tiptoed into her room, so I quietly changed into my sarong and climbed under the mosquito net beside her.

I was awakened some hours later by a cacophony of noise that sounded like shouting, banging and even gunshots.

Norma quickly rolled onto the floor beside the bed and put her hands over her head.

'Get down!' she cried.

But I wanted to know what was happening. 'I'm going to see what's going on!' I said, crouching down and making my way towards the door.

'Are you mad? Just get down,' she said, tugging at my arm.

I heard the voices of other hostel residents, and I snuck out to see if they had any idea what was happening. A few people were milling in the corridor whispering to each other.

'It's a riot. Students again,' said another resident.

'What's brought this on?' I asked, peering out a window. The hostel had been built on a rise and we could see the streets below us. I was worried by the number of people out there, especially as some were brandishing what looked to be guns.

'I heard that something is going to happen at daybreak,' said a Swiss pharmacist we knew who was working temporarily at the hospital.

'There are always rumours. But there seem to be so many people running around; where are they going?'

I caught sight of Evan rounding the corner of the corridor. He hurried towards me and even in the darkened space I could see his face was pale. 'One of my orderlies has told me that he heard that Sukarno is being released from the palace. That's what's causing the riot,' he said when he reached me.

'What does this mean?' I said.

'I think that if he's released there will be a lot of bloodshed,' replied Evan. 'Too many people don't want to give him any chance of returning to power.'

Suddenly the night sky was lit up by a flash of fire.

'They're throwing fire bombs, torching cars or even houses,' said Evan, standing back from the window.

'We should stay here inside where it's safe. These mobs can get out of control quickly,' said the Swiss pharmacist.

'We have friends down there in the town. I hope they're okay,' I said anxiously.

'They should be, just as long as they're not on the streets. I'm going back to my room,' said the pharmacist.

Evan and I waited in the darkness a little time longer, and as the sound of the mob disappeared into the distance we headed to our rooms.

Norma was now lying back on the bed. I climbed in under the mozzie net, but couldn't settle. I kept thinking about the stories the ambassador's wife had told us about the coup little more than two years before, and how the riots had gone on for weeks. I was fairly convinced that this was an isolated event, but it was unnerving to say the least, so I found it impossible to sleep.

I don't know how much time passed while I was just lying in the dark, but suddenly there was a commotion and I heard Mark's voice. He was shouting frantically for me and Evan. I leaped out of bed and ran down the short hallway as Evan, half asleep, stumbled to the entrance of the hostel, with me close behind.

Mark, looking dishevelled and dirty, rushed to Evan. When I got closer, I could see that Mark's clothes were soaked in blood.

'Quick, Evan, Susan. You have to go to the hospital's emergency ward!' he cried.

'What's happened? Are you all right? You're covered in blood,' exclaimed Evan.

'I'm fine. It's Jimmy. I've just left him at the hospital, he's in a bad way. Susan, you have to go to him. He's been stabbed!'

My head spun and I felt weak at the knees. I groped for something to hold on to and Mark supported me as I slumped to the floor. He glanced at Evan.

'Susan, I'm going to go to help Jimmy, okay?' Evan said. 'There's a short cut through to the back of the hospital. I'll go ahead and you follow.'

I nodded, dumbly, and then Evan, bare-chested and in cotton shorts, took off around the side of the hostel and into the hospital grounds.

My head was swimming, but I needed to know what was happening.

'What happened to Jimmy?' I asked Mark, my voice cracking. 'Will he be all right?'

Mark took a deep breath, steadied himself, and held my hand tight. 'It's pretty bad, Susan.'

I burst into tears. 'What happened, Mark?' I sobbed.

He took another breath. 'You heard the mob, didn't you? Well, a few rioters came down our street but they didn't stop. The Tans told us not to put a light on and stay still and quiet. A bit later, there was shouting and banging on the door and threatening voices, shouting that unless the door was opened up, they'd burn down the house.'

He paused and I stared at him in shock. 'The Tans' house? Why?'

Ignoring my comment, Mark continued in a voice which suggested that he couldn't really believe what had happened.

'Mr Tan opened the door a crack and told them to go away, but they pushed the door open and knocked him down and started kicking him and shouting. I think there were three of them. Jimmy and I rushed forward to try to make them stop.' Mark was speaking in a rush, the words tumbling over each other. I just listened, tears rolling down my face, but my body was taut with apprehension.

'They kept saying they wanted the gold they knew he was hiding, but Mr Tan kept insisting that he had none. It was in the bank. They were kicking him in the head, so Jimmy lunged at one of the men and tried to stop him. There was sudden confusion . . .' Mark squeezed his eyes shut as though to block out what he had witnessed.

'Mark . . . what happened?' I felt cold, my voice choking, and everything seemed to be happening in slow motion.

Mark looked at me as if he was in terrible pain. 'Then one of the men, not much more than a kid, lunged at Jimmy with a knife, yelling wildly. Jimmy fell. It was as though everything froze. Then one of the other men shouted, "*Orang kulit putih*", white man. They had attacked a white man, and they knew this would cause big trouble, so they ran.' He drew breath. 'Mr Tan quickly found a *betjak* and we put Jimmy in it and came straight to the hospital. He'll be all right, Susan. He'll be all right.' But the way Mark said this, it seemed it was himself he was trying to convince, not me.

I felt my strength come back to me and Mark helped me to my feet.

'I have to go to him,' I said. I got dressed and Mark, Norma and I took the short cut to the hospital.

There we sat and waited. Norma was able to find out that they were operating on Jimmy.

I sat, stony-faced, holding Mark's hand while Norma brought us some horrible coffee. She fidgeted, occasionally patting my arm and muttering comforting phrases. As I looked around, I realised that the emergency waiting room was full of injured people. The night's disturbances had left their mark.

I closed my eyes and leaned my head against the wall. Pictures of Jimmy ran across my mind like a slide show; Jimmy sitting beside me in a *betjak*, his warm leg pressed against mine; leaping from bed in Lake Toba to open the shutters, the golden streaks of sunshine striping his lean naked body; laughing as I tried my first frog's leg; his intense expression as he studied the carvings at Borobudur; looking across the table at me with an amused quizzical smile as I poured out my dreams and silly child-hood reminiscences; holding hands as we strolled through the streets of Bogor; comforting me after the incident of the peeping tom and when the mad woman attacked us in the Botanic Gardens. Suddenly I thought, is the crone's curse coming true? It was all too much. I buried my face in my hands and I cried and cried.

I felt a gentle hand on my shoulder and Evan stood before me in a faded hospital gown. My eyes went to the blood stains on it. I lifted my face to his.

His blue eyes were dull, as though the sun had gone behind a cloud. I looked at his lips as he tried to frame words. Then his fingers tightened on my shoulder and he slowly shook his head.

Norma gasped and her hand flew to her mouth as tears flooded her eyes. Mark's head dropped, and his hands covered his face as he choked.

I simply stared at Evan in disbelief, waiting for him to say, 'It's all right. Jimmy is fine.'

But no words came. Then Mark leaped to his feet and slammed his fist into the wall.

'*Bastards!*'

I stood up and gripped Evan's hand. I couldn't think of a thing to say. This was all happening to someone else, not to me.

'I'm so sorry. By the time he got to the hospital he had lost so much blood . . . Do you want to see him?' Evan asked gently. I really didn't. I wanted to remember handsome smiling Jimmy as I knew him. But then I thought of what a coward I was. I had to tell him goodbye. I nodded.

'I'll come with you if you like,' offered Norma. Mark and Evan asked if they could come as well.

'Yes. Thanks,' I muttered.

He was lying under a green cotton sheet. His eyes were closed and his hands were neatly clasped over the top of the sheet. He looked young, innocent and strangely peaceful. I touched his hand. It was smooth and cool.

I had no words to say. Mark put his arm around my shoulders and led me away. When I got back to Norma's room, I couldn't stop crying. I simply could not take in the fact that Jimmy, my Jimmy, was dead. It was as though I was in a terrible dream, just waiting for someone to wake me up. But no one did.

*

I was glad I'd had that short time in the hospital saying goodbye to Jimmy. After that, officialdom swung into action and I had no part to play. The American Embassy in Singapore arranged for his body to be taken back to the States, as his family wanted him buried there. The six of us could do little more than light candles in the beautiful old Bogor Cathedral. I wrote a letter to Jimmy's family, explaining how Jimmy had died and just how special he was to me. His mother wrote back, thanking me for my letter, but after that there was nothing to say.

I spoke to Mr Robinson on a scratchy phone line and he was full of sympathy, asking me what I wanted to do.

I chose to return to my *kampong* to try and find some solace in the calm routine of a simple life. There I tried to cope with the fact that I'd lost the man I'd secretly allowed myself to think might love me all my life. The villagers gave me the space to be alone and I was grateful for this healing time.

But when a letter arrived from my mother full of trivial, happy news, unaware of what had happened, I suddenly desperately wanted to go home, to my family and the familiar safety of my Australia, where violence didn't come in the middle of the night.

Mr Robinson was understanding and agreed that I could leave the programme early.

My friends and I had a quiet last dinner together. Evan, David, Mark, Alan and Norma. They all said that they were disturbed by the events, but they all wanted to stay on in Indonesia, even Norma, and they did.

After they finished their term they received individual letters of thanks and glowing references. But although Australians continued to work as volunteers in Indonesia, funding for this particular programme was withdrawn. We were its only participants.

Of course, Sukarno was never released; it had just been another of those rumours that continually swirled around Indonesia. He died three years later, still under house arrest.

Jimmy's murderers were never caught. Mark told me that he was pretty sure that one of the men involved had also been part of that unpleasant incident in the markets all those weeks before. He said he thought they'd used the riots as a cover to try to extort money from Mr Tan. It seemed to me that Jimmy had paid a very high price for their greed. I still couldn't believe he was gone.

*

Susan stopped talking and there was silence in the room.

Then Megan asked in a quiet voice, 'Bunny, do you think that curse, that spell the old woman put on Jimmy, was the reason he died?'

Susan shook her head. 'I don't think so. It was just a bizarre coincidence, darling.'

'What a tragedy, Mum. I had no idea that your time in Indonesia was so sad,' said Chris.

'Did Poppy know about Jimmy?' asked Megan bluntly.

'Yes, of course I told him all about it. Years later, he offered to take me back to Indonesia. A healing journey, he called it. But I didn't want to do that. The past is the past and I couldn't relive my times with Jimmy with anyone else except Jimmy. Not even Poppy.'

'Maybe you shouldn't go to the reunion then,' said Chris quietly. 'I understand now why you haven't gone to previous reunions.'

'Oh, darling, I'll never forget Jimmy or the violence that caused his death. I put it behind me a long time ago but when I think about it, it still hurts,' said Susan, drawing a knitted throw around her and folding her hands. There didn't seem to be anything else to be said, so the three of them sat quietly again for a few moments before the clock on the mantel chimed. It was getting late, so Megan disappeared to bed to read. Chris tidied up the kitchen then, as he went down the hallway to his bedroom, he passed his father's office and saw that the desk lamp was on.

Peering in, he could see his mother standing and staring at a painting which was almost hidden amongst the many other framed photos and memorabilia that covered the wall. It was the painting of a lake, a large mysterious pool of clear blue, floating between dark green hills in silver moonlight. Chris realised that this must be the painting she'd bought of Lake Toba, almost a lifetime ago.

Slowly Susan turned and gave him a soft smile.

Chris nodded in return and went to his room and lay in the darkness, listening to the gentle sounds of night in Neverend.

6

SUSAN WORKED HER WAY around the verandah with the watering-can, drenching her hanging baskets. She paused as she spotted Chris in his fluoro safety vest walking slowly towards the house, having finished work for the day. She sighed as she saw his slumped shoulders and downcast eyes. He looked tired and down in the dumps and her heart ached for him.

'Hi, darling. Can you put the kettle on, please? I'm ready for a cuppa,' she said as he climbed the steps onto the verandah.

'I'm ready for a double scotch, I think,' Chris sighed. 'That road to the plateau is starting to get to me.'

'Actually, you might need a stiff drink. Jill rang today. She spoke to Megan and she asked to speak to you as soon as you got back from work. She sounded very cranky.'

Chris groaned. 'Oh no, what now? Where's Megan?'

'In her room. Doing her homework, she says.'

'Right. I think I'll get us some tea first.'

A little later, holding a mug of tea, Chris tapped on Megan's bedroom door and stepped into the room. 'Hi, sweetheart, I'm home. How was your day?'

'Horrible.'

'Why was that? School again?' Chris perched on the edge of the bed where Megan sat cross-legged in front of her laptop.

'Not school. It's Mum. She's having a rave.' Megan rolled her eyes.

'So, are you going to tell me?'

Megan lifted her mobile phone. 'It's the bill for this. It's sort of gone up since I've been here, Dad. The account is still in Mum's name and she says she's not paying it. She wasn't very nice about it.'

'How much is it?'

'A lot, I guess. More than double what it was last time.'

'Ouch, that's bad,' said Chris, frowning. 'I had no idea the phone plan was in your mum's name. We should have reorganised it; I didn't think. Why has it gone up so much?'

'I dunno,' said Megan sulkily. 'Movies. Apps, I guess.'

'Can't you look at that stuff on your laptop?' Chris stood up and folded his arms. 'Didn't you get a message from the phone company to say that you'd exceeded your limit?'

'I suppose, but I miss my friends! There's no one here to talk to and the phone's my lifeline. Anyway, Mum wants you to call her.'

'I'm not surprised. Was there anything else she wanted to talk about?'

'No. She just ranted.'

'Okay, I'll leave you to get on with your homework and make that call to your mother,' said Chris tersely. He'd have a further talk with Megan after speaking to Jill.

*

Chris held the phone slightly away from his ear.

'Are you listening, Chris? This simply can't go on. You said you wanted to be responsible for her, so why am I getting her damn bills?'

'I'm sorry, Jill. I'm not totally across everything yet. I'm dealing with things as they come up. I'll handle this right away and make sure the plan is changed or stopped.'

'I think you and your mother are letting Megan get away with blue murder!'

'That's not true, Jill. Mum might be very loving but she doesn't let Megan get away with much. We are both very clear about what her boundaries are. But, according to Megan, she hasn't made any friends up here so the phone is her lifeline and that's why the bill is so high. I'm sorry that I didn't realise you were still responsible for paying for it. We'll get Megan a new plan straight away so this doesn't happen again.'

'I hope you can afford one. Have you got a job yet?' Jill said cuttingly.

'I'm working. We're managing,' said Chris. 'I'll try to get Megan out of the house more so she's not on her phone so much. That should help keep the bills down.'

'Well, that might be difficult. By the amount she seems to use her phone, it would seem that she's not at all interested in life in Nowhereville.'

'Jill, it's all a big adjustment for her. She is actually doing well at school. Her grades are excellent. And I'm doing the best I can. I'm hoping this arrangement will be temporary, but so far living in Neverend hasn't been too

174

bad.' Chris took a breath. 'I'll sort the phone out. It won't happen again.'

'Okay, well, I'm glad she's still doing well at school at least.' Jill sounded somewhat mollified. 'Tell Megan I'll Skype with her later in the week.'

Chris rang off and stood for a moment, considering the conversation.

'How did that go?' asked Susan, coming into the room.

Chris filled her in on the situation with Megan's phone bill. 'I have to say that I felt a bit guilty at not realising that Jill was still being billed for Megan's mobile, but she settled down when I said I'd pay it,' Chris told Susan.

'Really Megan has to pay the bill,' said Susan, pointedly. 'She can't be so selfish. Fancy just ignoring the phone company's warning that she had exceeded her limit. It's totally irresponsible.'

Chris sighed. 'I know that, Mum, but I'm not sure how she'll get the money to repay me. I don't give her that much pocket money and she's too young to get a job in one of the local cafés or shops.'

'She can certainly help me in the garden, but that won't be very lucrative.' Susan tapped her fingers together and thought for a moment. 'Hmm, I've got a solution, I think. Mollie Watson could use someone to give her a hand out at her place. She's broken her wrist and can't do as much as she would like. Megan can ride that bike the Fergusons lent her down there – it's only about three kilometres – and feed the animals and help with anything else that Mollie needs done.'

Chris nodded slowly. 'That sounds promising. I'm not sure how she is going to take to farm work, though.'

'She'll be perfectly fine. She just needs to accept a bit of responsibility. Kids can't have everything their own way all the time, you know that. Megan might not like the idea, but just tell her she hasn't a choice,' said Susan, crisply.

*

'But Dad, I don't know what to do with farm animals. It sounds yucky. Couldn't I just help out here or something?' wailed Megan, sitting up straight on her bed.

Chris stood firm. 'No! Your grandmother has managed to arrange a job for you so that you can repay that monstrous mobile phone bill, and you should be grateful.'

When Megan stared sulkily back at her father and didn't answer, Chris snapped. 'Give me your phone. It's confiscated for the time being. Email your friends and tell them that you're off the air for a bit.'

'What? No way! What if it's urgent?' Megan's voice rose.

'Tell them to call the landline. You're sounding like a spoiled brat, Megan. Tomorrow afternoon you're to put on some old clothes to work in, and we'll take you out to meet Bunny's friend. If you work afternoons after school and Saturdays, you'll pay off this debt before you know it. And won't that feel good?' Chris walked back to the kitchen, leaving a fuming Megan behind. She slammed her bedroom door with a bang.

'Well, that cleared the air,' he said to Susan, his voice filled with irony.

'I've never heard you raise your voice to Megan before. Probably shocked her a bit. I suppose she's always seen you as the father who comes along with presents, spoils her and leaves again. Not quite that way now.'

'We're both learning,' he sighed. 'So, off to see Mollie tomorrow?'

'Indeed. She's looking forward to having regular help until her wrist heals.'

Chris nodded, and gazing down the hallway at Megan's closed door, he realised he felt real satisfaction about the way they'd handled the issue, in spite of the drama it had caused. He turned back to Susan, who changed the subject.

'Chris, I have formally accepted the invitation to go to the reunion,' she said.

Chris smiled, pleased to hear she'd reconsidered. He thought she'd enjoy connecting with the people of her past, despite the sad ending to her trip to Indonesia. 'Are you going to drive down to Sydney, or fly?'

'Fly. Airfares are pretty cheap these days and if I drive I'll have to overnight in Sydney and I see no point in doing that. No, I shall just be away for the day, and I have to say that now I have made the decision, I'm quite looking forward to the lunch. I am curious to see everyone again after all these years.'

*

'You look the part,' said Susan the next day as Megan appeared in the kitchen in cut-off shorts, an old shirt of Susan's and a pair of gumboots.

'I look stupid in these.' Megan lifted one booted foot.

'You'll look worse if you come home from the farm with your favourite shoes covered in cow poo,' said Chris cheerfully as he joined them.

'Dad, I can't believe that you're coming too. It's so embarrassing. It's like you're chaperoning me.'

'Rubbish. I haven't seen Mollie Watson for years. I used to ride out to her place all the time when I was your age, and the Watsons were always pleased to see me. I'm looking forward to catching up.'

As the three of them drove out to the Watsons' place, Megan asked, 'So who is this lady?'

'Mrs Watson,' said Susan, 'is a lovely person. Her husband, Don, was a great friend of Poppy's. Don ran quite a few head of cattle back then, but Mollie sold off some of the land after Don died and really only keeps a couple of horses and some goats. She sells the kids.'

'The baby goats? What for?' asked Megan.

'For their meat,' her grandmother replied.

Megan made a face. 'To eat? Oh, yuck. Poor things. That's awful.'

They were driving along an old road lined on either side with poplars that cast their dappled shadows across the paddocks. Susan braked and turned into a driveway marked by an old milk can with *Watson* painted on its side that served as a mailbox. She drove up the short driveway to a rambling farmhouse.

Mollie Watson was tall and lean with curling brown hair speckled with grey. One arm was in a sling, but she was carrying a bucket in the other. She put it down to wave as Susan parked near the house.

'Hey, Susan. Chris, it's good to see you,' she said, embracing them both. 'Let's go in and have a cuppa. I'll show you round what's left of the farm later, if you like.' She looked past Susan and Chris to Megan, who was standing at a distance with her arms crossed. 'Hello, Megan,' she said, looking her up and down. 'Ah, smart girl, you came dressed in the right clothes. Here, Megan, could you carry this bucket for me, please? It's got the chook food in it. The hens' yard is over there. You can put the food in their feeder and check if there are any eggs in the laying boxes. We'll be in the kitchen.' She handed the bucket to Megan as if they were old friends.

'Pushing her in the deep end,' said Susan with a smile as an uncertain-looking Megan headed towards the chook house. The hens, which had been pecking about in the back garden, recognised the feed bucket and followed behind the young girl in hysterical excitement.

'Best way, I think. She'll be fine. Once she sees the new baby kids, she might even come to like it here. How about we have that tea and then you two can come back for her in a couple of hours? I'll have worn her out by then,' said Mollie, grinning.

'That's fine, but don't give her an animal to bring home, Mollie!' said Chris. 'We don't want any more complications in our lives.'

*

When Susan and Chris went back to collect Megan later on, she was full of chatter about the animals on Mollie's farm.

'I had to feed one of the little kids with a baby's bottle, because his mother wasn't interested in him. He was so sweet. Wish I could bring him home and look after him,' she said, beaming.

'No way. Besides, you don't want to get too attached. You know what happens to them. Anyway, it will be romping around before you know it. So how was the rest of the work?' asked Susan.

'It was fine, a bit smelly in the hen house, though, and the chooks are stupid. But I managed. I helped Mollie – she asked me to call her that – chop up her vegetables for dinner. It's hard for her with only one hand.'

'I suppose it is. Will you be right to ride your bike over tomorrow?' asked Chris.

'Should be okay,' Megan replied.

Chris changed the subject. While Megan had been at the Watsons' farm, he'd had a call from the real estate agent in Sydney that was weighing on his mind. 'Megan, something has come up. I'm a bit worried about the tenants I have in the Neutral Bay flat. I've been able to get a cheap flight to Sydney, so I've arranged with the agent to do an inspection on the place so I can see it for myself. I'll be going on the same flight as Bunny, so will you be okay to look after yourself until we get back on the six o'clock flight? It'll be dark by the time we drive home from the airport.'

'That's cool, Dad. Not a problem. This is the big reunion lunch? Are you excited?' Megan asked Susan.

'Well, maybe not excited, but now that I'm going I am looking forward to seeing everyone.'

'What are you going to wear?'

'Oh, Megan, I haven't even thought about that.'

'But you have to look really knock-out. Why don't you go to the hairdresser, and get your nails done and stuff? That's so fun to do.'

'Megan, it's not a ladies' luncheon, it's just some long-ago colleagues,' laughed Susan.

'Anyway, your grandmother always looks lovely,' Chris said. He gave his mother a quick glance. He realised he hadn't looked at Susan properly for a long time, in the same way that most people stop looking at familiar faces objectively. But, he thought, Susan was still a very good-looking woman. He felt a rush of affection for his mother. She'd been reluctant to attend the reunion but she'd decided to go and he hoped she would enjoy herself.

*

It felt strange to be in the city again, Chris thought. They had taken the earliest flight so that Susan would have time to browse through David Jones department store before her lunch appointment. Chris walked down to York Street to catch the bus to Neutral Bay for his appointment with the real estate agent.

The agent had mentioned on the phone that Chris's tenants had been somewhat erratic in their rental payments, and Chris was concerned that if they were

180

as careless in maintaining his apartment as they were in paying him, then he would have to get the real estate agent to cancel their lease. But when the agent let Chris into the flat, they were both amazed by its cleanliness and neatness.

'Chris,' said the agent, 'I know that these people can be a bit on the slow side in paying their rent, but they always get there in the end, and you have to admit that they keep your place in immaculate condition. I would advise you to put up with the irregular payments because you may not get tenants who are as good at looking after your place as these people are. Besides, cancelling leases can lead to a lot of expense and trouble for you.'

Chris looked about his small home and knew that the agent was giving him good advice.

'Now that I've seen the place, I can only agree with you,' said Chris, relief evident in his voice.

The agent drove Chris back to the bus stop and Chris quickly caught a bus back into the city. Checking out his flat had turned out to be unnecessary, but it had set his mind at ease. Now, he wondered how he could fill in the rest of the morning before he met up with Mac again for lunch. He decided that perhaps the most constructive thing to do would be to visit the newspaper offices around Sydney to let people know that he was still out there, looking for work.

Over the past few weeks he'd continued to try to line up interviews and reconnect with people, but had been fobbed off at every turn. Maybe it was time to be more brazen and if he turned up in a friendly, casual manner, old colleagues would be more inclined to talk to him.

But getting into the offices of the main news organisations proved to be challenging without his media pass, especially as he found that many of his former workmates were no longer working there. Everyone he knew seemed to have disappeared. He finally got past security at the newspaper company he had worked for prior to joining Trinity Press when a photographer he knew from years ago recognised him and let him in. They had a brief conversation which did not encourage Chris at all. They shook hands and Chris took the lift up to the newsroom.

As he stepped out into the open space, he was stunned not only by the empty desks and offices, but by the general air of desultory tedium in the room, the lack of energy, and the absence of any buzz of things happening. It seemed even worse than the newsroom at Trinity Press. He stopped by the desk of a former colleague.

'This is a surprise, Chris. How're you doing? What brings you in? Still at Trinity?' she asked.

'No, I left them a while ago. I'm just touching base with a few people, seeing what's around. Seems to be a bit of a slow news day,' Chris commented, looking around the newsroom. 'This is not exactly the high-energy place I remember.'

'The twenty-four-seven news cycle doesn't stop, and there's fewer of us to cope with it.'

They chatted a few moments longer and Chris quickly understood that there were no immediate openings, and even if there were he would have to join the very long waiting list of hopeful journalists.

Back on the street, he called Mac to arrange somewhere to meet for lunch.

'The Greeks okay?' asked the retired newsman.

'Terrific. Meet you there at one.'

The colloquially named Greasy Greeks, whose real name was something fancy that no one could recall, was cheap as chips with hearty authentic Greek food. Over a bottle of red and a huge plate of moussaka, Chris told Mac what he was doing and how fruitless it was searching for work as a journalist.

'Yeah, it's tough, all right. So much good talent wasted. And the older we get the faster change seems to happen. Back in the old days, you left school, worked hard in a solid business, got promoted and stayed there till you retired. In those days, companies valued loyalty. Nowadays it's very hard to stay ahead of the game. The future looks so uncertain, especially in the newspaper business,' Mac grumbled.

'So what do I do? I don't want to be a courier for the rest of my life.'

Mac put down his knife and fork. 'Maybe create your own work.'

'I can't very well start my own newspaper!' said Chris.

'No, but you could start by coming up with an idea for a story and then pitch it to one of the weekend magazines. That will give you the chance to write something of substance and get your name out there again. I know freelancing has its downsides, but newspapers love freelancers. No overheads. Are we having dessert?'

'Couldn't touch another thing,' said Chris. 'I have thought about it, but freelancing pays so poorly. I'm really not sure that is what I want to do, but thanks, Mac, maybe I should reconsider.'

'Think of it as an ad for Chris Baxter. Let people know that you're still a bloody good journalist,' said Mac as he finished off the last of the red wine. 'Let me know the next time you're in Sydney, won't you? Good to catch up.'

*

On the train to the airport, Chris asked Susan, 'So? How was it?'

'Amazing. I don't know where to start.' She gave him a dazzling smile. 'It was good. I almost did a double take when I saw everyone. Those days were all so very long ago that they could be part of a dream, but seeing the others today made it all real again. You go first, though, how was your day? What are you going to do about your tenants?'

'Nothing. They are really looking after my place, so it would be foolish not to keep them on. I had lunch with Mac, which was nice. He's still very cluey. Had a suggestion or two for me, which was good because I visited the old press office where I worked before Trinity and there was nothing going on in the way of work there, I can tell you.'

'You poor thing. I suppose with just Megan and me for company you must miss your colleagues almost as much as you miss your old job.'

Her remark touched a nerve, but he pushed the feelings away. 'Enough about me. How were your old friends? Do you wish you'd kept in touch?'

'Not really. But it was funny in a way. Once I got over the shock of seeing them as old men, when in my head I've always thought of them as young, we did slip back into feeling comfortable and familiar with each other. I'll tell you more when we're on the plane.'

'But you're pleased you went?'

Susan was silent for a moment, then nodded. 'Yes. Yes, I am glad.'

Settled in their seats after take-off, Chris turned to his mother and asked, 'So are you going to give me a few more details, or do I have to imagine what happened?'

Susan chuckled. 'As I said, it was strange to see them again after all this time. Everyone looks different, which is hardly surprising, but they are still just the same in many ways. Mark is still handsome in that silver fox sort of way. He went into his father's firm, but he has just retired and is now chairing a wonderful philanthropic organisation which helps disadvantaged teenagers get jobs in the hospitality trade as well as finding them apprenticeships in other industries. He seems to have all manner of projects on the go.'

'He sounds very altruistic. I don't think you've ever told me his full name. Would I have heard of him?'

'He's Mark Chambers.'

Chris looked at her, eyes wide. 'Mum! He's well known. When I was at university he used to give guest lectures on the economic problems of developing countries and his work with disadvantaged groups is widely known. What about the others?'

'Oh, well, I guess if you've heard of Mark, then you might know of Evan. He's a surgeon – Dr Evan Llewellyn.'

'The heart surgeon! Everyone's heard of him. Wow. He's great media talent. Comes across as very caring and manages to make complex medical procedures understandable. He has kept the medical profession on its toes for years.'

'That's him. Lovely man.'

Chris was astounded. 'Mum, you must have known how famous and successful these men became after your time in Indonesia! Why didn't you say something?'

Susan shrugged. 'What on earth for? I'm not a name dropper and they stopped being part of my life a long time ago. And I don't think of them as being the big names that they've become.'

'What about David, would I know his name too?'

Susan shook her head. 'Probably not. It's David Moore. He still looks amazingly fit and is as funny as ever. He more or less carried on with the work he did in Indonesia. He spent his working life with the FAO, the Food and Agriculture Organization that is part of the UN. He's lived in many developing countries, helping farmers develop more productive ways of growing food. But you might recognise the name of the other man I was in Indonesia with, Alan Carmichael.'

'Mum! Are you telling me that you know Alan Carmichael, the billionaire?' Chris was incredulous. How could his mother, a former teacher from the modest town of Neverend, know someone as rich and as powerful as the property developer Alan Carmichael? And to have never mentioned it! It was almost comical.

'I suppose there's no need for them to big-note themselves when they all had pretty spectacular careers, one way or another,' he said with a laugh.

'That's exactly right. There was no boasting. I think it must be restful for them to be surrounded by old friends they can relax and be frank with, rather than by people wanting something. Although Mark did want something. He managed to extract a rather large sum from Alan for his youth foundation.'

'Good for him. And your other friend, Norma, was she there?' Chris opened a bag of nuts and offered it to her. Susan waved them away.

'No. They told me that she'd gone to an earlier reunion but then they'd lost touch.'

'Does anyone know what happened to her?'

'She stayed in the nursing profession when she came home but I'm sure she has retired by now. No one has heard from her in years. I can't remember when I last had even a Christmas card from her and neither can the others.'

'Did you talk about the old days?'

'Not really. We talked more about current events and politics in light of what we knew about things back then. We all agreed the present links between Australia and Indonesia are a bit too fragile for our liking and that made me sad. We wondered what had happened to the people we knew in Java. Alan told me that he has a mansion in Bali. Evidently he flies there on his private jet. That made us all remember the night we met K'tut

Tantri and her stories about her paradise on Bali that was ruined.'

'Did Alan Carmichael give you his opinion about Bali?'

'Yes, he said that he'd been there a few times in the mid-seventies and loved it, which is why he decided to build himself a place on the island, but he said that over the years it has changed so much that now it's more like Brighton Pier.'

'Sad how beautiful places get spoiled. I suppose they just get loved to death,' said Chris.

'I imagine that Alan's place is well out of range of the popular tourist spots. David told me that Alan has his own beach and the place is surrounded by acres of padi fields and privacy.'

'Gosh, Mum, they're certainly an impressive lot. Serious movers and shakers,' said Chris, thoughtfully. 'And the time you spent together in Indonesia is an interesting link between you all.' He stopped and chewed on a nut for a moment. 'You know, there could be a great story here. It's inspiring, when you consider it. Mac suggested that I pitch an idea to one of the weekend magazines to keep my name out there, and I think that telling the tale of a group of young people working together selflessly to improve the lives of our near neighbours, who went on to become prominent Australians, could make fascinating reading. If I did want to write about it, do you think your friends would talk to me about those days?' As the idea took shape in Chris's mind, he suddenly felt energised, better than he had in months.

'I don't see why not.' Susan smiled warmly at her son.

*

Chris was immensely pleased when they walked into the house. The outside lights had been turned on and Megan's

187

music was cheerfully banging away, while a tantalising aroma wafted from the kitchen.

'My goodness, what smells so good?' asked Chris.

'I defrosted that chicken soup Bunny made last week. I'm hungry, though I suppose you had fantastic lunches?'

'I did rather,' said Susan, sinking into her favourite chair and putting her feet up. 'But soup and a bit of toast sounds perfect.'

'Would you like a glass of wine, Mum?' asked Chris.

'Yes, please.'

'So? How was it?' Megan sat on the footrest and lifted Susan's feet into her lap. 'Was it exciting? What were they like? Did they all say how fabulous you look?'

Chris set a glass of wine beside Susan as Biddi jumped into her lap. 'Thanks, Chris. Yes, Megan, they were very nice to me. We all looked older, of course, but essentially no one was very different from how I remember them.'

'And it turns out that Bunny's old friends are all quite important people,' added Chris.

'Are they? Would I know them, Bunny?'

'Maybe not. I'll tell you all about them later, if you want,' replied Susan.

'How was your day, Dad?' Megan asked, solicitously.

'Turns out that I had nothing to worry about regarding the flat, and I had lunch with Mac who gave me a good idea, and now, thanks to Bunny, I have a lead for a story I'm going to pursue. How was your day?'

'School was the same old, same old. My new friend Jazzy and I hung out. After school I biked over to Mollie's. I'm getting on quite well with Squire the horse now. Mollie's Shetland pony is cute, too.'

'Oh, that Gem is a naughty little pony. Do be careful of her. How are the baby goats?' asked Susan.

'Gorgeous. Adorable. I might ask Mollie if Jazzy can come over with me on Saturday.'

'Who's this Jazzy? Is she in your class?' asked Chris, pleased to hear that Megan had made a friend at last.

'Yep. She started at the beginning of the year, so she's new too. Her parents live way out somewhere in the country, so Jazzy boards in town with a family they know.'

'Oh, which family is that?' asked Susan.

'Forgotten, but could she stay here Friday and Saturday night?'

'Yes, of course,' said Susan, pleased, like Chris, that Megan had found a friend.

'Oh, and Carla rang, said she'd be in town on Friday, too. She said she might stay for a few nights.'

'Wonderful. We haven't seen her since Christmas,' said Susan. 'Let's eat. Can you serve up the soup, please, Megan? Then I'm having an early night. It's been a very interesting day. Lots to think about. Megan, I'm impressed by the way you looked after things so well here. Thank you, darling.'

'Any time, Bunny. I'm more grown up than you guys think.'

*

Late on Friday afternoon the guttural rumble of Carla's beloved motorbike announced her arrival. By the time Megan and her friend Jazzy arrived, Carla and Susan were busy cooking and chatting in the kitchen with Chris.

'This is Jazzy,' Megan announced, and made all the introductions.

Jazzy had short braided hair, a small jewelled nose stud, and goth eye make-up, which Chris assumed had been added after school hours but which in no way detracted from her stunning beauty. She gave everyone a big smile.

'Hi, Susan, Carla. Hey, Chris. Man, that's a superior bike parked in your driveway. Is it yours?'

189

Susan winced at the overfamiliarity. 'No, it belongs to Carla, who is also staying for the weekend. And why don't you call me Bunny, as Megan does. There's some tea and scones I made earlier, if you'd like.'

As Jazzy followed Megan down the hall, they all heard her whispering, 'Tea and scones! What are they? The CWA? I thought you said they were cool.'

'There's always juice in the fridge, if you want that,' said Megan.

Susan raised an eyebrow.

The girls kept to themselves in Megan's room, playing music, though it must have been Jazzy's selection as it was raucous and growling heavy metal Chris hadn't heard before.

After dinner that evening, the adults sat on the verandah while the girls stayed in Megan's room watching a DVD. Susan was the first to retire and Carla and Chris talked a while longer before Carla said her good nights and walked across the back patio to the guest cottage. Chris sat staring into the darkness, wondering if an article for a weekend magazine would really change his fortunes, before also turning out the lights and heading to bed.

He tapped on Megan's door on the way past. 'Not too late, you two, you have to be out at Mollie's in the morning.'

'Okay. G'night, Dad.'

'Good night, Chris,' chorused Jazzy.

Both girls were still asleep the next morning when Carla came in to announce that she was heading off to see some of her friends in Coffs Harbour. Then she asked Chris if he could come and check something on her motorbike that was concerning her.

'What's up? I'm not much of a mechanic. I'd have thought you'd know more than me,' Chris said as they made their way out to Carla's bike.

Carla began zipping up her jacket. 'Chris, I wanted to speak to you on your own. Last night I read for a while and it was quite late when I turned out the light. Shortly after that, I thought I heard someone in the garden. I immediately thought about my bike parked in the drive-way, so I stepped quietly outside to check on it and then I smelled something. When I looked around I saw young Jazzy standing beside the hedge and I realised she was smoking a joint.'

Chris was startled. 'Oh, shit! Was Megan with her?'

'I don't think so. But Megan does seem rather struck by this girl, Jazzy, so I thought I'd better let you know. Maybe you need to have a talk with your daughter.'

'Jazzy is Megan's first real friend in Neverend, but maybe she's not the right sort of friend. This is awful. I'll speak to Mum; she's good with teenagers. She'll put a stop to her seeing Jazzy right away.'

Carla poked him in the chest. 'No, Chris, you'll do no such thing. You have to speak to your daughter yourself. The buck stops with you. Leave your mother out of it. You sort this out with Megan.'

Carla buckled on her helmet and rode slowly down the driveway and out into the lane, leaving a stunned Chris behind.

A few moments later, his shock began to turn to anger and disappointment. Surely Megan could have made a better choice of friends. He went into the kitchen and poured himself a coffee, glad his mother was in the shower. He glanced down the hall at the closed door of the room where Jazzy was staying. He turned and knocked quietly on Megan's door and let himself in.

'Are you awake? I need to speak with you.'

'Sort of, come in.' When she saw her father's face, Megan sat up in bed and asked in alarm, 'Dad, what's up?'

'Megan, I have to talk to you about this Jazzy girl.

191

Did you know she was smoking pot? And what about you? Are you smoking dope too? I need you to be truthful or things will get far worse.'

Megan looked stunned. 'What? No, Dad. Never. How can you accuse me like this? What's happened? What did Jazzy do?'

'It seems that your new friend Jazzy was having a quiet joint behind the hedge last night. She brought pot into your grandmother's home. God knows what sort of stash she has with her,' said Chris, his voice rising. 'You simply can't mix with this girl. I forbid you to see her, and you are certainly never to bring her into this house again.'

'What? You *forbid* me? She's my friend and I don't care what she does!'

'Well, I care what *you* do. Just tell me if you are smoking pot or not.'

'You obviously think I am!' Megan was close to tears. 'I didn't know she'd brought pot into Bunny's place, but I can't believe that you assume that I knew or that I was smoking it. You're so unfair, Dad.' She jumped out of bed and ran to the bathroom, as Susan appeared in the hallway wrapped in a bathrobe.

'What on earth is going on? Why the shouting? I just saw Jazzy running down the driveway.'

Megan, her face streaked with tears, flung herself onto Susan. 'Dad's accusing me of being a drug addict! He won't listen to me, he just assumed . . . it's not fair . . .' She broke into sobs again.

'Chris! What on earth?' Susan put her arm around Megan and stared at Chris in shock.

'Carla spotted Jazzy smoking pot last night,' he said.

'And did she see Megan as well? I bet the answer's no. For goodness sake, calm down and stop shouting and carrying on like a pork chop! I will get dressed, Megan can shower, and then Megan, when you're ready, come and have your breakfast.'

Susan quietly shut the bathroom door behind Megan and hissed, 'Chris. For goodness sake, let's talk about this.'

When she'd dressed, Susan and Chris sat together at the kitchen table. Chris rubbed his head miserably. 'I never thought she'd be influenced like this. Is she that unhappy? I have to put my foot down, show her who's boss. I've been too soft.'

'That's rubbish. You have to talk calmly to her and not go on the attack.'

'I feel so guilty for failing her.'

Susan threw up her hands. 'How do you know you've failed her? You haven't let her get a word in. You're handling this very badly. You've had no practice, but that's not an excuse. You need to shape up. This is called a reality check.'

'I've got enough reality at the moment, thanks.'

'I'm going to walk into town and get the newspaper, and see if I can find Jazzy. You handle Megan. Listen to her, for heaven's sake, and don't just jump to unwarranted conclusions.'

'I don't want Jazzy around Megan. Her problems aren't ours.'

'Chris, you can't be so judgemental. You should know better than to be so biased. We don't know the girl at all. Hear what Megan has to say. Hear all sides of the story.'

'All right,' said Chris, calming down.

After his mother had left, Chris sat looking at his cold toast and coffee, feeling overwhelmed. He wished that Susan could sort the issue out. She had years of experience with teenagers. But Susan and Carla were right. He did need to step up. Megan was his daughter and he had to handle the crisis himself. He had to try at least.

Chris heard Megan's chair scrape on the kitchen floor as she sat down at the far end of the table and poured herself a bowl of cornflakes. He lifted his head and gave her a weak smile, but she wouldn't meet his eye.

'Megan, I apologise for shouting and jumping to conclusions. I love you and I do trust you. But I was frightened. Shocked. This is the sort of thing that happens to other people.'

'Dad, I know Jazzy has problems, so I guess she escapes them by smoking the occasional joint. I don't think that's such a big deal. She's lonely and unhappy. And she's bored. But it hurt me that you'd think I'd do the same.'

'I know. I was wrong. I shouldn't have accused you of doing such a thing. But I don't want you to be influenced by other people's habits, whatever their reasons are for taking drugs.'

'Carla said at Christmas time that she used to make pot cookies.'

'That was years ago and I doubt she'd condone it now. Anyway, you can talk to her about it when she comes back. What I'm worried about is that you have a friend like Jazzy who could lead you astray. Does your pal Ruby do drugs?'

'No way. But Dad, drugs are everywhere, at sports events, parties, even in some schools. There's always some new craze or some drug or pill floating around. It's all a bit hard to avoid. Dad, you have to trust me that I'm just not into that sort of thing. I think taking any sort of drug is stupid. You have to believe me.'

'I'm glad that you're aware of it and know what to avoid. I just feel that you're far too young for us to be having this conversation.'

Megan rolled her eyes. 'I'm fourteen, Dad. I'm not a child. They teach us all about it at school. I've talked about drugs with Mum, too.'

Chris felt suddenly inadequate. He realised that Megan was not only well aware of the problems associated with recreational drugs, but had discussed the issue maturely with her mother, while he had panicked, jumped to all the wrong conclusions and yelled at her when she hadn't done anything wrong. He'd bungled things badly. How would he earn her trust again? There seemed to be an ever deepening chasm in their relationship. Before he had a chance to say anything further, Susan walked back into the kitchen, put her handbag and the newspaper on the table, and felt the teapot.

'Way too cold. I'll make another pot. Anyone joining me?' she asked, brightly.

The other two shook their heads.

'Did you find Jazzy?' asked Megan.

'Yes, I did,' she said as she refilled the kettle. 'She heard the row between you and your father and she guessed that she was the cause. She told me that I used to teach her mother, Janelle Whittaker. Janelle was a few years younger than you, Chris. A lovely girl. Quiet, always well behaved, so I have to say I'm a bit surprised by Jazzy's conduct. But Jazzy apologised in a very pleasant way and seemed genuinely contrite. She wanted to go back to where she's been boarding. I don't think she wants to face you, Chris.'

'I see,' said Chris. 'I think I've stuffed up. I shouldn't have made such a fuss.'

'Yes, you should have, but perhaps with a little more tact,' said Susan, ruefully.

'You say that Jazzy's boarding. Whereabouts?' asked Chris.

'That's what I was trying to tell you, Dad,' Megan interjected. 'Jazzy's parents live right up on the plateau and so she has to board with a family in town. Sometimes her parents can get down and take her home on the weekends, and sometimes they can't.'

'Jazzy certainly is a lot wilder than her mother,' said Susan.

'Jazzy is so homesick. She likes to act cool, but that's because she's so miserable. I don't think she's really like that at all. She really misses her little brother and sisters and her parents, as well as her animals. Anyway, that's why I think she smokes pot – it helps take her mind off how unhappy she is,' explained Megan.

'I see, but I don't think that smoking pot is going to provide her with any lasting solutions. So, who's she boarding with?' asked Susan.

'The Sedgemores,' replied Megan.

'Are they the same Sedgemores who used to have kids boarding with them when I went to school, Mum?' asked Chris.

'The very same,' replied Susan.

'They must be a hundred in the shade by now,' said Chris in amazement.

'The Sedgemores are good people, but you're right. They aren't young, so I can't imagine that they would provide exciting and stimulating company for a fifteen-year-old,' said Susan.

'If I'd known how unhappy Jazzy was, I think I would have been a bit more understanding, instead of thinking the worst about her,' said Chris, remorsefully.

'Shall I call her and ask her to come back?' asked Megan. 'Explain that you didn't mean to lose your cool?'

'Megan, just because I can understand Jazzy's motives doesn't mean I can condone her pot smoking,' replied Chris.

'Oh, for goodness sake, Chris, don't be so prim,' said Susan, tartly. 'If we don't get Jazzy to come back here, then we can't help her, and believe me, she wants to be helped.'

'All right, you two, I give in. Do you want to take Jazzy out to Mollie's place and then bring her back here for dinner, Megs? Tell her that you've got me sorted out and that the path is clear.'

'Dad, you are the best. I'm going to ring her right away.' With that Megan leapt from her chair and raced to use the landline. In less than a minute, Chris could hear her chattering brightly.

'Are teenagers always this mercurial?' he asked his mother.

'You're lucky that Megan is. Some teens can hold a grudge for a very long time.'

Megan arranged to meet Jazzy down at the river.

'I hope she'll come back with me and talk to us all. She said she might, but you'll understand if she doesn't want to?'

'Sure thing,' said Chris.

'But do try to encourage her,' added Susan. 'We're not going to preach or anything like that, we just want to see if we can help her somehow.'

'Being nice and friendly will help her heaps,' said Megan.

'How are you going to get to Mollie's farm? I'll drive you if you like,' said Susan.

'It's okay, thanks. We'll walk and take turns on the bike.'

Carla arrived back before the girls returned, and Chris filled her in on what had transpired.

'You did the right thing. Sounds like Jazzy is struggling. Hard on her being separated from the rest of her family.'

The three adults were on the verandah when the girls came home that afternoon, wheeling Megan's bike.

'I'm so glad you decided to join us for dinner,' said Susan with a sincere smile. 'You both must be starving and it'll be a while until the meal's ready, so why don't you get yourselves a snack?'

The girls went inside and soon reappeared with large homemade milkshakes. Jazzy seemed much more subdued than she had the previous day.

Carla broke the ice, cutting to the chase. 'So, your parents are out in the bush, are they? Too far to travel to school each day?'

'I used to go to the local high school on the plateau, but my mother thinks that Neverend High is much better 'cause that's where she went, and she thinks that I'll get better educational opportunities if I go there, too.'

'Do you like Neverend High?' asked Carla.

'It's okay. The teachers are good, I suppose.' Then, unbidden, tears started to roll down Jazzy's cheeks. 'When I went out to Mollie's farm today, all I could think about was home. I just love being on the land.'

'Yeah, you like shovelling cow poo and horse poo,' said Megan, trying to lighten the mood.

'I *do* love it. I miss it so badly, it hurts.'

The others looked at her.

The poor girl, thought Chris.

'Did you like the school on the plateau?' asked Susan.

'It was all right. I had some nice friends there. Not that you're not nice, Megan, and you too, Bunny,' said Jazzy in a little voice, and then started to cry again.

'But if your parents knew how unhappy you are in Neverend, surely they would let you transfer back to your old school,' said Susan.

'I couldn't tell them. They're making big sacrifices to pay for my board so I can go to school here. I don't want to disappoint them,' Jazzy sniffed.

Susan said nothing more and Carla had the tact to change the subject and talk about a rally she was going to in South Australia the following week.

'I think I'll go in and start the dinner,' said Susan, walking towards the kitchen. 'No, I'll be fine by myself,' she added when the others started to get up, 'you lot just talk and I'll call if I need help.'

As soon as Susan left, Chris spoke quietly to Jazzy, explaining that while he could not approve of her smoking pot, he should not have overreacted. He assured her that if she didn't bring marijuana into the house again, she would always be welcome to visit.

Jazzy smiled weakly. 'Thank you, Chris. I won't ever do anything like that again. You are great people and I'm glad that Megan invited me to stay over.'

An hour later, Susan announced that dinner was on the table.

'I could eat a horse,' said Chris. 'You were ages getting dinner ready. You should have yelled for help.'

'Actually, dinner was quick and easy. What held me up was a very long phone call to Jazzy's mother.'

'You rang my *mum*?' said Jazzy in a shocked voice. 'You told her about the pot! I thought you were my friend.'

'Bunny, how could you do such a thing?' asked Megan in an incredulous voice.

Susan held up her hands. 'Listen, both of you. I didn't mention the marijuana. I rang Janelle to tell her that she has one very homesick daughter. I told her I remembered her from school and that I was aware I was interfering but I felt I had to tell her that sending Jazzy to Neverend High was having a detrimental effect on her. I told Janelle I understood her motives, but it wasn't necessarily the best way to go. I said that in my opinion not only was the plateau high school a good school, but I also said that if Jazzy was happy in her home environment, then she would achieve more than if she was unhappy at another school, no matter how good that school was.'

Jazzy mulled this over for a moment. 'I didn't want them to know that, but I think I'm glad you told them,

Bunny. What did they say? They weren't angry, were they?' she asked anxiously.

'Your mother was shocked to find out how miserable you are. You've covered it up pretty well. But she thanked me for ringing, because neither she nor your father knew how you'd been feeling. She said that now that they understand the true state of affairs, they'll come down on Monday morning to talk to you and Mrs Hardwick with a view to having you transferred back to the school on the plateau.'

'No way!' Jazzy leaped to her feet. 'Oh, Bunny, did she really?'

'Yes indeed. I also think your parents were reassured by my opinion about the quality of the plateau high school. It is unfortunate, in a way, that Neverend High has such a good reputation, but other schools around here do a good job too. I was quite fond of your mother. She was always a sweet-natured person, very kind and caring. I was sure that if I could talk to her, she would reassess your situation. The important thing for her, Jazzy, is that you're happy.'

'Oh, Bunny, I am. I can't thank you and your family enough for what you've done for me. Would I be seriously rude if I asked to go back to the Sedgemores' place straight after dinner? I want to be packed and ready to go, first thing on Monday morning.'

'I'll drive you there on the back of my bike,' said Carla.

'Wow. I've never been on a big bike like that, only the farm bikes, and they haven't got much power at all. That would be really cool.' Jazzy beamed at everyone.

*

After Carla left, with Jazzy holding tightly on the back of the bike, Megan disappeared into her room. Chris helped his mother with the dishes.

'It was pretty cheeky of you to ring up Jazzy's mother like that, Mum,' said Chris. 'She might not have reacted so well to someone calling her up and interfering with her family.'

'Yes, I was being very forward,' admitted Susan. 'But the funny thing is, even though it is years since I taught Janelle, I still felt as though I had a responsibility to her, so I just had to let her know about her daughter. Besides, if you're part of a community, you have to accept responsibility for some of its members.'

'It was a bold move, Mum,' said Chris. 'But I'm glad it worked out. I suppose Jazzy will be back home in a few days a much happier girl.'

Later Chris tapped on Megan's door and found her curled on the bed, her face buried in the pillow she was hugging. She looked up at her father, her eyes red, dried tears on her cheeks.

'What's the matter, sweetie? I know it's been a tough day. But I thought you'd be happy for Jazzy.'

'This has been more than tough – it's been an awful day. I mean, like, so hard. First I find out my new best friend is smoking pot, then you accuse me of taking drugs, and then everyone worries about Jazzy and now she'll most likely end up going home. And then I email Ruby and she's too busy to talk to me. I don't have any real friends.' Her rushed words tumbled out. 'I hate it here.'

Chris sat on the edge of the bed. 'I guess it must seem that way. Do you want to go to Perth and see your mum in the next school break? Or what about you go and visit Ruby? Do you want me to talk to Mrs Hardwick at school? Maybe she can talk to the other students.'

'You can't do that. You can't make people be friends with me!'

'Megan, I don't think people don't like you or don't want to be friends. They're just getting on with their own lives, school, family, sport, as we all do. Maybe you just have to make more of an effort to get to know them.'

'That's right! Blame me,' Megan said, turning her head away.

'Don't be so defensive, honey. Hear me out. Take me, for example. I've lost my job and I have been feeling more and more frustrated, hurt, depressed and a bit frightened about what I'm going to do next. But I have decided that I have to be proactive, to actually start to do something for myself, rather than asking other people to do something for me. Maybe you could do that, too.'

Megan looked at him again and rolled her eyes. Despite her demeanour, he could tell she was taking in what he was saying.

'So instead of waiting for work to come to me, I'm going to try to create my own work by starting to find my own stories and write as a freelancer. It's not exactly what I want to do, but we can't always stay in our comfort zone. Sometimes we have to jump-start our lives.'

'And how do I do that? I'm at school!'

'I guess that when an opportunity comes along, even though it may not be exactly what you want, grab it and see where it leads you.'

'Easy for you to say, but so far there haven't been a lot of opportunities for me. Nothing is going to happen and I'll be an outsider forever.'

Chris sighed. 'I doubt that very much, Megan. Hang in there, something will come along and all that's happening now will be forgotten.'

'Yeah, right, Dad. As if,' she sniffed.

Chris felt frustrated by Megan's relentless negativity, but he couldn't help but feel sorry for her. He knew that it was always difficult being the new person, and he hoped that his daughter would be able to make friends soon. He hated to see her so unhappy. They sat in silence for a few moments, digesting the conversation.

'Dad, I suppose I could take Mollie up on her offer,' Megan said thoughtfully.

'What was that?'

'Well, you know Squire, Mollie's horse? I've been brushing him down because Mollie finds it too difficult, and I can tell that Squire likes me. Anyway, Mollie said that if I wanted, she would teach me to ride him. So, I'm wondering if I should be game enough to try it. He is a lovely old horse.'

'Hey! Amazing! Fantastic idea. That's something I've never done,' replied Chris enthusiastically.

'Mollie says that she has helmets and boots that'd fit me. I don't need anything else, much, for just riding around the paddock.'

'Well, there you go. Before you know it you'll be competing in the local gymkhanas!'

Megan laughed. 'I doubt it.'

Chris leaned over and gave her a quick kiss. 'It's going to be all right, Megs. We'll muddle through. Both of us.'

*

Chris began to spend time at his computer after work, researching the Neighbourhood Aid project that had so captured his mother's imagination and taken her abroad for the first time. There were other volunteer groups like hers which had operated in various countries and continued to do so, but what stood out about his mother's 1968 programme was the calibre of the people who had taken part in it. He was yet to pinpoint the specific focus of his story, but he quickly realised that he had a lot of material, not only about the volunteering itself but also about the subsequent activities of that particular group. He knew he'd have to budget for trips to Sydney and Melbourne and possibly Canberra to search archives and conduct interviews, but it felt good to sink his teeth into the process of digging, discarding, probing, talking and analysing. He was determined to write an in-depth, pertinent backgrounder that would hopefully make editors sit up and take notice.

Megan, too, seemed in better spirits. At dinner two weeks after Jazzy's visit, she announced she had news.

'It's so awesome. Simon Fowler is coming here! To Neverend, can you believe it? To judge a school contest!'

'What? You mean the Hollywood actor?' said Chris. 'Why would he come to Neverend?'

'Simon's a local boy, Chris,' said Susan. 'Comes from just outside Coffs. I suppose he's here visiting family. A few members of the Neverend school staff probably taught him. They might have kept in touch and that's why he's coming to the school.'

'Just about everyone watches his show "The Way We Go". This is so cool. Nothing like this ever happened at my old school,' squealed Megan. 'I suppose you know all about this, Bunny, but Dad, Neverend helps out a school in PNG. The school there doesn't have much in the way of equipment and Neverend has sort of adopted it. The money raised from this contest is being used to buy books and pencils and that sort of thing and it all gets packaged up and sent to New Guinea.'

'That's right,' added Susan. 'Every year the kids in the junior, middle and upper schools write and star in their own short plays. The three plays are judged and the best performance wins a trophy. Everyone has to take part in some way or other and of course the age differences are taken into account in the judging, so that it's fair. It's been going on for some years now, but I have to say that usually the judges are not nearly as famous as Simon Fowler.'

'So what part have you got, Megan?' Chris asked.

'Yeah, well, not what I wanted. I'm on the writing

team. It's a bit disappointing because it would have been so cool performing for Simon Fowler, but as you say, Dad, I'm grabbing the opportunity. Not that I can see it as much of one, but at least I'll be able to skite to Ruby.'

A couple of days later, when Chris arrived home, he was confronted by a group of earnest teenagers sitting around the kitchen table, deep in conversation. When Chris greeted them, they all politely acknowledged him, but Megan made it clear that they were working really hard on a script and that it would be good if they weren't interrupted. Chris smiled to himself and, after he'd made himself a cup of tea, quietly retreated to the study.

Over dinner, he asked Megan how things were going.

'Brill, Dad, just brill. You have no idea how clever we are. This play is going to be so funny that everyone will wet themselves laughing.'

'I hope not, but I get the picture.'

'And Dad, these guys are into everything at school and they want me to join in.'

'What sort of things?'

'Josh plays in the school orchestra and when I told him that I could play the clarinet, he said I should join, too. He even said that since he plays the saxophone, maybe we could start up our own jazz group. How cool would that be?'

'I thought your mother stopped paying for your music lessons because you wouldn't practise,' observed Chris.

'That's because I didn't do anything interesting with my music. This is way different. You wait. I'll practise and practise and I'll get picked for the orchestra. And you know what else? When I told Elle – she's the one with the really red hair – that I was in the netball team at my old school, she said that I had to play netball for Neverend. She's the captain of the middle school team.'

'That's great, Megan. You'll be really busy.'

'That's not all. Bryan is in the debating team and he said that I was obviously really quick-witted and that I should try out for that, too.'

'Are you going to have time for all these extra-curricular activities, Megan?' asked Susan with a faint smile.

'Absolutely. And I'll fit in riding Squire, too. I'll still go out to Mollie's, even when her arm gets better and she doesn't really need my help.' Megan sighed elaborately. 'So much to do, so little time.'

Chris and Susan burst out laughing. It was hard to believe it had only been a couple of weeks since Megan had told them that her life had no future. Things had clearly turned around very quickly.

Just then, the phone rang and Susan went to answer it. She was gone for a few minutes, and when she returned she told Megan that Jazzy was on the line and wanted to talk to her. Megan smiled and went into the hall to talk to her friend.

'What did Jazzy want?' Chris asked Susan.

'She phoned to thank us for helping her and to tell us that she was really happy to be home again. She also said that her parents were grateful for me calling them and telling them how unhappy she was. Wasn't that nice? I spoke briefly to Janelle, who suggested that sometime in the future, Megan might like to go and stay with them for the weekend. Easy enough to do when you're up and down that plateau so frequently. Still, it's up to Megan.'

'Hey, guys,' said Megan, returning from the hallway. 'Jazzy wants me to go and stay. I told her I was flat out at the mo, but that as soon as I had time, I would love to visit her. That's okay with you two, isn't it?'

Three weeks later, Megan burst into the house, her face flushed with pleasure. 'We won. The middle school won the trophy and you know what? Simon Fowler said that our play was so funny that us writers could have a future as scriptwriters in Hollywood. How cool is that!'

Chris congratulated his daughter. 'Well done, darling.'

'Another budding writer in the family,' Susan said, giving Megan a hug.

While Chris was relieved and happy that Megan had found her feet and was starting to settle in so well at Neverend, Chris knew much of it was due to his mother's sensible and steadying influence. For a moment he remembered being the son leaving home and stepping out into the world, convinced he would achieve great things. He'd felt invincible, he'd had talent and skills, and he'd known he would make a name for himself. And he had.

And now? He was over forty and yet here he was feeling like he was starting out in life all over again. But he was not the carefree young man he'd been back then, unburdened by ties or fears. He felt disillusioned, wounded and, despite the love and support of his family, lonely. He knew he had obligations, but the reality of responsibility was a heavy mantle, and for the moment the path ahead was dimly lit.

7

AFTER SPENDING TIME INVESTIGATING their successful careers, Chris was beginning to feel as though he knew these men who'd been with Susan in Indonesia almost as well as she did. Susan had asked him to keep her name out of the article. She told Chris that she didn't want the attention. In a small town, she didn't want to dredge up the past for people to gossip about. Chris was happy to respect his mother's wishes and he knew he had a good story anyway.

When he had initially googled the group, he'd found a passing reference in Evan's citations, which were quite voluminous, to his work as a volunteer. Not much had been written about David, though Chris did find a paragraph about his work with the Food and Agriculture Organization of the United Nations, which said that he had been partly inspired to work in poorer countries by his experience in Indonesia. In the published material about the other two men, there was no mention of their time in Indonesia. And despite his best efforts, he couldn't find anything on Norma.

Chris knew not to rely on what he found on the internet for his article, knowing how fallible it could be. He'd been taught by Mac to be prepared to verify every word he wrote. Fact-checking could be tedious, but Chris slept well at night. He knew many journalists were so rushed these days that they didn't have the luxury of time to check much at all. But Chris knew that, once out there, incorrect facts became self-perpetuating. He contacted an old friend, Wendy, who was in charge of Trinity Press's archives, to dig deeper.

'Everything is available in online files now,' Wendy told him. 'There was one mad librarian here in the 1980s who tried to throw out all the original old cuttings books – you know, where the articles were cut and pasted up – so there could be some articles missing. You have some big names on your list, so you could also look up the various professional magazines. There should be something in those. Are you writing about these people for anyone in particular?'

'Not really. It's for whoever takes it, pays me, and keeps my name out there,' said Chris. 'Thanks for your help, Wendy.'

'If I come across anything related to this star-studded cast of yours, I'll get in touch.'

The financial papers, specialist magazines and reports relating to medicine and business filled in a few more gaps about the careers of Evan, Alan and Mark, but still nothing turned up on Norma. Chris even came across a few old radio and TV interviews, and he found that hearing the men's work described in their own words was particularly helpful. Chris began to see that perhaps Mark's philanthropic work and Evan's outreach programmes could well have had their roots in the work they'd done in Indonesia.

Alan's career had come a very long way from building rural roads and bridges in Java. He had become a major real estate developer, particularly known for the large-scale shopping centres that he'd spawned in sprawling suburban Australia. But although Chris could find plenty of information about Alan's company, International Industries, and its developments, he could find very little actually published about the chairman himself. Even in media interviews over issues which involved his company, it was always one of his representatives who fronted the microphone and cameras. Indeed, Chris found several references to Alan Carmichael's aversion to the media as well as some comments by one or two disgruntled shareholders over his failure to engage with them. But a glance at the share price index of International Industries showed that shareholders had little to complain about as the share price headed steadily north.

Chris saw that since there was already a lot of information available about the careers of these men, he needed to take a more original approach. He decided to concentrate on each individual and piece together a story which he could link back to their time as idealistic volunteers. Surely, Chris thought, their experiences in Indonesia all those years ago must have helped shape the pattern of their lives and careers. He hoped that he would be able to interview them and get their personal observations to confirm this idea. But before he had even sought his first interview, serendipity struck.

Susan came into the office as Chris was sorting through his papers. She looked surprised and somewhat pleased.

210

'Hey, what's up, Mum?'

'We're having a visitor for afternoon tea.'

'That's nice. Who?'

'You'll never guess. David Moore. He did say he might look me up one day in his travels, but I didn't take him seriously.'

'Well, that's very fortuitous! Maybe I'll be able to pick his brains for my article,' said Chris.

'I've got time to bake a cake before he gets here, or do you think that's too old-fashioned?'

Chris smiled. 'Mum, if David Moore doesn't appreciate your cake, there are two other people in this house who will.'

*

David Moore arrived as Chris was getting out mugs for coffee. He heard his mother's laughter as she brought David inside.

'Well timed, Chris is making fresh coffee. Or would you prefer tea?'

'I still love Java coffee, thick and strong. But I'll take whatever is going.'

As they came into the kitchen, Susan said, 'Chris, this is David Moore. My son, Chris.'

They shook hands and Chris instantly liked the easy manner, friendly smile and down-to-earth air David Moore radiated. He was solid and suntanned, with greying hair and a firm handshake. 'Good to meet you,' Chris said. 'No Java coffee, I'm afraid, but I'll double the dose of what we have, if you like.'

'Thanks. What a great part of the country. Neverend's a bit of a secret,' said David.

'We rather like to keep it that way,' said Susan. 'Where are you heading?'

'To a place about one hundred and fifty kilometres

west of here. There's a property whose owners have developed an innovative system of regenerating the land. By improving its soil, saving water, and using natural methods, they have created a sustainable agri-business that's really flourishing. I have to go to see it for myself.'

'That does sound interesting,' said Chris. 'I'd like to visit that property myself.'

'You're into farming?' asked David.

'Gosh, I know woefully little about farming, but I'm a journalist and by the sound of it that place could make a good story!' said Chris. 'I'm always on the lookout for things to write about for various magazines and suchlike.'

'Ah, that's right. Susan mentioned you were a writer. Yes, Core Creek Organic Farm is very innovative. They produce superb quality beef cattle as well as having a fantastic set-up with their production of free-range eggs. Two thousand chickens roam around the paddocks during the day and are provided with sheds on wheels for nesting safely at night. It sounds terrific.'

'Certainly does.' Chris poured the coffee and handed the mugs around and they chatted easily for a while. Finally Chris decided to broach the subject of the article. 'David, I know that you've come to visit Mum, but I've an idea for a story based on you and your colleagues' experiences in Indonesia in the late sixties. Would you have a moment after coffee, for a few questions about your time there and how it related to your subsequent career? If that's okay with you?' asked Chris.

'Chris thinks he can sell a story about those days,' explained Susan.

David didn't hesitate. 'Sure thing, Chris, if you think people would be interested in what we did all those years ago, but first I want to know more about you, Susan. We didn't catch up properly the other week,' said David.

'Of course,' said Chris. 'I'll leave you two old friends to it. I'll be in the study when you're free to talk.'

*

About an hour later there was a tap at the door and David stuck his head into the office.

'Am I interrupting? I've just had a tour of the garden. And I'll have to make tracks soon, so if you want that chat, fire away.'

'Great. Take a seat, David,' said Chris as David settled himself in a large brown leather chair. 'Would you mind if I recorded our conversation?'

'That's fine,' said David, smiling. Chris clicked the recorder on.

'I must say, although I was aware my mother had been in Indonesia, I'd never paid much attention to what it was all about until Mum got that invitation and my daughter insisted on hearing the full story,' he said. 'I was deeply impressed, not just by what you all did, but what you have all become. You are a pretty formidable group of Australians.'

'Yes, the others have made great names for themselves. My contribution has been far more modest, I'm afraid. I stuck closely to the core business I was keen on.'

'I can't agree with you there.' Chris smiled. 'I've done some research on you and you are an internationally respected agriculturalist.'

'Agronomist, actually,' David corrected. 'There's a lot of science involved in maintaining our natural resources in order to sustain our global society. I work across a wide range of fields from biotechnology, genetics, soil to water preservation and improvement, and plant technology.'

'That's a long list.' Chris consulted his notes. 'And you worked for the Food and Agriculture Organization?'

213

'Yes, the organisation is under the auspices of the United Nations and, as you can imagine, it has a broad mandate to contribute to better lives for rural communities and raise levels of nutrition around the world.'

'Are you still working for it?'

'No, although I like to keep my hand in by doing consultancy work, so I'm still travelling the world. I also have a townhouse in Brisbane, near my brother and his family. And I bought an old farmhouse near Siena, while I was living in Rome, and I try to escape there each year for two or three months. I can please myself pretty much as to what I do, because marriage and kids seem to have passed me by when I wasn't looking,' said David.

Chris decided to get to the point. 'Do you think that your time as a volunteer influenced your decision to continue working with poorer communities?'

David nodded. 'I already loved agronomy even before I went to Indonesia, but my time there made things very clear for me; it made me realise how I could best utilise my skills. The people were so warm, so grateful for assistance, and so generous. But I learnt a lot from that experience as well. Working in the villages explaining how crop yields could be improved was an opportunity almost beyond price. I always felt I got far more in return than I gave.'

Chris paused, digesting David's words. 'Do you think that the others felt the same way you did?'

'Chris, I can't speak for the others,' said David, shaking his head, 'but I would be surprised if they had not been affected in some way by that experience. Mark was always generous. I think he tended to overcompensate a bit because he came from a privileged background. Mind you, Mark is pretty smart, he became a leading economist after all. And Evan epitomises the Hippocratic Oath. He developed wonderful skills as a surgeon but he doesn't just use them here in Australia, he continually gives back

214

to underprivileged communities overseas. He frequently goes to developing countries to help train their doctors and performs quite sophisticated heart surgery in those countries under less than optimum conditions. He's a tireless fundraiser, too, trying to buy equipment for ill-equipped hospitals.'

Chris scribbled down a few notes to himself as Mark spoke. 'What about Alan? Do you think that his Indonesian experience influenced his career?'

'I don't really know. Alan stays very private about his life,' said David.

Chris decided to change tack. 'It was actually quite a long time ago you were all together, yet you maintain links. Why is that?'

'I don't know how to describe it. I guess there are times in your life where you share something with others that binds you together. Perhaps meeting up every five or so years makes us feel young and adventurous again. Know what I mean?' David chuckled.

Chris smiled. 'Yes, I do. I was really close to a few friends when I was a kid and I have discovered that I still enjoy their company and all those old memories.'

David nodded and then paused for a moment lost in thought. 'Maybe we stay in touch because we don't want that experience to fade from our memory but, otherwise, we don't intrude into each other's lives.' He paused again. 'And yet, here I am intruding into Susan's life.'

'Afternoon tea is scarcely intruding,' said Chris.

David looked down at his hands. 'I always had something of a soft spot for Susan. And now I find she's just as lovely and unaffected as I remember.'

Chris acknowledged the compliment to his mother and said, 'I feel a bit guilty that I never showed any interest in her time in Java. It sounded as though she was swept off her feet by Jimmy, her American boyfriend. His violent death must have been a terrible episode. I didn't know about it until quite recently.'

'Yes,' said David, his face darkening. 'Jimmy was a very nice man. His death was a dreadful shock to all of us. Things changed after that. Susan wouldn't stay in Indonesia, which was hardly surprising. It was terrible. But I'm glad that she married your father and had a happy life in what seems to be a very special place.'

'Yes. Mum and my father always said they found their own piece of paradise here.' Chris consulted his notes, looking at the last question on his list. 'David, do you know what happened to Norma, the midwife?'

'We rather lost track of her, though I'd be surprised if she had changed her field of work. She was devoted to her mothers and babies. However, I'm not sure if she felt the same way about Indonesia.' David glanced at his watch and stood up. 'If there's anything further I can help you with for your article, let me know, although I'm not sure what else I can tell you. You talk to the others. All of us will have a different slant on that time.'

Chris clicked the recorder off. 'Thanks so much for your time, David. Next time you come by, stay for dinner and the night, if you like. You saw the guest cottage out the back. Maybe you and Mum will remember a few more stories over a bottle of red,' said Chris with a smile.

'Now that sounds like a plan,' said David, reaching out and shaking Chris's hand. 'Good luck with the story, Chris. It's hard to know sometimes what interests other people. Personally, I'm not particularly interested in hearing about peoples' holidays to the "real" Bali, or the discovery of a sensational "undiscovered" surfing spot.' David made the quote marks in the air with his fingers. 'Of course, I've come to recognise that glazed look when I start to tell people about my experiences in Java in the sixties. But you're probably a better storyteller than I am.'

They both laughed and, as he saw David out, Chris hoped that the other men would be as easy to interview and as affable as David had been.

*

The well-known and respected Evan Llewellyn was easy for Chris to research. When the doctor had returned from Indonesia he had begun training as a surgeon, specialising in the field of cardiovascular surgery. Chris found a quotation from an article in which Evan had said: 'You need calm nerves and a steady hand. I find I go into a kind of zone where you are utterly focused on what you're doing and stay calm under pressure, but I'm prepared to improvise quickly if things don't go according to plan.' Chris wondered about the origin of Evan's ability to stay calm under pressure as he added the query to his notes.

Later that evening, as Susan was organising the dinner, Chris read the article to his mother.

'Is that how you remember Evan? Cool, calm, collected?' asked Chris.

'I do actually. Gentle but firm. Organised and very caring. What else have you found out about him?' asked Susan.

'When he was head of the Royal College of Surgeons, he gave a speech about the continuing need to give back to society. Evan, Mark and David all seem to be on a similar wavelength.'

'Yes, it would seem that while they have all done well, they have never lost touch with those less fortunate,' said Susan.

'Evan's son has followed him into medicine.'

'You're not writing about their personal lives, are you?' asked Susan.

'No, that won't be the focus of my article.'

'And what have you found out about Alan?'

217

'Not much. His company is clearly very successful, but like a lot of other shrewd high-flying businesspeople he likes to play his cards close to his chest. Presently his company is in the middle of a contentious building deal in Victoria. Evidently there is a lot of opposition to a proposed giant multi-storeyed shopping complex. A lot of the locals say that the building is not in keeping with the rest of the area and such a development will kill off the main street merchants.'

'Oh, yes, at our lunch he did make a passing reference to the usual nightmare of planning permissions and fascist local councils – to use his expression – but he didn't elaborate. What have you found out about Norma?' asked Susan.

'Nothing, unfortunately. I can't seem to track her down and I'm running out of time. So for this article, I think I'll just concentrate on these four distinguished Australians that I have got information on. I know David isn't a household name but I checked out his record through the FAO, and it's impressive, world class. They all seem to be working still. David's a consultant, which involves travel and advising. Mark's charitable foundation sounds pretty full-on. Evan is training other doctors, and corporate giants like Alan never retire.'

'Maybe Norma is doing something significant, too, that we don't know about,' said Susan.

'Maybe,' said Chris. 'But if I can't find anything on her, there's not much point including her at present. I'll keep looking but if she's moved or changed her name, I might not be able to find her in time. And besides, I know what editors are like and they like names and the bigger the better. That's what sells stories.'

'Fair enough, sweetie. Good luck with it.'

Chris had gathered as much information as he could without speaking to the men involved, other than David.

No point in approaching them if the magazine wasn't interested. He knew he didn't need a long pitch document – editors were busy people – but there had to be enough detail to whet their appetite.

THE TIME OF THEIR LIVES

They gave their time, their compassion, their knowledge, to work as Australian volunteers in Java. Indonesia was reeling from the effects of coups and crises after a new crusader – President Suharto – had replaced the charismatic Sukarno.

It was the 1960s, an infamous era in Indonesia's history, the horrors of which are still coming to light after four decades of Suharto's corrupt and brutal reign.

In the fragile hiatus between riots and the stumbling steps of a nation torn between embracing East or West, four Australian university graduates arrived, not to preach or teach, but to live and work with local people, offering their knowledge and friendship one to one.

The Neighbourhood Aid project, which had been inspired by President Kennedy's Peace Corps volunteers, was a brave and innovative scheme to bridge the gaps in understanding and develop a shared future between two neighbours who were yet to know each other as friends.

These four men were strangers, but this brief time was to influence their lives and begs the question: Was it this experience which made them the men they are today?

Dr Evan Llewellyn. Renowned cardiovascular surgeon.

Mark Chambers, OAM. Economist, founder of the All for One Foundation.

Alan Carmichael, AM. Chairman, International Industries.

Dr David Moore. Agricultural specialist, formerly of the Food and Agriculture Organization.

Four distinguished Australians who are leaders in their fields, respected and honoured, successful and philanthropic.

Christopher Baxter travels back with them to that formative year.

'Well, I'd buy the magazine to read this,' laughed Susan as Chris showed her what he was about to submit.

'If they go for it, I just hope your friends will be as forthcoming as David was,' said Chris.

'One can but try,' said Susan. 'They probably don't think the experience was as interesting as you make it out to be. A mere pit stop in their life stories.'

'So did your time there influence your future?' he asked.

'Yes, but not in the way you might think. After Jimmy's death, all I wanted was a quiet life. I'd had quite enough adventure. Teaching attracted me as a safe alternative and your father and Neverend confirmed my decision. This place has brought me joy and serenity.'

Chris emailed his story proposal to the editor of *Sunday Scene* magazine, the weekend magazine of the newspaper for which he worked before joining Trinity. He crossed his fingers and tried to appear as calm as he could while he waited for an answer, although he couldn't put the story entirely out of his mind. He kept seeing ways of expanding the piece, and not just from the perspective of Australia's relationship with Indonesia and her adjoining neighbours, Timor Leste and Papua New Guinea. His interest was also piqued by the people who had shared his mother's adventure. There seemed to be so much to learn about their lives. Maybe the newspaper would ask him to do a couple of follow-up articles.

For the next few days, Susan was busy with a Landcare project, helping restore a nearby creek that was choked with weeds and exotic plants. Laden with hat, sunblock, waders, gloves and a packed lunch, she set off early each morning and came home late in the day utterly exhausted.

With Megan's after-school activities, Chris's long trips in the courier van and Susan's many commitments, meals had become a bit hit and miss. But the three of them pitched in to get something on the table each night.

'I'll chop up the vegetables,' said Chris one evening a few days after he'd submitted his pitch. 'These domestic chores help me think.'

'Have you heard anything from that magazine yet, Dad?' asked Megan.

'No. They probably have an editorial meeting once a week or so, planning stories. They work months ahead unless it's something topical which can't wait.'

The phone rang and Susan went to answer it. She didn't return for some time. When she did, she said, 'Sorry to disappear while you two are getting dinner, but that was David Moore. He gave me some very helpful advice about our Landcare project.'

'Oh, yes, I suppose he could. How did he know about it?' asked Chris as he sliced up some bread.

'He didn't. He just called for a chat so I picked his brains.'

'That was handy,' said Chris as Megan put the lamb cutlets on to grill.

'Yes. He said he was driving down from Brisbane soon, so he asked if he could drop in again.'

Chris recalled that he'd pressed David to come and have dinner with them if he could, but he was a little surprised David had taken him up on the offer so soon. 'He's certainly reconnected with you! I don't suppose you've heard from the others?' he asked.

'No, I haven't. Can you mash the potatoes, please?'

Chris drained the potatoes and began to mash. His

thoughts turned again to the article. Digging into the research work filled him with pleasure and he felt lighter than he had in quite some time.

*

The next day, as Chris drove the courier van down from the plateau and back into mobile phone range, his phone beeped. A few minutes later he was able to pull over and he saw he had a text message from the magazine editor.

Your story sounds intriguing, Chris. I'll have a look. Cheers, Fenton.

'Is that a commission or not?' wondered Chris aloud.

'That's a bit vague, isn't it?' said Susan when Chris told her the news that night.

'Once Fenton reads my story, he'll make sure that the paper buys it,' said Chris, confidently. 'He knows my work and if I say I've got a good story, he'll go with it.'

'That's great, darling. Better get cracking.'

So Chris sent out emails and was able to make appointments to speak with both Evan and Mark on the phone.

Alan Carmichael proved elusive. After many attempts, Chris finally got through to his personal assistant, who fobbed him off. Evidently, Mr Carmichael never gave interviews to the media.

Chris found Evan and Mark both to be charming and polite, though Evan said he was pressed for time and offered to do a second, longer interview at a later time. Over the phone, Mark Chambers was more voluble, telling Chris some colourful stories about his time in Indonesia, but he was more interested in talking about his current activities. 'In answer to your question about how Indonesia affected my career, I would say not all that much. It's not that I wasn't moved by events there, but I think that I had already decided that I wanted to use my

222

family's wealth to help people. My time away there just confirmed that.'

Chris mentioned to Mark that he was having a difficult time pinning down Alan Carmichael.

'That'd be right. Alan's very publicity shy. If he knows that you are Susan's son, he might be more inclined to talk to you.'

'Do you see Alan outside of your group's reunions?'

'No. Once or twice we've crossed paths at various functions. I've met his new wife. Much younger than he is. American, I seem to recall.'

'Was Alan always so intensely private?' asked Chris.

'Sort of. We never shared a lot of personal information when we were in Indonesia. Just the basics. Where we were from, what we'd been studying, bits about our family, but nothing really in depth. Not that men are known to have really intimate conversations, are they?' Mark laughed.

'You're probably right. So what is it that you all had in common, do you think?'

'Drive and energy and the desire to make things better. Perhaps we thought that we could make our mark early in our careers by working in Indonesia before we came home to a more settled and structured life. I'm not sure I can speak for the others from this distance, but that's how I felt. Does that help you at all?'

'Yes, it does. I appreciate your insights, Mark.'

'Good luck with your piece. I hope it inspires other people to go and be a volunteer. It's so very rewarding. And I wouldn't give up on Alan. Why don't you send him a personal note? Those PAs can be tough watchdogs for their boss, and a letter explaining who you are might do the trick!'

Chris took Mark's advice and sent Alan a brief letter. He also borrowed Mark's line, saying that he hoped his

223

article might inspire more Australians to volunteer abroad. To his relief, the strategy worked and Alan's PA called to arrange a time for a telephone interview.

'Mr Carmichael can speak to you at two next Wednesday afternoon, and is prepared to give you fifteen minutes of his valuable time.'

Chris arranged to finish work early on Wednesday, and he put together a list of questions for Alan which he hoped would complete his article.

Promptly at two, Alan came on the line sounding cheerful and friendly.

'It was good to see Susan at lunch the other day. She's looking well. Hard to believe how the time has passed.'

Chris acknowledged the compliment and then plunged ahead with his questions. 'Do you remember why you joined the Neighbourhood Aid project?'

'I've really forgotten now, but it probably seemed like it would be a bit of an adventure. I think my university professor said it would give me hands-on experience and the chance to think creatively when things were not all laid out for me. Suggested that it would look good on my resume, too. He was right. Civil engineering in the sixties in Indonesia certainly taught me to use my imagination and improvise,' Alan said with a short laugh.

'And that's helped you in your professional life?'

'I think it has. Having the right equipment, plans and feasibility studies are all important, but there's generally a curve ball tossed into the mixture at some point in building anything which requires managing,' he said. Chris thought about the opposition to the Victorian project he had read about and wondered if that was the sort of problem Alan meant.

Alan went on, 'You mentioned in your note that you hoped your article might attract more interest in volunteering. While I like to think my time in Indonesia was

224

valuable for me, I don't think perhaps it's for everyone. Some people are self-starters, others need direction. I pride myself on being in the former camp. Of course, one also has to be mindful of the effects these sorts of projects have on volunteers' health, safety, comfort. I'm sure that your mother has filled you in on what happened to some of our group. Nevertheless, I can say that we were enthusiastic, and had the energy and motivation to manage on our own. If people have these qualities, they should give it a go.'

'Have you ever kept in touch with any of the Indonesians you knew there?' Chris asked, ticking off the questions on his list.

'No. It was a long time ago. Apart from my holiday home in Bali, I really have no interests there at all.'

Chris pursued a few more avenues about Alan's career and views on Australia's relationship with its Asian neighbours, but Alan side-stepped them all. Chris visualised him glancing at his watch as he gave non-committal answers.

'Don't know if I can help you with anything else. As you know, I meet up with the others every few years. Nice to talk about old times with other successful people who shared the same experience, but Neighbourhood Aid was a very short episode in my life. Please give your mother my best wishes and tell her that I hope to see her at the next lunch, when Evan organises it.'

At exactly 2.15 pm the interview was over. Chris considered it no more than a casual conversation. Glancing at his notes, he had some answers but it was clear that Alan Carmichael was adept at deflecting or simply ignoring questions. Years of practice, no doubt.

Still, Chris thought he had enough quotes for the article, and the inclusion of someone as high profile and media shy as Alan Carmichael, the billionaire developer, would give his piece some added weight.

*

'Dad, Bunny says to take a break and come and have some dinner. It's on the table.'

'Okay, Megs, I'm just putting the finishing touches on the article.'

'Is it good?'

'Well, it's often hard to judge. I'll read it through again and then I'll ask Bunny to read it as well. Tap into her critical expertise. Can't let all those years of experience go to waste.'

This Chris did, and early next morning Susan put the printed pages on the kitchen table and took a sip of her tea.

Chris stopped buttering his toast. 'So?'

'It brings back a lot of memories. You've framed the article well, looking at the men's original motivation. It's a very multi-layered story, well researched, powerful and really interesting. I think it will make most people sit up and say, "I never knew that about those men!"'

Chris looked pleased but said, 'You're biased, of course.'

However, he immediately emailed the story, together with a short note, to Fenton at *Sunday Scene*. He knew he wouldn't hear back from the magazine for a few days, so he returned to work and tried to put it out of his mind. But as usual, once he'd sent the story off he started to think of other things he should have put in, other avenues that he might have investigated. He knew the story was possibly too long, but it was hard to let bits of it go.

The following Monday afternoon he and Susan wandered down to the local netball courts to watch Megan play. There was action on all eight of the courts, and the shouts and squeals of the netballers could be clearly heard, shattering the tranquillity of the afternoon. Enthusiastic spectators urged their teams on. Chris watched Megan flinging herself into a spectacular intercept, which brought cheers from her friends on the sidelines. The afternoon was relatively balmy for the time of year. The liquid amber trees had lost their summer leaves, their naked branches stark against the skyline, and yet here he was, still without a jumper. He was clapping loudly after Megan's team scored another goal when he received a text message from a staffer at *Sunday Scene* asking him to call the editor when it was convenient. He quietly walked away from the game and rang Fenton.

'Thanks for getting back to me, Chris. Just wanted to let you know we'll take your piece, although it's a bit long. Might have to be edited somewhat, but nothing too drastic. The photo editor will be in touch for some pictures. What have you got?'

Chris punched the air with his fist but then answered: 'I hadn't really thought much about photos. There must be a lot of suitable ones of these men you can easily access. They are hardly strangers.'

'Chris, if we wanted to use file photos, I wouldn't be asking you for yours. The article has to have relevant photos from that time. See what you can do.'

Chris went back and stood beside Susan and told her jubilantly, 'They're taking the story. Be a few weeks before it appears, though. And there's a bit of a problem.'

'Well done, Chris!' Susan beamed at her son. At the same moment, Megan's team scored another goal and Susan and Chris cheered and clapped enthusiastically. 'So what's the problem?' she asked.

'I'll explain when we get home. Let's watch Megan. She's certainly playing well.'

'Stop worrying. The magazine's going to publish the story and that's the main thing. Can I mention it to David? He's coming down this way in a week or so, remember? He said he'd like to look at my Landcare project.'

'That sounds like a good idea,' Chris said. 'No, of course you can mention the fact that the story has been accepted. He's part of it.'

*

After Megan's team had won the closely contested game, the three of them walked home and Susan made a start on dinner. Chris wandered into the kitchen after her.

'Now, tell me what the problem is with your article,' Susan asked as she began chopping herbs.

'Fenton wants photos. Not recent ones, which I have no trouble getting, but ones of your group in Indonesia. Have you got any?'

'Oh, back in the dim dark ages before smart phones I had a Kodak Instamatic camera. I think Norma had one too. Mark had a movie camera. I know I came back with several rolls of film that I'd taken.'

'Do you still have the photos?'

Susan finished chopping the chives. 'They're in a box somewhere.'

'What's going on?' asked Megan as she sashayed into the kitchen and dropped a couple of her textbooks on the table.

'I don't think you should be doing your homework here. I'm getting dinner and the table's messy,' said Susan.

'It's easy stuff. What're you talking about?'

'Your grandmother is going to dig out some photos of her friends back in Indonesia for my article.'

'Cool, can I see them? They must be really, really old.'

'We did have some technological breakthroughs back in the olden days, primitive as they might have been,' said Susan, dryly. 'Let me put this in the oven and you two clear the table while I go and hunt for them.'

After Susan had gone, Megan said, 'I bet she knows

228

exactly where they are. Living in one place nearly all your life must make things easier to find.'

'I'm not sure about that,' said Chris with a chuckle.

About ten minutes later, Susan reappeared and gently placed a shoe box in the middle of the table. She untied the ribbon around the box. 'I haven't looked at these for . . . well, I can't remember how long. Oh, my.' She peered at the first photo she'd pulled from the box. 'Bingo, Chris. Right on top. Here we are.'

'Let me see, let me see!' Megan hung over Chris's shoulder as he took the picture.

'Wow, oh my God, look at you guys! There you are, Bunny. Oh, you look so cute.'

'Let me guess who's who. That's obviously Norma. Was she a redhead?' asked Chris, peering at the black and white photo.

'She's got lots of curls. Like Little Orphan Annie.'

'Not quite as resilient, though,' laughed Susan. 'She was always so afraid of getting sick. Okay, who are the others?'

'Hard to pick them, just going by how they look now. And check out that crew cut, why would you do that to yourself?' said Chris.

'That's Mark. He said it felt cooler even if it did make him look like a Yank. I think he got the idea from Jimmy.'

'Is there a picture of Jimmy?' Chris asked gently.

'Yes, in here somewhere.'

'So who are the others?' asked Megan.

Chris took a stab at it. 'I'd say that'd be Alan, he looks grim-faced. I don't think he's changed all that much, if the few recent photos of him are any indication. And the smily one is David. He hasn't changed much either. So that one must be Evan.'

'Correct. Chris gets the prize,' laughed his mother, then she sighed. 'It's nice looking at all these again.'

Megan dipped into the box. 'Ooh, look at the big water buffalo. And is this the village where you lived?'

'Yes. See that hut in the corner? That's where I stayed. Very primitive, wasn't it?'

'What about this one, is this Lake Toba?' asked Chris. 'Extraordinary. I love the bungalows with the high curved roofs.'

'And that's a picture of the nearby town.'

'Certainly not much of a metropolis.' Chris studied the photo.

They were all dipping into the box and spreading the photos across the table.

'Look, Megs . . . here I am in my *sarong kebaya*.'

Chris glanced at his mother, touched that she was enjoying reminiscing and sharing.

'Oh, Bunny, you look so beautiful! I'd love to wear something like that!'

'I still have the lace *kebaya* top somewhere. Not that I would fit into it any more. But the embroidery was pretty, so I kept it. We can make you a sarong out of a length of batik if you like.'

'And who's this?' asked Megan.

Susan smiled wistfully at the photo. 'That's Jimmy and me at Lake Toba. His friend took it.'

Chris stared at his young mother standing beside the tall, smiling American. He put the photo to one side as they all delved into the bottom of the box.

'Wow, you're all dressed up here. Is this when you went to the embassy party?' asked Megan, showing the photo of the group to Chris.

Susan glanced at it. 'You're right, Megan. That was the reception at the Australian Embassy when we met the amazing K'tut Tantri.'

'You had some interesting times. Where's this photo taken?' asked Chris, picking out another picture.

'That's Bogor Palace and the gorgeous Botanic Gardens. Jimmy and I loved wandering through them.' For a moment Susan stared into space, then she shook her head slightly as if to clear unwanted images. 'Take anything that you think will be useful, Chris.'

'Thanks, Mum. This will be more than enough.'

*

After Chris had sent the photos to the magazine, he received a short message from the deputy editor to say that the story would be printed in three weeks' time.

But in fact the article came out a week earlier. The protests against Alan Carmichael's Victorian development had escalated and clearly the *Sunday Scene* thought Chris's piece was now very topical.

Susan got up early, walked down to the news-agency to collect the paper and pulled out the magazine section. She stopped from time to time on her way home to read it.

When Chris came into the kitchen and saw the paper on the table, he asked, 'Well, Mum, how was it?'

'I don't think you're going to like it.'

'What now?'

'It's okay as far as it goes, but having read the original, it's a real shame. This version has been cut right back.'

'Oh, damn.' Chris sat down and read the piece from beginning to end with a sinking heart. His story had been pared back to the bare bones. It was more than frustrating; it was very disappointing after all the hard work that he had put into it.

'How many words are left untouched, do you think? You won't get paid much,' said Susan.

'It's more annoying that the detail and background to it has been slashed. Only a page and a quarter with three photos! And what is even more irritating is that they have heavily featured everything that I wrote about Alan Carmichael at the expense of the others. David hardly gets any mention at all. What a wasted opportunity.'

'I suppose that's because Alan's in the news right now.'

'But Mum, what he said was so lightweight, and the magazine has made him sound as though he is delivering the Ten Commandments. It's not the emphasis I wanted at all.'

'You never know, darling. At least you've made contact with the paper and they might commission more from you,' said Susan.

A week later Chris was still smarting over the fact that his story had been so heavily cut. He was staring moodily out the kitchen window, cradling a coffee, when Susan entered carrying the remains of a meal.

'Aren't you playing golf with Shaun and your other mates this weekend?' Susan asked. 'That will cheer you up.'

'No. I don't think so,' Chris said, sighing. 'I'm not sure that I want to be locked into golf on a regular basis. They don't mind. I'm always welcome if I want a game. But you know what they say about golf, it's a good walk spoiled.'

'Why don't you pop down to Sydney and catch up with Mac or your other friends?' suggested Susan, clearing away a few dishes.

'Hmm. I'd like that. But I suppose I really shouldn't spend the money.'

'Don't be silly, spend that extra money from the article on yourself. Do something to liven yourself up. Megan and I feel we have to tiptoe around your long face these days.'

Chris gave a small laugh. 'Sorry. I am being boring, but I do feel a bit down in the dumps. Having my article hacked to pieces is bad enough, but the fact that I haven't had one nibble about another story, let alone a job, feels like the last straw.'

'Well, moping isn't going to help,' said Susan briskly. 'Go to Sydney. Megan and I have more than enough to fill our Saturdays, so you won't be missed at all.'

Chris laughed. 'All right! All right. I will. I'll see if Mac is free.'

The next Saturday morning Chris got off the airport train at Hyde Park and walked in the sunshine through to Phillip Street, where he met his two friends, Wendy from archives and his old editor John from Trinity Press. Over coffee and croissants he caught up with their plans, and heard about what other colleagues were doing. They dissected the current political scene, exchanged anecdotes and had a few laughs. Then he caught a bus to nearby Paddington and found the small but excellent Italian restaurant Mac had suggested.

Spotting Mac at a table near a window, he was surprised to see an attractive young woman seated beside his old mentor.

'Chris! Great that you're here. Hope you don't mind, I asked my daughter Georgia to join us. I'd promised Georgie a birthday lunch and this is the first chance we've had to celebrate.'

'How do you do. Happy Birthday,' said Chris, sliding in beside Mac in the curved booth and offering Georgia his hand. He felt a trifle disappointed by Georgia's presence, as he'd wanted to have a serious talk with Mac about his article and run a few other ideas past him. However, as she greeted him warmly and shook his hand, he looked at her with more interest. She was in her mid-thirties, he guessed, and was quite striking with her dark hair and unusual green eyes. When he tried to recall what Mac had told him about his daughter over the years, he realised Mac had made few passing references, as they'd always just talked shop. Georgia hadn't featured in any of their many conversations. Clearly,

Chris thought, as he glanced at Georgia again, this had been a terrible oversight.

'My birthday was over a week ago. Dad has just found a space in his diary,' said Georgia, good-naturedly.

'That's not true,' protested Mac. 'You're the one with the packed diary.'

It wasn't until they had finished ordering that Mac enquired about Chris's article.

'So Chris, you mentioned that they butchered your story. The way it goes, I'm afraid.'

'I realise that, but it's so frustrating. I feel that there is so much more to tell about these amazing people. I have a feeling I've hardly scratched the surface.'

'I enjoyed your story. Actually, I always enjoy your writing. I used to read your column from the States all the time,' said Georgia. 'What really surprised me about this story was the fact that a group of young Australians worked in Indonesia at such a dangerous time. I went to the Ubud Writers Festival in Bali this year. Stunning location. No wonder they get all the top-name international authors to go. Everyone wants a luxurious jaunt there. Very different from how it was in 1968, I imagine.'

'That festival does sound nice,' said Chris. 'I'll have to try and go one year. Actually, my mother would love it.'

'I was working, so I didn't get to see as many of the events as I would have liked. But the hotels and resorts were stunning and the social get-togethers were fun,' Georgia said with a grin.

'Working there? In what capacity?' asked Chris.

'I'm a literary agent. I had a couple of authors speaking.'

'That sounds interesting. How long have you been an agent?' asked Chris.

'I started when I was living in London a few years ago and then when I came home I found another job with an agency in Melbourne. Then I was headhunted by a literary agency here in Sydney. They didn't have to twist my arm too hard to convince me to come home,' added Georgia. 'I missed my old man.'

'As if, Georgie,' snorted Mac. 'You're too wedded to your job to have much time for your old man.'

'He's good company,' said Chris with a smile. 'And he gives good advice.'

'I agree,' said Georgia with a fond glance at Mac. 'Now tell me, Chris, I get the idea, from what I read, that there seems to be a lot more to your story. I think it's intriguing that a random group of men flung together on a particular project in Indonesia would all go on to such success. Dad says your mother was there too.'

'Yes, and another woman, a midwife. I can't find her in time for the article and Mum didn't want to be in it.'

'But those men are significant names,' said Georgia. 'So why do you think there's more to tell? What did they cut out that was so important?'

As the waiter poured their wine and they picked at the overflowing platter of cheeses, olives, dips, slices of ham and salami and pickled antipasto, Chris began to tell Georgia what had been cut out of his article and what else he felt should be written about the men.

'It was so annoying that the magazine chose to ignore someone as interesting as David Moore in order to concentrate on Alan Carmichael, when David is just as accomplished in his own way. I think . . .'

Chris suddenly paused mid-sentence, sipped his wine and then took a chunk of bread and dipped it into some excellent olive oil. 'Sorry I'm going on so much. Let me get my dismembered story out of my system and I won't mention it again.' He reached for more bread.

'Your article certainly has a fascinating cast. While it might be irritating that Alan Carmichael ended up being the star of your show, getting any sort of response from him is a coup. He's notoriously private. So, well done, you. A couple of well-known writers have approached him with a view to writing an authorised biography. No joy there, however,' said Georgia. 'So what's next?'

'I'll try to hunt around for another story, but I won't put so much blood, sweat and tears into it,' said Chris.

'You won't be able to help yourself,' said Mac.

The waiter came over and topped up their wine and Georgia returned to the subject of Chris's article, asking him questions about what else he knew about the background of the Neighbourhood Aid project.

'So what are you thinking, Georgie? Is there any more to this story?' asked Mac.

'More than what?' asked Chris. 'I haven't been approached for any sort of follow-up piece.'

'I'm not thinking of another article,' explained Georgia. 'I'm thinking there might be something here for me, for a book. You've thrown out some tantalising morsels. Maybe there's something more to this.' Georgia paused and cocked her head to one side. 'I think you need to keep digging.'

'Georgie has good instincts about this kind of thing,' said Mac, smiling at Chris. 'If she thinks there's more to it, usually there is!'

'A book? Wow, I never considered that. How do you judge if a book is going to work?' Chris felt the adrenalin begin to kick in, and a feeling of excitement gnawed at him.

'Pitch your ideas to me in writing,' smiled Georgia. 'Throw in everything you know, what you want to know, and where you figure the book might end up. The main thing, though, is finding a hook. Something to make a publisher sit up and take notice.'

Chris took a sip of wine. 'I would love to scratch

below the surface a bit more and find out what makes these men tick. But who would want to read it?'

'Australians like to read about other Australians, especially if they are successful,' said Georgia. 'We're a curious lot. Bookshelves are full of biographies of footballers and cricketers, not to mention politicians. These four will make a nice variation on the theme. Still, don't get too excited yet. I'll have to pitch it to some publishers and they can be a hard bunch to impress.'

'What if they bite?' asked Chris, trying to sound calm.

'You'd get an advance. Nothing too extravagant, especially given the shaky state of publishing at present, though it's coming good. But an advance could help cover your research costs. Give you a bit of breathing space. Once the book is published, you pay back the advance out of the royalty payments. But Chris, an author gets a very small percentage of the book sales, so don't go buying a house in Tuscany just yet.'

'She's right. Only a handful of authors in Australia do well enough to make a living from their books alone,' said Mac. 'Most have to take other jobs to keep a roof over their heads.'

'Even so, writing can be satisfying, I'm told,' said Georgia.

'If you don't starve first,' said Mac. 'Speaking of starving, look at this food. Magnifico!'

The conversation became more general as they enjoyed the food. But while he made small talk, Chris's mind was whirring with the idea of writing a book.

They had ordered a fruit platter, but before it came the waiter placed a slice of cake complete with a flaring sparkler in front of Georgia. Mac and Chris sang 'Happy Birthday' lustily, while the birthday girl blushed with embarrassment.

'What are you doing this afternoon, Georgie?' Mac asked her as she polished off her cake.

'Well, not eating, that's for sure. I'm off home. Thanks for lunch, Dad. I'll leave you two to talk newspapers.' She shook Chris's hand. 'I meant what I said about a book. Keep digging and let me know if you think you've got something. If you have any questions, give me a call.' She handed him her business card, kissed her father on the cheek and left.

'Another coffee?' said Mac.

'Why not? What do you think about the idea of a book?' asked Chris.

'It sounds good to me. No harm in putting together what you can and letting Georgie see if anyone bites. As she said, these are prominent men. They'll have some sort of pulling power.'

'You must be glad to have her home.'

'I am. I confess I miss her mother, so it's good to have Georgie around. She's got a dinky little house in Balmain that she paid a ridiculous sum for. Not that I see all that much of her. She likes to deal face to face with the people she's representing, so she tends to zip about the country all the time. Very independent young woman. Career-focused. But Chris, if she takes you on, she'll do a good job. She's a hard taskmaster, but she knows her stuff.'

'I have to say, Mac, I'm rather taken with the idea of doing a book. Something I can get my teeth into. My foray into freelance journalism got short shrift, so this idea appeals to me.'

'Well, go to it, lad, and if you need me, feel free to ask. But trust Georgie. She'll rip into you if the book's not measuring up, but she also has the knack of making you see your story from quite a different angle. Anyway, if you like this book idea, give it your best shot.'

*

'Do you realise you haven't stopped talking about the book since you got home last night and now for ...' Susan glanced at her watch, 'half the morning?!'

'Sorry,' said Chris, grinning as he sipped his coffee. 'I'm just so enthused about the idea. I doubt I'll turn into a fulltime author, but if I have a book published it could open a lot of doors. I'm so glad I had lunch with Mac. I had a great day seeing old friends. I needed the break. Now I think I feel keen enough to be beaten by the boys at golf next Saturday.'

'Great. I'll be out for the day too. That's the day David Moore will be here to help with our Landcare creek project.'

'Really? Well, I could talk to him a bit more too, if he has time. Is he staying over?'

'I offered him the guest cottage. Our Landcare group is very excited that someone with an international reputation is coming to give us some advice on restoring that poor old creek.'

'Terrific. And what's Megan up to today?'

'She's going out to Mollie's. She so loves her riding lessons.'

'I must go out and watch her sometime,' said Chris. 'Now I can't keep up with all her activities.'

'You're right. If she's not riding or playing netball or part of a debating team, she's practising in the school orchestra. And there's that jazz band that she's joined with a couple of her friends. I've heard them play. At this stage all I can say about them is that what they lack in the way of talent is made up for by sheer enthusiasm. I'm so glad she's got herself involved in all these projects. They certainly keep her busy,' said Susan.

David Moore arrived on Friday afternoon and suggested he take them all out to dinner to repay Susan's hospitality.

'Oh, I have a school orchestra practice,' said Megan. 'Thank you anyway, Mr Moore.'

Chris hesitated, then said, 'Thanks, but if you don't mind, I think I'll stay in. I'm working on a plan for a book I'm thinking of writing.'

David raised an eyebrow. 'You're writing a book? That sounds interesting.'

'I'm sure Chris will fill you in when he gets the chance,' said Susan.

*

When Chris got up the next morning Susan and David were ready to leave.

'We're off. I'm not sure when we'll be home but do you think you could do us a barbecue tonight? There's plenty of meat in the freezer and it's all labelled, so you just need to defrost it. David's kindly said he'll supply the wine, but will you get some fresh sourdough bread from the bakery? That would be good.'

Chris waved a hand. 'Leave it to me. I'll get it before I head off to golf.'

Megan appeared in the kitchen dressed in the stretch jeans she called her riding pants, a T-shirt and an old flannel shirt of Susan's. She was carrying a riding hat and wearing some battered riding boots that Mollie had given her. 'Hi, everyone. Any porridge?'

'Sorry, darling, no time. Have some cereal with a banana,' said her grandmother.

'I'll make you some porridge,' said Chris.

'I don't have time to wait for that, thanks Dad. Gotta go. Why don't you come out to Mollie's this afternoon and see me and Squire in action?'

'Love to, sweetie. Depends what time we finish golf.'

'Okay, whatever. Have a fun day, Bunny,' Megan added as Susan, holding a piece of toast, gathered her things and she and David, looking slightly bemused by all the early morning activity, headed out the door.

'See you all later,' she called back happily.

Chris watched his mother walk to her car. Even though she was wearing well-worn moleskin pants, boots and a pale blue shirt with a navy sweatshirt knotted over her shoulders, her expensive sunglasses pushed up on her head, Chris noticed that she'd taken great care over her make-up and was wearing her pearl earrings. He glanced at his daughter and smiled to himself. What his mother wore might be described as country chic, but Megan looked downright country. Apart from her multi-coloured nail varnish, there was no evidence of any trendy favourites or brand names. He wondered what Ruby and her Sydney set would have said about this transformation.

'Have a good day, Megs. I'll try to get out to see you, honey. I won't linger at the nineteenth hole with the boys, just tote up my losses, pay up and leave.'

'Dad, maybe if you played more, you wouldn't always lose,' said Megan, cheerfully.

'You have a point there,' agreed Chris.

He stuck to his plan, and while he enjoyed the golf, Chris excused himself early, saying he wanted to head out and see his daughter's riding lesson.

Driving to Mollie's farm, he marvelled again at the beautiful countryside, mellow in the late afternoon light. The shadows had begun to lengthen across the hills, and all the paddocks were lush, glowing emerald from recent rain. A sense of permanence and stability filled the valley as it sat at the edge of the ancient rainforest, while the nearby ranges concealed cascading waterfalls and uncharted territory. And tucked beneath those ranges in the crevices of the landscape, small villages and communities were filled with people leading full lives.

He turned off to Mollie's farm and headed up the rutted driveway to the farmhouse.

He parked the car and headed down to the paddock, where he could see a small knot of people. He smiled proudly as he looked at Megan on horseback, confidently trotting around the makeshift arena.

He continued to watch her from a distance, trying to reconcile this straight-backed girl, head held erect, legs tightly hugging the flanks of the sturdy horse as she bounced in unison with the movement of the animal, with the girl of just a few months ago, hunched over her laptop, slouching around the house, slumped on the sofa watching a video or playing with her phone. Chris saw that his daughter had suddenly become someone with different priorities. She was still determined, quick-witted and funny, with intriguing tastes and interests, but now Chris knew she was more grounded and seemed happier with her life.

He walked towards the others and watched Mollie giving Megan directions, but then he was surprised to see that to one side of the paddock, leaning on the rails, were his mother and David.

He joined them. 'This is a surprise, seeing you both here. How's she doing?'

'We finished early enough to come over. Aren't you thrilled, Chris! Look at her. Who'd have thought it! Surfer girl to horse rider in such a relatively short time. I'm so proud of her.'

'You'd think she'd been born in the saddle,' added David.

'Of course, she still likes to go surfing at the nearby beaches, so she hasn't given surfing away entirely,' Susan told him.

Chris said nothing as he lifted his arm to let Megan know that he was there, but she was concentrating so hard she didn't notice.

'She has a good seat, holds herself well,' said David.

Chris nodded in agreement, but suddenly he felt inexplicably miffed by David's presence, although he couldn't work out why. A few minutes later, Megan joined them and she hugged Chris.

'I'm so pleased you made it, Dad. I'm getting trotting sorted out and I love cantering. Mollie says I should learn to jump, when she thinks I'm good enough.'

'Do you want to do that?' asked Chris.

Megan nodded. 'It would be the best ever.'

'What do you think, Mollie?' Chris asked as Mollie walked over to join them.

'She's a good student, Chris. Only have to tell her something once. So when I think she's ready, I'll be happy to teach her to jump.'

Susan smiled at Megan. 'Can David meet Squire?'

'Yep. I have to brush him down and stuff. You can watch if you like.'

So they all hung over the paddock fence to watch Megan expertly unharness and groom the placid Squire.

David turned to Chris. 'I saw your article. Thanks for including me. Brought back a few memories.'

'It wasn't even half the original piece I wrote. The paper slashed it back for space, as they do. I actually wrote a lot more about you and your work than was published,' said Chris.

'Never mind. But I thought what I read was interesting. That period of Indonesia's past is fast becoming ancient history.'

'Chris is going to write a book about it all,' said Susan.

Chris wished his mother hadn't said that, not before he had formulated clear ideas about what he actually wanted to say. 'Yes, I think there's a bigger story there. Essentially it will be about the four of you and your time in Indonesia and how your careers developed after that, if you have no objections. So, if you think of anything, anyone to interview, any anecdote, do let me know.'

'That's very flattering. I don't feel that I have done anything special to warrant being part of a book. Will people want to read it?'

'Chris is getting an agent. He's spoken to her already and she assures him that people will be interested,' Susan explained to David.

'I hope that's right. She hasn't read anything yet,' said Chris.

'Well, best of luck,' said David. 'If you still want to do a story about Core Creek Organic Farm, let me know. I'll be happy to give you some contact details.'

'Thanks, but I'm a bit disillusioned with freelancing at present, so I'm concentrating on this book idea.'

'It's starting to get dark, so we'd better get home and clean up before we have that barbecue,' said Susan. 'See you back at the house. Bye, Mollie, see you next week at book club.' With a wave, Susan and David headed back to Susan's car.

'Do you want a ride home, Megs?'

'No thanks, Dad. I have my bike. I've just got a couple of things to do for Mollie. I'll see you there.' She gave him a big smile. 'David's nice, isn't he? Bunny said they had a great day cleaning up the creek. That's good, isn't it?'

'Yes, I'm sure he had a lot of useful advice for them all,' Chris said primly.

'Daaaad . . . I meant about Bunny and David!'

'What about them?' Chris glanced at her.

'That they like each other and want to do stuff together. I mean, you can see he adores her!'

'Rubbish. They're just old friends. You're being a teenage romantic.'

Megan chuckled. 'C'mon, Dad, I think it's lovely she has a special friend.'

'I think you're reading too much into this. It's not the beginning of some romantic entanglement,' said Chris, although privately he wasn't so sure. 'Be careful riding home on your bike. I thought you looked very at home on a horse.'

'Thanks, Dad.'

As Chris walked to his car, he wondered why he hadn't noticed the interaction between David and his mother. He knew he was being silly, but he felt out of sorts about it. Perhaps somewhere in his head, he couldn't help but feel that Susan was being disloyal to his father. The only man he'd ever seen his mother relating to was his father and since his death it had never occurred to Chris that she would ever feel remotely interested in the company of another man. But, he reasoned, she was a free agent. If his mother chose to enter into another relationship that was entirely her prerogative. But then, he rationalised to himself, this was probably just a brief interlude brought on by their recent reconnection. Soon David would return to his travelling and his work and the life he'd lived these past decades, and Susan would continue her full and contented life in Neverend. There was probably nothing in it at all.

Chris's thoughts circled back to himself and the way his world had narrowed. He was becoming insular, where once he had been engaged in a broader way. He couldn't bring himself to think of Neverend as just a backwater, but still, it would be good to involve himself in a project which would expand his horizons. Yes, he decided, he was looking forward to the challenge of writing this book.

8

As CHRIS DROVE SHAUN'S courier van, he found his mind continually drifting to other places, events and imagined scenarios. He felt as though he was experiencing a parallel universe; sometimes it was an era that had existed before he was born, a time and place which had come alive through his mother's Indonesian stories and photos. Other times, Chris felt that he was running up against his own childhood, for as he drove around the district, he realised that little had changed in the Henry Valley and surrounding hills. Even Neverend had hardly altered in the last forty years. Then he would be drawn back to the present as he tried to apply himself to the book he had committed to write. This was at once challenging and daunting, but Chris knew that he had to seize the opportunity that Georgia had given him. This book would be the way forward.

About a week after David's visit, Chris was nearing the town at the end of his shift when his mobile phone rang. It was Megan.

'Dad, can you pick me up from Mollie's, please? She's been going through some of her old things and she said I could take what I wanted. I can't carry it all back home on my bike.'

When Chris arrived at Mollie's farm, he stared at the saddle, boots, bridle and stirrups, what looked to be an oilskin coat, two riding hats and a saddle blanket.

'Megan, what do you want with all this equipment?'

'Dad, you never know when this might come in handy. Riding is a serious business,' Megan told him gravely.

Chris was amazed by his daughter's enthusiasm for riding, but as Susan had pointed out to him a few days earlier, it was likely to wane when the next trend beckoned.

'Teenagers tend to move from one craze to another,' she'd said. 'Who knows what will be next? Come the Christmas holidays, it could be back to surfing or kayaking along the river.'

Chris helped Megan put the riding gear into the back of the van, but the thought that he and his daughter might still be here next year and maybe the year after that, or even longer, depressed him. It made him feel as though he was going backwards. It wasn't that he didn't like being here – for a while now he'd recognised what a pleasant lifestyle Neverend offered – but increasingly he was missing a serious career, a sense of achievement and being someone whose work was recognised and valued. He knew that if he was honest his feelings were partly about his ego and the status his career had given him, but the fact was that he felt he was stagnating. He was over forty years old and had a very hazy future. He tried to push these nagging thoughts to one side. Book, book, book, focus on the book, he told himself.

The research for the book was progressing. Evan and Mark had been very cooperative and Evan had even sent him a few personal notes and letters he had written of his time in Indonesia. Both had been pleased to speak with him on the phone, and had returned his emails so willingly that Chris didn't feel as though he was intruding on their time and memories. Alan Carmichael, however, was proving to be much more elusive. Since their phone conversation, he hadn't acknowledged any of Chris's overtures. Chris was beginning to realise how fortunate he'd been getting even that brief interview with him for the magazine article.

That evening, Chris looked out of Susan's living room windows at the soft folds of the hills, mellow in the late light of day. The weather was cooling and a thin wisp of smoke coming from the far end of the valley caught his eye. Chris vaguely recalled the long bike rides he'd taken with his mates on the narrow dirt roads that linked the old farms in that out-of-the-way area. He recalled Archie Doyle, a mate from school who'd lived on one of the small farms, and remembered going out to his place one day to pick apples from a heavily laden tree. Archie was a good footballer and had left to go to Newcastle to try his luck there. Chris wondered what had become of him. He'd have to ask Shaun, Duncan or Alex about him. They'd know.

Megan was tired and dirty and smelled faintly of hay and horses as she bubbled with the news of the day's events.

'Aaaaand, Ruby is so jealous about Squire, she says she's always wanted to ride. First I've heard of *that*. But I promised that next time she comes up she can have a go.'

'Are you are going to have a shower before dinner? You can't come to the table like that,' Chris commented.

'In a minute, Dad. Actually, that reminds me, Ruby wants me to go down to Sydney, for her birthday. She'll be fifteen and that's huge.'

'That's nice of her. When is this extravaganza?'

'Saturday week. I could fly down, couldn't I?'

'We'll see. Where's it going to be held?'

'At Ruby's. Her parents have a big undercover area around the pool. It will be too cold for swimming, but it will be great. Her mum said I can stay with them for the weekend. Ruby's father is making mocktails.'

'You mean expensive, doctored-up, fancy non-alcoholic drinks with names like Naked Lady and Surfer Stud,' laughed Susan, looking up from the book she was reading on the couch.

'Really, Mum, how do you know these things?' Chris feigned astonishment.

Suddenly Megan's expression changed. 'But I've got absolutely nothing to wear. I've got no new clothes and everyone's seen all my stuff already, it's so old. I can't go. Everyone will think I'm so uncool.'

'Why don't you and Bunny go into Coffs to buy something?' asked Chris.

'That's a great idea, I'm sure we could hunt for something dressy there,' said Susan.

'Oh, you two don't understand,' said Megan, tugging at the sleeves of her dirty shirt. 'What will all my friends think if I don't wear something really up to date? I can't look like I'm from Hicksville. And where will I get the money for those sorts of clothes? I've only just paid off my phone bill, so I'm still broke. I'm not going to go to Ruby's party if I'm going to be embarrassed.'

'Megan, I'm sorry,' said Chris. 'But I can't splash out hundreds of dollars for party clothes. I just don't have that much spare cash at present.'

Megan looked at her father and gave him a small smile. 'That's okay. I understand. I'll just tell Ruby I'm too busy to come. Anyway, how would I get to Sydney? You probably can't afford the airfare either.'

'Don't tell Ruby anything just yet,' said Susan. 'Give me a day or so to come up with an idea.'

'Maybe if I did have something to wear, we could all drive down to Sydney together,' suggested Megan, hopefully.

'Not me,' replied Susan. 'David's coming down from Brisbane that weekend.'

'Again? More Landcare work?' asked Chris, turning to face her.

'What's wrong with that?' Megan demanded. 'They like working on the Landcare thing together.'

Chris was silent a moment. Then he was conscious that Megan was giving him a death stare. He shrugged and said, 'I suppose I can talk to David about the book while he's here. Pick his brains a bit more.'

'No, you can't,' said Megan, haughtily. 'You're coming to Sydney with me. Please, Dad. Bunny will think of something for me to wear that will make them all sit up and take notice. You will, won't you, Bunny?'

'I'll do my best,' said Susan.

'All right,' Chris relented. 'If I get my book outline finished, I'll be able to talk it over with Georgia when I'm in Sydney. I'll give her a call.' He looked at his daughter. 'Maybe, if I'm there for two days, I might even ask Mark if he can spare some time to see me. But Megan, I reckon if you went down there looking as glamorous as you do now, you'd set a new trend. Go and clean up before dinner.'

'Yeah, right.' But she smiled as she glanced at her mucky jeans, dirty riding boots and an old fishing jacket she'd thrown over her shirt. The jacket had a lot of pockets and funny mesh loops and a faded badge sewn on the sleeve. It was weatherproof, kept the wind out and she liked its faintly fishy odour. She was still smiling as she headed for the shower.

After dinner, Chris phoned Georgia, apologising for the lateness of the hour.

'No problem, Chris. I'm fine with it. How's your outline coming along?'

'Thin on the ground in some respects, but I'd like to run it past you. I could be coming down to Sydney the weekend after next. If I do, could we meet?'

'Sounds like a good idea. You can email me what you've got so far and I can take a look at it and then we could discuss it over a meal, if that suits you.'

'I'll let you know our plans as soon as I can,' said Chris, suddenly hoping that Susan would produce an outfit for Megan that would convince his daughter to go to Ruby's party.

*

'So we all have plans. That's good, isn't it?' said Susan the following afternoon when Chris filled her in on what he was intending to do. 'We'd better get that party outfit sorted out.'

'Have you got any ideas yet, Bunny?' Megan pleaded.

'I have, but I don't know if you will want to take up my suggestion. As you would say, it's a bit "out there",' said Susan, using her fingers to make air quotes.

Megan frowned. 'What do you mean?'

'I understand that you won't be able to compete with your Sydney friends when it comes to designer brands, but I've thought of a way of getting around that. You could dress in something really exotic, something that doesn't have a brand name at all. Something that will knock your friends' socks off.'

'What do you have in mind, Bunny?' asked Megan, hesitantly.

'I was thinking of something to do with Indonesia. I know I have some batik somewhere and I still own a lace *kebaya* top. You could go dressed as a Javanese girl.'

'That sounds like a fabulous idea,' agreed Chris, nodding encouragingly at Megan, who still looked dubious.

'I also have some Indonesian jewellery, a lovely intricate necklace and earrings. You can put your hair up and wear flowers in it,' added Susan. 'It's not fancy dress, it's just different.'

'Will I wear a sarong?' asked Megan.

'I'll hunt out my old batik lengths and make you one.'

'I'm not sure,' said Megan, slowly. 'Maybe everyone will laugh at me.'

'I think it will be fun, but how about we have a dress rehearsal before you make a final decision? I'll have a burrow in my boxes after dinner,' said Susan.

'That sounds a lot better than the last fancy dress costume you did up for me, Mum,' said Chris, the memory suddenly springing into his mind. 'Megan, Bunny made me a swaggie's outfit. You know the sort of thing, bush hat with corks dangling from it, a billycan on a stick, patches sewn on my clothes. I cringe just remembering it!'

'But you won a prize, didn't you? Don't put Megan off, Chris. Take no notice of him, darling. You won't know yourself when I've finished with you,' said Susan as she gave her granddaughter a hug. 'Trust me.'

A few hours later, as Chris finished the last of the dishes and was thinking of heading to bed with a book, Susan appeared from the shed. She'd been hunting around among the various boxes which stored the overflow of Baxter possessions, such as Christmas ornaments, keepsakes from Kate and Chris's school days, a clock Susan said she planned to restore one day, various sewing and knitting projects and a tin trunk of photo albums and other memorabilia. Susan placed several folded lengths of batik and the lace *kebaya* on the kitchen table, along with a box and some papers. Chris hung up the dishcloth and smiled at Susan.

'Mum, that lace top is beautiful,' he said. 'Megan will be thrilled with all this tomorrow morning. Can I open the box?'

Susan nodded.

Taking an intricate piece of jewellery from the box, Chris marvelled at the workmanship. 'Wow, this is pretty fancy. I suppose it's not real gold? Looks tarnished.'

'Of course it's not real gold, but it is gorgeous. It's an Indonesian wedding necklace. It was a farewell gift from the villagers I lived with, but a bit too elaborate for me ever to wear. I think it will be great for Megan's outfit. And Chris, look how lovely these batiks are.' She stroked the soft fabric. 'They shouldn't be hidden away, they're excellent quality, hand done, not like the mass-produced ones now. But I have no idea how I can display them.'

'And these papers? What are they?' said Chris turning his attention to the documents at the bottom of the box.

'Oh, I thought you might like to see them,' explained Susan. 'I wrote to Jimmy's family after he died and that's the letter I got back in reply. And a year or so later, I can't remember exactly, Jimmy's brother wrote to me as well. That's his letter underneath. There're also some of the letters I wrote home and a few other little souvenirs from my time in Indonesia.'

'I'd love to see these. Thanks.'

As Susan packed up the batik and other items, Chris kissed his mother good night, gathered up the letters and went to bed.

But his light stayed on for some time.

When Susan got up the next morning, Chris had already started tapping at his computer.

'You're working early, Chris. Inspiration in the night?' she said, putting the kettle on.

'I don't know, but I've learned something very interesting. Mum, did you know much about Jimmy's family?'

'They seemed like very nice people from what I gathered. They were well educated and comfortably off. Why do you ask?'

'Well, it's this letter Jimmy's brother wrote to you after he had visited Indonesia sometime after Jimmy's death.'

'I remember it now. He said he'd gone to see if he could find out anything else about what happened to Jimmy, but he hadn't been able to discover any more than I'd told him. Still, it was nice of him to write to let me know.'

'You have probably forgotten Jimmy's brother's name. It was a long time ago, but Jimmy's brother has done exceedingly well for himself. He's a lot more than just comfortably off, now.' Chris picked up the letter to show to his mother. 'Jimmy's brother is Thomas Fairfax Anderson . . .'

'Jimmy and Tom, yes, that's right,' said Susan, as the kettle boiled.

'Mum, Thomas Fairfax Anderson is one of America's wealthiest men and one of its most influential financiers,' Chris said, pointing at a picture of an older man on his computer screen. 'You can't live in the States for any length of time without being aware of Thomas F. Anderson. He brokers the most incredible deals. He's behind really, really big contracts which build toll roads, airports, inner-city redevelopments. He has arranged money for film studios to develop high-tech animation. He has a finger in

254

almost every major infrastructure development in the US, because he organises the finance. He's a major broker and he's on the Forbes list of the one hundred richest men in America. Mum, it's amazing that this man was – is – your Jimmy's brother.'

'Heavens, Jimmy said that his brother was interested in business, but I had no idea,' said Susan, her eyebrows raised. 'Do you think you might contact him for your book?'

'I don't think so. After all, none of you can actually claim to have met him and he wasn't in Indonesia with you, so I don't think he's really relevant to this story. Just an amazing connection.'

Susan shrugged. 'Never mind. Still, it is interesting.'

Later that day Susan brought out her old sewing machine to run up the sarong for Megan. She would have to take in the *kebaya* carefully by hand. After school that afternoon, Megan tried it on excitedly.

'Please stand still, Megs. I can't get an accurate length and you don't want to trip over it. I'll put a fold at the front so you can walk easily, but it will still hug your little waist and hips.'

'Do you think I can buy some sandals in Coffs?' Megan asked. 'I love the pattern on this sarong, the flowers and birds. Oh, Bunny, everyone is going to be green when they see me in this! It's just beautiful. Now I can't wait for Ruby's party.' Her eyes were bright with happiness.

'You can't wear purple and black nail varnish with the outfit, but gold nail polish would work well. Let's practise with your hairstyle a couple of times, so you can pin it up yourself.'

'Ruby's mum will help me,' said Megan, twirling, the colours of the rich fabric shining in the lamplight. Susan smiled.

'Now that you're definitely going to the party, have you given any thought to what to give to Ruby?' Susan asked.

Megan stopped twirling. 'It's hard. I'll have to ask some of the others what she's into now, but that could also be pointless because I have so little money. I did think I might give her one of Jazzy's pictures. Jazzy's making these gorgeous little paintings of animals wearing flowers for clothes. In her pictures the plants are taken apart and the different pieces of the flower are made into outfits, like hats and boots and jackets, and in one picture the animals, little fat frogs, are wearing ball gowns. It's a bit hard to explain but the pictures are amazing – clever and funny. I love them. And she has the animals in silly fun situations. If I get one for Ruby, I think I'd get the one that has these cute frogs and a grasshopper dressed up in their plant outfits and shopping at the "Endangered Greengrocer's Stall". But then again I might get the one with the animals at "The Frogs' Ball".'

'They sound intriguing,' said Susan. 'How do you know about them?'

'Jazzy puts them on Facebook. Do you want me to show you?'

Megan raced to her bedroom, returning with her laptop. 'I've brought them up on the screen. Come and look.'

Chris and Susan peered over Megan's shoulder at Jazzy's quaint pictures.

'Megan, these are wonderful!' said Susan.

'They are,' said Chris, genuinely impressed by what he saw. 'Whimsical, charming, funny, clever. I thought Jazzy would be into dark gothic art.'

'Oh, she does that too.'

'How do you propose to get one of these master-pieces?' Chris asked.

'Weeeell, I thought that maybe when you do a delivery on the plateau in the next few days, you could go to Jazzy's place and pick it up for me and I could give you the money?' Megan looked beseechingly at her father.

Chris smiled at her. 'I think I could manage that.'

*

When the Saturday of the party came around, Susan, along with David, who had arrived late the previous evening, went outside to wave Chris and Megan off. After hugging Susan tightly, Megan jumped into the car and immediately plugged in her iPod earphones.

'Enjoy Sydney, and good luck with the agent. Are you feeling confident?' David said to Chris.

Chris put the last bag in the boot. 'Not sure yet. I have a few ideas. Alan is a big missing piece in the puzzle, though. Cooperated for the article but now I can't get any kind of a response. I doubt he would've spoken to me at all if it hadn't been for Mum.'

'I think you should persevere. Once he's found out that Evan, Mark and I have agreed to help with the book, he might come around.' David scratched his chin. 'But I have to admit that Alan was always his own man. He had his own ideas and really didn't care what others thought.'

'In what way?'

David hesitated. 'I've always had the impression that Alan sometimes sails close to the wind in his business dealings.'

Chris looked surprised. 'Do you know that for sure?' he asked.

'It's only an idea, but Alan's clever and I think he finds opportunities others might have missed or he looks for loopholes in the law that no one else has thought of going through. I wouldn't like to suggest that what he does is illegal, but I've watched his career for years and some of the things he's pulled off have surprised me.'

'That's really interesting. I'll keep trying to make contact with him. Enjoy the weekend, both of you.' Chris slammed the boot closed and went around to the driver's side door.

'We will. I'm planning a bit of a dinner party for tonight,' said Susan cheerfully.

'Oh, the Landcare group. Sounds like you two have done a good job with the creek,' said Chris.

'Drive carefully,' said Susan. 'And give Mark my best wishes when you see him.' Then, as Chris climbed into the driver's seat and turned the key in the ignition, she and David went back into the house.

*

Shrieking and squealing, Megan and Ruby hugged as if they hadn't seen each other for years.

After he'd had coffee with Ruby's parents, Chris fare-welled Megan and headed over the Harbour Bridge to Elizabeth Bay, where he checked in to a small and inexpensive hotel for the night.

Time melted away like the froth on top of their coffees as he and Georgia finished up their dinner later that evening. Chris had gone through his book proposal and Georgia had made several suggestions about the various ways of approaching it. She had talked about other recent non-fiction books and what had made them work, tossing around ideas that could be useful for Chris. Chris had made rapid notes as the meal progressed and then they'd begun to talk about other things: their jobs, working overseas and why they were drawn to their professions.

'With Dad being in newspapers, I always seemed to have a toe in the media world,' said Georgia. 'Our house was full of writers, journalists, even playwrights. So many of them had tales of woe about missing out on a deal or being cheated or no one understanding their work.' She gave a smile. 'I think that's where it started for me. I hated to see talented people not being treated with respect or not making good business decisions because they weren't savvy enough. I have a good analytical mind, and while I can easily see the big picture, I also love the detail.'

'I suppose you have to look at both when you're working with authors.'

'I do indeed.' Georgia smiled and nibbled at a chocolate mint.

'And what do you do with yourself when you're not looking after authors?' asked Chris.

'I love photography. I like to view the world through my lens. It's my hobby. Well, my passion, to be honest.'

'Have you produced any photographic books?' Chris asked.

'Oh no. My work keeps me way too busy. Besides, I'd need some sort of theme, something really interesting. Here I keep seeing the same things over and over. I'm not seeing anything new.'

'You do sound like someone who's working in the city,' laughed Chris. 'I can tell you that moving to the country certainly slows things down. I find that I'm observing things I might not have noticed before.'

'Smelling the roses, eh?'

'More time to sit and look at things properly. It's good in some ways, but I'd be less than honest if I didn't confess that I miss the adrenalin rush of being on a deadline unless you count my weekly column for the *Coastal Star*.'

Georgia laughed. 'Well, if we get a publisher interested in this book, you'll be on a deadline. Having a journalist's background, I know you'll deliver. But equally, you have to think of this not just as a news article. You need to get below the surface, explore their motivations, cause and effect. The choices they made and why, and where those choices led them. Readers are interested in what makes famous people tick.' Georgia's eyes sparkled with enthusiasm. 'I think you should talk to as many people as you can who have been associated with these four men: entrepreneurs, top financial people, other professionals in the same field. See what they think of them. Find a new angle that will make the world sit up and take notice.'

'Good grief, that's a big blank canvas,' said Chris, his eyebrows raised. 'A can of worms, as your dad would say! Challenging, but I can't wait to get my teeth into it. I just wish I had the funds to drop everything and start seriously researching right away.'

'Let's see if we can get an advance first so that you can start to manage your time. I reckon if you can come up with something that is not already in the public arena then I'll be able to sell your book.' Georgia raised her glass. 'Here's to you. But don't give up the day job just yet!'

They touched glasses.

'I haven't felt this good since I arrived home from the USA expecting to head off to Bangkok,' said Chris. 'I can't thank you enough, Georgia.'

'I'm glad I could help.' Georgia smiled and sipped her wine.

'Actually, Georgia, David said something to me this morning which was very interesting.' Chris explained what David had said about Alan's business dealings.

'Really? See if you can find out if there is anything to David's suspicions. Did he say anything else?' Georgia asked.

'Not really. He's staying at my mother's for the weekend. He's been to visit Mum a couple of times since they met up again.'

'That's nice. Does David live near Neverend?'

'Not exactly. He drives down from Brisbane.'

'Well, that's a bit of a hike. He must be keen,' said Georgia with a grin.

Chris said nothing as he emptied his wineglass.

'What's he like?' prompted Georgia.

'Well, he's nice. Decent. Good company,' admitted Chris.

Georgia leaned back in her chair, noticing Chris's reticence. 'But you're not happy about him?'

'It's silly, I know, but I feel he's invading our family. I've never imagined my mother relating to a man other than my father, and I don't feel entirely comfortable with the idea. I know I'm being childish,' said Chris sheepishly.

Georgia shrugged. 'Maybe you're just being protective. Wait till your daughter has serious boyfriends.'

'Oh, no thank you! Thank goodness she's into horses for the moment.'

'Your daughter's a lucky girl. I think it's every teenage girl's dream to have a horse. I know I loved pony stories when I was a kid, but when I said I wanted to have riding lessons, Dad just gave me a funny look. So I gave that idea away.'

Chris chuckled. 'I can imagine Mac doing that.'

Georgia insisted on paying for dinner and, as they walked out into the evening, cool gusts of wind lifted the tendrils of her hair.

'That breeze certainly holds the promise of winter to come,' she said. 'Where are you headed now, Chris?'

'Nowhere special. Back to the hotel, I guess. Mark has agreed to see me tomorrow morning, but until then my time is a blank canvas.'

'Feel like walking off our dinner?'

'Sure, where do you want to go?'

'I'm not fussed. It's a lovely evening, so why don't we walk through the Botanic Gardens?'

So they walked to Macquarie Street and through the

261

gardens to the Art Gallery of New South Wales, then down to Woolloomooloo, past the Finger Wharf, and on to Kings Cross, where Georgia caught a taxi home and Chris continued on to Elizabeth Bay.

Later Chris couldn't recall in detail what they'd talked about, but Georgia was easy company.

The next morning Chris called Georgia from his hotel.

'I wanted to call and thank you for dinner,' he said.

'It was my pleasure. I was very pleased with our conversation and I was particularly interested in what David told you about Alan. Maybe there's nothing in it, but I think you could do a bit of exploring. Have a look at some of Alan's developments and see if there might have been some corners cut. If you can find anything, it would really help sell your book.'

'I'll do my best. Also, I've been thinking about what you said about your photography, Georgia,' Chris took a breath. 'And I'm sure that if you came to Neverend you would find plenty to photograph. The area is absolutely full of photogenic places. Maybe you should consider making the journey.'

'That's a nice idea. I don't know when I'd have the time, but I'll keep it in mind. Let's talk again soon. Goodbye, Chris.'

Shortly afterwards, Chris checked out of the hotel and headed to Sydney's North Shore to meet Mark. He drove through the leafy streets of one of the area's most prestigious suburbs until he found Mark's large house, set well back from the road and hidden behind a big hedge. Chris turned down the gravel driveway beside banks of flowering camellia bushes just past their prime, until he reached a parking area beside a beautifully restored Federation house. When he got out of the car, he could see a carefully maintained lawn tennis court as well as a delightfully large swimming pool.

'Crikey,' said Chris to himself, looking up at the massive facade of the house.

He rang the front doorbell and Mark opened the door almost at once.

'Hello,' he said. 'So you must be Chris. It's nice to meet you face to face. I hope you didn't have any trouble finding the place.'

Chris shook Mark's hand. Mark was as Susan had described him, still very good looking, with a lot of thick silvery hair. Chris knew that he had to be at least seventy, but Mark looked years younger. He was wearing a pair of jeans and a casual polo shirt.

'I think we might sit in the family room at the back of the house,' said Mark. 'It gets the sun at this time of day when the lounge room can be rather dark.'

As Mark guided Chris through the beautiful house, it was hard not to stare. The entrance hall, flanked by tall mirrors, was dominated by a large chandelier. As they crossed the lounge room to get to the back of the house, Chris was charmed by what he saw. The enormous room was dominated by a large fireplace and its walls were lined with Australian landscape paintings. Chris was sure they were originals. The moulded ceiling, its decorations etched in gold, was magnificent, and through the open French doors on the other side of the room, Chris could see a billiard room. Everything, Chris thought, was decorated to perfection. The room was elegant and restrained. There was nothing flashy about Mark, but Chris knew everything he could see was very, very expensive.

'Would you like some coffee?' asked Mark as they made their way into the biggest kitchen Chris had ever seen. One end of it comprised the cooking area, featuring a full-sized Aga cooker and a large island complete with high bar stools, while in the middle area was a casual dining table that could seat ten, and at the far end of the room were two very comfortable sofas. When Chris nodded, Mark made his way to an elaborate Italian coffee machine.

'Please, take a seat on the lounge. So much more comfortable than perching on those kitchen stools. So, how is Susan?' he asked, switching on the machine and fetching milk from the enormous steel refrigerator. 'It was lovely to see her at the lunch and I don't think she's changed at all. Well, that's silly. Like the rest of us, she's older, but I think that her personality is just the same as it was forty-five years ago. A charming woman. I read your article in the *Sunday Scene* and I thank you for the kind comments you made about me. Very flattering.'

'I believe I only told the truth,' replied Chris.

Mark smiled. 'I don't think I'm quite as wonderful as you made me out to be, but you are right about the fact that I like to work to help people who have not had all my advantages.'

'This is certainly a lovely house,' said Chris.

'My wife and I bought it not long after we married and we've added bits to it, like the pool and these extensions, but we've never wanted to move. This place has always felt like home. Lorraine is out at present, but I'm sure she'll be back soon. She wants to meet you.'

Chris felt quite touched by Mark's genuine ability to make him feel so welcome.

'I'm looking forward to meeting her.'

'Ever since you let me know that you might do a book about the four of us, I've been going through my personal papers, wondering if they could be of any use to you.'

'Mark, that is very generous of you. Of course they will be useful. They will certainly save me a lot of time running around. Thank you.'

'Not a problem,' said Mark, and then cocked his head as they heard the distant sound of the front door opening and closing. 'Here's Lorraine now. Hello, darling, glad you got back in time to meet Chris.'

Chris stood up to meet the tall, willowy woman who entered the room. She moved gracefully, like a model, her hair still a pale blonde and her clothes, like the house, expensive and tasteful. She held out her hand.

'Thank you for saying all those kind things about my husband in your article, Chris. I think you were very generous in your praise. And now Mark tells me you want to expand that article into a book? Such a good idea. I'm sure you'll want to talk to Mark about it. Why don't you stay for lunch? Nothing grand. The staff don't work on Sundays, but we'll manage.'

Reluctantly, Chris explained that he wouldn't have time as he had to pick up his daughter from where she had been staying at Newport and then drive the six hours home.

'A pity,' said Lorraine. 'Perhaps next time.'

'I'll go and get the boxes of notes I've set aside for you,' said Mark. 'There is quite a lot about the Indonesian programme in there that could be useful.'

After coffee and a chat, Mark walked Chris to his car. 'Lorraine is right. Please drop us a line next time you come to Sydney. We'd like to know you better. Maybe you would consider staying with us.'

Chris looked across the manicured grounds to a cottage which stood at the end of a long bed of roses.

'You have a guest cottage, I see,' he said.

'Actually, that's the staff quarters. No, if you stay with us, we have plenty of room in the house,' said Mark with a smile.

As Chris drove away, he tried to remember if he had ever met such a charming couple, so generous and thoughtful and as kind in person as they were in their public actions.

*

Megan slept most of the drive home. Three other friends of Ruby's had stayed over after the party, and they'd been awake nearly all night talking and sharing photos from the party on their social media sites. Chris knew Susan would be happy to know the Javanese outfit had been a huge hit.

Just before the Port Macquarie turn-off, Megan stirred.

'Want to stop for a break?' Chris asked.

'I guess,' yawned Megan.

Chris pulled over to a servo and ordered himself a coffee, while Megan had a milkshake.

'So you had a great time?'

'I did. It was great to catch up with everyone. Lots of fun. Ruby just loved the picture I bought from Jazzy for her. Said it was really clever.'

But there was something in Megan's voice that puzzled Chris.

'You don't sound all that enthusiastic, or is that because you're tired?'

Megan shrugged. 'Dad, it was great to see everyone and they all made a fuss of me, which was nice, but after a while, we really didn't have anything much to talk about. I mean, I have Squire and netball and the school orchestra and our jazz band, but the others weren't really interested in what I'm doing; all they seem to be into is posting things on Facebook or talking about the latest gear they've bought that cost a fortune. They don't do anything else, really, and in the end, I just found them boring. They used to be my best friends. Do you think there is something wrong with me?' she sighed.

'Of course not. You just have different interests now. I would say that your horizons have expanded since you came to Neverend while your Sydney friends are all just as you left them. You've found that there is more to life than just shopping and social media. You want to be involved, and I really admire that.'

Megan smiled but didn't reply. Five minutes after they hit the road, she was asleep again.

'I had a fun weekend too,' Susan told Chris when they finally arrived home. 'I enjoyed putting on a dinner party for David so he could meet a few of my friends. I haven't done that since Christmas.'

'Oh. I thought it was just the Landcare people,' said Chris, trying to keep his voice light.

'Yes, but I also invited some friends from the book club and a couple from the golf club. David said that he really enjoyed meeting everyone and they all liked him.'

'I see,' said Chris, but he said no more.

A few days later, Chris had a phone call from Georgia.

'I haven't ever told you about my difficult author, have I?' she said. 'He lives outside Woolgoolga and he refuses to come to Sydney. He says he'd like to see me. So, as we haven't met for a few months, I thought I could fly up to Coffs, go and see him, and then drive over to Neverend. It'll just be for the day, I'm afraid, but I'm bringing my camera, so I hope you'll be able to show me this photogenic landscape you've bragged about.'

Chris was pleased that Georgia had taken him up on his offer to visit Neverend and the days sped by.

Chris had arranged to swap a shift with another of Shaun's drivers so that he could show her around. Georgia had no trouble finding Susan's place and Susan had lunch ready for her.

'This area is enchanting! I see why you settled here, Susan.'

'Yes, I fell in love with it almost as soon as we arrived here. It's such a vibrant, interesting community. I couldn't ask for more.'

'Lucky you, growing up here,' Georgia said to Chris, who smiled at her.

'My sister and I rather took it all for granted, as you do. But we had it all: rivers and rainforest, waterfalls and surfing beaches.'

'Where did you grow up, Georgia?' asked Susan.

'Inner Sydney. But Dad and Mum had a holiday house on the coast a couple of hours' drive south of Sydney which we all loved.'

'I was planning on taking you on a bit of a tour to show you some of the area,' said Chris. 'How much time have we got before you fly back to Sydney?'

'I'm booked on the eight o'clock flight.'

'Plenty of time, and I'll make an early dinner for you so that you can easily catch your flight, and you'll have the chance to meet Megan as well,' said Susan.

*

Georgia held her camera in her lap as she stared out the car window. She'd been silent for some time as Chris wound through the valley, following the course of the Henry River.

'Let me know if you want me to stop so you can take any shots,' said Chris quietly.

Georgia turned to him. 'Sorry, it's just so pretty. So tranquil. I was simply enjoying the scenery. I know I should be snapping away but I feel as though I just want to take it all in. Balm to my soul.'

Chris smiled. 'I'm glad you're enjoying it. I'm taking this drive along the valley rather than going up the plateau road, which can be a bit hair-raising.'

'Who lives around here?'

'All sorts; families running dairy or beef herds, hobby

farmers starting up gourmet enterprises, a few old hippies, and even a few wealthy folk in their hideaway holiday homes.'

'A diverse lot, it seems.'

'I'd love to mooch around and just knock on doors and see who is out here,' laughed Chris.

Suddenly the car began to wobble and one of the wheels started to make a flapping noise.

'I think we have a flat tyre,' said Chris grimly. 'The dirt roads around here play havoc with them. Sorry about this, but I should be able to change it pretty quickly.'

Chris pulled the car off to the side of the road, beside a leaning fencepost with the name 'Applebrook' faintly painted on the rusting mailbox which sat atop it.

'Goodness,' said Chris as he got out of the car and looked at the property. 'It doesn't look as though much farming goes on here anymore. The fences are neglected and the paddocks seem to be full of weeds, unless Scotch thistle is a new gourmet crop.'

'Pretty trees, though, and I bet it has an old-fashioned garden,' said Georgia. 'Look, there's smoke, so someone must live here.'

'Could be someone burning off.'

Through an overgrown arbour gateway smothered in tangled roses, they glimpsed an old weatherboard house in need of a coat of paint, and in the distance they could both hear the sound of someone chopping wood.

'What a classic house. What a shame it's in such a sorry state,' said Georgia.

As Chris opened the boot to get out the spare tyre, there was a desultory 'woof', and a large arthritic dog ambled towards them. When he realised that they were strangers, he managed a more serious bark.

The chopping stopped and from behind the house came an elderly woman carrying a hatchet.

'Can I help you?' she asked.

For a moment, Chris and Georgia were at a loss for words as they stared at the slightly stooped but still imposing woman who came towards them. Thick, coiled grey braids framed her weather-beaten face beneath a well-loved straw hat. A knitted scarf was wound around her neck and she wore fingerless gloves. Her worn corduroy pants were teamed with a hand-knitted mulberry cardigan and a pair of mud-splattered gumboots. She radiated a firm energy and her blue eyes studied the two of them curiously as her old dog sniffed their heels.

'We didn't mean to disturb you; we've got a flat tyre. It won't take me long to change it,' said Chris.

The woman glanced at their car. 'So you have. Where are you headed?'

'My friend is showing me this scenic route,' said Georgia with a smile. 'I've never been here before. You've obviously been here a long time.'

'I have. Where are you from? You a local?' she said to Chris.

'I live in Neverend. I'm Chris Baxter and this is Georgia McPhee,' said Chris, offering the woman his hand.

'Jean Hay,' said the woman, shaking Chris's hand. 'Baxter, yes . . .' she paused thoughtfully. 'Were your parents teachers at the high school?' When Chris nodded, Jean continued. 'I remember them. I used to be very active in the town, once. Popped in for Red Cross and CWA meetings all the time, and I'm sure your parents taught a couple of my children and maybe even my grandchildren.'

'Seems like the locals know everyone in Neverend,' said Chris with a smile.

'Living in Neverend doesn't necessarily make you a local,' Jean pointed out.

'I was born there,' Chris explained. 'And I've come back to live here for a while.'

'Good decision. After you've changed your tyre, would you both like a cup of tea?' asked Jean, gesturing to the house.

'We don't want to put you to any trouble,' said Georgia.

'It's that time of day,' Jean said with a slight smile. 'I'll just fetch my kindling.'

'Please, can I help?' said Chris quickly as they followed the woman around the house to the rear garden. In the tangle of undergrowth and fruit trees they saw a patch of vegetable garden. Near it was a chicken run, where several large brown hens pecked about beside a water tank. An old outside toilet was almost buried under a choko vine. Jean headed towards the woodshed and Chris could see that she'd been splitting pieces of wood into kindling chips. With a sudden swing she slammed the small axe into the chopping block where it bit into the wood, leaving it standing upright.

'We'll carry the kindling for you,' said Georgia.

'Would you like me to split any big pieces?' asked Chris.

'I have enough to be going on with, thank you. Soon as you've changed your tyre, come inside.'

With Georgia's help it took Chris only a short time to change the tyre, and then they made their way to the front door. As they stepped onto the solid boards of the partially latticed verandah, Georgia said softly, 'Aren't these rose and green leadlight windows beautiful?'

Chris nodded, then tapped on the door and called out.

'Let yourselves in. I'm in the kitchen.'

'I hope we're not intruding,' called Georgia as they made their way down a hallway to the back of the house, where they entered a large country kitchen that looked as original as the day it had been built. Jean was sitting at the kitchen table, pulling off her gumboots.

'Not at all. No problem changing your tyre? That's good. You look a nice couple, and I'm generally a good judge of people.' Jean smiled. 'Now, I'm going to make some tea and toast, I'm a bit peckish. Would you care to join me?'

Using a metal hook, Jean opened the heavy enamel door of the old stove and threw in a piece of wood. She left the door open as the fire in the small box blazed, and, filling a large aluminium kettle with water, she put it on top of the stove.

'Can I help?' asked Georgia as the woman took down a brown china teapot and spooned tea leaves into it.

'Cups are on the shelf over there.' Jean pointed to some open shelves which were lined with paper, the edges cut in a lacy frill.

'How long have you lived here?' asked Georgia as she looked around the kitchen.

There was a single, elderly tap over the sink, suggesting that Jean had no running hot water. The china Georgia took down from the shelf was old and crazed and neither Chris nor Georgia could miss noticing the old rabbit traps that were hanging on the back wall.

'I was born here,' said Jean. 'My parents built this house for themselves as soon as they got married. They were among the first settlers this far along the river. After my parents died, my husband and I lived here. But Ernie's gone now as well.'

'So you live alone?'

'I'm used to my own company. I don't go to Neverend much anymore, but I have grandchildren who come to see me regularly. And I have the radio and TV for company.'

Looking from the kitchen through the hallway to the living room, Chris could see that probably little had changed since Jean's parents had lived here.

'Your house has so many interesting things in it. Did they belong to your parents?' asked Georgia, who seemed eager to have a look around the quaint house.

'The house is pretty much as my mother left it. She did the embroidery you can see on the cloths on those little tables and the crochet and needlepoint cushions. Don't know how her eyes held up with the old lamps. My husband and I added a few personal things. Of course my family think most of it is junk and the lot should go to the tip. I should get around to having a sort-out one day and see if the Historical Society is interested in some of my bits and pieces.'

'Oh my goodness, I'm sure they would be. May I look at the photos hanging in the hallway there? I'm keen on photography,' said Georgia.

'Certainly, I'll show you. Chris, would you mind doing the toast? Butter's on the table.' Jean handed him a long-handled fork with a slice of thick bread on the end. 'Pull up that chair if you like, and put the bread in front of the fire. I've got a toaster, but I always think toast tastes best done over a wood fire. Don't you?'

'Always reminds me of camping,' agreed Chris, looking rather amused by the situation as Jean led Georgia down the hallway.

Later, seated around the kitchen table with the earthenware pot of tea snug under its woolly tea-cosy and their toast slathered in Jean's homemade marmalade, the three chatted like old friends. Georgia talked about being a literary agent and Chris told Jean about his time as a foreign correspondent. When the teapot was empty and nothing remained of the toast but crumbs, Georgia asked, 'Could we look around the garden? And would you mind if I took some photos of it, Jean?'

'I'm not sure the place is very photogenic, but I'm happy for you to do that.' Jean drained her cup of tea.

'Are there any jobs you'd like me to do for you?' asked Chris. 'Though you seem remarkably capable,' he added.

'Thank you. I'm fine. The gutters have been done. I have enough chopped wood, and my neighbours keep an eye on me. Mind you, now I'm pushing ninety, I do have to accept that I have a few limitations. Come along out the front.'

Chris and Georgia exchanged astonished glances as they walked through the well-loved old house crammed with family memorabilia.

'Just look at the sunlight coming through those glass panels. May I take this picture?' asked Georgia.

Jean nodded, so Georgia used her wide-angle lens to capture the front sitting room with its solid cedar furniture, small side tables, bookcase and a large old-fashioned radiogram. The neat open fireplace had a mantelpiece on which photos in old-fashioned silver frames and glass ornaments were lined up in profusion on either side of an old mantelpiece clock. Above a well-worn but comfortable-looking settee with its embroidered cushions, the casement windows allowed the light to flood in through the rose-coloured stained glass panels, transforming the room with a rosy hue.

'I think your whole house should be photographed, just as it is,' said Georgia. 'It's so very evocative. I would love to do it.'

'You are welcome any time, dear girl, provided I'm allowed to dust and put out some flowers beforehand,' said Jean.

After they had finished their tour of the house and garden, and Georgia had taken more photos, they reluctantly said their goodbyes.

'We have to be on our way, Jean. I've a plane to catch and Chris's mother is expecting us for an early dinner – not that we'll have all that much room for it, now,' said Georgia.

Jean and the old dog, which had been lying on the verandah in the sun, walked Chris and Georgia to the car. Chris looked across the road towards the dark flowing river.

'This is a truly lovely spot your parents chose to settle in, but it must have been hard work for them to clear the land,' he said. 'Do you still own all of their original acreage?'

'No, over time we've had to sell bits of it off. Can't be more than seventy acres left, and I don't use that for anything at all now. Bit of a shame, really. It's beautiful soil going to waste. Still, that won't be my problem much longer.'

'Nonsense,' said Chris. 'You look as fit as a flea. You'll be around for a long time yet.'

'I hope that you meant what you said about my photographing your place properly. This visit has been so short, I have not had a chance to do the place justice,' said Georgia.

Jean impulsively gave Georgia a light hug. 'I certainly meant it.'

'Then we'll be seeing you again,' said Georgia.

'Thank you so much for being so kind,' said Chris.

They got in the car, and as Chris started the engine and turned back onto the road, Jean waved them goodbye before she and the old dog slowly walked back to the weatherboard house.

*

'You two have been chattering non-stop ever since you got back. You said you had afternoon tea, so I'm only making a pizza and salad for you before you have to catch that plane, Georgia. It's almost ready,' said Susan, coming into the front room where Georgia was positioned to get the best view across the river and the paddocks where the

275

cattle, dark silhouettes against the emerald paddock, were grazing lazily.

'Oh, that's perfect. Thanks, Susan, everyone's been very good to me.'

'That's just the local country hospitality,' said Chris with a smile.

'Hello everyone,' said Megan, bursting into the room. Chris introduced Georgia to his daughter.

'So,' said Megan, bluntly, 'do you reckon Dad's on to a good thing with his book?'

'I think he could be. He just needs to do a bit more research and I'm sure I'll be able to find a publisher interested in what he has to say.'

'Awesome.'

'How was band practice?' asked Susan.

'Megan's in a jazz band with a group of her friends,' Chris explained to Georgia.

'What instrument do you play?' asked Georgia.

'The clarinet, but I'm thinking of learning the sax,' Megan replied.

'That's the first I've heard of it,' said Chris.

'I used to play the flute. I wasn't much good, but the best thing about a flute is that it's portable, not like a piano or double bass,' said Georgia.

Megan laughed. 'Absolutely.'

Susan served up the pizzas and the four of them sat around the kitchen table, laughing and talking.

'I'm sorry everyone,' said Georgia at last, 'but if I don't get going right now, I'll miss my plane. It was so nice to meet both of you, Susan and Megan. I hope that next time you come to Sydney, you'll let me know so that I can return your hospitality.'

While Megan and Susan cleaned up the kitchen, Chris had a last word with Georgia as he walked her out to her car.

'It's been such a nice day. I can't thank you enough,' said Georgia warmly. 'I think your mother and Megan are lovely.'

'They are. It's been a bit of a challenge getting to this point. Leaving Sydney was a big wrench for Megan, but she has settled into the school really well, which is a relief.'

Georgia reached out and touched his arm. 'Listen, Chris, I know the past few months have been hard on you, but I'm sure that things will come good. Mind you, I don't want you to get the idea that becoming an author will be the answer to your prayers. That's a tough life, too. But I think giving it a try is worthwhile.'

'I appreciate all your help, Georgia,' said Chris, trying to stifle a slight feeling of panic. He had been putting all his eggs and hopes into the book basket. Perhaps he was being over-optimistic and unrealistic about where this idea would take him.

Georgia hadn't quite finished, though. 'Something else occurred to me today. Now that I've met your mother, I'm having a bit of a re-evaluation about your approach. What I'm trying to say is that while you are focusing on four very successful men, there was actually a group of six who went to Indonesia. I know you tried to find the midwife, but I think you should try again. After all, she stayed in Indonesia longer than your mother. See what she has to say. Women can be more observant and sensitive to things than men, and she might be able to provide you with some new information that could be pertinent. She's been a nurse, so try the nursing associations. I'm sure with some more digging you can find her. You're a journalist, you're used to finding people.'

Chris was pleased that Georgia had suggested another thread to pursue for his story.

'You're right. I'll make some more effort to track Norma down and I'll keep trying with Alan Carmichael.

I really need to crack that nut. I'll be in touch when I have anything new. Thanks again for making the time to come to Neverend.'

'It's been a day of riches for me and very enjoyable. Thanks, Chris.'

'Come back soon. Come for a weekend.' As Georgia climbed into her hire car, Chris leaned over and kissed her cheek. It seemed a very natural thing to do.

As he waved Georgia goodbye, he thought about how much he'd enjoyed the afternoon with her, and he realised that he hadn't spent time with a woman as smart and charming as Georgia in a long time. He suddenly felt lonely.

*

Chris took up Georgia's suggestion and decided to contact the various nursing associations to try to track down Norma. Initially they were unable to find any trace of her, but he pushed them to keep looking.

Once again Chris approached Alan through his PA, who again fobbed him off. So Chris wrote Alan a letter as he had done for the article, explaining that he was going to expand his original story into a book about the careers of the four men. He hadn't really expected anything to come of it, so he was surprised when Alan called him personally a few days later.

'So, tell me about this book you're doing,' he said.

Chris explained what he wanted to write.

'You're not including your mother and the midwife?'

'I certainly hope to use their experiences to fill in background detail about that time in Indonesia, if I can, but my mother is not at all interested in my telling her story, and I haven't yet been able to track down Norma. To be truthful, I think it's the high-profile names which will garner a publisher's enthusiasm.'

'Who is going to buy and read this book?' asked Alan crisply.

'Good question. I think Australians like to read about other Australians, especially successful ones, and you have been very successful. So I'd like to explore your career path. I know, for instance, that you started your company from scratch. I hope your story will give inspiration to other Australians.'

'Perhaps,' said Alan Carmichael. 'I'll be in touch.'

Chris felt elated. While Alan's tone had been curt and Chris hadn't had a chance to pin him down for an interview, the billionaire had at least called, so Chris felt hopeful that Alan would agree to further questions.

Chris now started to delve into the background of all his subjects in earnest, their schools, their universities, their old friends. He managed to work out what had become of the Neighbourhood Aid project, and found that it had merged with a couple of other aid organisations, and so he requested information about their Indonesian operation and its volunteers. He received some documents in the mail, but was told any personal files would have to be accessed under Freedom of Information procedures.

Chris was beginning to enjoy himself. He relished the familiar feelings that digging for information brought him; mainly frustration, but also elation as small pieces of a puzzle began to emerge.

But one morning there was a letter in the mail that chilled him. Chris read it twice, absorbing its contents.

Susan noticed the expression on his face and asked, 'Have you hit a snag? You look concerned.'

'A snag is putting it mildly. This is a letter from Alan Carmichael's personal lawyers notifying me that if my book defames Alan in anyway, they will be taking legal action. Apparently they're going to be watching me very closely.'

'What?!' Susan looked stunned. 'Why would Alan do this?'

'He's famous for being a private person,' sighed Chris. 'And he's got his professional reputation to protect. Mum, what does he think I'm going to write about him that would cause him to act in such a heavy-handed way?'

'Wealthy people are known for being litigious,' said Susan.

Chris's shoulders drooped. 'How can I fight this? This book is going to be very hard to do without Alan Carmichael's cooperation.'

'Would it help if I spoke to Alan?' asked Susan, distressed on her son's behalf at this turn of events.

'I don't know, Mum. Maybe I should speak to Georgia first.'

Georgia was businesslike. 'These things happen, Chris. Legal wrangling is part and parcel of publishing. I suggest you get a lawyer to respond to Alan's letter on your behalf. Don't worry, though. With some good legal advice, you can work around defamation and still do the book.'

'I don't know, Georgia. Alan's a billionaire. He's probably got a dozen lawyers. I don't have the sort of money to take on someone like him! Maybe I should drop the whole idea,' said Chris.

'Well, I don't think that you should give up so quickly. For the time being my advice is just to get on with researching the other three. They're interesting enough for a book, even without Alan, but I still think that you need to protect yourself by responding to that letter,' replied Georgia. 'You really should approach a lawyer.'

Chris thought for a moment. 'My friend Duncan's brother is a solicitor in Coffs Harbour. I could get him to reply to the letter. Maybe he would only charge me mate's rates,' said Chris.

'That sounds like a plan. I suggest you get on to it right away.'

'Okay, thanks, Georgia,' said Chris, feeling calmed by Georgia's efficient manner.

But after he'd hung up the phone and stepped outside to take a deep breath, Chris shivered. It was not from the frosty air and curling mist weaving its way across the valley, but from the worry that things were not going the way he had hoped. He needed this book to be a success, and now he was having doubts it was ever going to work.

But then a slow burn began in the pit of his stomach. I'm going to write this book, he thought, no matter what. It might be risky, but I'll be careful. I'm sure that I can pull it off.

Chris walked back inside with a firm tread and a determined expression on his face.

9

THERE WAS A COMFORTABLE silence in the car as Chris drove Megan to the plateau.

They were used to each other now, thought Chris. A few months ago he'd have felt the need to make small talk with his daughter, but these days the awkwardness that had prompted him to constantly engage with her had gone. Megan evidently felt the same way, for while she had her earphones draped around her neck, she wasn't listening to anything but simply gazing contentedly out the window. She was going to Jazzy's place for the weekend, the first time they'd spent time together since Jazzy had left Neverend to return home.

Chris glanced at Megan's pretty profile, and as she caught the movement she turned and smiled at him.

'Looking forward to this?' her father asked.

'Yep. Jazzy and I have been emailing about plans. She's still very cool. It will be fun to spend the weekend with her, and I'm looking forward to seeing her animals. What are you going to do, Dad?'

'Write. Looking forward to some peace and quiet,' he said.

'Well, if Bunny goes away too, you can have the house to yourself.'

'What do you mean? Why's Bunny going away?'

'Oh. Hasn't she told you? Well, maybe it's not definite, but I think that David was hoping to come down and they're going to some farm place . . . that organic one?'

'Core Creek Organic Farm? Mum hasn't mentioned it.' Chris felt annoyed that he'd been left out of the loop. Going away with David for the weekend was a big step in their relationship. 'I think she could have said something to me,' he said crossly.

'Oh, Dad! C'mon . . .' laughed Megan.

'No. I'm serious. David seems to be a nice man but, well . . .' Chris stopped, trying to work out how he really felt about it.

'But what? What's wrong with Bunny having David for a friend? I think it's great . . . she's all sparkly when he's around. You can tell she likes him.'

'I keep thinking about my dad,' said Chris, quietly.

'But Poppy died yonks ago!' Megan stared at him in genuine surprise. 'I can't believe you're sounding like such a grump.'

'All right, all right,' said Chris, tersely. 'I was very close to my father and I think he and your grandmother had as near to a perfect marriage as I can think of. Maybe she should stay loyal to that marriage. Anyway, perhaps Bunny and David's relationship doesn't mean anything.'

'It might not, but so what if it does? Did you get upset when Mum married Trevor?' Megan asked.

'Of course not. That was different. I was very happy for your mother. If she's happy, then we all are.' Chris grimaced as he realised how silly that sounded.

'Then why can't you be pleased for Bunny? Don't you want her to be happy, too?' said Megan, archly. 'I think you're being a dick.'

'Watch your language, Megan! That's not a suitable word.'

Megan pulled up her earphones and pushed them into her ears, turning on her music and effectively shutting him out.

Chris spent the rest of the drive to the plateau trying to sort out his feelings about Susan and David. His head told him that Susan was perfectly entitled to make her own decisions about David, but his heart made it hard for him to accept the relationship. As he had admitted to Georgia, he felt that David was invading the cosiness of their small family and he resented it.

As soon as Chris pulled up at Jazzy's place, Megan dashed out of the car and hugged Jazzy, who was standing outside her house waiting for them.

'Hi, Megan. I thought you'd never get here. Come and see the alpacas. There's a baby one and it's so cute.'

'Hi, Jazzy. Is your mum here?' asked Chris.

'Yes, Chris, she's inside.'

'Have a fun weekend, you two. See you Sunday afternoon.' Chris smiled at Megan but she just nodded and linked her arm through Jazzy's, replying with a short, 'Okay. See ya.' The two girls headed towards the small herd of curious alpacas grazing in a nearby paddock.

Chris ignored the cold shoulder and knocked on the front door. Jazzy's mother, Janelle, welcomed him and they chatted briefly about the girls' plans for the weekend as he dropped in Megan's bag. Janelle asked him to stay for a drink, but Chris declined, explaining that as the evenings were closing in early, he wanted to get straight back to Neverend before it got too dark.

He was heading down the mountain when Susan rang. He answered the call with the hands-free.

'Hi. I'm on my way home.'

'Did you get Megan safely delivered?'

'Yes, I left them admiring a mob of cute alpacas. Janelle told me Jazzy wanted to take Megan to the rainforest tomorrow. Have a bit of an explore.'

'Are they going down to the waterfall?'

'I have no idea.'

'Chris, I've been meaning to chat to you about this weekend. David has decided to go over to Core Creek Farm, so he's asked me to go along. I'm keen to see the place, so I'm going with him. I just wanted to let you know.'

'This is all a bit sudden, isn't it? Are you comfortable going away with a man for the weekend?' Chris asked tightly.

'You are joking, aren't you? You make it sound like a dirty weekend,' snapped Susan.

Chris recalled what Georgia had said. 'Sorry, Mum. I guess I'm just being protective.'

'Chris, I don't need protecting. I've managed perfectly well all these years on my own, even when you were overseas.' Susan's voice was clearly angry now.

'I realise that. I suppose I'm thinking of Dad.'

Susan softened. 'Your father was a loving and bighearted man, but I have had a life beyond the life I had with him, you know. David is an old friend and it's so nice to have the company of an interesting man who is not part of my life here in Neverend.'

'Fine. I get it, Mum.' Chris refrained from saying anything more about what he thought of David. He felt suddenly tired. 'I'll be interested in what you think of

Core Creek farm. I'd better go; I'll see you tonight,' he said as evenly as he could.

'That's why I rang – we'll probably miss each other. David is picking me up at five and we're heading off. You might not get back here before then, so I'll feed Biddi before I go.'

'Okay, have fun.'

That night Chris had the house to himself, but he found it hard to concentrate on his book as his focus was constantly interrupted by thoughts about his mother and David. He told himself that he was being idiotic and selfish about the whole thing, and that his father would have been nothing but happy for Susan to find another companion, but Chris couldn't shake the thought that he really didn't want anyone else intruding on their little household.

The next morning he decided to press on with the book while there was nothing to disturb him in the quiet house. It was late afternoon when the phone broke the silence with its shrill ring.

When Chris answered it, he could hear a woman's voice, high-pitched and agitated.

'Chris? It's Janelle here. I think you'd better get back up to the plateau.'

'What do you mean? What's wrong?' Chris knew at once that whatever Janelle was going to tell him would not be good news and his own voice sounded strained and tense.

Jazzy's mother took a breath, obviously trying to steady her voice. 'You need to come to the rainforest, to the tourist centre there. The girls have had an accident.'

Chris felt his chest tighten. 'Are they all right? What's happened to them?'

'They went exploring around the waterfall and Jazzy hurt her leg. Megan went back up to get help.'

'Is Jazzy okay?'

Janelle's voice sounded frightened. 'We don't think anything's broken, but it's Megan. She's missing.'

Chris's heart leaped into his mouth. 'What do you mean? Didn't she go for help? She always has her phone on her.'

'Apparently her phone fell into a pool and so Megan went for help. About fifteen minutes later, Jazzy was found by some bushwalkers and they brought her up to the top but when she got there, Megan hadn't shown up. That was half an hour ago and there is still no sign of her. The staff at the tourist centre have notified the police. Look, I'm sure that they'll find Megan soon, but Chris, you need to be there.'

Chris hung up the phone, found his car keys and was on his way to the rainforest tourist centre in a matter of moments. He drove up the narrow winding road to the plateau like a madman. He swept around a hairpin bend at such speed that the car moved into the middle of the road. Realising then that he was being stupid driving at high speed on such a dangerous road, he slowed down.

It was a drive he'd never forget. All he could do was think about Megan. What if something really terrible had happened to her? He would never forgive himself for the spat they'd had the day before. Megan had been right to point out his overreaction to his mother's relationship with David Moore. He shouldn't have been so childish as to allow them to part on bad terms. He hadn't even kissed Megan goodbye. But maybe, he thought, by the time he got to the tourist centre above the rainforest, she'd be sitting there laughing over her adventure.

When he screeched to a halt in the parking lot of the complex, his heart sank at the sight of all the emergency vehicles: SES vans, ambulance and several police cars as well as police emergency units, even a rescue helicopter. There were numerous people milling about.

He jumped from the car and ran inside the tourist centre. At one end of the centre was a souvenir shop, whilst at the other was a coffee shop where the first thing he saw were a couple of paramedics talking to Jazzy. She was huddled under a blanket, her leg stretched out in front of her, resting on a chair and Janelle was sitting beside her, holding her hand.

Jazzy's mother saw Chris straight away and motioned him over.

'Jazzy, are you all right?' asked Chris. 'What happened? How did you get separated from Megan?'

Jazzy lifted a tear-stained face. 'I'm all right. They say that I only have a badly sprained ankle. Megan and I, we were at the base of the waterfall, climbing around the pools there. Megan was taking a selfie of us and I slipped on the muddy ground and twisted my ankle. Our phones were out of action so Megan said she'd go for help. She must have got lost trying to find her way back . . .' Fresh tears started to run down her face. 'I'm sorry, Chris. She thought she was doing the right thing . . . Megs will be all right, won't she?' Jazzy looked desperately at her mother.

'I can't understand how Megan could get lost. Surely she would have just followed the track back here,' said Chris, his voice rising in panic. As soon as he said that, a young policeman came over to speak with him.

'Are you Mr Baxter, Megan's father? I'm Constable Bright. You need to speak to the police commander.'

Chris followed the young constable over to another policeman whose authoritative demeanour, and the fact that he was surrounded by all the other emergency service personnel, indicated that he was in charge of the operation.

'You're the girl's father? I'm Area Commander Watson. I'm in charge of the search. We have a lot of people out looking for your daughter. I'm sorry to say we haven't located her yet, but it's only a matter of time. There are more people on the way to help in the search.'

'I saw some of them in the car park,' said Chris. He looked around the centre's coffee shop, which seemed to be a hub of activity.

A man who was introduced as the controller of the state emergency services stepped forward and placed his hand sympathetically on Chris's shoulder. 'We think that Megan may have taken one of the small unmarked tracks in the park that don't go anywhere specific. If she has, then the situation is a little more difficult, especially as night is falling and we have been told that your daughter only has on a light jumper and jeans. I gather that she doesn't even have a jacket. But Mr Baxter, the police rescue squad and SES here on the plateau are very experienced in finding lost bushwalkers and we're doing all we can.'

'Could the chopper I saw out the front see her?' Chris asked, desperately.

The man shook his head. 'It's been up looking, but it's too dark now, and if the weather closes in as is forecast, it will simply be too dangerous for it to fly. It will go up again at first light – but hopefully by then it won't be needed,' said the controller. His calm voice conveyed his experience and knowledge of emergency situations.

'But she can't spend the night down there in the cold,' cried Chris. 'And what if she's fallen and hurt herself? I've been in that rainforest enough to know that the terrain there can be quite treacherous.'

'Try to stay calm, Mr Baxter. We have people down there, and others coming with lights,' said the SES controller.

A park ranger who was also among the group added, 'Hopefully she'll find somewhere to stop and hole up, rather than blindly walking around in the dark. An overhang or cave, perhaps. Is she an experienced bushwalker?'

'God, no! She'll be terrified.' Chris glanced outside the room at the gathering rainclouds and failing light. 'What can I do?'

'Mr Baxter, we would prefer that you leave the search to those who are experienced. I know that doing nothing is a hard ask, but we don't want you stumbling around, getting yourself lost as well. We've got a well-organised search under way, so get yourself a coffee. It might be a long night, but I'm confident your daughter will be okay.'

Chris walked outside into the blustery wind and headed along the wooden walkway that ran above the rainforest canopy. In the distance the darkening clouds were backlit by menacing flashes of lightning. During the day and in the sunshine, this walkway presented a spectacular outlook, but now Chris could barely bring himself to look down into the tangle of dark vines and undergrowth that lay below him. How scared Megan would be, all alone, cold, possibly hurt and with the night sounds of strange animals about her. He wanted to plunge down into the rainforest, scream her name and hear her shout back to him, 'Over here, Dad.' How he'd hold her close. They'd had such a short time in which to really be together. After years of absence, long-distance conversations and flying visits, he'd finally come to truly know his daughter. He'd grown to love her funny, sometimes prickly and precocious personality, her ability to make him laugh, her gift for getting along with people of all ages, her enthusiasm for new ideas and her determination to accept challenges and turn them into conquests. He knew he had given up a lot for his daughter but he recognised that, despite the upheaval in his life, deciding to have Megan live with him was the best choice he'd ever made.

He pulled his phone from his pocket. He knew he needed to call Jill, although he dreaded how upset she was going to be.

The phone in his hand rang, making him jump.

'Chris, it's me,' said Georgia's cheerful voice.

'Oh, Georgia . . . it's Megan. It's so, so awful.' Chris's voice cracked.

'Chris! What's wrong? Are you all right?'

'No, I'm not. It's Megan. She's lost in the rain-forest . . .' he began.

There was a gasp at the other end of the phone. 'Oh, no! Megan's the girl lost in the bush? I've just heard about it on the radio. What's going on? I'm so sorry. Can I do anything?'

'Find her?' said Chris, futilely.

'Are you all right to tell me what happened?' asked Georgia, her voice full of concern.

Chris briefly filled her in.

'Chris, they'll find her and she will be okay. Do you hear me? I know it. She might be scared and cold but she will be all right. Just hang in there.'

'Georgia, I feel so wretched. Megan and I had an argu-ment before I dropped her off, about Mum and David. Everything Megan said was right, and I behaved like a prat. I'm so stupid. And I didn't even kiss her goodbye! I'm useless as a father, my life is falling apart and I feel that I'm a total failure.' Chris was distraught.

'Chris, listen to me.' Georgia spoke sternly. 'You are a good and devoted father. *Devoted*,' she reiterated. 'Look what you gave up for her. An interesting job you really loved, a job that gave you status, a good salary and a lifestyle that many others would kill for. I would say that what you've done for your daughter is gutsy, caring and even courageous. Not a lot of men would be as unselfish as you've been. You gave Megan what she most wanted and that was to be with her dad. I'm quite sure the fact that she's so happy and well-adjusted is due in no small part to what you've done for her. Everyone quarrels with those they love, but that does not mean that the essential relationship is undermined. Are you listening to me?'

Chris took a deep breath. 'Thanks, Georgia. Those are kind words, but all I want is for Megan to come home so I can prove to her that I really love her.'

'Chris, you already have! Listen, I rang to say I've had a call from one of the publishers. He sounds really interested. Now hang in there and call me when Megan is safe. I don't care if it's the middle of the night.'

'Oh, Georgia, I hope it's not that long.'

'Me too, Chris. Take care.' She hung up.

Chris turned and walked back towards the brightly lit café and tourist centre. He felt a bit embarrassed at the unprofessional way he had dumped his emotional baggage onto Georgia, but she had given him words of hope.

In the café he could see even more people crowding in. There appeared to be a television camera as well as a group of people who were clearly journalists, all trying to get information from the police commander and the SES controller. Chris's phone rang again. He quickly answered it.

'Mate, are you playing golf tomorrow?'

'Shaun, I'm so sorry, I don't think I'll be able to. I'm in the middle of a nightmare.'

'What's up? You sound crook.'

'It's Megan. She's lost in the national park up here on the plateau. She went down to the waterfall with her girlfriend. Her friend is fine but Megan . . . she's lost somewhere out there in the rainforest in the dark and cold and it's going to start raining any minute.'

'Jesus, is that lost girl Megan? Are you up there? We're coming. Don't worry, mate. We'll find her. What do you need? Got jackets and gear?'

'No. When I heard, I just grabbed the car keys and came. I'm at the rainforest tourist centre. SES and cops and ambos are all here as well as the media.'

'Hang in there. We'll be there as soon as we can.'

Shaun hung up. Chris stared at the phone. No ifs, buts, maybes, good luck, hope it works out, but just drop everything straight away, get the boys and we'll be right there. Shaun's instant support rallied him and Chris walked into the centre with a firmer stride. With a heavy heart he pressed Jill's number, but there was no answer. He then tried Trevor's phone and quickly broke the bad news to him when he answered.

'Look, Trevor, if it wasn't for this weather she'd probably have been found by now – I'm sure it's only a matter of time. There is a whole team of emergency service workers out there looking. Tell Jill that I'll call her as soon as I hear anything.'

'Yeah, Chris. She's going to be horribly upset when I tell her. She's at the dentist's, that's why her phone's off.'

'I'll call back soon and talk to her. By then, hopefully Megan can talk to her, too. Thanks, Trevor.'

After he hung up, Chris sat with his head in his hands.

He had been sitting still for a few minutes just trying to regain his composure when a television camera man and a young woman waving a microphone rushed forward.

'How do you feel, Mr Baxter? Has your daughter ever run away before?'

'What the hell? Of course not. And she hasn't run away. Who are you, anyway?'

'Sandy Lean, local television. I just wanted to ask . . .'

'Not now. Please.' Distressed, Chris turned away. He knew that the local media monitored the emergency services' radio transmissions and that they were up there on a cold Saturday night just doing their jobs, but that didn't make things easier for him.

'You bearing up okay?' asked one of the paramedics kindly.

'I just hoped we would have found Megan by now,' Chris replied.

'With this weather closing in, it makes it a bit more difficult, I'm afraid.'

'Can I get you a coffee? A sandwich?' asked the woman behind the counter of the café. 'We're staying open for a while. There'll be a few volunteers coming in to help us. The people out searching can always do with a hot drink and a bite to eat.'

Chris nodded. 'A coffee would be nice. Thank you.'

Taking his coffee, he moved to a table far away from the searchers, who were poring over the maps of the area with the police commander.

Slowly he called his mother's mobile.

'Hi, Chris. We're at the farm. Shame about this weather. Is it wet at home? What are you up to?'

'Mum . . . there's a problem,' he started.

'Chris, what's wrong?'

Quickly Chris told his mother what had happened.

'Oh, Mum, Megan'll be so scared out there in the dark, and so cold. She's only wearing a light jumper and jeans.'

'Chris, Megan is sensible. She'll find some shelter and wait until they find her. Don't worry, darling. They will find her,' said Susan in such a firm voice that Chris knew she was trying to hide her own fears. 'We're coming straight back. Where are you?'

'At the rainforest tourist centre.' Chris felt relieved that his mother was coming back to be with him, so he added, 'Thanks, Mum.'

After he hung up, Chris sat with his hands clasped together, his coffee untouched beside him, and tried to hold himself together as darkness fell.

*

Once the ambulance crew were satisfied that Jazzy was all right, Janelle took her home. Jazzy protested that she wanted to stay until Megan was found, but Chris assured her that he would contact her as soon as Megan was located.

'None of this is your fault, Jazzy. You should be home, resting that ankle of yours. I'll call as soon as I know anything, I promise.'

After Jazzy had left, Chris sat glumly in the corner of the café, the rain falling steadily, wishing he could take part in the search, do something, anything. Suddenly he was shaken from his dark reverie by a hand on his shoulder.

'We're here, mate,' said Shaun quietly.

Chris jumped to his feet and grabbed Shaun's arm. 'You're in your SES clothes. I'd forgotten you were part of it,' he managed to say. Chris looked over at his other friends, who were also dressed in their orange wet-weather gear, talking with the SES controller.

'We've all been members of the SES for years,' said Shaun. 'All of the Neverend SES is here. Look, I brought you some gear. As soon as we get the map coordinates the police commander wants us to search, we can get going.'

Dumbly Chris took the rain gear, hard hat and boots Shaun handed him.

'Frenchy, they won't let me go. Worried that I'll do something stupid and get lost, too.'

'Just get that gear on. We'll fix it,' Shaun assured him.

Chris was so relieved to be doing something practical he couldn't express his gratitude in words. But there was no need.

Alex, Duncan and Shaun were listening intently to what the SES controller was saying. They made room for Chris between them.

'Here are your coordinates, Frenchy. Stay within them. You've got your radios and phones. Let's hope that equipment works down in those valleys. Keep in touch or in sight of one of your party at all times. This is rugged territory and we don't want anyone having an accident of their own and drawing on resources that are needed for the search. Remember, Megan might be some distance away from you, or hoarse from shouting, and while she could hear you, you mightn't hear her. It's even harder in the rain, which mutes noise. So everyone, listen very carefully when you're out there.'

'I just don't understand why you haven't been able to find her. How many paths could she have taken?' asked Chris.

The controller was sympathetic. 'It's very easy to get disoriented, especially in these conditions. She could be going around in circles and not realise it. We're all covering as much ground as we can, Mr Baxter, and now that the SES from Neverend has arrived, we can cover even more. But please, I don't usually let untrained people take part in such a difficult search because they could become a liability – we don't want to have to send a search party out looking for you. Your friends, however, assure me that you will stay with them and not wander off, so I'll let you go with them. And remember, everyone, this is dangerous terrain with a lot of steep cliffs, so watch your map.'

*

If Chris turned to his left, he saw the wavering watery light of Shaun's torch. To his right, he knew there was the rising slope of the mountainside, steep and covered in wet rainforest. In the slimy, dripping darkness he kept his eyes down, looking where to tread so that he didn't slip on the treacherous path. As Chris stepped carefully, hearing the distant shouts of the other men calling for Megan, he ached with pain and fear for his daughter alone in this primeval forest.

Shaun called out to Chris. 'I'm going to go along this side of the creek. Keep me in your sight.'

'Okay. How deep is the water?'

'It's all right, mate. I'm just trying to see if there might be a track of some sort over here,' Shaun called back.

Awful images kept running through Chris's head. Megan could have slipped and injured herself. She could have fallen into the creek. As the rain got heavier, he knew the tiny stream would swell quickly and the memory of his struggle in the flooded creek all those years ago when he had rescued Shaun flashed unwanted into his mind.

Chris lifted his head and howled, '*Meeeegaaan . . .*'

He lost track of time, concentrating on his footfalls and watching for the glow of Shaun's torch. He was moving higher up the bank now among massive tallowood and blackbutt trees, their great canopy of branches acting like leafy umbrellas, lessening the downpour. In the background was the distant roar of the falls. Chris looked back across to where Shaun's light was moving and he was startled to see that the distance between the two of them was lengthening, so he turned downhill, pushing through the slippery undergrowth towards his friend. The last thing everyone needed was for him to get lost as well.

God, where could she be? Chris lifted his head and shouted his daughter's name again and again, his voice becoming raspy. He gripped the stick he was using to stop himself from slipping and concentrated on catching up with Shaun. Then he froze. He'd heard something. Faintly, he heard the sound again. His heart leaped.

'*Heeelp. Someone help me.*'

Chris knew he had found Megan. He wanted to crash through the wet foliage and rush to her, but he held his ground as he had no idea which direction the faint cry had come from.

'MEGAN, it's Dad, where are you?' he shouted as loudly as he could.

'*Dad . . . Dad . . .*' The voice was still very faint. Megan was some distance away. Quickly Chris shouted to Shaun, 'Frenchy, I can hear Megan.'

Straight away he heard Shaun's voice replying, 'Chris, I'm coming.'

'*Daaad . . .*' Megan's shout was quickly lost in the swirling rain.

Moments later, Shaun reached Chris. 'I heard her, mate,' Chris told him in excitement. 'Megan, stay where you are, I'm coming,' he shouted.

Faintly they both heard her call back, and turned in the direction of the sound. '*Dad, please hurry.*'

'Okay, that's certainly Megan. We'll find her quickly now. I'll radio in straight away with the good news and give them our map coordinates,' Shaun said triumphantly.

'Mate, I can't wait for that,' said Chris as he heard Megan's cry again.

Disregarding his instructions to stay with Shaun, Chris hurried towards Megan's cry, slipping and falling in the mud. Cursing, he pulled himself up and leaned against a tree to catch his breath. Then he heard other voices ahead of him. Dear God, was it over? Please, please let it be all right. He could see a light blinking between the gaps in the trees and stumbled on.

'Megaaaan . . .' he called.

'*I'm here, Dad...*' Her voice was nearer. Then he heard Alex calling out.

'Up to the right, Chris. Follow the light.'

He was still among the tall old trees, trying frantically to make his way towards the lights. Then through the curtain of rain he could see a bright light and the figure of someone carrying a bundle wrapped in an oilskin.

'Look up here. We've got her, Chris.' Alex's voice was elated and cracking with emotion.

'Where are you, Dad? I want my father,' sobbed the voice inside the raincoat.

'Megan, oh, my girl. I'm here...'

He reached Alex, who gave him the wet and shivering girl. Megan put her arms around her father's neck, sobbing and muttering incoherently. Chris held her tightly to him, his fingers in the dripping tangle of her hair, her body saturated and cold against his. Chris clung to her, feeling both the joy of relief and the fear of what might have been.

By now Shaun had caught up and immediately unrolled a silver insulation sheet.

'Here, Megan, let me get this around you. It will help warm you up,' he said kindly.

'Darling, we have all been so very worried. Are you hurt at all?'

'No, but Dad, I was so scared . . . I'm sorry.'

'Shh. There's nothing to be sorry about. It's over now. Just as long as you are okay. That's the important thing.'

The insulation blanket crackled as he crushed his daughter to his chest as though he would never be able to let her go. He looked at his friends over the top of Megan's head. 'Thank you, all of you.'

'No worries,' said Shaun with a grin, trying to disguise the relief he felt. 'I owed you one anyway.'

'I'm just glad she's in one piece,' said Alex. 'They won't be long bringing down a rescue litter for you, Megan. Bit far for you to walk. And you're probably suffering from hypothermia, so we have to look after you.'

Megan nodded, her teeth chattering, and buried her head in her father's shoulder once more.

*

A cheer went up when Megan and the stretcher party reached the café. Chris had held her hand all the way back, reluctant to let her go. Then from the sea of smiling faces and bright lights Susan dashed forward, followed by David. She hugged Megan, who started to cry again. Chris, very relieved to see his mother, let go of Megan's hand, slumped into a chair and started to shake. He was handed a mug of hot sweet tea as a doctor started to examine Megan.

'Oh, Bunny, I'm so sorry you had to come back. Sorry, David,' said Megan, tears running down her cheeks.

'Of course we had to come. I was so worried about you, and you are far more important than some old organic farm,' said Susan.

'Your grandmother loves you very much. There was never any question about us coming back. You come first and that's how it should be,' said David.

'Thank you, Dad. I knew you'd come,' said Megan in a little forlorn voice.

'That's what fathers are for, my darling.'

'Oh my God. Jill.' Chris pulled his phone out and rang Jill's mobile.

'Jill. It's me. It's all right. Megan's been found.'

'Oh, thank God,' said Jill. 'Chris, I've been frantic with worry. All I knew was that Megan was lost and I couldn't get through to you. Why was your phone turned off?'

'I've been out of phone range for a couple of hours, searching for Megan, but she's fine now. I'll put her on in a minute.' Briefly Chris told Jill what had happened and then waited for the tirade he knew would follow.

'How could you be so stupid letting her go bush-walking on her own! You are so irresponsible, Chris. How could you? I knew you wouldn't be capable of looking after her. For God's sake, put her on.'

Trying to remain calm, Chris said, 'Jill, she didn't go out on her own. This was just an unfortunate accident. Everything's all right now.' Without waiting to hear any more, Chris handed Megan the phone. 'It's your mother.'

She made a face and whispered, 'Is she mad?'

'Only at me. It's not your fault, just tell her you're okay.'

He leaned back in a chair and shut his eyes. It had all been nightmarish and now he was exhausted. He couldn't wait to go home and get to bed.

Chris listened to his daughter as she placated her mother, assuring her that she was fine.

Finally Megan hung up, and Chris opened his eyes and looked at her expectantly. 'She's okay now,' Megan reported. 'She was frightened and a bit mad at you. You know she gets cranky when she's stressed.'

'People react differently when things go wrong,' said Susan. 'Don't take it to heart. She probably wishes she wasn't so far away.'

Watching his mates get themselves cups of tea and coffee, Chris felt so grateful for their efforts that he was suddenly at a loss for words. These men were his friends. He'd known them since they were all young boys together. And for him they had unhesitatingly dropped everything to help. He knew that if he needed them again they would do the same, as would he for them. They were solid and dependable and he hoped that one day he might have the chance to repay them. Chris went quickly to shake hands with the police commander and thank him for his help, and then he moved among the members of the SES and the police rescue squad, the paramedics and the doctor as well as the volunteers who had provided food and hot drinks for everyone, letting them all know how thankful he was. So many people had been involved in looking for his daughter. He found it hard to find the right words to express his gratitude.

The doctor spoke quietly to Chris.

'Your daughter needs to go to the local hospital for observation, Chris. She has mild hypothermia and she shouldn't go home until her body temperature is back to normal. It might be best to keep her in overnight.'

'I don't want to go to hospital. I want to go home,' cried Megan when she heard.

'Darling, we can't take any chances with you. You need proper medical attention. But I'll be with you all the time, so don't worry,' said Chris. 'I promise I won't leave you.'

Before Megan was loaded into the back of the ambulance, she insisted that Chris ring Jazzy to let her know that everything was fine. It was only a brief conversation. 'Jazzy is really pleased, but she's really, really tired. Her mother had to wake her up. I said you'd ring her tomorrow, when you're home.'

Chris sat beside Megan in the ambulance as they drove to the small community hospital, while David took Chris's car back to Neverend. Once Megan was admitted to a ward, she went to sleep straight away. About ten minutes later, Chris suddenly realised that he had forgotten to tell Georgia the good news. By now it was after midnight, so he walked quietly out of the ward and sent her a text message. She rang back immediately.

'Oh, Chris, that is such good news. I couldn't get to sleep because I've been so worried. Where are you now?'

Chris explained that he was spending the night in a chair beside Megan's hospital bed.

'What a wonderful father you are,' exclaimed Georgia. 'You must be dog tired yourself.'

'I'll survive, just as long as I have my daughter safe and sound. I'll ring you tomorrow and tell you what happened, if that's all right with you.'

'It certainly is. Goodnight, Chris, and I'm so relieved it all turned out in the best possible way.'

Chris hung up, thinking to himself what an extremely nice person Georgia was, before he went and spent an uncomfortable night in the chair beside Megan's bed.

*

After Megan was discharged the next day, Susan and David drove up to take them both home. Chris and Megan spent the afternoon sleeping.

The following morning, Megan seemed little the worse for wear and she happily went to school, ready to tell everyone about her great adventure. Chris returned to work and spent the day thinking about how very lucky both of them had been.

A few days later, having come home from work early, Chris looked at the blank page that was supposed to contain his notes about Norma. All he really knew about her was that she had been devoted to her profession. Susan was sure that, because of this, she would have maintained some relationship with one of the state nursing organisations.

Chris had already rung all those he could find, but had not been able to track Norma down. On impulse, though, he decided to try again. It wouldn't hurt, and it was possible he would get someone else who might be of more help. He knew it would be a pity not to be able to get in touch with Norma.

So Chris rang the state's Nurses and Midwives' Association again. This time Sarah, the woman who answered his query, seemed very happy to help him when

Chris explained what he was after. 'It's all computerised now, so if she's been a member in the past, we should be able to find some trace of her.'

'I was hoping that would be the case,' said Chris and gave her Norma's name.

'I can't find anything under that name. Do you know if she got married? She might be registered under her married surname. Sometimes nurses work under their maiden name and sometimes their married one.'

'I suppose she could have. She was a friend of my mother's. They lost touch but Mum never heard that she got married. I don't think that my mother thought of her as the marrying kind.'

'Look, leave it with me and I'll do a bit more of a search.'

'You're very helpful. I do appreciate it,' said Chris gratefully.

Chris headed to the kitchen to get a cup of coffee. Susan was rolling out pastry for an apple pie.

'Do you think Norma got married?' he asked her.

'Not that I ever heard. She was such a dedicated midwife. Loved her mothers and their babies. She never once mentioned any boyfriend back in Australia. Norma was a rather serious, no-nonsense sort of person. I mean, that's not to say she wouldn't have fallen in love, but somehow I just can't imagine it.' Susan suddenly looked at Chris. 'Gosh, you don't suppose she has died?'

'It didn't seem odd to you that she never kept in touch with any of your group?'

'Not really. I didn't, either.'

'Maybe she didn't go to the reunions because you didn't.'

'Oh. I hadn't thought of that. But we weren't very close. I wasn't in Indonesia for all that long, but Norma stayed until her term was up. We did make an effort to get along, even though we had little in common. We all did our best to do that.' Susan lifted the rolling pin and patted the pastry, then smiled at Chris. 'We all believed in what we were doing. Do you believe in what you're doing now?' she asked quizzically. 'Do you think you still have some wild living to do? Or are you over travelling, living abroad, dashing from job to job? It's not my business, you know I'm here for you and Megan no matter what, but I can't help wondering about your future.'

'You know, Mum, this business with Megan has made me rethink things somewhat. I rather enjoyed my peripatetic life and liked having no ties, leaving my responsibilities for Megan to Jill, but now I see that not only was I selfish, I was missing out. I love having Megan around. She is an absolute joy and I can't imagine being without her.' He smiled. 'But, Mum, if truth be told, it's the financial issues that concern me most right now. When you have money, you have a lot more options. Without it, your horizons are limited.'

'True. But as long as you sort out your priorities and decide what it is that makes you happy in life, you'll get there.'

'Well, Megan is my priority, and that's that,' Chris replied with conviction.

Susan nodded as she pressed the top of the pastry over the pile of apples in the pan. 'Which is the way it should be, but Chris, be aware that time can suddenly evaporate. One day you will look back and wonder where it all went, so don't leave your decisions too long.'

'Do you feel like that, Mum? That time's a-wasting?'

'Sometimes I think about that idealistic young girl who went to Indonesia with dreams and an eagerness to make the world a better place. And I saw poverty and struggle, evil and corruption but also hope and inspiration and people with good hearts and patience who believed things would change. But when my heart was broken by terrible events, I raced back to the security of my country. Over time I found peace and joy and happiness. But sometimes I wonder if I should have tried to stick things out. Fulfilled that young girl's mission.' She paused thoughtfully, and Chris went and put his arms around her.

'Mum, you are a good person. You've lived a valuable life, contributed to the society that is Neverend, raised a family, and been a decent person in every way possible, big and small. I'm proud of you, Mum.'

Susan wiped her eyes with the tea towel. 'Thank you, darling, that means a lot to me. I guess we can't all be as successful as Alan, as generous as Mark, as compassionate as Evan, or as interesting as David, but if we do our bit for the people around us, well, that's what counts.' She turned and slid the pie into the oven.

*

Over dinner a couple of nights later, Susan remarked, 'I had a call from Carla this morning, and I mentioned your book. I hope you don't mind. I told her about the trouble you were having with Alan Carmichael.'

'No, of course I don't mind your mentioning my book. Tell me, does she know him, by any chance?'

'No, but it seems that she has a friend who was, or still is for all I know, involved in that protest against Alan's Victorian shopping complex. Evidently he's an ex-councillor in the town where the complex is being built and he's had some dealings with International Industries.'

'Really? Now that's interesting. I wonder if the dealings were good or bad. I might give Carla a ring.'

'I thought you might. Her number is in my address book, on my desk.'

'Excuse me, girls. I've a call to make. And don't eat all the leftover apple pie.'

Chris spent a long time on the phone and came into the living room afterwards deep in thought.

Susan turned down the volume on the TV. 'Was Carla any help? You spoke a long time.'

'Actually, we were talking about her friend Greg, who is a councillor for the town where the mall is going up. She believes from what Greg has told her that there could have been some manipulation going on over the rezoning of the building site.'

'Wouldn't be the first time that there was doubtful rezoning in local government areas,' said Susan.

'I don't know how true it is. I mean, David said that he thought Alan sailed a bit close to the wind at times, so I reckon it's worth a trip to Melbourne to check it out. I can kill two birds with one stone if I set up an interview with Evan as well. I'm looking forward to meeting him.'

*

The following Friday, having squared things with Shaun, Chris flew to Melbourne to meet Carla and her friend Greg Rowland as arranged. They settled into a corner of one of the city's many coffee shops to talk.

'Are you still a councillor?' Chris asked Greg, after they'd ordered coffee.

'Not since the last election. I decided not to run again because I'm getting on a bit, but I'm still pretty up-to-date with what's been going on.'

'Yes, Greg thought he'd better slow down,' said Carla, enigmatically.

Greg didn't really look the way Chris imagined one of Carla's friends would look. He was no biker, as evidenced by the neat tie he was wearing under a vest. He'd combed his thinning hair carefully and he held his coffee cup with soft hands.

'Carla says that you have something to do with this protest against Carmichael's shopping mall,' Chris said.

Greg straightened his tie. 'A lot of the locals don't like it, don't want it. They think that the mall will change the character of the town. The main street is full of heritage buildings and it's a lively place. A shopping mall will draw the traffic away and the town will lose its vibrancy and be left with empty shops. The area where the mall is to go was originally zoned residential, but then there was a submission to have the zoning changed. Some of the councillors, like me, were opposed to the rezoning, but we were outvoted. We were told that the mall would bring a lot more shoppers into the town and so the economy would grow. Now that the decision has been made, many of the locals are up in arms. They think the place will be an eyesore.'

'It won't be the only town where this has happened,' said Chris.

Greg nodded. 'Of course, the argument is that the development will create more jobs, so there will be more housing and infrastructure and the town will boom, but I've seen enough of these developments to know that while they create, they also destroy. There are so many towns and cities in Australia where the growth of shopping malls has ruined the essence of the places they are meant to serve.'

'Hence the rallies against its construction,' said Carla, pointedly.

'And what does Alan Carmichael say?' asked Chris.

'I'm not sure that he even bothers to take an interest in it,' replied Greg.

'You said that you thought some of the councillors had been bribed to change the zoning,' said Carla in rather a triumphant voice.

Greg held up a hand. 'I know I did, because I couldn't understand why they went along with the rezoning when it would, in my opinion, be detrimental to the future of our town. But honestly, when I think about the councillors who supported the mall, I realise that they simply believed all the bulldust that International Industries told them about how the changes would improve the town's economy. I can't say for sure that they were bribed and I certainly couldn't prove it. In all likelihood these men were too naïve and trusting.'

Chris felt quite deflated by Greg's declaration. He had been sure that Greg could tell him something that would give his book some spice and make it more attractive to a publisher. Instead, he had nothing to show for the trip.

'I think that our little mall and our protests are only small fry to International Industries anyway. You know that they have gone into the States in a big way, don't you? I believe that Alan Carmichael aims to build shopping malls all over the US. The company must have deep pockets,' said Greg.

'Or know where to access the big money for the large-scale plans he has in mind,' added Carla.

'It all sounds very ambitious,' said Chris. 'That certainly seems to be a major expansion of Alan Carmichael's business.'

'It's the lack of consultation that's got the community riled up,' said Carla, who was obviously not put off by Greg's admission that the town council's decision to back the building of the mall probably had not been corrupt. 'Someone needs to do a bit of digging to see if there's anything untoward about how the zoning got changed.'

'Maybe you're right,' said Chris, without any real enthusiasm. If a member of the town council who was actually opposed to the building of the mall thought that everything was above board, he doubted there was much of a story to chase.

'We were hoping you might have a bit of a go. You're the investigative reporter,' said Carla.

Chris flung himself back in his seat, lifting his arms. 'Hey, no way. I'm out of that business.'

'But aren't you writing about Carmichael and those other fellows your mother knew?' persisted Carla.

Chris hesitated. 'It's not that sort of story. I mean, I'm not sure that there is a story here at all, but I'll talk to my agent about it.'

After leaving the coffee shop, Chris checked his watch. His appointment with Evan wasn't until later that afternoon, so he decided that he had time to call Georgia.

'I promise I won't be a pest of an author and bother you all the time, but I met a former councillor from the Victorian town where Alan Carmichael has his development for a mall,' said Chris. And he outlined what Greg and Carla had said.

'Mmm. Does your mother's friend Carla actually know anything, or is she just hot under the collar about the development?'

'The latter, I think,' said Chris.

'Well, it wouldn't be the first time a mega business deal was connected with murky goings-on. Unfortunately, this sounds like bit of a dead end. All the same, maybe you could look at some of Carmichael's other developments and see if you can find a pattern. Keep me in the loop and let me know if you find anything.'

As soon as Georgia had hung up, Chris regretted not saying something more to her. He had rung her on a pretty lame excuse just so he could talk with her, and he had said virtually nothing. She had gone out of her way to see him at Neverend and had shown such concern about Megan,

Chris wondered if there was a chance she was interested in him as more than just a client. But then again, Mac had said she was intensely interested in all her clients, so he probably wasn't so special after all. Nevertheless, Chris thought about their time together in Neverend and how much she had seemed to enjoy his company – almost as much as he had enjoyed hers. If he could just make his book really attention-grabbing, then perhaps he could persuade her to visit Neverend again.

*

Dr Evan Llewellyn had agreed to meet Chris at his rooms at the hospital where he was a leading consultant. As he was ushered into Evan's office, Chris liked him immediately. The doctor rose and came around his desk, hand outstretched. His jacket was rumpled and his tie askew, and his big smile and friendly eyes met Chris's as he shook his hand. If he were my doctor I'd want to hug him, Chris thought.

'I was so thrilled to see your mother again. Susan was always friendly and great company and nothing has changed even after all these years. Please sit down, Chris.'

'She has very special and happy memories of her time with you all,' said Chris.

'Well, at least until Jimmy's tragic death; I suppose you know all about that. It's little wonder she went home early.'

'I only recently found out about all that. That was a part of her life she never liked to talk about,' said Chris, pulling up a chair and taking out his notebook and a pen.

'They were terrible times for the people of Indonesia. Sadly we still see similar events happening in other countries today where groups want the power and the profit for themselves at the expense of the poor and the decent who just want to do the best for their families. Water?'

311

'Yes, please. Did you find it traumatic when you were there? Did you expect the place to be as unsettled as it was?' asked Chris.

'We did a couple of crash courses before we started our work, but we were woefully unprepared. The poverty, the Indonesian way of life, their culture and the continuing political upheaval was all a bit of a surprise to us. But there were also the good things about the encounter, such as the warmth and hospitality of the people and the knowledge that, as undertrained as we were, we were helping improve lives. It was a worthwhile experience. You may not know it, but I still do a lot of work in emerging countries improving health standards where I can.'

'Yes, Evan, I've read about the wonderful things you've been doing. I do find it quite intriguing how successful you, Mark, Alan and David have been in your careers. And I know from when I spoke to you on the phone for the magazine article that you think your time in Indonesia contributed to your success.'

'I always wanted to be a doctor, but that period of my life in Indonesia made me view the world from a slightly different perspective. I think it made me realise how privileged we are to live in Australia. It also made me aware that one person can make a difference. It saddens me today that many Australians take the great advantages this land offers for granted and are not prepared to share our good fortune with people from other countries who do not have it.' He shook his head and took a sip of water. 'I'm also saddened that there isn't a greater closeness between Indonesia and Australia. I thought by now everyone in our country would be studying Indonesian, that there would be a huge two-way exchange of ideas and that Australians would have a better knowledge of the multi-faceted culture of the islands of Indonesia instead of seeing the place just as a cheap holiday destination or a valuable source of raw materials. And the powers that be think money and aid will fix any problems and have little respect for the country.' He lifted his hands. 'Oh dear, I seem to have got a bit carried away, but I do think that we have gone backwards in our attitude to Indonesia. That seems to me to be a great pity. I was told by my parents always to be nice to our neighbours, especially the ones right next door.' He grinned apologetically.

Chris consulted his notes. 'Evan, I'm not entirely sure where I want this book to go. I think I want to use it to inspire other Australians to try to make a difference as well. David and Mark are very willing to help me, but Alan definitely wants nothing to do with my project, even though I have assured him that I would not be writing anything defamatory.'

'That's a shame about Alan. He's done exceptionally well for himself, hasn't he?' said Evan.

'Do you know that he is going to expand his construction business into the States?' quizzed Chris. 'Is that correct? I've heard a couple of negative things about his business dealings. David thinks he might have sailed a bit close to the wind at times.'

Evan raised an eyebrow. 'Really? Well, I suppose that's big business for you. Personally, I think that the fact he gave up a year of his life to work in Indonesia for a pittance would indicate a good heart. And a few years ago he gave me a very generous donation for my overseas work, and I think he said he's done the same for Mark.'

'I see,' said Chris thoughtfully. 'There was something else I wanted to ask you, Evan. When I wrote the magazine article, it wasn't very long, so I didn't really bother looking for Norma, as I felt I had enough information without her. Now that I'm expanding the article into a book, I really want to find her. Do you know what became of her? None of the others do.'

'No, I don't either, but I think you're right to talk with her if you can find her. She had quite a different temperament from your mother. Very straightforward to the point of bluntness about what she thought.'

Chris laughed. 'That's what everyone tells me. I hope I can find her, she sounds like a valuable resource. By the way, you may not know this, but Jimmy's brother's Thomas Fairfax Anderson. You lot were certainly moving in exalted circles, even if you didn't know it.'

'Really? I had no idea. So Jimmy's brother's one of the top financial bods in the US. I'm amazed. Puts me in my place,' said Evan, clearly impressed.

'I think your place is pretty important, too,' Chris replied.

They talked a while longer until Evan's phone rang.

The doctor answered it and after listening for a moment said, 'I'll be there shortly.'

Chris gathered up his notes. 'Thank you for giving me your time. I'm very grateful for these extra insights, and it's been an honour to meet you.'

Evan shook Chris's hand. 'Any time, Chris. If I can be of more help, just shout. And do give my warm regards to Susan. Tell her to make sure she's at the next reunion, won't you?'

When Chris arrived at Tullamarine Airport, he called his mother to let her know that the plane was on time and he'd be home in a couple of hours.

'You have had the nicest men in your life. Evan was absolutely lovely. He was so warm and told me a lot about himself, and he said he's willing to let me see his own notes and for me to speak to whomever I like about his career. He's happy to be an open book, just like Mark and David.'

'Pity about Alan,' laughed Susan. 'Maybe he'll come around. Did Evan know anything about Norma?'

'No, but like everyone else he thinks she would not have given up midwifery.'

'And what about Carla and her friend, did you see them?'

'Yes, that was interesting, but very inconclusive. Carla has a conspiracy theory about the council rezoning land to enable the Victorian development to go ahead, but her friend Greg thinks that his fellow councillors were just dazzled by International Industries and so gave the company everything it wanted.'

'I don't think Alan would do anything illegal. Big companies can't expose themselves by breaking the law. Wouldn't be worth their while,' said Susan.

'Oh, Mum, I think that's pretty naïve. Big business has power and influence and they will use it to further their profits. Some of them are prepared to break the law to get what they want. I'm not saying that Alan is behaving in this way, but I might just have a look at some more of his developments. Is Megs there?'

'Not home yet. Netball practice.'

'Give her my love. I'll see her soon.'

*

Chris was standing in the bookshop at the airport when his phone rang. He was surprised to hear Alex's voice.

'Mate, bad news. It's Frenchy, he's had a bit of an accident in the van down on the river flats. Ran into a ditch on the side of one of those gravel roads. Just as well he wasn't on the plateau road, otherwise it could have been more serious.'

'That's awful. How bad is he?'

'Pretty bruised and he's got a couple of cracked ribs. They had to take him to Coffs for x-rays, but I gather there's nothing too serious. He was lucky, by all accounts. Karen is with him at the hospital, and we have the kids at our place. Police have had a quick look at the van. Said it was unroadworthy.'

Chris was aghast. 'That's bullshit! Frenchy treats his vans almost better than he treats his kids. They're his livelihood, so they're always in tip-top condition.' Chris lowered his voice. 'Listen, I'm in Melbourne, about to board my flight home. I'll be home in a couple of hours, so if I can do anything tonight, just let me know.'

'He'll be fine. I just thought you'd want to know.'

'Yes. Thanks, Alex.'

Chris hung up, feeling quite shaken and even guilty. He should have been driving that van, but when he'd taken the day off to fly down to Melbourne Shaun had taken over his deliveries. He was puzzled about the van, too. He knew that there would be nothing wrong with it, no matter what the police said. Shaun must have been travelling too fast along the gravelled surface of the road and skidded on a bend. Easy enough to do. He'd go and see the police tomorrow after he'd visited Shaun and try to find out exactly what had happened.

10

CHRIS STROLLED DOWN NEVEREND'S leafy main street just as the café, coffee shop and patisserie were all opening up. He ordered a croissant and an espresso and sat in the crisp morning air with his newspaper as the sun began to filter through the camphor laurel tree that sheltered the table. Neverend might not be as trendy as Melbourne, but as Chris sipped his coffee and read the paper while the sun warmed his back, he felt happy to be there. He exchanged greetings with other locals he knew who were also enjoying this morning ritual, then he rang Shaun.

'Still a bit bruised and battered, mate, but glad to be home. Should be back at work by next week, right as rain. Thanks for ringing,' said Shaun, ebullient as ever.

After he'd finished his coffee, Chris headed to the nearby police station to ask about Shaun's van. The station was housed in its original building constructed more than a century ago. Chris went round to the side door and stepped into the foyer.

'Morning, Chris.' The local police sergeant Pete Pollard greeted him from behind the station's front counter. 'You heard about the van?'

Pete was a burly local lad who had returned to Neverend after working for several years in the police force in other parts of the state. Chris had known him since schooldays and along with the rest of the community thought of the police officer as a thoroughly decent man.

'Hi, Pete. Yes, do you know what happened?' asked Chris.

Pete leaned across the front counter, twiddling a pen between his thick fingers. 'Pretty straightforward. Whoever changed the tyres on that van did a poor job. Two of the wheels had loose nuts. No wonder the wheel almost came off. First rule when you change a tyre is to tighten the bolts.'

'Well, of course, Pete, we're not idiots! There's no way Frenchy would have let that happen.' Chris furiously tried to remember who had last changed the tyres. 'That van went in for new tyres weeks back and I've been driving it ever since. Surely I would have noticed if the wheels had started shaking or wobbling ages before this happened?'

'Possibly,' said Pete, shrugging. 'But all I can say is that those nuts were loose when the accident occurred and Shaun was damn lucky he wasn't driving the van down the plateau road. Then the accident could have been fatal.'

Chris shivered. He couldn't shake the guilt he felt knowing he should have been driving the van.

'So what happens now? Can we drive it when the repairs have been made?'

Pete squinted at him. 'You're sure that neither you nor anyone who works for Shaun would have tampered with those wheels, Chris?'

'I can't speak for everyone, Pete, but I certainly didn't touch them and I doubt anyone else would have. There was no reason for it at all.'

'Then maybe the nuts weren't replaced properly all those weeks ago and just took a long time to work loose.'

Chris nodded slowly in agreement. It wasn't very likely, but there seemed to be no other explanation.

The vehicle was in one of the local repair shops and so Chris farewelled Pete and walked over to see the damage.

'Pretty lucky, your boss. Not too much harm done, either to the van or to Frenchy, I hear,' said the mechanic. 'Bit of work needed on the driver's side where he careened into bushes and boulders at the edge of the road, but it shouldn't take long. I'll give you a ring when it's right to drive. Insurance will cover most of the costs.'

'Thanks,' said Chris, folding his arms. Another wave of guilt swept over him. It should have been him behind the wheel. He'd talk to Shaun about hiring another van while this one was being repaired so that he could start back on the run immediately. He might have to do a couple of extra shifts to cover for Shaun's absence, but that wouldn't be a problem. It would make him feel better to do some extra shifts for Shaun. Chris stepped out of the shadows of the mechanic's workshop and back into the sun.

*

Life quickly settled back into its routine. In his spare time between driving the courier van and writing a weekly column for the *Coastal Star*, Chris sorted through notes and printouts, shuffling the pages of the men's lives like a deck of cards, trying to put together a coherent picture.

Although there were still plenty of gaps, he saw that he had an interesting composite of three of the men, David, Evan and Mark. Unfortunately, there were a lot of blanks around Alan's story and Chris wondered how he was ever going to fill them.

Nevertheless he enjoyed researching material he wouldn't normally include in a journalistic article. The broad canvas of a book gave him the freedom to delve a lot deeper. He also found that his writing style was changing from succinct journalese to a more reflective and questioning prose.

Chris had begun to look at the men's families to see if their parents had also been high achievers. He already knew that Mark had come from a wealthy background and that Evan had come from a family of doctors. David's family had humbler origins, although it was clear that his parents had valued education very highly for, like David, all of his siblings had acquired university degrees in an era when tertiary education was not common. When he dug a bit deeper into Alan's background he learned that Alan's father had been quite entrepreneurial, but it appeared that he had been a risk taker. The business he'd built up in the 1950s and '60s had done well, but he had gone into a venture in the early 1970s that had failed, bankrupting him. Alan had initially worked with his father, but after the bankruptcy he'd gone his own way, starting up his own construction company, which had done very well.

The more Chris looked at other people's lives, the more he questioned his own. Sitting in the office one afternoon, the sun fading over the horizon, he pondered the influence he was having on Megan's upbringing. What ethics, compassion and thoughtfulness was he encouraging in his daughter? Was he adequately supporting her ambitions and giving her confidence in her undertakings? What was the example he was setting for her?

As if on cue, Megan poked her head around his office door, breaking his train of thought.

'Hi, Dad. I've brought Toby home from school to help with homework.'

Chris smiled to see her face. 'That's nice. Bunny's shopping in Coffs, so get yourselves a smoothie or something else vaguely healthy.'

Later, when Chris headed for the kitchen to make himself a coffee, he heard the teenagers' voices on the verandah and went out to say hello. The pair had their heads bent over a book, papers and notes spread across the low table in front of them.

'Hi. What's the subject under debate?'

'Hi, Dad. You know Toby. He understands algebra and is trying to teach me.'

'I'm glad you can do that, Toby. Algebra's not one of my strong suits.' Chris liked Toby, who was a member of Megan's jazz group. The boy was the same height, maybe a little taller than Megan, but he had a slim build, pale skin and a thick crop of dark curls. He wore heavy-framed glasses that gave him a studious appearance, but his brown eyes were large and full of friendly warmth.

'Actually, I find that if you just become familiar with all the rules and maths jargon, suddenly it clicks,' said Toby.

'That's a good way of explaining it. I guess I didn't persevere long enough to become fluent in maths speak. Did you two get something to eat or drink?'

'We're fine, thanks, Dad.'

'My coffee is probably ready. See you later. Nice to see you again, Toby.'

'You too, Mr Baxter.'

After dinner that evening, Susan and Megan cleaned up the kitchen by themselves so that Chris could get more work done on the book. Then they watched a TV programme together before retreating to their respective bedrooms.

'How's it coming, Dad?' asked Megan as she passed the study.

Chris stretched his arms above his head. 'Slowly. But I'm feeling good about it. I still need to find a lot more info, but I can see a bigger picture emerging.'

'Great. Glad it's happening. See you in the morning.'

'Thanks for your encouragement, sweetie.' Chris smiled at her. 'And good night to you, too.'

Chris worked for another hour or so until he came to a point which he felt was a good stopping place, so after saving what he'd written, he turned off the computer. In the kitchen he poured himself a glass of water and padded through the house onto the darkened front verandah. He took a deep breath and inhaled the cool and fragrant night air while he watched the clouds drifting across the moon as it rose behind the hills. This was a ritual he performed almost every night, but tonight, while the smells and soft sounds were familiar, there was something that did not quite fit into this normal pattern. Chris peered into the gloom and in the pale light he was just able to make out the silhouette of a car parked on the grass verge diagonally opposite his mother's house. During the day, tourists often pulled up on this verge to admire the spectacular views across the valley, but at night, not only was there nothing to see, but stopping there was dangerous, for if a driver misjudged the edge of the narrow road in the dark there was a thirty-metre drop straight onto the road below.

What an odd thing to do, Chris thought to himself. He shrugged and was about to turn away when something suddenly occurred to him. Was the driver of that car watching the house? Feeling uneasy, he went inside and drew the curtains across the sitting room windows.

*

The following morning, Susan asked, 'Who closed the curtains last night?'

'I did,' said Chris as he crunched on some toast. 'There was a car over on the grass verge, just in front of the house. I thought someone could have been in it, watching us.'

Susan rolled her eyes. 'I think you have an overactive imagination. This is Neverend, where we don't lock our houses or cars, not Sydney or Washington DC. Get a grip,' his mother teased.

'It just seemed odd,' he said defensively.

When Chris opened his emails after work that day, he found a message in his inbox from the helpful Sarah from the nurses' association.

I think I might have found your missing midwife! Shall I email the info or do you want to call me? I'll be here till five.

Chris picked up the phone immediately.

'Hi, Chris, I'm glad you called. I think I've found who you're after. It's taken a bit of unravelling, because she was last registered under her married name.'

'That's brilliant work, Sarah. I can't thank you enough. What's her address?'

He lifted his pen ready to write it down.

'Actually the most recent address we have for her is an overseas one. Looks like she was living in some place in Java, Indonesia, called Bogor.' Sarah rattled off the full address and Chris noted it down.

'What year was that, 1968?'

'No, it was 1994.'

Chris raised his eyebrows in surprise. 'That's interesting. What about now?'

'Nothing since then, I'm afraid,' said Sarah. 'We sent mail but it came back. No forwarding address.'

Chris felt deflated. 'That's that, I suppose. Dead end.'

He'd felt so close to finding Norma. 'Thank you for your help, Sarah. Oh, by the way, what is Norma's married name?'

'We have her down as Norma Mary Marzuki.'

'What an unusual surname,' said Chris, writing it down. 'Where do you think it originates?'

'It could be Indonesian since our records show she was living there for a while. Sorry I can't help you more.'

'Sarah, you've been a champion, thanks again.' Chris rang off and sat still for a minute, digesting this piece of information. He was quite intrigued. It seemed that Norma had returned to Java and married. Maybe she was still living there. This news was going to surprise Susan.

He glanced at his watch and saw that it was nearly 5 pm. Susan was playing golf, while Megan was at netball practice. He felt he had to tell someone about this interesting discovery, so he decided to call Georgia.

'Are you in the middle of something? Heavy negotiations?' he asked as soon as his agent answered her phone.

'I wish. I spend such a lot of time just waiting for people to return my calls. What are you up to? It's freezing down here today.'

Chris smiled as he imagined her lovely face and sparkling green eyes. 'It's a lovely sunny day here, although I have to admit that the nights are starting to get quite cold. We've had the fire roaring every evening this week. Listen, Georgia, I rang because I wanted to share some fascinating news about Norma. It seems that she went back to Bogor in Java and she may have married an Indonesian, although her new name is so unusual that her husband could be Russian or Hungarian for all I know. Unfortunately, I have no idea if she's still living in Indonesia or has moved back to Australia, or gone somewhere else entirely.'

'Heavens, that certainly is news, even if it is a bit nebulous. What does Susan say about it?'

'She's out, so no one knows yet except you. I just hope I can track Norma down.'

'Well, if you could, it would be more grist to the mill. Oh, and Chris, while we're talking, I'd like to have a couple of sample chapters when you can, just to see how things are moving. There's a definite keenness out there for your book in principle, but publishers need to see content and your writing style before committing. The sooner we get a deal, the sooner you'll get some cash in your pocket.'

'That'd be nice,' sighed Chris. 'I've been looking at the formative years of these guys, and it's really made me think. Their families all seem to have been quite an influence.'

'Is that so unusual?' asked Georgia.

'No, of course not, but it's made me wonder about my own life and my family.'

'Like how?' asked Georgia, gently.

'Like, I wish I'd talked to my dad when I had the chance, found out more about the influence his parents had on him. I've been wondering what effect the way I live my life is having on Megan's future . . .' He stopped, feeling a little awkward. 'Oh, all that kind of stuff.'

'Have you come up with any answers or decisions?'

'Not really.'

'The fact you're thinking about these things is good. I bet Megan's big adventure has helped you focus your mind on her.'

'That's very true,' laughed Chris, trying to lighten the conversation, but then added, 'Seriously, these last few months with my daughter have been some of the best times of my life, and when she was lost, it wasn't just Megan who was frightened. I was pretty scared, too. I couldn't bear the thought that I might have lost her.'

'I can understand that,' said Georgia. 'I don't think any parent would want to go through what you did.'

'No, certainly not,' Chris murmured, pushing the memories aside.

'Any joy with Alan Carmichael?' Georgia asked, as though sensing the need to change the subject. 'Have you heard anything more from his straight-shooting solicitor?'

'No, not since I answered his letter through my mate Duncan's solicitor brother in Coffs. He told Alan that I would be continuing with my book with or without Alan's cooperation but that I would be careful to avoid defaming him.'

'Good for you. That was a wise move. When are you coming to Sydney next? I'd love to catch up.'

'No plans. Why don't you come to Neverend again? There's a long weekend coming up.'

'I'll think about it. A break could be just what I need.' Chris could hear the smile in her voice.

'And bring your camera.'

*

Susan was as surprised as Chris had been when he told her what he had found out about Norma's return to Indonesia and her marriage.

'That is so interesting. She was so dedicated to her profession that I never really thought of her as the marrying kind. I'd love to be able to talk with her again, if you can track her down.'

After a quick google didn't produce anything useful, Chris checked the Australian White Pages website and saw immediately that there was only one NM Marzuki listed. The address given was in Melbourne. Chris rang the number but there was no answer, so he left a very brief message. A couple of hours later his call was returned.

'Mr Baxter?' The voice on the phone was quietly modulated.

'Yes, speaking.'

'This is Norma Marzuki. I believe you wanted to speak to me.'

Chris caught his breath. 'Yes, I'm so pleased you've called back. As I said in my message, I'm Chris Baxter. You were in the volunteer programme in Java in '68 with my mother, Susan . . .'

'Of course I remember Susan, although I haven't seen her since then. How is she?'

'She is very well. She'll be so pleased that you've made contact with me. I know she'd love to see you again and especially find out about your life. She understands that you returned to live in Indonesia?'

'Chris, what made you want to find me? Was it on behalf of Susan?' Norma broke in.

Chris hesitated. 'Not primarily. I hope you don't feel I'm intruding, but I'm actually writing a book about the four men who were with you in Java, and I would like to hear what you have to say about your time there and perhaps your opinion of those men and their work in Bogor.'

There was a slight pause. 'So you're a writer.'

'I used to be a journalist, but the media business is a sea of shifting sands these days, so I'm trying to write a book. I'm presently living with Susan and my fourteen-year-old daughter in my mother's house at a place on the New South Wales north coast called Neverend. Look, I'd love to talk to you in person; can I meet you? I realise you live in Melbourne, but would there be a problem in my flying down?'

'I'm not sure that I can be of much help. I haven't kept in touch with the others, and I can't say that I've taken much notice of their subsequent careers, apart from Evan's. I have very much admired his medical achievements over the years. I did turn up at the first reunion, as

327

I was working in Sydney at the time, but Susan didn't go and I have to say that I felt a bit lonely there without her company.' Norma paused. 'Funny that. I never considered that we were particularly close when we were in Indonesia, but I've often thought of her. Anyway, when I moved away from Sydney for work, I didn't bother to go to any more reunions again.'

Chris was rather surprised at her comment about his mother. Norma didn't sound like the self-contained woman Susan had described. Perhaps his mother had had more of an influence on Norma than she realised. 'Norma, I'd love to know your story. Where your life path has taken you . . .'

'Oh, no. I'm not at all interesting,' Norma said quickly.

Chris felt a mild panic rise in him at her hesitancy and knew that her willingness to talk was slipping away. 'Norma, Mum would love to catch up with you, and I would so appreciate anything that you can tell me about those Bogor years.' His gentle and persuasive tone quickly came to the fore.

There was another pause on the end of the line before Norma said, 'I've got to be in Sydney for a few days next week. If you could get down there, perhaps we could meet on the weekend. Do you think your mother would be interested in doing that?'

Chris was filled with relief. 'We'd planned to make a trip to Sydney in the near future, as it happens,' he quickly fibbed. 'And I know Mum would jump at the chance to see you. Next Saturday all right with you? Could we exchange mobile numbers so that we can stay in contact?'

Before Norma had time to make any further excuses, they'd set a time and hung up.

Chris felt elated as he rang off and went to find Susan. 'Guess what, that was Norma on the phone, Mum.

She's agreed to a meeting, next Saturday in Sydney. I think she mainly wants to see you, so I said you'd be there with me. Do you think you can come?'

Susan smiled broadly. 'Of course, I wouldn't want to miss it! I'm very curious to hear about her going back to Indonesia, as well as her marriage. But we can hardly leave Megan by herself.'

'Megan would be more than happy to stay over-night with one of her friends. I'm sure something can be arranged.'

'Maybe Toby's parents could put her up,' Susan suggested. 'Those two are pretty thick these days and I know Toby's parents well. You chat to Megan and then I'll give Toby's parents a call.'

'That sounds like a plan to me. Do you want me to call Mark and tell him we've found Norma and that we're coming down to Sydney to meet her?' asked Chris. 'He did offer to put us up any time, so perhaps if we accept his invitation you could catch up with him too and meet his wife, Lorraine.'

Susan waved a hand. 'I wouldn't dream of imposing on him,' she said.

'Mum, he wouldn't have offered in the enthusiastic manner he did if he didn't mean it.'

Susan relented. 'I suppose so, and I would like to meet his wife. Oh, all right, you can call.'

'Wait till you see Mark's mansion,' added Chris.

*

Mark's wife Lorraine, elegantly slim in slacks and a cream cashmere sweater, her pale gold hair swept up in a French roll, met Susan and Chris at the front door of the North Shore house. She ushered them into the enormous family room at the rear of the house, where lunch was beauti-fully laid out on a table.

'I'm afraid it's just me at present,' Lorraine said, indicating with a gentle wave that they should take a seat. 'Mark was called away suddenly to an emergency meeting of the board of the Art Gallery of New South Wales. Evidently there's a problem with a forthcoming exhibition that needs to be solved straight away. Anyway, he'll be home for dinner, so you can talk to him then.' She smiled.

'It's very kind of you to put us up like this, Lorraine,' said Susan.

'I'm so happy to meet you, Susan,' Lorraine said warmly. 'I've brought you out here as the sun just streams through these windows in winter, making this a very pleasant spot.'

'It's a gorgeous room,' said Susan, unable to help glancing around at the stunning interior of the house. 'You and Mark have a really beautiful home.'

'Thank you, Susan,' Lorraine said. 'Mark talks fondly of the time you all spent in Java. It must have been an incredible experience.'

'Yes, it was an amazing time. Have you been to Java?'

Lorraine shook her head. 'No, although we've been to Bali a couple of times. The grandchildren love it there.'

'Bali seems to be all anyone thinks about when talking of Indonesia,' said Chris. 'Even though it is just *one* of the seventeen thousand islands.'

'I think Mark likes to go there just to practise his Bahasa. Do you still speak it, Susan?'

Susan laughed. 'I haven't spoken Bahasa since I left Indonesia! And that was such a long time ago that I don't think I remember any of it.'

'We can go for a holiday and you can brush up on it,' said Chris. 'When I have the money,' he added quietly.

'Actually, I was thinking of learning some Italian and going to Italy for a holiday,' said Susan, casually. 'A friend of mine has a holiday house there,' she explained to Lorraine, obviously referring to David's farmhouse.

'I wasn't sure how long it would take you to drive down, so I thought I'd just get some quiche and salad made up for us. Something easy and quick. I hope you don't mind,' said Lorraine, as she poured their coffee from a shining chrome pot. 'It's good to hear that you're thinking of learning another language, Susan. Mark has business dealings with Indonesia on occasion and he says there's not much point sitting around the negotiating table if you're the only one in the room who doesn't understand what's really being said. Language is the key to understanding people, culture and friendship, don't you think?' Lorraine passed around some crusty fresh bread.

Susan nodded, taking a piece of bread and spooning some salad onto her plate. 'Yes, I agree. We all found speaking the language made a huge difference to connecting with people. Being there to help and working from the heart are important, but from a practical point of view, knowing the language is essential. Without that knowledge I am sure we would not have been able to form the wonderful bonds we did with the local people.'

Chris cocked his head to one side. He had always thought he knew his mother inside out, but recently she had begun to surprise him, and he could glimpse the young woman she'd been all those years ago.

Later that afternoon, the two of them met Norma for coffee in a café in the Sydney CBD. They were seated at a table beside a window when Norma walked in. Chris knew immediately who it was, though he wasn't sure how.

'That's her, isn't it?' he whispered to his mother.

331

Susan nodded, turned, smiled and gave Norma a short wave.

Norma was a solidly built woman with short faded red hair abundantly flecked with grey. She looked efficient and businesslike.

In her usual affectionate manner, Susan rose, reached out and embraced Norma, and although Norma looked slightly taken aback, she returned the hug.

'Norma, it's been so long! I can't believe that we're actually meeting up after all this time. This is my son, Chris, who cleverly tracked you down.'

Chris stood and shook Norma's hand. 'It's such a pleasure. I'm so grateful you could come. We've been looking forward to this meeting.'

'I went to the last reunion hoping that you would be there, but of course you weren't,' said Susan, retaking her seat. 'I was disappointed, but that was silly of me. After all, it was the first reunion I had ever been to, so I could hardly expect everyone else to go just for my benefit.' Susan smiled. 'Still, it was lovely to catch up with the others. They have done such interesting things with their lives – which is what gave Chris the idea of writing a book about them. Listen to me! I'm just chattering on because I'm so happy to see you. Please, Norma, tell me what you've been up to these past forty-five years,' said Susan, her face beaming with delight as she talked with her old friend.

Norma relaxed. 'No, Susan, you first. You tell me all about your life.'

The three of them quickly ordered coffees as Susan told Norma about becoming a teacher, marrying and moving to Neverend, and staying there to raise a family and eventually becoming part of the town's fabric.

'I know that my life doesn't sound all that exciting, especially compared with the lives the boys have led, but it's been a very happy life and I've no complaints.'

'After your adventures in Indonesia, perhaps living in a quiet country town was the life that best suited you,' said Norma, gently.

Susan smiled gratefully at Norma and then said, 'What about you, Norma? I was so intrigued to learn you went back to Indonesia and that you married. When did all that happen?'

Norma paused, looking down at her coffee. 'When my contract was up and I came home from Indonesia, I worked here in Australia, first as a midwife and then teaching midwifery. I moved around a bit, but to my surprise I never felt really fulfilled. I thought that working with like-minded people in clean, well-run hospitals with up-to-date equipment was what I wanted, especially after the difficulties we had working in Indonesia. But eventually I realised that it wasn't. While the work was in many ways satisfying, I found that it wasn't challenging enough. I knew that there were literally hundreds, even thousands of women in Australia who could perform my job as well as I could, but I knew that in Indonesia that simply wasn't the case. Then out of the blue I heard about an opportunity to join a team establishing a birth centre and postnatal clinic in Bogor, of all places, so I went back.'

'Good heavens,' said Susan. 'That is simply amazing. I have to say that out of the six of us, you are the one I thought least likely to go back to Indonesia. So how did the clinic go?'

'Very well. The centre was very successful. The death rate amongst newborn babies plummeted in Bogor and so the model was adopted by other towns in the region. I began to train women to be midwives, and they took their skills back to their own communities. It was a very productive period of my life.'

'I bet it was,' said Chris, thinking what an extraordinary woman Norma was.

'Norma, that sounds wonderful,' said Susan, genuinely delighted at the success of her old friend. 'I think I was startled initially when Chris found out that you'd gone back to Indonesia, but I do remember how committed you were to the mothers and babies you worked with, so I guess your decision to return is not all that surprising after all. And tell me, when did you get married, and who did you marry?'

Norma paused while she took a sip of her coffee, as though trying to gather her thoughts.

'My husband's name was Anwar Marzuki,' she said in a low voice. 'He was an Indonesian doctor at the Bogor hospital. You would never have met him, Susan; he started work in the hospital quite some time after you had left Indonesia. He was such a fine man and he was an excellent doctor, very committed to raising health standards in Bogor. I admired him greatly.'

'He sounds very dedicated,' said Susan.

'He was,' replied Norma. 'Unfortunately, our marriage didn't work out.'

'Cross-cultural marriages are difficult, I imagine,' said Susan, tactfully.

'Yes,' said Norma, frowning slightly. 'His family were devout Muslims, although Anwar himself was not quite so religious. I didn't want to adopt his religion and this led to friction with his family. To escape it, we eventually decided to come to Australia, but after a couple of years Anwar decided that living the good life in Melbourne was doing his own country a disservice and so he returned and we divorced.'

'Have you been back to the Bogor area since then?' asked Susan.

'No. If truth be told, I never expected to stay in Bogor as long as I did, but after Anwar and I divorced, I decided that that part of my life was over and it was time to move on.'

'But I bet you never lost your passion for your work. Good on you,' said Susan with a grin.

'No, I didn't,' said Norma, the corners of her mouth lifting. 'I used my experiences in Bogor to help NGOs set up similar clinics through other parts of South East Asia and the Pacific. I'm here in Sydney for a few days because I'm supervising a student's PhD on the Indonesian family planning programme that was aimed at promoting a two-children-only policy.'

'Was that successful?' asked Susan.

'Yes, in some ways. But it was also extremely intrusive and often came close to forcing contraception on women.' She gave a tight smile. 'All part of the authoritarian social engineering by Suharto's New Order. Women were dumbed down to be no more than adjuncts of the militarised and patrimonial state he built. Thank heavens they don't have that programme anymore,' she said, her eyes hard. 'I'm also on a couple of working panels over the next week, to discuss what improvements can be made to the current working model of postnatal care in emerging nations.'

'That's fantastic! You must have phenomenal energy,' said Susan, draining her cup. 'I'd kill for another coffee. Anybody else?'

All three of them ordered more coffee and Chris quickly took the opportunity to ask Norma some questions.

'From the work you're involved in, I guess you think that we should be paying more attention to our neighbours in this Asian Century,' he said.

Norma nodded. 'I think that if we don't engage and exchange more ideas, especially on a friendly basis, we will miss a great opportunity,' she said. 'While it is true that Australia is a Western-style country, sometimes we forget that we are located in southern Asia. This country looks north to Europe and the USA and in doing so skips over one of the rising world powers. Indonesia will be one of the biggest world economies by 2020.'

'Hard to believe, considering the way it was when we were there,' sighed Susan.

'Norma, can I ask you what your opinion was of the men who were in the Neighbourhood Aid programme with you? I have to tell you that anything you say is in the strictest confidence. I just want to get a feel for the men I'm writing about,' said Chris.

'Chris, your mother was a very good friend to me,' said Norma. 'I don't know if she ever told you, but I was very sick for quite some time when we were in Java. I thought I would have to return to Australia, but your mother nursed me and cooked for me and made sure that I got better. We hadn't known each other very long and yet she was more than happy to put herself out for me. I owe her. So if you are sure that my name will never be attached to any comments I make, I will tell you what I knew about these men and the work that they did. Have I your word that my privacy will be respected?' She raised her chin and looked him straight in the eye.

Chris felt a tingling sensation. It was the sense he sometimes felt right before a story cracked wide open. Perhaps Norma was the key after all. He returned her gaze and said, 'Absolutely, Norma. If you like, I'll send you anything I write before it's published so that you can make sure.'

'Don't worry, Norma,' said Susan. 'Chris will keep his word.'

Norma nodded her head. She paused, waiting for the waiter to serve their coffees, then took a sip before starting to speak.

'Well, of course, I couldn't fault Evan and his work. He was so young and had barely qualified, but he had a gift for medicine. I expect that was partly because he came from a medical family, but it was something more than that, too. He had a knack for creating extraordinary relationships with his patients. It's hard to explain, but he was able to radiate such confidence they sometimes seemed to want to get better just to please him. I remember him telling me that he used to be frustrated when people came to him convinced that they had been cursed and would likely die. Yet his quiet assurance often seemed to have the desired effect on his patients and they survived whatever spell had been placed on them.'

Norma looked at Chris and smiled.

'I see that you think that they would have recovered anyway, but that was not always true, was it, Susan?'

'No,' said Susan. 'Sometimes belief in the supernatural can be very strong.'

'I didn't know the others quite as well as I knew Evan,' said Norma. 'From what I could see, David loved being out and about with his farmers, helping them improve the yields of their crops. He was always enthusiastic about his work and as I remember he had a great sense of humour, sometimes at my expense,' she added.

Susan laughed. 'He still has that sense of humour and I'm sure he meant no harm when he directed his wit towards you.'

'Yes,' said Chris. 'We've seen quite a bit of David lately and he's still travelling the world, helping raise crop yields in poorer countries.'

'Good for him. I remember Mark quite well too. I felt he could have been the odd one out, coming from such a wealthy family, but he fitted in well and quickly gained the respect of Bogor's small traders. He wasn't easily frightened, either.'

'What do you mean by that?' asked Susan, frowning.

'Even after all the trouble at the Tans', he wouldn't

move out. He continued to live with them. Said that if they had to stay in their house, then he would too.'

Susan was silent for a few moments, then she said, 'I didn't know that.'

'No reason you should,' said Norma. 'You'd gone home by then, which was the right thing to do. You suffered a terrible experience. That's why I've been so pleased to hear that your subsequent life has been so happy.'

The three of them sat for a while, saying nothing, drinking their coffees in silence, each deep in thought.

Then Norma spoke. 'I used to see quite a bit of the Tans, after I went back.'

Chris glanced at her. The way she said this seemed to hint at something.

'Goodness,' said Susan. 'How were they?'

'Old Mrs Tan had died, but Mr Tan remembered me. One of his daughters was running the family business because he had no sons, and we became quite good friends. She was a very good businesswoman.'

Quietly Susan asked, 'Did they ever mention Jimmy?'

'Yes, of course, Jimmy . . .' She stopped talking as she and Susan looked away, both clearly remembering the terrible event of Jimmy's murder.

'Those protests,' said Susan, softly.

'Rabble rousers using those riots as a cover.'

'What do you mean?' asked Chris.

'The people who killed Jimmy weren't taking part in a political protest, they were using the chaos of that night to target the Chinese. It was common knowledge that most Chinese hoarded their money, mostly in gold. They didn't trust the banks,' Norma explained.

Susan sighed. 'Yes. Jimmy died because the Tans were raided and Jimmy got in the way of a robbery. It was tragic.'

Norma opened her mouth to say something, seemed to think better of it, and took a sip of coffee instead.

'Mum told me you lived at the hospital, is that right, Norma? She said it was only Mark who lived with the Tans, so why did you go and see the Tans when you returned to Bogor?' asked Chris.

Norma looked down at her coffee. 'The Tans were old friends of Anwar's and his family, so we used to visit them on occasion. I got to know them well. Anwar had a lot of other friends in Bogor, friends who over time told him stories about the night Jimmy died.' She took a breath and looked at Susan. 'It turns out that events weren't quite the way we had accepted them at the time.'

For a moment there was complete silence around the table. Then Susan spoke.

'Norma, will you tell me what you know? It might have been a long time ago, but I still want to find out what really happened that night.'

Norma held up a hand. 'All right, Susan, I'll tell what I've learned about his death. But it won't be easy for you to hear.' Norma paused and Susan looked at Chris and then back at Norma and nodded. 'For starters,' Norma began, 'you probably didn't know that when Jimmy came up from Jakarta that weekend to see you, he told Mr Tan he was going to propose to you. He showed him a picture of a ring and asked him if he could copy it. He knew Mr Tan was a good goldsmith.'

Susan made a small sound and her hand flew to her mouth. 'I never knew,' she whispered.

But Norma continued talking, obviously keen to tell Susan everything now she'd started.

'Anwar had some friends who were businessmen. I think they liked to be seen with Anwar because he was so admired in Bogor. They probably felt that his status rubbed off on them. One day we were having lunch with a couple of them and something came up about the six of us and the work we'd done in '68. I mentioned Alan

Carmichael to them and said that I thought he was now a rich businessman. They were very impressed. Then one of them said, "Mr Carmichael a very good friend to Indonesia. He try very hard to get rid of bad Chinese, communist Chinese." We all knew that Alan hated the Chinese and used to tell us that Indonesia would be better off without them. Then the other man said that Alan had actively worked on getting the Chinese out of Bogor. I had no idea what he meant, so I didn't say anything.'

Chris glanced across to his mother. She hadn't taken her eyes off Norma's face and he realised that neither woman was aware of his presence, so intent were they on Norma's story and remembering back to all those years before.

Norma continued, 'I was puzzled about the comments from these men, so I later asked Anwar if he understood what they were talking about. Anwar said that he would make some inquiries to find out. A few days later he came back and told me what he had discovered. I found it quite shocking. Alan had made no secret of his dislike for the Chinese, but what Anwar discovered was that when Alan was in Bogor, he was actually involved in pursuing them.'

'But how could he do that? Surely we, someone, would have noticed?' Susan asked, her voice filled with horror.

Norma shifted in her seat and then drank from the glass of water that had been put in front of her, gathering her thoughts. 'As you know, there were gangs that intimidated the Chinese. Remember that day at the markets, when Mark and you and I saw them extorting money from the Chinese traders there? Well, evidently some of the manual labourers who worked for Alan were members of those gangs and he actually encouraged them in taking this sort of action against any of the Chinese.'

340

Chris simply stared at Norma. 'What sort of people were they that Alan was involved with?' he finally asked.

'Chris, it was a time of madness. It was like a fuse had been lit and there was no stopping the explosion that would follow. There was sporadic but unpredictable chaos, and it could be quite indiscriminate. Anyone could be denounced as a communist and killed. So many people were frightened that they might be singled out, quite erroneously, that they often turned in other members of their own family to save themselves. And there were gangs that took part in these killings with impunity. Sometimes they were complete strangers to the victims. Sometimes they all dressed in black carrying swords, sometimes they wore camouflage outfits and carried guns; it varied. But they all hated communists and thought of themselves as patriots, and that the killings were justified. Thousands of innocent people were victims of these gangs. But the Chinese were the biggest target for the anti-communist riots, and as they often had money and valuables in their homes, the gangs particularly went after them,' Norma explained.

'And Alan believed in all this?' asked Chris, trying to reconcile what he was hearing with everything he'd learned about the well-known property developer.

'This was the 1960s, Chris. Throughout the West there was a fear of communism. This was the time when the Vietnam War was at its height. Communism, it was thought, would run right through South East Asia, conquering country after country, even invading Australia if not actively stopped,' said Norma.

'Yes, many Australians believed that this domino effect could easily happen,' Susan chipped in. 'So it was thought that anyone who was connected with communism, either in Australia or in nearby countries, was a threat to Australia's freedom. Communism was an idea which could not be allowed to flourish, something that had to be actively fought.'

'So you're telling me, Norma, that Alan was involved in the violence against people who were thought to be communists in Bogor, especially the Chinese?' said Chris.

'Yes, but there is more to the story. Anwar found out that Alan was forewarned that there would be riots that terrible night and that using the ensuing chaos as cover, several Chinese homes would be invaded and robbed. One of those homes would be the Tans'.'

'What!' Susan's stunned expression turned to fury. 'Alan knew that the Tans would be attacked and he did nothing? He never told us. He did nothing!' said Susan, her voice rising.

Chris reached over to take his mother's shaking hand.

'Norma, are you sure about this information? This is dreadful,' he said, shaking his head. 'Mark lived with the Tans. I thought he and Alan were supposed to be friends. Why wouldn't Alan tell him what was going to happen, or at least drop some sort of a hint?'

'You'd have to ask Alan that,' said Norma, evenly. 'But I suppose if he had said something to Mark, or Jimmy for that matter, then they would have known about his relationship with those terrible gangs and he might have been sent home in disgrace. But also remember, generally white people were never targeted by these gangs, because they knew that then the police couldn't just turn a blind eye. They would have had to become involved. Maybe Alan was just taking the chance that nothing would happen to either Mark or Jimmy.'

'But the police never caught whoever stabbed Jimmy,' said Susan quietly, almost to herself.

'Norma, may I ask why you didn't tell my mother all this before now?' asked Chris, gently.

Norma hesitated and looked at Susan. 'I suppose I

knew that this could only upset you, as it did me. It's in the past. I may have been wrong to keep this information to myself, but I did. Why bring up something that can't be changed, especially something so painful?'

Susan nodded, her face flushed, and while Chris felt enormous sympathy for his mother and what she had just learned, he couldn't help feeling a tingle of satisfaction that his story had taken such a huge leap forward.

Susan was still trembling and shaking her head at the news. 'I can't believe Alan would deliberately not warn us, the Tans, Mark and Jimmy . . . No, it's unforgivable that he didn't say something. I think that he's responsible for Jimmy's death.' Susan's eyes filled with tears.

'I'm so sorry, Mum.' Susan leaned against her son for a moment. Then Norma reached into her handbag and handed Susan a tissue, which she accepted gratefully, sitting up straighter again.

'I just think it's so sad,' Susan said, dabbing her eyes. 'It was such an unfair, random act of brutality. Poor Jimmy. Maybe his family should also know what really happened. Jimmy's brother, Thomas, wrote to me, you know,' Susan said to Norma. 'He went to Indonesia, to Bogor, a year or so after Jimmy's death, trying to find out more about what had happened to Jimmy, but by then it was a closed chapter. An unfortunate incident, as far as the authorities were concerned.'

They were all quiet a minute. Then Susan reached out and touched Norma's arm. 'I know you didn't have to share this. But I'm glad you did. Thank you.'

Norma nodded and gave a small sympathetic smile. 'I'm sorry this has upset you, but at least now you know the truth.'

'Oh, Norma, it was a special time back then, wasn't it? For both good and sad reasons. I have never forgotten a moment of it. I learned a lot about life, which made me grow up. Those first impressions and images of such a different, exciting, amazing place and people have always stayed with me,' said Susan.

Norma agreed. 'We were lucky to glimpse the heart of a country. And I never regretted marrying Anwar. He was a remarkable man, but our backgrounds were too different. Sometimes your own customs, heritage and childhood claim you, even when you don't want them to, isn't that so?' said Norma.

Susan glanced at Chris and he smiled at her.

'Yes, that's true, but often you're not aware of it until you make that return journey,' Chris said. They sat quietly for a few moments, lost in the momentous and emotional moment they had just shared. Chris could see his mother looked tired and spent and he thought that perhaps it was time to wind things up.

'Thank you for giving me the privilege of meeting you,' said Chris to Norma. 'I'd like to keep in touch, if I may.'

'Perhaps,' Norma replied, her face now closed.

Susan managed a smile. 'Yes, thank you for telling me the truth. It's not always an easy thing to do, but I appreciate that you have.'

Chris settled the bill and then Norma clasped Susan's hands, inclined her head towards Chris and then rose and walked out into the gathering gloom of the winter's evening without a backward glance.

*

Chris had asked Georgia out to dinner, but she'd suggested he come to her house for a meal, so Susan took the train back to Pymble to spend the evening with Mark and Lorraine while Chris went out to Balmain. On the way he picked up a good bottle of wine and bought a bunch of dramatic oriental lilies.

Georgia's terrace cottage was tucked at the end of a quiet cul-de-sac in the harbourside suburb. It had a tiny backyard surrounded by a high brick wall and contained a tumbling garden lit by well-concealed lighting.

'It's very Mediterranean and secluded. You're not overlooked at all,' said Chris as he gazed at it. 'And I can hear boats on the harbour.'

'I have some harbour glimpses from upstairs. Come and see.'

As they went back inside and up the narrow staircase, Chris couldn't help but admire Georgia's eclectic décor, a happy marriage of shabby chic, modern art, antique etchings, and a retro modern dining room and kitchen.

The bedroom was next to a surprisingly large bathroom, all crisp white tiles with a dark blue trim.

'I sacrificed a minuscule second bedroom for a decent bathroom where I could swing a cat, if I had one,' said Georgia. She indicated the bedroom window. 'There's the view.'

Peering out, Chris could see the spangled city lights across the water. 'That's gorgeous,' said Chris. 'My place at Neutral Bay is not nearly as exciting.'

'But you've got Neverend as well, and that's really lovely,' said Georgia. 'Now let's go open that wine, I'm dying to hear about Norma. Did you learn anything interesting?'

Settled in a deep chair with Georgia stretched out on the sofa, the long coffee table between them, Chris relayed all that Norma had told them that afternoon. Georgia listened quietly and when he finished, said, 'Wow. Your poor mother. That's a lot to take in.' She paused and took a sip of wine. 'And this also puts a bit of a new slant on the story. Are you going to tackle Alan with this information?'

Chris shook his head. 'Bit hard if he refuses to make contact. I believe Norma, but I can't prove any of it.

Anyway, I really can't write about it. Alan would sue the socks off me. Still, it does make one think about what sort of man Alan Carmichael must be.'

Georgia straightened up and put down her wineglass on the coffee table. 'Speaking of your book, I have something for you. Come into my den.'

Her office had been converted from the small dining room. Bookshelves lined one wall, and there was a large filing cabinet and neat piles of what appeared to be manuscripts on her desk. Another wall was covered with framed photos. One in particular jumped out at Chris.

'The old house! Jean Hay's place. What a great shot.' He leaned forward to examine the muted pink print of the sitting room in the old house. It was full of colour from the light as it shone through the rose glass panes in the windows. 'This is the sort of picture you want to walk into so you can look at every little thing in the room. It's beautiful, Georgia. You certainly do have an excellent eye for photography.'

'I'd love to go back and spend more time there,' she sighed.

'Any time. We'd all be very pleased to see you up in Neverend again.'

Georgia went over to her desk, pulled an envelope from the top drawer and handed it to Chris. 'Congratulations.'

'What's this?' He opened it and pulled out several sheets of paper. He glanced quickly at the top page, and then realised what he was reading. 'Oh, is it for real . . . ?'

Georgia stood in front of him, her eyes dancing with pleasure. 'Yep. It's your contract. An advance will follow once you sign on the dotted line. It's not a big advance, because the publishing company is only a small outfit. They publish mainly Australian non-fiction and they liked the sample chapters that I gave them and are willing to back you.'

Chris felt overwhelmed. In his excitement, he swept Georgia into his arms and kissed her. But his quick kiss of joyful delight suddenly turned into something more. His mouth lingered on hers. He dropped the pages of the contract onto the desk and wrapped both his arms around her and kissed her longingly.

Georgia returned his kiss, holding his head close to hers before lightly pulling away and saying breathlessly, 'Ah, you'd better sign the last page of the contract and initial the others before we get too sidetracked.'

Chris leaned over the desk, picked up a pen and quickly signed the contract.

Georgia laughed. 'You didn't read it!'

'I trust you. You're my agent.' He reached for her again. It felt so good to hold her close.

Finally Georgia drew away from his arms. 'I'd better check the dinner. Unless you want curry for breakfast.' She grinned playfully at him and kissed him quickly once more.

'Sounds perfectly fine to me,' Chris returned, but he followed Georgia into the kitchen and watched as she fussed at the stove.

When she had put the lid back on the saucepan, Chris stood behind her and wrapped his arms around her as Georgia leaned into his embrace.

'Was that a genuine invitation?' Chris murmured. 'Are you sure you know what you're getting into? I'm not just a dinner and breakfast kind of guy.'

'I know that,' she said calmly, and turned to face him. 'Stick around as long as you want.'

'I might just do that.' He kissed her more gently this time. 'I'm going to make a couple of calls. I won't be long. Why don't you refill our glasses?'

Chris went into the lounge room and called Megan's mobile.

'Hi, Megs. How're things at Toby's place?'

'Hi, Dad. Fun, we're all playing Scrabble and we can't stop laughing. I think that Toby's father cheats. He puts down words I don't think are proper words and he won't let us use a dictionary. How's it going in Sydney?'

'Really, really well. I'll pick up Bunny at about nine in the morning, so we'll be home around mid-afternoon. I'll give you a ring when we're back, but if you want you can let yourself in and wait for us.'

'So where are you, Dad? Where's Bunny?'

'Bunny is with her friends Mark and Lorraine at Pymble. I'm having dinner at Georgia's place. I'll tell you my exciting news when I get back.'

'Oh, really! You're with Georgia. Is that your exciting news?' Megan teased.

'No. Oh, all right then, I have a book contract. Now I'll really have to work hard!'

'Congrats, Dad! I knew Georgia would pull it off. Say hi for me. Gotta go – I'm being called. It's my turn.'

Chris then quickly rang his mother to make his apologies to Mark and Lorraine and told Susan that he would pick her up in the morning to drive back to Neverend. His mother made no comment other than to say that she would be waiting. Chris rang off and then returned to the kitchen to find Georgia waiting with two full glasses of wine. He smiled at her and watched as a broad grin spread across her face too.

*

The next day, it wasn't until the car was well out of the city heading north on the Pacific Highway that Chris asked, 'So how was your evening last night, Mum?'

'Very interesting. I told Mark and Lorraine about what Norma had said. Lorraine was furious. As she pointed out, it could just have easily been Mark who was killed that

348

night. Mark was very subdued. He said that nothing could change what had happened, but I know that he was very unimpressed by what Alan had done. I don't know if he will continue their relationship now that he's learnt what really happened that night, but I would be surprised if he did.' Speaking to her friends about the events surrounding Jimmy's death seemed to have helped Susan. Chris could see her steadiness had returned. 'How was your evening?' she asked him.

'Lovely. Do you want to see the book contract? It's real.'

'No. I believe you, and it's brilliant news, but what I really want to know about is you and Georgia. Is this becoming serious?'

'Okay, Mum, while we're on this subject, how serious are you and David?' he countered.

Susan's mouth twitched as she suppressed a smile. 'Don't be cheeky. I'm your mother.'

Chris softened and shook his head slightly. 'It's been a long time since I've felt like this about someone. I'm scared to think where it might go. I'm nervous and I hope that she feels the way I do.'

'That's nice to hear, Chris,' said Susan. Then she hesitated. 'Georgia is a lovely woman, but is it wise to mix business and pleasure like this? She's your agent and you're her client, after all.'

'I know what you mean, Mum, but I'm not sure that it's actually going to go anywhere,' said Chris. 'I mean, I can't offer Georgia anything. I'm struggling to find meaningful employment, living with my mother hours away from Sydney and I have a teenage daughter to boot.'

'You're a challenge all right, but Georgia obviously has enormous faith in you and your abilities. Speaking as a mother, I see a kind, loving, generous man who gave up a selfish lifestyle to do the right thing by his daughter, and that makes you pretty special in my book. I bet Georgia sees the same things.'

Chris took in these comforting words. He was also remembering how exciting and wonderful it had been to make love to Georgia the previous night. It had been a long time since he'd felt the depth of emotions he felt for Georgia. His mother was right, he had to stop doubting himself. Still, he couldn't help but wonder what was next. The advance from the book contract was very small, so there would be no big change in his lifestyle anytime soon, but it was a step in the right direction.

He decided to change tack and said, 'Now that we've discussed my relationship with Georgia, what about you and David? Where's that going?'

'It's not going anywhere. It just is. We're happy as we are. Leading our own lives, chatting on the phone and spending time together when we want to. A connected past is a great bond.'

'But it's not much of a history. Do you think he had the hots for you back then?'

'Don't be vulgar, we didn't use such expressions as "the hots".' She smiled. 'Well, not publicly.'

They both laughed.

'I'm glad you're happy, Mum. I made a terrible mistake about you and David. I should not have interfered. It's your life, after all, and David is a great guy. I really do understand that having had a wonderful relationship with Dad doesn't preclude you from having another one with someone else now. Dad would not have wanted you to be living alone and unhappy if there was a better alternative, and I don't either.'

'Thank you, Chris, and you're right. My relationship with David is my business, but I'm pleased that you understand it and you approve.'

'You seem to be able to form such loving relationships,

Mum. I always saw you and Dad as the perfect couple.'
Chris sighed. 'I assumed my marriage would be like that
too, but it fell apart. I seem to have messed up a lot in my
life, including not being around for Megan when I should
have been. I wonder if I'll keep on making these mistakes.'

Susan shook her head. 'Rubbish. It's never too late
to get onto the right path. You've done the right thing by
Megan now. She's a very different girl from the one she
was only a few months ago; she's considerate, interested
in doing things and not just in buying things. She's made
a lot of worthwhile friends and seeing you two together
makes my heart burst with happiness. Maybe you'll both
go on to lead your own lives in other places, but I think
this time here in Neverend has been good for both of you.'

'Thanks to you, Mum.' Chris smiled at her.

'It's more than just me. It's being in Neverend.'

'I guess we all need that sense of belonging,' said Chris,
thoughtfully. 'I've lived in so many places and yet never
really felt settled. I put that down to my job. But after
my divorce, I never felt comfortable getting into another
relationship, either. Maybe I didn't want to commit to
someone in a place where I felt I didn't belong.'

'I see what you mean,' said Susan. 'What a good thing
Georgia loves Neverend,' she added brightly.

'Mum, she's only been to Neverend once!' said Chris.

'You never know, she might come again,' said Susan.
She patted his knee. 'In the meantime, concentrate on
your book.'

'I intend to. So what do you make of Norma's news?'

Susan was thoughtful. 'It shocked and saddened
me. It's hard to believe that Alan's actions, or inactions,
created the circumstances in which Jimmy died.'

'I'd like to front up to him about it.'

'You know he would probably just threaten to sue
you,' said Susan.

'True, and if there is nothing to back up the story except hearsay, then he would win.'

'You know what I'm thinking? I'd like to contact Jimmy's brother Thomas and tell him what happened. I expect that Jimmy's parents would probably be dead by now, but Thomas is still very much alive. I'm sure he would be very interested in what we found out.'

'That is a good idea, Mum,' said Chris. 'And I think I might be able to help you with that. I know someone in Washington who went to work for Thomas in a pretty senior position. Why don't I email him and find out how to contact Thomas's PA directly? That way your email should get to him.'

*

Megan bounced out to meet them as the car drove up the driveway of Susan's house. Chris waved his book contract at her as he and Susan got out of the car.

'I'm going to make this book happen . . . and sell heaps and heaps of copies!' he told her as she raced down the steps to meet them.

'Good on you, Dad.' Megan hugged them both.

'Thanks, sweetie. So everything was okay while we were away? Biddi got fed and you stayed at Toby's last night? I must call his parents and thank them.'

'They're really nice. A bit nerdy. I mean, they're really smart. They hardly watch TV or anything. But it was okay.'

'Who won the Scrabble?'

'Toby's dad. But I didn't do too bad.'

'*Badly*,' Chris corrected. 'Well, maybe we could have a game one night with Bunny. I bet your grandmother would win.'

Susan laughed and started towards the house with her bag.

'Dad, since you're home well before dark, could you

drive me over to Mollie's?' Megan asked. 'I'll have time for a ride if you do.'

Chris hesitated. He was tired after the six-hour drive and didn't really want to go out again that day, but there was something about Megan's demeanour that suggested she wanted to have a private talk with him.

'Sure. Throw your gear into the car.'

As they headed along View Street, Chris asked again about Megan's weekend, but when he turned onto the road heading out of town along the river, Megan suddenly pointed out the window, catching her breath.

'Look, Dad. That car. See it?'

'What about it?' A dark blue car with tinted windows was parked under the heavy foliage of an old tree. The car suddenly looked familiar. Chris went cold.

'That car was in our street yesterday and I am sure it followed me when I rode my bike to Toby's.'

'Was it there this morning?'

'I didn't come home till this afternoon. Not long before you arrived.'

Chris decided to make a rapid U-turn so that he didn't have to go past the car, and headed back into town. But a few seconds later, Megan cried out, 'Dad, it's following us.'

Chris looked in his rear-vision mirror and saw the car immediately behind him. He put his foot down and headed towards the main street, busy with locals and tourists.

Looking over her shoulder, Megan squealed as she saw the blue car rocket up the main street close behind them. Then suddenly it made a hard right turn onto one of the side streets and disappeared from view.

Chris pulled over to the side of the road.

'Do you think he was following us, or just being an idiot, Dad?'

Chris evaded her question. 'Let's not worry about some hothead. You still right to go to Mollie's?'

'Yes, please,' said Megan, firmly.

'Great. Let's go. Squire will be waiting for his carrot,' said Chris, trying to sound cheerful. But as he pulled back onto the road he was silently considering whether or not to mention his concerns to the local police. He had no doubt that the blue car was the same one he'd seen outside their house a couple of evenings ago, but why on earth would someone be watching their home?

I I

IN THE SPARKLING LIGHT of Monday morning, as he looked from the lounge room windows across the valley to the bush of the distant plateau, Chris's fears from the previous evening seemed irrational. His mother had picked some of her winter crop of tomatoes and was roasting them in fresh basil and garlic, and their glorious tang drifted out to him from the kitchen. He could hear Megan singing along to a favourite Harry Styles song as she got dressed for school. A willy wagtail landed on the verandah railing and sang cheerfully.

Morning in Neverend rolled along at its usual peaceful pace.

Chris headed into the study to do some work on his book. After a fruitless few minutes, he pushed his laptop to one side and decided to tidy the cluttered papers, folders and notes on the desk. Perhaps by creating order he'd be able to focus his scrambled thoughts. He stacked his reference materials, transcribed notes from interviews and scribbled jottings into neat piles. He looked at the screen of his laptop, which was also smothered with files and folders. Maybe the first thing he'd do when he got his advance would be to buy a decent computer. This one had been dragged around the world and was probably nearing its use-by date. He glanced at the time, closed down the computer and went out to say goodbye to Megan and get ready for work.

'See ya, Dad.'

'You off too? Bye, Chris,' Susan called to him.

'Yes, see you later, Mum. Anything on your agenda today?'

'I've got a Red Cross meeting, lunch with my friend Valerie, then I thought I might go into Coffs to look at some material. Pasta all right for dinner?'

'Sounds good. I'm heading to the plateau, so would you like me to get anything from the foodie place up there?'

'No thanks, all good. See you this evening. How's Shaun, by the way?'

'Not bad. Still hobbling a bit and missing his golf.'

As Chris drove towards the plateau, his mind sifted through the various aspects of his book. Norma's story about Alan painted a picture of a single-minded, even cruel man, and it seemed to Chris, based on the limited knowledge he had of Alan's business dealings, that Alan had carried these traits into his corporate life. But where to go from here, Chris wondered. Without corroboration from Alan, he couldn't use the information he'd been given by Norma, and Carla's friend could not supply him with any evidence of wrongdoing at Alan's Victorian development either. All Chris could say for certain was that Alan was shrewd and used his powerful position to his advantage, and there was nothing unique about that.

Such intense musings helped the time pass and soon Chris had arrived on the plateau with its rolling pastures, still surprisingly green even in these early winter months. He made his deliveries, pausing to talk only briefly with his regulars, then stopped for a quick sandwich and coffee at one of the little cafés in the main street. It was still early afternoon, but rain clouds had begun to heap on the horizon. Chris was pleased that he could begin the winding journey back down the mountain on the hazardous road before any rain started.

There seemed to be little traffic using the road and he hoped the quarry trucks had finished for the day. He switched his news station to the classical music one so he could fully concentrate on the road, although he admitted to himself that he was far more confident about the drive than he had been when he started the job.

About five minutes later, as he rounded the first of the road's notorious hairpin bends, he caught a glimpse in his rear-vision mirror of a car behind him.

'Sorry, mate,' he said aloud. 'Nowhere for you to get past me for quite a while. You'll just have to be patient.'

A light misting of rain blew across the windscreen. Chris turned on the wipers, only to find they wouldn't work. The rain wasn't heavy, but he didn't need such a malfunction right now. Around and down, around and down, the van twisted its way towards Neverend. The thick foliage that covered the hillside on the opposite side of the road and the densely wooded ravine beside him were becoming wetter as the rain increased. The road was greasy and as he slowed to round the next bend, he was relieved to feel the van's brakes grab the wet bitumen without any trouble.

As he drove on in the deteriorating conditions, he thought he might have to pull over, but when he tried the wipers again, he found that they would at least work on intermittent speed. He decided to press on. He briefly looked into the rear-vision mirror again and caught another glimpse of the dark car still behind him, its headlights on low beam. The driver was clearly getting impatient with Chris's reduced speed, for the car had edged closer to the van.

'Calm down, mate,' said Chris. 'There's a place where I can pull over in just a minute. I'll get out of your way then.'

But suddenly the car shot out from behind the van and drew level with Chris, who eased up sharply to let the car get past.

'You're nuts!' yelled Chris angrily. 'You can't overtake here. If something is coming the other way, you're dead meat.'

Then to his horror Chris realised the car wasn't trying to overtake him, but was staying beside him and nudging closer to the van.

'Hey, you stupid bastard . . .'

Chris glanced across at the car in disbelief. He couldn't see the driver through the car's tinted windows, but he suddenly realised that it looked like the same car that had been outside Susan's house the previous week and had intimidated him and Megan the day before.

As the blue car and the van rounded the next bend, side by side, there was the frantic honking of a horn. A gravel truck was slowly climbing the mountain road in the opposite direction and the blue car was right in its path. Chris braked, struggling to control the van on the slippery road, and the blue car squeezed between the van and the truck and roared off into the distance. Chris drove on slowly, sweating and shaking.

Was that just a crazy driver in a hurry, or had it been a deliberate attempt to push him off the road and into the ravine that ran alongside it?

Chris drove on. The windscreen wipers were now barely coping as the rain got heavier. He concentrated on the difficult road, very relieved that he was nearly at the bottom of the mountain. He made a routine glance into his rear-vision mirror to see what was behind him and was astonished to see that he was again being followed by the blue car. He realised at once that the car had simply pulled over into one of the tourist lookouts at the side of the road and waited there for Chris to drive past. The blue car was rapidly gaining on him and Chris knew that if it again tried to push against the van on the slippery road, he might well lose control and he and the van would go over the edge. He decided to try to outpace the blue car. He floored the accelerator, but the blue car stayed right on his tail. The workhorse van was proving to be no match for the more powerful engine of the blue car, but Chris was on very familiar terms with the road and he knew that in less than three kilometres there was a side road where he could turn off. He just had to stay in front of the blue car until then.

The two vehicles thundered down the mountainside, the blue car continually trying to draw level with Chris. Cars coming the other way blew their horns in alarm and pulled over to the side of the narrow road to avoid being hit.

This idiot will kill someone, Chris thought angrily. Most likely me.

The road began to level out, but the blue car did not let up. Chris knew that the small side road was approaching. As late as he dared, he shifted down his gears and did a hard left onto the narrow road, which was almost hidden beneath an archway of trees. The blue car, taken by surprise by Chris's actions, shot past the turn-off and disappeared into the distance. Chris pulled the van up in front of the small general store that stood a few metres away. He was shaking as he rolled down his window to gulp breaths of cool, damp air. There was no doubt now in his mind. The driver in the blue car had been trying to push him off the mountain.

He got out of the van and leaned against the door for a minute until he got his breathing under control. Then he went into the store and pulled a bottle of water from the refrigerated cabinet and, holding it in trembling hands, drank it down.

Ten minutes later he got back into the van and drove the rest of the way into Neverend. He kept glancing in his rear-vision mirror, but the blue car didn't reappear.

Chris parked the van in Shaun's shed in town and grabbed his jacket, then walked slowly home, oblivious to the showery weather. He was deeply concerned. He knew now, beyond any shadow of doubt, that he was being targeted by someone. And he was also sure that the loose wheel nuts which had caused Shaun's accident had been meant for him. Moreover, it was not just he who had been targeted. Susan's house and Megan had also been watched. What was he to do?

Chris didn't mention what had happened over dinner that night, but when it had all been cleared away, he glanced at his watch and said, 'I'm going for a stroll. I'll be back by eight, everyone.' He stepped outside and, after checking the guesthouse and his car, walked down View Street towards the town. The street was deserted and he glanced back at the house, its lights shining a welcome cosiness.

Anger welled up in him. How dare someone threaten his home, which should have been the safest place in the world? He walked past the Neverend Hotel and the shopping centre and approached the police station. He was relieved to see through the glass door that Sergeant Pete Pollard was on the evening shift.

The sergeant waved when he spotted him and came over to let him in. 'G'day, Chris. I've got the kettle on. Or do you want a soft drink? What can I do for you?'

'Tea, coffee, either would be great.' Chris took a deep breath. 'Pete, I know how this is going to sound, but I think that my family and I are being targeted by someone.'

'Take a seat and tell me what's been going on.'

As Pete made instant coffee, Chris gave him a brief run-down on what had happened to him that afternoon, and the previous incidents in which he had seen the blue car watching the house and then been followed and intimidated by it. Pete set a mug of coffee down in front of Chris and sipped his own. 'So you don't think that the car this afternoon was just being driven by idiots out to scare you?'

'Well, they certainly scared me. But I don't think it was a random action. I don't think Frenchy's crash was an accident, either. I should have been driving that van, not him.'

'What sort of car was it, Chris?'

'Some sort of Japanese car. I really didn't take it in. Mazda, Toyota? Probably a Mazda. Pretty sure it was a hatchback, too. And I know you'll ask me about the number plates, but I can't help you there. I didn't see them, and when I think about that, it's because they were smeared with mud.'

'So, mate, is there anyone you can think of who would want to frighten you and your family?'

Chris sipped his coffee. 'I don't think so. I mean, most people I might have had problems with are overseas, and those problems were a long time ago. I can't see anyone chasing me to Neverend to get me. Besides, I don't think that anything I did or wrote was enough to have me killed. None of this makes sense.'

'This book I hear you're writing; would that make you any enemies?'

'Pete, three of my subjects are more than happy to help me. I did initially get a letter from Alan Carmichael's lawyer about defamation, but I got Duncan's brother in Coffs to send one back to say that I would be going ahead with the book, but I wouldn't be writing anything that was likely to offend him. I've heard nothing since.'

Pete gave a low whistle. 'Carmichael is a big name. You don't do things by halves, my friend, but I can't see him chasing you down the plateau road. And as you say, he's the sort who uses lawyers when he doesn't like something. Have you told your mother about all this?'

'No, but I will. I'll tell her to be on the lookout for dark blue cars,' Chris said bitterly.

'Well, I'll make sure that we keep an eye on your house and we'll watch out for dark blue cars as well, but I'm not sure we can do much more at this stage.'

'You know, Pete, I don't like the idea of being threatened in my own home town. It makes me angry to think that someone is trying to invade my space,' said Chris. 'But thanks for your help. I'll tell Mum that someone from the cop shop will be poking around the house regularly. Mind you, I'm not sure that Mum would be easily intimidated, but best we don't take any chances. And thanks for the coffee, mate.' He drained his mug and stood to leave.

The sergeant opened the door and put his hand on Chris's shoulder. 'Take care, Chris.'

As he walked back to the house, Chris felt comforted by Pete's support and relieved that he had reported the events, but still uncertain about what his next move should be. It felt good to stretch his legs. The rain clouds had cleared and the sky was bright and clear, studded with a zillion stars. The Milky Way was a brush stroke across the velvety night canvas. This was the kind of sky you never saw in a city.

On an impulse, he didn't walk straight back to View Street but continued on the lower road, towards the river. The old white bridge spanned the silky silent water. How many times had he fished from this bridge, swum beneath it with his dog and his mates, or driven across it; a link with home and other places, always the beginning and end of a journey. Here, in the darkness, he had no sense of anyone watching him; no car in the shadows, no danger, no threats. All around him felt safe and peaceful. But for how long, he wondered. He had to make some decisions.

Megan was his priority. He didn't want to alarm her by suggesting that the Baxters were being targeted, but he wanted her out of Neverend for the time being. School holidays started the following week. He'd send Megan to her mother. Jill had wanted Megan to go over to the west for quite some time, so that would work out well. He couldn't move his mother, so he would have to alert her. He was sure she would take it in her stride, maybe even decide that now was the right time to go away with David. He would also tell Georgia what was going on. He felt the need to share his concerns with her. He turned and walked towards home.

Megan and the cat were curled up beside Susan, riveted to the flickering TV screen. Chris didn't want to talk about all that had happened, so he poured himself a Scotch, something he rarely did, and went into the study and rang Georgia.

She listened quietly, letting out a shocked expulsion of breath when he finished.

'Dear God, Chris, that's really serious. Have you any idea who would do something like that? Who's got it in for you?'

'Quite frankly, I'm at a loss about that, but I know it was no subtle hint. I was almost pushed off the road. It's some kind of miracle I wasn't killed, and you know, if I had been, everyone would just think it was an accident that happened in the wet on a slippery mountain road. But now I'm more concerned for Megan and my mother.' And he told her that he had decided to send Megan to Perth for the holidays.

'That's a good idea. I don't suppose there is anything I can do, but if you think of something, just give me a shout.'

'Thanks for that. It's good to know you're in my corner. Someone to talk to so that I don't have to worry Mum too much. 'Night, Georgia, talk soon.'

*

'Do I have to go to Perth?' wailed Megan the next morning when Chris told her of his decision.

'Of course you do,' said Susan briskly. Chris had explained to her late the previous evening about the incidents with the blue car and she was in total agreement that Megan should be sent away for the time being. 'Your mother misses you. I bet she'll plan some fantastic things to do. Perth is beautiful. Isn't that right, Chris?'

'A lovely city, and Freo, Fremantle, is great fun.'

'I'll miss Squire. You know I don't want to leave him. And what about my friends? We have heaps planned for these holidays. And you said Georgia might come up to visit soon and I want to see her.'

Chris smiled to himself. Six months ago, Megan had hated the thought of living in Neverend. Now he couldn't get her out of the place.

'Mollie will ride Squire for you and I'll check on him and take him carrots,' said Chris. 'And your friends will still be here when you get back, and you can see Georgia another time. Your mother wants to see you, so over to Perth you go.'

Megan shrugged and shuffled off to her room where, no doubt, Chris thought, she would tell her friends about her unreasonable parents.

'Do you want to drive my car?' Susan asked as soon as Megan had gone.

'Thanks, Mum, but if they're watching me, they'll spot that soon enough. Anyway, I hope they've gone by now. Perhaps they think they've made their point. I just wish I knew what it was.'

Chris didn't want to feel he had to keep looking over his shoulder, so he had no intention of changing his routine, although he was thankful that he had no immediate reason to drive up to the plateau. He debated over whether to worry Shaun by telling him about the various incidents, or say nothing on the presumption that nothing more would happen. But in reality, Chris was concerned that another vehicle might be sabotaged, so he decided that he had little choice other than to confide in his friend.

The screen door banged behind him as he entered Shaun's house and called out a greeting.

'In here, mate. Watching the footy.'

'Don't get up. How're you going, Frenchy?' Chris grinned at Shaun, who had his foot up on a cushion and a folding table beside him with a can of beer, peanuts and the crossword.

'Help yourself to something from the fridge. The missus is out shopping. Everything go all right today? Get everything delivered?'

'Sure did. Needed to get the windscreen wipers fixed first. A light beer sounds good, you ready for another lager?'

'Why not? I'm not going anywhere.'

Chris brought the beers back from the kitchen and gave one to Shaun.

'When do you see the doctor again?' asked Chris as he twisted the top from the bottle and sat down.

'Tomorrow, but I'm doing really fine. I'm just making the most of the time off while I can,' Shaun grinned. 'What're you up to?'

'I have a few things on the agenda. I was hoping to get a couple of days off next week. Do a swap with someone. I need to do a bit on this book. I seem to be falling behind. I'm thinking of talking Georgia into coming up, as well.'

'No worries. I'll be back driving by then, so we won't be a driver down. We'll work around you. Make up for all those extra shifts you've done while I've been laid up. Is this Georgia girl getting serious? Or is it work?'

'Bit of both, I guess. If she came up we could talk about my book, or go out to Jean Hay's place so that Georgia can take more photos of it. She thinks it's very photogenic. But mate, I have to talk to you seriously.'

'What's up?' Seeing Chris's concerned expression, Shaun leaned forward. 'Anything I can do?'

'You've done more than enough for me, mate. I feel really badly because I think your accident was due to me.'

'Whaddya mean? Don't tell me you changed those damned tyres and didn't tighten the bolts? I don't believe it.'

Chris shook his head. 'No, no. But I'm convinced that those nuts were loosened deliberately in an attempt to hurt me. I was expected to drive that van, you were collateral damage. And that's not all,' he said. He went on to describe the events involving the blue car.

'So are you telling me that someone is trying to kill you? Have you any idea who? Chris, the whole thing sounds crazy. Things like this don't happen in Neverend. But then, I guess I do have a few cuts and bruises to show that maybe they do.'

'Look, Frenchy, if you think I'm a danger to the business, and you want to let me go, then just say so. I would understand.'

'Don't be stupid. What sort of mate do you take me for? Talked to Pete Pollard yet?'

'Yep. He said he'd keep an eye on the house.'

'Good bloke, that. We might have to beef up security at work. We don't have much. There's a man in Coffs who has security dogs. Could get him to bring them over to patrol the yard for a bit, to protect the vans. I think a couple of Dobermans would make intruders think twice. What are you going to do about Megan and your mother?' asked Shaun.

'Mum said she'd be fine and I'm sending Megan over to Jill's in Perth for the holidays.'

'That's a good move. Look, Chris, it's a bit of a worry that all this has happened to you, but if we all take sensible precautions and keep our eyes open, things will work out,' said Shaun.

Chris stood up and put his hand on Shaun's shoulder. 'You're a good friend. I really appreciate what you've done to help me. The last thing I want is to make trouble for you. And I'm sorry you had this prang that was meant for me.'

Shaun rearranged his leg on the cushion and smiled. 'Ah, it's given me a good excuse to bludge for a couple of days. Do me a favour and get me another beer on your way out.'

Chris chuckled. 'Sure thing. See you soon.'

'Say hi to that Georgia for me!' He called as Chris let himself out. Shaun looked concerned as he picked up his beer.

*

After dinner that evening, Chris's mobile rang.

'G'day, kid. Mac here.'

'Hi, Mac, gosh it's good to hear your voice,' said Chris as he walked into his study.

'Chris, Georgie filled me in on what's going on. Serious

367

stuff. I didn't call straight away; did a bit of homework. I think you're going to be shocked by what I've found out.'

'How so?'

'Well, Georgia mentioned to me that you've had a bit of trouble with Alan Carmichael over this book of yours. Now, it's well known in some circles that the man is less than forthcoming about his business interests. Then I remembered a journo I used to know a few years ago. He had a good nose for any corruption going on in the building industry. Anyway, he was investigating one of Carmichael's shopping centres in Queensland – that is, until he was killed in a hit-and-run accident on the Gold Coast. The police never found the driver of the car that hit him.'

Chris was taken aback. 'That's terrible,' he said, shaking his head. 'But it could have been pure coincidence, Mac. Don't you think you're drawing a long bow, linking Carmichael to what happened to me? I mean, it doesn't seem feasible that a business tycoon like Alan would try to harm me.'

'That's not all, Chris. Once I'd remembered that case, I did a bit more research. And guess what? I found another similar story. This time it was a journalist from Adelaide and it only happened a couple of years ago. Evidently he was looking at a questionable rezoning application for another of Carmichael's projects in one of the suburbs when he was killed. The brakes on his car mysteriously failed and he ran into a telegraph pole.'

Chris said nothing as his blood ran cold. Two journalists who'd been investigating Carmichael's activities, both killed in road accidents.

'I think that Carmichael is bad news, Chris,' said Mac emphatically.

'But Mac, it could still all be a coincidence,' said Chris, though he wasn't sure he believed this himself.

'You know what they say, once is an accident, twice is coincidence, and three times is a pattern. I reckon that this is definitely part of a pattern. Two deaths that we know of and the attempt on your life, and the connection between all three is Alan Carmichael,' said Mac seriously.

'There's another death connected to him as well,' said Chris. 'The murder of my mother's friend Jimmy Anderson in Indonesia all those years ago. Carmichael has to bear a lot of the responsibility for that, too.'

'Well, the way I see it, Carmichael doesn't like people nosing around his operations, so someone doing a book that rakes over his past is not going to be welcome.'

'You know, when I spoke to him first for the magazine article, he was polite and in no way threatening.'

'Changed, though, when he found out that you were going to write a book, didn't he? Got his lawyer on to you, and then you made it clear that you weren't going to be warned off. I can't help but think that Carmichael has it in for you.'

'If you're right, Mac, then what am I going to do?'

'Up to you, Chris. Do you call his bluff and ignore what's been going on? Or do you let Carmichael know right away that you're dropping him from the book?'

'What a mess. Maybe I shouldn't have been so bull-headed and told his solicitor I was going ahead with the book with or without Alan's agreement. I wonder if I should talk to Evan or Mark as well as David.'

'And what are they going to say? They might be horrified by what Carmichael is doing, or at least what we think he's doing, but all they can say is that you either take a chance and press on, or back off.'

Chris's heart sank as he realised there was really only one path he could take. 'I suppose you're right. Mac, if I was working on my own, I'd keep going, but here with Megan and Mum . . . I can't take that chance.'

'Do you think you should talk things over with Georgie before you make a decision?'

'Of course I'll speak with her about my decision and what that will mean for my book, but the bottom line is that I can't risk my family's safety. I'll notify Carmichael's solicitor right away and tell him that I'm backing off from including him in the book in any way.'

Mac was quiet a moment. 'I think that it's probably for the best, Chris.'

Chris rang off and then dropped his head into his hands. His life seemed to have become a pattern of one step forward and three back. He picked up his phone and called Georgia to tell her what Mac had found out and what he had decided as a result.

'So do you want to drop the book?' she asked quietly.

'Well, not the whole idea, I can't! I mean, this is my future. I need to do it. But the trouble is that without Carmichael in it, the book loses much of its impetus. He's the big name.' Chris swallowed the lump in his throat. 'Oh, I don't believe this. I feel I'm not getting anywhere.' He drew a shaky breath.

'Yes, you are. The other three people you are writing about are important Australians too, so maybe the publisher won't have a big problem with your omission of Carmichael, although I agree it is a pity. Let me talk to the powers that be and see what they say.'

'Oh, Georgia, I feel every time my life starts to get back on track, something gets in the way.'

'That's nonsense. If both you and Dad think that Carmichael is behind this intimidation, then you are doing the right thing by backing out to protect your family. You have no choice. But I'm confident that I will be able to talk the publisher into letting you continue with the book. Things will work out, I promise you,' said Georgia emphatically.

'You're so supportive, Georgia. I really appreciate it. Now I just have to get Megan organised to go to Perth. The flights are a bit fiddly. I can put her on the plane to Sydney, but she has a few hours' wait there for the Perth flight. I suppose she'll be all right.'

'I can understand that you might feel nervous about letting Megan out of your sight, especially after her rainforest adventure, but it's hardly a major problem. What if I meet Megan at the airport in Sydney and keep her company until her Perth flight, and then I get the next flight up to Coffs? I'm sure I can swing that.'

'Are you sure? It seems a lot of bother, but Megan would love to be able to spend some time with you. And so would I, Georgia. That'd be wonderful if you came up. Thanks. I can't wait to see you.'

'I'm opting out for a few days. I managed to finalise two deals and get the contracts signed, so I'm due a bit of a breather, plus I'll visit Mr Difficult Author in Woolgoolga to justify my trip. And I've treated myself to a new camera lens.'

Something occurred to Chris. 'Hang on, Georgia, I'm wondering if it might not be safe for you to come until I send a message to Carmichael's solicitor to say that I'm dropping him from the book. I'll get on to Duncan's brother to do that first thing tomorrow. Even then it might be a bit risky,' Chris said quietly.

'I'm still coming up,' said Georgia, defiantly. 'Anyway, I miss you,' she added. 'There. I promised myself I wouldn't say it, and I have.'

Chris felt a warmth surge through him. 'That's the best news I've heard in weeks,' he said. 'And I miss you, too.'

'It's going to work out, Chris. Really,' said Georgia softly.

*

371

Chris felt that he had never been so pleased to have a weekend arrive. The past week had been a nightmare, but there had been no further incidents. Now he was happy just to be able to spend the next couple of days at home. However, on Saturday afternoon Alex persuaded him to go to a local football match. He arrived home from the game to find Susan sitting in the kitchen looking thoughtful, an untouched cup of coffee beside her.

'Hi, Mum. I popped in to see Frenchy on my way home. Sends his regards.' He glanced at Susan. 'You look distracted, what's up? Is everything okay?' Chris suddenly felt worried.

Susan touched his hand reassuringly. 'Yes, everything's fine. I just had the most amazing phone call, that's all. I'm trying to tell myself that it really happened.'

'Really? Who was it from?' asked Chris, curiously.

'I'm still a bit stunned. Thomas Anderson rang me here.'

Chris had to sit down. '*The* Thomas Anderson? Jimmy's brother? Thomas Fairfax Anderson. Good grief. What did he have to say?'

'He said that as soon as my email was brought to his attention, he had to ring me straight away. He was pretty shocked.'

'I'm not surprised, after what Norma said. I suppose that even after all this time he would want to know what really happened to his brother. How did he react to the news that Jimmy's death could have been prevented?'

'He said he always felt that the family never received a proper explanation about his brother's death, which is why he went out to Indonesia himself. He also said that the family was pretty sure Jimmy had formed a romantic attachment with me, going by his letters home and my letter to his parents. That was why he wrote to me all those years ago. Now he says he's very grateful that I took the time to write to him, to let him know what I'd found out from Norma.'

'Well, I hope he felt some closure, to use the cliché?'

Susan shook her head. 'I don't know about that. I feel like I've stirred up a hornet's nest. I could tell on the phone that he was very tense.'

'About what?'

'Alan Carmichael, of course. I made it quite clear in my email that while those violent gangs had been responsible for Jimmy's death, Alan was connected with them and had prior knowledge of what would occur that night. I did say I was shocked and surprised by this new information, and so I thought he, too, might like to know Jimmy's death was not an open-and-shut case of misadventure. It saddened me that it might have been prevented. Actually, I rather think I suggested that Jimmy's death was due entirely to one man's fanaticism.'

'So did he ask you any questions specifically about Alan?'

'Not really. I got the impression that he might know who Alan was already. Maybe he'd looked him up after I mentioned him in my letter. I suppose these wealthy businessmen all know of each other.'

Chris shook his head. 'Mum, Alan is a big fish in a small pond. Thomas Fairfax Anderson is an enormous fish in a very big pond. I mean, he has to be in the top dozen or so of the richest men in America. Carmichael's International Industries is not in his league. So how did the conversation end?'

'He'd like you to ring him so he can chat to you.'

'Me?'

Susan explained, 'When he asked how I'd found out this information, I told him that you had been researching a book which included the period we'd all spent in Indonesia, and how your research had led you to Norma

373

and her story. He asked when your book was coming out and I said you were having a few problems which could delay its release, problems we both thought were caused by Alan Carmichael. I didn't elaborate.'

'Thomas Fairfax Anderson wants me to ring him. That's amazing. Did he leave a number?'

'Yes. His direct line.'

'Good grief, Mum. You seem to be connected with the most incredible people. Maybe my conversation with Thomas Anderson could put a whole new slant on things.'

'I'm not sure how, but give him a ring.' Susan gave her son an encouraging smile.

Taking a cup of coffee, Chris looked at his watch and hurried to his study.

As he waited for Thomas Fairfax Anderson's personal assistant to see if Mr Anderson was available to speak with him, Chris sipped his coffee. He knew he shouldn't hold his breath. Anderson's call to Susan might just have been a knee-jerk reaction, in which case Anderson might not really expect him to call back from Australia. But less than a minute later a slightly breathless voice came on the line.

'Tom Anderson here. Sorry for the delay, I've just arrived back from my gym. Trying to stay fit at my age is getting harder to do. Now, it's Chris, isn't it? Susan's son?'

For one of the few times in his professional life, Chris felt overwhelmed. 'Ah, yes, sir. Chris Baxter. I really appreciate you taking my call.'

'No, I'm very grateful that you called back so promptly.' Anderson paused. 'Terrible business what happened to my brother in Indonesia. I loved him. Reconciling his death was always difficult for my parents. Although they were proud that Jimmy had joined the Peace Corps, they never understood why he stayed on in Indonesia after the other members of the corps had returned home when all that political turmoil broke out. Jimmy assured them that he was far removed from the troubles, but clearly that was not so. I don't think my parents ever got over his death.'

'I can understand that,' said Chris quietly.

'I've learned from your mother that Jimmy's death was not a random incident but the result of a planned robbery that went wrong. I'm actually glad my parents aren't alive to know this terrible truth.' He paused for a moment. 'And what's even more galling is that the man who was involved in Jimmy's death is someone who has gone on to make a successful career for himself as a property developer, someone who has acquired wealth and status after denying my brother the same opportunity. I find this a hard pill to swallow.'

'I can well imagine. Are you aware that I've had problems with Carmichael?'

'Your mother alluded to that, but suggested that I talk to you about it.'

'To be frank, Mr Anderson . . .' Chris began.

'Please, call me Tom.'

'Tom,' said Chris. He briefly explained how he had been writing a book about the men who had been with his mother in Java in 1968.

'Three of those men have been very cooperative, but Alan Carmichael has not. When he learned I was writing the book, he shut the door on me.'

'It is his right to maintain his privacy, of course,' Anderson said. 'I've had many people wanting to write my biography, but I have discouraged them because when I want my story told, I'll do it myself. Not that I have any time to write a book.'

'Yes, I understand that. But Carmichael had his lawyer send me a letter warning me about writing the book. Perhaps foolishly, I sent him a letter back saying that I would go ahead with the book with or without his cooperation, although I would refrain from saying anything defamatory about him.'

'Did he accept your compromise?' asked Anderson.

'I didn't hear anything more from his lawyer, but my family and I have subsequently been intimidated,' said Chris, and then explained about the loosened wheel nuts and the mysterious blue car.

'Can you prove that Carmichael was behind them?'

'No, I can't, but a friend of mine, an ex-journalist, has discovered that two other investigative journalists who were separately looking into Carmichael's business affairs over the years were killed in road accidents.'

'Now that is a coincidence. You're quite sure of those facts?'

'Absolutely, and I didn't want my family or my friends exposed to any more intimidation, so I had my lawyer send another letter saying that I was no longer interested in including Alan Carmichael in my book.'

'I see. Has anything suspicious happened since then?'

'No, but the letter has only just been sent. As a further precaution, I'm sending my daughter over to the other side of the country to stay with her mother.'

'Pleased to hear that. So tell me, Chris, how do you feel about what's been happening to you?' asked the financier.

'Very angry, as you can imagine. My agent is hopeful my book will still be published, but I feel it has been substantially weakened. Because of his position, Carmichael knows that he can do what he likes, including mounting a long and expensive litigation which I can't afford to fight. Now I'm beginning to think that he is literally getting away with murder.'

'How have your other books been received, Chris?'

'This is my first one. I was previously a journalist,

however times are tough in the media and I'm a single father with a teenage daughter, so I was hoping to switch to writing books so I can give Megan a stable home life.'

'I see. It's a shame that you won't be challenging Carmichael, but that is a difficult thing to do without concrete proof, and as you have explained, that is very hard to get. Thank your mother again for letting me know what happened to my brother, and I hope things work out for you, Chris.'

'Thanks again for taking my call,' Chris replied and rang off, pleased that Thomas Anderson had taken the trouble to speak with him, but disappointed that the conversation had not led to anything.

'What did he say?' asked Susan as Chris walked back into the kitchen.

'Nothing much really, but he was pleasant and polite in that friendly American way.'

'Well, I'm glad I wrote to him.' She looked at her son. 'Now what?'

'Y'know what, Mum? I'm going to take a bit of a break. Megan's off to Perth and Georgia is coming up, so I'm going to spend a couple of days with her. I've even organised some time off, so I'm going to take each day as it comes.'

Susan smiled. 'That's a very good idea, especially as I shall be away myself. David and I plan to go over to Core Creek farm again. He says he's interested in looking for some land to buy.'

'What, to farm?'

'Yes. He thinks he would like to develop a project of his own. Tells me that he's getting sick of travelling.'

'Well, good for him. Seems a lot for him to take on, though.'

'Rubbish. Your sixties and seventies can be very productive and exciting times. We're looking at an interesting project that will keep us on our toes.'

'We? Are you investing in this?' asked Chris, a little concerned.

'Not at all. But I'm excited by David's ideas. He's interested in bush foods and he wants not only to grow them successfully, but to find an innovative way to market them. He's met a couple of young indigenous agriculturalists who have been growing bush foods for years, and they want to work with us.'

'And you want to be part of this? You're amazing, Mum. Always up for something new.' Chris grinned admiringly at his mother.

'It won't be all work,' said Susan. 'We're planning to do some travelling around Europe too.'

Chris gave her a hug. 'Yes, I remember your hint about Italy. I think it's wonderful.'

'What's wonderful?' asked Megan as she came into the kitchen.

'Bunny and David are thinking of starting their own farm.'

'What! And leave Neverend?' Megan looked stricken. 'Are you going to sell this house?'

'Of course not, sweetie,' soothed Susan. 'David is just looking for some land for an agricultural development.'

'Well, don't you do anything while I'm away, will you,' insisted Megan. Then she added, 'If you have a farm, can I ride there? Maybe keep Squire there?'

'Megs, Squire belongs to Mollie,' Chris reminded her gently.

Seeing Megan's worried expression, Susan said, 'Oh, who knows what plans David has. He once mentioned alpacas. But I promise that we won't do a thing without first talking to you. You just have fun with your mum.'

'Okay. What about you, Dad, what are you doing?'

'I'm hanging around, sweetie. I'll be looking after Biddi and Bunny's garden while Bunny and David swan around the countryside looking at acreage. When Georgia comes up, I'll show her the sights. We didn't get the chance to do much last time she was here.'

'I'll miss all the fun.'

'Don't be silly. David and Georgia will be here again,' said Susan briskly. 'You're the one going on the exciting trip. Be sure to send us photos!'

Megan simply rolled her eyes. 'Of course I will. Ruby and Jazzy and Toby want updates every day.'

*

Chris felt his spirits lift and a smile break out as he saw Georgia exit the plane. He hugged her warmly as he took her bag.

'Was Megan okay? Thanks so much for meeting her and getting her onto the Perth flight.'

'No problem, and she was absolutely fine. She had a nice fat book and said it would keep her occupied for hours. And she had her music, of course.'

'I hope she has fun. I know she misses Jill, even though they're in regular contact. Okay, let's hit the road. I thought you might like to explore Neverend a bit more before we go back to Jean's place. I know my town is only forty-five minutes away from this airport, but believe me, it's a world away.'

'Fine. The metropolis and environs of Neverend it is.'

'By the way, we have the place to ourselves. Mum and David are off seeking land.'

Georgia shook her head after Chris explained Susan and David's new idea. 'What a pair. Mac won't venture further than his favourite restaurant, pub and the old press club hangout with his mates.'

Chris chuckled. 'You must bring him up sometime. Expand his horizons. He and Mum would enjoy each other's company and I think he'd get on with David, too.'

'You're comfortable about your mother's relationship with David now?' asked Georgia.

'I am. Of course, that has a lot to do from you, and Megan, for that matter,' Chris replied.

'I'm glad we helped you see things from a broader perspective.'

'True, but it's also because I don't feel so . . . isolated any more. I feel positive, hopeful, joyful, thanks to you,' admitted Chris. 'Even if I don't have much of a job happening at the moment,' he added ruefully.

'So what did Thomas Anderson have to say?' asked Georgia.

She listened as Chris told her about their conversation, and laughed when he finished up with, 'He also hinted that he didn't need a biographer.'

'Pity about that. That would have been some coup.'

Chris concentrated on the road for a moment before sighing. 'Yes. I know. Maybe I'm over the idea of doing biography. Everyone has something they want to keep secret. I'm beginning to think it's a rare person who is willing to expose every facet of themselves, their life, warts and all. People want to present to the world the image of themselves they like best, and not the person that others actually see.'

'But Mark, Evan and David aren't like that.'

'No, you're right, they're not, probably because they have nothing to hide. Honestly, Alan Carmichael has made me look at things in a very pessimistic light. I thought journalism was tough, but this book business has me stumped.'

Georgia sighed. 'Chris, I'm afraid that it's just got a whole lot harder. I spoke to your publisher this morning. I explained that for reasons that I could not divulge you would no longer be including Alan Carmichael in your book. At all.'

'And what did the publisher say?' asked Chris, a lump of lead settling in his stomach.

'Basically, that without the big name of Carmichael there could be no book. I argued that the other three Australians were worthy subjects to write about. Unfortunately, he was adamant. You agreed in your contract that the book would feature Carmichael, but now you can't deliver what you agreed to. Chris, I am so sorry that your book has come to this. I really, really tried to talk them into honouring your contract, but they just wouldn't agree to it.'

Chris pulled the car over to the side of the road and sat silently for a few moments. If he was truthful with himself, he was not surprised. Carmichael was a very big presence in Australia and to be unable to write about him after promising to do so . . . well, he could see the publisher's point of view. But it was a hard blow.

'So that's that, then. Just as well I didn't get that advance. I might have spent it. I guess a new computer will have to wait. Carmichael has certainly stuffed up our lives, first my mother's and now mine. I just wish there was some way I could expose all the evil he's done, but I can't. I don't want to put my family's lives at risk ever again. I feel so angry. I don't think that I'll ever get back on track and I'll be driving a courier van for the rest of my life, all because of that man,' said Chris angrily.

'Look, I know this is really hard to take, but I'm sure we'll be able to come up with another idea. What is it that you really want to do, Chris?' Georgia asked calmly.

'I just love to write. Writing is all I've ever wanted to do, even when I was very young.' He swallowed. The rage and unfairness he felt seemed to roll over him in waves. 'So should I start my own town newspaper?' he snapped angrily. 'Reveal the underbelly of beautiful Neverend? The secret of Mrs Hampton's scone recipe? Who's borrowing whose bull in the dead of night? The incestuousness of a small community where everyone knows everything about everyone? Maybe do an exposé on our troubled youth, hampered by lack of jobs and exposed to a drug culture?' He drew a breath and then started to speak more calmly. 'But you know, Georgia, I find joy in this small town. Neverend has evolved into a beautiful yet hip and artistic place with great local food and eateries, music and even fabulous coffee. And I've seen buskers a lot worse than the ones who perform in our main street. This town's community spirit embodies the philosophy of accepting new arrivals and alternative lifestyles. It's a place where a bearded bloke wearing combat boots and a yellow taffeta cocktail dress can sell his homemade muesli and no one thinks it an odd thing for a veteran of the Iraq War to do. What the town doesn't accept is new money trying to change the old ways, or slick tourism pushing out the locals. Rather, it embraces who we are and what we have with vigour and passion. Is that enough to fill the daily newspaper?'

'Whoa! You don't seriously want to start up a newspaper, do you?' said Georgia incredulously.

'No, of course not. I'm sorry, Georgia. I was just letting off steam,' said Chris. But even as he made the excuse, he realised he was telling Georgia not about himself, but about his affection for his town, Neverend. For years it had been the home that he had dismissively taken for granted. Now he knew that it was a special place, and he was lucky to be part of its makeup. He was grateful for that, especially in light of Georgia's dismal news.

'I know how frustrated you must be.' Georgia touched his arm.

'I think that frustration hardly covers what I'm feeling at present.'

She was silent a moment and then asked, 'You've never told me about your assignments when you were working as a foreign correspondent. What were some of the tough ones? I know you loved the States, and if you were working as a foreign correspondent today would you have liked working in Asia?'

Chris started up the car again, very glad for this change of subject.

'I loved everywhere I was posted,' he said, enthusiasm creeping into his voice. 'I loved the challenge of a new place with different attitudes and customs. An unknown country, people who think differently from us. And you know, I always seemed to luck out with stories. Things just fell in my path. Your father used to say that maybe I was simply open to new things, prepared to follow a hunch and trust my instincts. Once, in the middle of Mexico's badlands, I happened to meet, through a series of accidents, the head of a drugs cartel who also happened to be the richest man in Mexico. He invited me to drink tequila with him. Once I was in a supermarket in the deep south of America and I saw a man buy enough food and personal items for a whole school. So I followed him home to find he had thirty kids and five wives. Ah, Georgia, I have a zillion stories that I can bore you with,' said Chris with a wry smile.

'I don't think they sound very boring at all. So you don't miss that life?' she asked.

'Sometimes,' he admitted frankly. 'But now only in short bursts. If I'm honest with myself, in between the excitement there was a heck of a lot of tedium.'

'I'd like to hear more.'

'Ah, some other time. Ask my mother. I sent her long emails, and I think she used to print them out and keep them. Shall we stop in town for a swish lunch or are you ready for a sandwich on the verandah?'

'Do you have to ask?'

'Sangers it is. With fresh bread baked this morning, Mum's corned beef and homemade tomato relish, all

383

washed down with a crisp Pinot Gris. You live high on the hog when you come to Neverend,' said Chris with a laugh, feeling a little more cheerful.

*

Chris and Georgia didn't leave the house for the rest of the day. Chris still felt very depressed when he thought about the book and Georgia did her best to cheer him up. They made meals and cuddled in front of the fire with the cat between them. It was a novelty sharing a bed and waking up together in the morning and then showering together; it was a tantalising glimpse of how good their relationship might be. But Chris didn't want to allow himself to think past the moment. Especially now.

Over breakfast, Georgia raised another thorny issue as she helped herself to some of Susan's marmalade to go with her toast.

'Chris, I'm not sure that this is going to work.'

'I don't understand, Georgia. I thought we were getting along really well. Do you want to go home?'

'No, Chris, you've missed my meaning. We're getting along too well, and for the record, I have to tell you that I don't make a habit of sleeping with my clients. But I'm your agent and I think that our private and professional relationship is becoming a little confused. Moreover, I'm also the agent who has badly let you down. I seriously think that you should look for someone else to represent your interests, someone who is more detached.'

'So what you are saying is that we aren't mature enough to be able to separate our private lives from our professional ones? Do you really think that you would not be able to give an honest appraisal of my work because I could take offence and ruin our relationship? Well, that's nonsense. I can accept brutal honesty if I know that it is sincerely meant. I can also accept bad news when I know that you did your best for me. I think that we can still work together, but if it turns out that you're right, and our relationship begins to suffer, then I will look for another agent. Of course, they won't be half as good as you.' Chris smiled at Georgia and then gave her a kiss. 'Is that a deal?'

'If you say so, Chris.' Georgia took a sip of her coffee. 'Don't you think you'd better get me up to Jean's place before half the day has gone?'

'Hmm. You're right. Time to hit the road.'

Georgia stood up. 'Chris, your life is what you make it. This setback is just that, a setback, nothing more, right? Think about what you want, what's important to you, and where you want to be not just next month or next year, but in five or ten years' time.' She headed out of the room and he heard her call out cheekily from the hallway, 'I know where I'd like to be.'

As they both headed off to get dressed, Chris's phone rang.

'Hi, Dad!'

'How's my favourite girl? What's happening, are you having fun? You're up very early.'

'Yeah, I am. We're all going over to Rottnest Island today, so we have to get an early start. It's too cold to swim, but it sounds fun.'

'How're you getting on with the boys?'

'They're okay. They kinda like me, I think. They're older now, you know.'

Chris smiled to himself, wondering how much two ten-year-olds could have matured in little more than six months. 'That's great. I'm having fun too, Georgia is here and I'm taking her out to Jean Hay's place today to take photos, then we might do a bit of a twirl around the district. Watch out for those quokkas on Rottnest, they can be scary.'

Megan giggled. 'Don't be silly, Dad. I've seen pictures of them and they are really cute.'

'Glad you are having a good time. I miss you.'

'Miss you, too, Dad. See ya.'

*

For the next two mornings, Chris and Georgia rose well before dawn, rugged themselves up and then Chris drove Georgia out to Jean Hay's place, Applebrook.

'I need to be able to photograph this place in different lights, so I need an early start. Thank you for bringing me out here at this ungodly hour.'

'Not a problem, although I have to say that I like picking you up and bringing you back home a lot more than dropping you off.'

'I like that bit, too,' said Georgia.

During the day, Chris found that he missed Georgia's company, but their time together at night more than made up for it, and he was increasingly aware how special Georgia was becoming to him. So it was with somewhat mixed feelings that he welcomed Susan and David back from their visit to Core Creek farm.

'So interesting and inspiring to see what they're doing,' said Susan.

'They're a big operation, very serious,' said David. 'I plan to be less ambitious. Maybe I could divide some land and use one part to grow organic food and the other to produce bush food.'

'I'd love to raise alpacas, for wool, not meat. I couldn't bear to send them off after seeing those pretty faces and knowing their personalities,' said Susan.

'We don't give the stock names,' said David with a smile. 'But I'm not sure about alpacas. Anyway, it's still a bit of a dream at the moment. After running big projects and overseeing other people's properties for so long, I'm

386

yearning to do my own thing. Mind you, I've produced some lovely grapes and olives in Italy, but I'm never there long enough to enjoy a whole season.'

'Surely you have the time to do that now?' asked Chris.

'I don't think I could persuade your mother to spend months in Italy.'

'You're right. A month or so would be great, but after that I'd miss Neverend, I'm afraid,' sighed Susan. 'I would like a new challenge, though.'

'It's fun to dream and a lovely excuse to tootle around the countryside,' added David.

Later Chris and David sat out on the verandah in the winter sun before Chris had to leave to pick up Georgia.

'I'm so sorry that the publisher decided not to go ahead with your book,' said David.

'Yes, I suppose these things happen. And I'm sorry that you won't see yourself in print.'

'Good heavens, Chris, as if I care about that. Do you think things will settle down with Carmichael?' asked David. 'Susan has told me about your suspicions.'

'Well, since I told him I wasn't including him in the book, I haven't had any strange vehicles following me, if that's what you mean.'

'I'm still pretty stunned to hear about what you've been through, and what happened back in Bogor. Jimmy's death was such a dreadful shock to all of us.'

'I was amazed that Alan was so anti-Chinese in those days. I wonder how he feels about the Chinese now?' wondered Chris. 'He's done business with them.'

'I expect that he sees them more as capitalists than communists now, so he feels it's okay to do business with them,' said David. 'But as far as your mother and I are concerned, Alan and his life have nothing more to do with us.'

'The same goes for me. I'm glad you and Mum seem to have joined forces,' said Chris carefully.

'I love your mother, Chris,' said David simply. 'I think I always have. Funny how things work out. Mind you, she has made it very clear that she is attached to this area, so I've decided that if you can't beat 'em, join 'em,' David laughed.

'Does that mean you're looking for land in this area? Would you build a house?'

'I'd like to be close at hand to any land we bought, but wherever it is, it can't be too far away from here.'

'That's sounds like a good plan to me.'

When Chris drove to Jean Hay's house that evening, he felt ridiculously excited about seeing Georgia. He parked outside the front fence and entered through the old gate under the sagging archway covered in a rose vine, although there were few leaves and no flowers on it. That needs pruning, he thought to himself.

Jean's old dog ambled over to greet him with a waving tail, sniffing Chris's hand before sinking back onto his bed on the front verandah.

The beautiful door with the rose-coloured glass panels was open, so Chris knocked and called out. When he received no answer, he walked down the hall to the rear of the house and heard Georgia's voice in the back garden. The two women were sitting in the sun in old wicker chairs.

Georgia jumped up and gave Chris a hug. 'We're enjoying the last of the afternoon sunshine. It's so sheltered back here.'

'Hi, Jean, how're you doing?'

'I'll make some tea and coffee, shall I, Jean?' suggested Georgia.

'Yes please, dear. You know where the biscuits are.' Jean turned to Chris as Georgia headed inside. 'It's been

388

so lovely having Georgia here. What a wonderful girl. You're a lucky man.'

'I know it. Did Georgia take a lot of photos?'

'Oh, I suppose so, dear. She went for lots of walks. Poor old Moses, my dog, couldn't keep up and came home. He's a bit like me. I'm not keeping up as well as I have been.'

'Are you okay?' asked Chris anxiously. 'Anything we can do?'

'Georgia has done more than enough. In the last couple of days she's vacuumed rugs and cleaned windows. She's done a lot of dusting, too. There are so many things I've neglected and Georgia's kindness has only reinforced that. I can't even pick all the mandarins from my tree. You must take some with you. They're the best they've been for years.'

'I'm sure you've just slowed down in the cold weather. Come spring you'll blossom,' said Chris.

'You know, Chris, Georgia has made me see this place through new eyes. I look back at its past. I like to think of all the memories and family history that is here. Georgia has such fresh young eyes, she keeps seeing the potential of this property.'

'That's understandable,' said Chris.

'She's full of ideas. Like the old barn. Georgia suggested that it could be reborn as a lovely family retreat, or a cottage.'

'Could you rent it out as a farmstay sort of thing, or use it as somewhere for the grandchildren to stay?'

'Heavens, do you think something like that would work? But I'm not sure I would like to take such a venture on at my age.'

'You could make a bit of pocket money renting it out,' said Chris encouragingly.

Chris got up as Georgia appeared and pulled over a

cane table for Georgia to set down the tea tray and then she poured Jean a cup of tea.

'Are you happy with the photos you took?' he asked her.

'I think so. I've resisted going through them. I'm trying to work by instinct and not be a slave to technology.'

'Goodness, we were so judicious with the pictures we took with our old Box Brownie. Couldn't snap away at everything, we would soon have run out of film. And you had to wait a week for the prints to come back to the chemist shop,' said Jean with a smile. 'A bit different now. Georgia took hundreds of photos.'

'But you took enough photos to have a wonderful record of this house and your family,' Georgia said to her. She turned to Chris and added, 'Jean is going to lend me her photos so that I can do parallel illustrations. It's going to make a wonderful book.' Her voice was filled with enthusiasm.

'A book! Wonderful idea,' said Chris. 'Do you have a good agent who could sell the concept to a publisher? I can recommend one.'

'Silly! Even if I do get it published, it won't make me rich, but maybe Jean will be able to get some of her fencing fixed. We're going fifty–fifty on any profits,' Georgia explained.

'My dear, that's not necessary,' Jean protested.

'We agreed to be partners,' said Georgia firmly. 'And Jean, this place could do with some work. New fencing, a bit of weeding, that sort of thing.'

Jean shrugged. 'I know, dear. It's a shame the land's not being utilised. There's seventy acres out there, all the way to the river flats, and it's being overrun with weeds. My husband was always very particular about invasive species, but I've had to let the place go, I'm afraid I just don't think I have the motivation to do any of that anymore. There comes a time in one's life when things start to become too much of a problem.'

'Jean told me that she is thinking of selling up,' said Georgia.

Chris stared at them. 'Really? Are you sure, Jean? That's amazing. This could be quite a perfect solution for someone I know.'

'What do you mean?' asked Georgia. 'Who do you know?'

Chris nodded his head, almost laughing. 'Jean, Mum and her friend David are looking for land somewhere in this area so that David can develop a bush food programme. Quite possibly your property would be suitable. May I suggest they come and see you?'

'Of course, dear. I'd love to see Susan. And really it might just be the right time for me to move on, although I would be very sorry to leave Applebrook.'

'David is an agronomist who lives to restore soils and keep creeks clear of weeds and experiment with sustainable crops,' said Chris. 'He would take very good care of this land.'

Georgia stared at Chris. 'What a fabulous idea. I do hope it works out for you all.'

Jean took Chris's hand. 'When you've been around as long as I have, you learn to trust and simply deal with what life throws you. Maybe this is exactly the right time for me to leave this place.' She patted his hand. 'I hope you don't mind, but Georgia was telling me about what happened with your book, Chris. You'll see, dear. Something will come along and things will work out as it seems to be for me, and you'll wonder why on earth you got so upset at the time.'

'I hope you're right, Jean,' said Chris.

Jean smiled and picked up her cup. 'Oh, I know I am, dear.'

12

IT SEEMED TO CHRIS that suddenly everyone else had a project, a plan, but he didn't. He felt raw, exposed and vulnerable. But he tried not to let it show.

Chris missed Georgia madly after she returned to Sydney. Her visit had marked a milestone in cementing their relationship. But Chris wasn't sure quite what lay ahead for them both, and he decided that it was best just to take things day by day.

Megan returned from Perth full of stories of her adventures. The first evening back she settled on the couch next to Chris while he was reading a book.

'I missed you, Dad.'

'I missed you too, sweetie. But you had fun, right?'

'Yep. Mum and I are besties now.'

'But haven't you always been pals with your mother?'

Chris asked.

Megan wriggled a bit, then said, 'I suppose, but it's different this time. Now we're, like, grown-up girlfriends. We talked about everything, even sex.'

'Did you? That's good,' said Chris warily. 'Do you have any questions you'd like to ask me?' he added, rather hoping that Jill had covered everything.

'Are you having a really serious relationship with Georgia?' Megan asked, earnestly.

Chris paused a moment. He really didn't want to have to explain his love life to his daughter, but he realised that she had a right to the truth about himself and Georgia.

'Yes, I am, honey, because we love each other.'

'Is Georgia going to come and live with us?' Megan asked.

'I don't think so. She has a job in Sydney. What if we moved back to the city?' he asked suddenly.

'No way! I'm not ever leaving Neverend. Tell Georgia she has to come up here. Okay, Dad?' She jumped up.

'Sure, I'll tell her you said so.'

When Chris later told Susan what Megan had said, Susan smiled.

'That's all good,' she said. 'Megan has settled so well in Neverend now. She knows she has two happy parents, even though they are on opposite sides of the country, and a network of friends around her. She's found where she likes to be. What about you?'

Chris sighed. 'I guess I don't feel quite the same way. I'm glad Jill is happy and that Megan feels secure with us in Neverend, but Mum, let's face it, I'm hardly doing well financially. I seem to be no further ahead with my career decisions than I was when I first arrived here more than six months ago. And I have no idea where my relationship with Georgia is headed, either.'

'I don't suppose Georgia would consider moving to Neverend?'

'Possibly. She works from home, and I suppose she can travel anywhere to see clients. But that's not the only factor in play. I want to be able to be at least an equal financial partner in this relationship,' said Chris. 'Losing the book deal has pulled the rug out from under me yet again.'

'Yes, I know things seem bleak at this stage, but I'm sure that will change. Something will turn up,' said Susan, comfortingly.

Chris was not so sure.

But then a change of luck came out of left field.

Chris and Susan were in Coffs Harbour on a shopping expedition, and they'd just popped into the large supermarket for some groceries when a pleasantly voiced woman, a bit younger than Chris, stopped Susan.

'Mrs Baxter! How lovely to see you. Remember me? I'm Bronwyn, Allsop. I'm Bronwyn Johnston now, complete with two kids. I was in your class for three years. I mean, they were different classes, not the same one three times over.' She laughed amiably.

'Of course, Bronwyn, how lovely to see you. This is my son, Chris,' said Susan warmly, gesturing to Chris.

Bronwyn nodded. 'I remember Chris from school, but you were a few years ahead of me, so I don't suppose you remember me.'

'But I do know who you are,' said Chris with a smile. 'I used to listen to you all the time on local radio. Haven't heard you lately, though – are you still with the ABC?'

'Absolutely, but I've been working on the south coast for a while. I'm just back here now. I've been promoted. I'm the local station manager.'

'Congratulations,' said Susan. 'That's wonderful. You have done well.'

'Thank you. I've followed your career, too, Chris. I've so enjoyed reading your columns in the *Coastal Star*. They are very entertaining and you certainly display an intimate understanding of this area. I suppose you'll be off to another posting soon.'

'I'm staying in Neverend for a while longer.'

'Chris has moved back home. He's writing a book,' Susan interjected.

Chris shrugged. 'Actually, the book deal fell through, so my principal job is driving a courier van for Shaun French.'

Bronwyn cocked her head and looked at him for a moment. 'Are you really planning on staying in Neverend? If you are, you might be just what I'm looking for. One of our journalists has taken up a position in Canberra, so I'm looking for an experienced journo to replace him.'

Chris hesitated. 'Unfortunately I've had no experience in radio, Bronwyn. I'm a print journalist.'

'Chris, a good journo is a good journo, regardless of the medium. You can always be trained to do radio.'

'Are you serious?' he asked, with an incredulous laugh.

Susan seemed to catch the hint of interest in his voice. 'Chris, I think that sounds like a terrific idea.'

Bronwyn leaned towards him. 'Look, why don't you put in an application? There will be lots of others applying, but you have a great deal of journalistic experience and you certainly know this area. I can give you a try for a couple of months and if it all works out the way I think it will, then you can become a permanent staff member.'

'Suits me,' said Chris casually, but his eyes were sparkling.

'Give me a call at the office after nine. As the station manager, I do the breakfast shift, so I'll be off air by then. I'd give you one of my cards, but I never have them on me.'

'Thanks, Bronwyn. I'll call you after nine,' said Chris.

'Great. Gotta go. My kids have probably filled the trolley with junk by now. Talk soon. See you, Mrs B.'

'It's Susan,' she called out as Bronwyn hurried down the aisle to find her children. Susan turned delightedly to Chris. 'Can you believe that, Chris? Such a wonderful opportunity, don't you think?'

'Mum, I may not be suitable,' said Chris, shaking his head.

'Don't be such a pessimist.'

'All right, I'll give it a whirl. Local radio might not be Washington DC, but reliable news is important whatever the subject and wherever it's broadcast,' Chris said, warming up to the idea. 'I have to say, Bronwyn seems bright and capable.'

'She always was a smart girl. I remember that there was a write-up about her in one of the local papers some time back. It seems that although Bronwyn was always being courted to move on to bigger things she and her husband prefer living in the country. Neither of them wants to move to the big smoke.'

Chris didn't answer, but he was thinking hard. While this offer could be the answer to his problems, would working in local radio be too stifling? He pulled out the shopping list.

'Have we got everything? Corned beef, tomato paste, laundry detergent, a job for Chris . . . Yep, looks like we can tick those off and head home.'

Susan laughed and tucked her arm through her son's as he pushed the trolley towards the checkout.

*

Georgia was thrilled at his news when he called her later on. 'That's wonderful, Chris. If it comes off, you can retire from the courier business and go back to what you do best, writing and reporting the news. A book can wait.'

'There's a lot that could go wrong, Georgie, but I am going to apply for the job. What's the worst that can happen? I'll be given a try-out and prove to be no good for radio.'

'I'm sure you'll be great. Anyway, we'll keep our fingers crossed that Bronwyn is bowled over by your talents. I'm proud of you, my darling. And I haven't given up on you as my client either.'

*

'Are you going to be a DJ on the radio? How cool!' exclaimed Megan that night at dinner.

'No, I'll be one of the station's journalists, writing the news and reading it on air.'

'That's cool, too,' said Megan, graciously. 'Wait till I tell everyone at school.'

'Whoa, I've just put in my application. I haven't got the job yet,' said Chris with a grin.

For the first time in ages, Chris felt re-energised and enthused. Radio would be a new medium for him to master and he would be a working journalist again, doing what he did best, keeping people informed about the issues that impacted on their lives.

*

One afternoon a few days later, Chris was at Jean's house chopping some firewood when his phone rang. He lowered the axe, mopped his brow and answered. He felt a thrill as Georgie's voice came on the line.

'Hey, you. Where are you? Can you chat?'

'Georgie, I always want to chat with you. When are you coming up? I miss you,' he said. 'And why are you calling me? What can't wait till tonight?'

Georgia took a breath. 'I'm actually wearing my agent's hat, Chris, not my "I love you" one. I was at a book launch earlier in the week and met the new CEO of Port Publishing, an independent outfit that manages to attract some pretty good writers. Paul likes to find people with something interesting or provocative to write about, politicians, academics, former diplomats, those sorts of people. Several of his books have done surprisingly well. Anyway, he agreed to meet me and I went to see him this morning.'

'What about? A new client?'

'No, a client I've had for a while. You. I pitched an idea for a book that I know you could write and he loved it.'

Chris was silent for a moment. 'Oh? And what sort of book would that be?'

'I know I should have run my idea past you and I'm sorry I didn't, but sometimes you have to strike as soon as you see an opportunity. I showed Paul those couple of sample chapters you wrote for your first book. He really likes your writing style,' said Georgia, enthusiastically.

'So what is it I'm going to write about this time around?' said Chris cautiously, wondering what Georgia was going to come up with.

'I mentioned some of the stories that you'd told me about your time overseas, not just the articles you've written, but the background to them, the digging you did to unearth them. You've had some extremely fascinating, funny, scary experiences and I think you should share them.'

'Who'd be interested?' began Chris.

'Don't be silly, young man,' said Georgia briskly. 'The work you've done as a reporter around the world is a dream job to most people. Many foreign correspondents are celebrities.'

Chris couldn't help but smile. 'Foreign correspondents are supposed to be out of sight, telling the story, not at the centre of it. Anyway, it's not always as exciting as it sounds.'

'You're a terrific raconteur, Chris. You can make anything sound exciting. You can tell the story behind the headlines. I think that the way you tracked stories down could be as interesting as the stories themselves.'

'I'm not sure. Is this pushing one's own barrow really me? Your father doesn't believe in journos thrusting themselves into the limelight. Besides, look what happened to my last book effort. Maybe I don't have one in me,' he sighed.

'Chris, have you any idea how many books get turned down by publishers?' said Georgia, sounding slightly exasperated. 'A whole lot more than get published. And it's frequently the case that a writer's first attempt ends in failure. But even if it does, just trying to write something is good practice. When you were working on your first book, one of the things you told me you got out of it was that you found your voice. You learned to move from being a newspaper writer to being a book writer, so that experience was worthwhile.'

'I suppose so,' Chris said quietly, but he was secretly pleased to know that Georgia had listened to what he'd said.

Georgia ignored his comment and continued, 'Only in novels does an author have a sensational overnight success. In real life, writing a book is a long, hard slog, and even then there is no guarantee of success. I think that you could make it as a writer, but only if your heart is really in it. So would you please write down a few thoughts that I can show to the publisher?'

'Hmm. Let me think about it.'

'An expression of interest from a dedicated publisher isn't to be sneezed at, Chris,' said Georgia, sternly.

Chris could hear the excitement in her voice, the eagerness, the enthusiasm. 'What an ungrateful sod I am. I don't deserve you. I wish I could kiss you. Okay, I'll give it a shot, Georgie,' he said contritely.

'Fantastic, I'm so pleased. Can you get down to Sydney any time soon and bring your ideas? I'll set up a meeting with Paul and we'll go in and see him.'

'Any excuse to see you! But seriously, I would love to have another attempt at a book. Thank you for this opportunity. I love you, Georgie.'

'I love you, too.'

Chris rang off and returned to his wood-chopping detail with renewed energy. New opportunities seemed to be springing up everywhere.

*

Chris began to put in long hours on his writing again, gathering together his old stories and looking at the emails that he'd sent his mother over the years, pleased that she had always been reluctant to discard anything. He was often deep in thought as he wandered around the house, out onto the verandah and into the garden before returning to his desk. Even Megan noticed his deep absorption in the task and teased him.

'Gosh, Dad, you're on another planet half the time! I hope the new book's coming together for you.'

'Yes, honey. I'm having a bit of fun with it, actually. It's bringing back a lot of memories.'

'That's great. When can I read it?'

'Oh, when I think it's worth reading, but I have to say that I'm enjoying the project.'

'That's a good sign, isn't it?'

'Yes. I hope so.' He gave her a hug. 'How're you going?'

'Good, Dad. Really good.' She held on to him for a moment and then skipped out of the room. Chris grinned watching her go and then returned to the satisfying work in front of him.

*

'Do you think you could set up a meeting with the publisher?' Chris asked Georgia. 'I have something to show you, and the airlines are having a special this weekend, so I thought I might get the earliest flight down.'

'Yes, I'll make the appointment for us first thing. After that, do you think you would have time to meet Dad? He wants to catch up with you, and of course he'd rather do that over lunch than on the phone.'

'And you?'

'I'll be making us a special dinner.'

'I like the sound of that. So next Saturday's a date, then?'

*

Chris strolled into Greasy Greeks feeling pleased with himself. The meeting with the publisher had gone well. Paul had shown obvious enthusiasm for his stories and there would be no problem publishing them because they weren't at all controversial. Certainly there wouldn't be any difficulties like the ones Alan Carmichael and his lawyers had posed with Chris's first book.

Chris saw Mac sitting at their favourite table. Walking over to join him, Chris glanced around the restaurant, recognising a few familiar media faces, although he didn't feel like one of them anymore. He realised he'd moved away from the hub of things. He was no longer the harried journo hunting for stories, chasing unpromising leads flung at him by the news editor, always facing a deadline.

Mac rose and held out his hand, a big smile on his face. Chris gave him a bear hug.

'What's that for?' mumbled Mac as he sat back down. 'I said I'm paying for lunch this time. Or are you trying to worm your way into the family?'

Chris laughed. 'Maybe, or maybe I'm thanking you for being such a good friend and having such a wonderful daughter.' He nodded at the room. 'You know, Mac, suddenly I don't feel like I belong here anymore. I'm not one of them now.'

'You and me both, sport. Not a lot of familiar faces around.'

'No, it's more than that. Last time we came here, I felt on the outer because I'd left my job. Now I feel as though I've moved on.'

'Driving a van? Or writing the great journo book?'

'Both, I'm multi-tasking,' Chris quipped as he started to read the specials scribbled on the front of the menu. 'The moussaka is always good here. I think I'll have that.'

'You always have that. Try something different.'

Chris chuckled. 'All right, I will.' Just as he put down the menu, a familiar face joined them.

'Hello, stranger.'

'John Miller!' Chris leapt to his feet to shake hands with his old editor from Trinity Press. 'How are you keeping?'

'I can't complain. Been a few changes at Trinity in the last few weeks.'

'Can you sit down and tell me what's happened? I'd be interested in knowing,' said Chris, genuinely pleased to see his old friend and boss.

After greeting Mac, John pulled up a chair. 'Well, the best news is that Honeywell has gone. You remember that pompous English twat? Had no idea what he was doing and under him the paper went into very rapid decline. Now the paper has to begin rebuilding quickly while there's still something there to regenerate.'

'I'm pleased to hear that piece of news,' said Chris, with a small smile.

'Running into you is fortuitous, Chris. We are now on the lookout for more really first-class journalists, of which you are most definitely one, so how would you like your old job back? If you still don't want to be a foreign correspondent, I would be happy to find you a job based in Sydney. Brad Jones is retiring early. He's got some serious health issues, and you could easily take his place.'

Chris tried to keep a straight face at John's surprising announcement. 'I'm sorry about Brad. Nice chap. John, I'll need to think about your offer, which I have to say is very generous,' he said carefully. 'How long have I got?'

'Maybe a week or so. But don't leave it too long. More journos than positions these days.'

'I'll think it over, and thanks again, I'll get back to you with my answer.'

Chris leaned back in his seat after John had fare-welled them and gone back to his table. He could hardly believe it. Two job offers in such a short time. Now he had options, but the trouble was, which option should he take?

'That's good news,' said Mac. 'Will you take the job?'

'Part of me is keen. I can't say that I'm not flattered that Trinity wants me back,' said Chris, slowly. 'However, that'd mean moving Megan back to the city and getting a bigger place. And Mac, there's a job available at the local ABC radio outfit and the station manager is sure that, even without radio experience, I'm the best candidate for it. Even though I'd not be making a heap of money, I don't need all that much, living in Neverend.' He paused as his thoughts turned over. 'And I've got the bit between my teeth with this book. And you know, I think that if I started fulltime newspaper work again, it'd be very hard on Megan. I know the sort of hours I'd have to work with Trinity. I'd often have to leave her on her own and I don't want to be a part-time father again. With the radio job, I'd be around for her. I also think I could work for a few hours each afternoon on my book. Coming home

at night from the newspaper and then trying to be crea-
tive . . . well, it wouldn't work. And frankly, Mac, I'm
pretty sure that Megan doesn't want to leave Neverend,
and I'm not sure I do either.'

Mac handed the menus to the waiter, who was
standing with pencil poised. 'Well, bugger me. You're full
of surprises. I'll have the moussaka,' he said to the waiter.

'Lamb shanks,' said Chris, then grinned at his old friend.

Mac leaned back in his chair. 'Are you sure you want
to work in local radio? Bit out of the mainstream for
someone of your abilities,' he said.

'I suppose so, but I intend to do the job as well as I
would if I were still a foreign correspondent for Trinity
Press. As I see it, it's the best job around that fits in with
my present life.'

'Georgie will be disappointed,' said Mac, pointedly.

'I know.' Chris was quiet for a moment. 'Am I being
stupid, Mac? Six months ago I'd have killed to have this
Trinity Press job offer, but now I know that it's not the
right job for me at this point in time. I wish I could be
closer to Georgie. Maybe she might be happy living away
from the city?'

'You'd have to ask her, mate.' Mac leaned across
the table and lowered his voice. 'Chris, I didn't just ask
you here for a chat, you know, although that's been nice.
There's another reason that I wanted to meet you for
lunch. I've still got good contacts around the traps, as you
know, old journo mates as well as friends in high places,
and I've heard a rumour that a certain multi-millionaire
who has been trying to expand his construction company
into the US is in a heap of financial pain.'

'Do you mean Carmichael?' Chris said incredulously.
'Are you bullshitting me?'

Mac put his hand on his heart. 'It's true. If you look
in today's financial papers, you'll see a couple of stories.

They're only small at this stage, but from what I hear, things are going to get a whole lot worse for Carmichael. The word is out that the American banks that were going to back his expansion are pulling out of their deal. Rumour has it that he's no longer sound.'

'What does that mean?' asked Chris.

'I think the bankers are questioning the viability of Carmichael's projects.'

Chris gave a low whistle. 'So where does he go from here?'

'Who would know? But if he doesn't get other financial backing pretty quickly, then he's going to be in a lot of bother.'

Lunch arrived and their conversation turned to other things, mainly how great it had been working as a journalist in the good old days; colourful characters, less stringent restrictions, a lot more free-wheeling opportunities to chase stories.

After lunch, Chris made his way to Georgia's place and they watched the nightly news snuggled together on the couch. The story about Carmichael was little more than a passing reference, but Susan was on the phone to Chris immediately.

'Chris! Have you heard the news? I can't believe it! Do you think Alan is in real trouble?'

'It didn't say much in the news today, but Mac thinks he is.'

'I might ring Mark right away and see if he's heard anything,' said Susan, and hung up.

'My mother is pretty shocked at the news,' Chris relayed to Georgia.

'I'm not surprised. I suppose we'll hear more about what's going on over the next few days,' said Georgia. 'By the way, what else did you and Dad talk about besides Alan Carmichael today?'

'Actually, something else did happen while we were having lunch. I was approached by my old editor in the restaurant and he offered me a job back at Trinity, working in Sydney.'

Georgia sat up. 'That's wonderful, Chris. How do you feel about that?'

'Truthfully? It puts me in a difficult position. It's certainly what I wanted to do a few months back.'

'And now?' Georgia cocked her head to one side.

Chris began hesitantly. 'Georgie, please don't be hurt, I want to see you all the time. But . . . it's Megan. I just can't drag her away from Neverend now. She's so happy there, what with her friends, her interests, and of course Squire. And if I take the Trinity job, I know that I wouldn't be able to give her the attention she deserves. I'm feeling very confident about getting the ABC position and then I'll have the security of decent money and a regular job and have a lot of time for Megan, too.' He stopped as she started to smile. 'Am I nuts settling for all that without you?'

Georgia looked fondly at him. 'Perhaps not. I've been to Neverend. I've seen how happy Megan is. And your relationship with your daughter is your first priority, and that's how it should be. Besides, as your agent, I can see that you have a much better chance of writing your next book in a stress-free atmosphere.'

Chris put his arms around Georgia. 'I love you insanely,' he said. 'I'm a lucky man, to have such an understanding girl like you.'

'Oh, I don't mind hanging out with a bloke who lives in the bush, drives a courier van and scribbles in his spare time, but who will soon be a radio star.'

'You're wonderful,' he sighed as he hugged her. 'I'll give this book-writing a decent bash. Second time lucky, but I couldn't do it without you.'

'Maybe I'd better stick around, then,' she said playfully. 'Keep an eye on my client.'

*

Early the following morning, Chris wrapped his arms around Georgia, feeling the warmth of her body through her bathrobe. Her hair smelled faintly of lemons as he kissed her scrubbed face. 'It gets harder and harder to say goodbye to you,' he murmured.

'I know. Me too. I'll fly up as soon as I can. Just keep writing. I love what you're doing.'

'I'll call you tonight. Let me know if your dad hears anything more about Carmichael.'

'Will do.'

Chris drove back to Neverend from Coffs airport, his mind whirring with all that had happened. As always, once he'd crossed the bridge over the Henry River and turned off the Pacific Highway towards Neverend, he felt his body and mind relax, slowing and settling as a peacefulness stole over him despite all he had running through his head.

It was the middle of the day, the winter sun lit up the trees and in the paddocks soporific cows stood motionless, time being of no consequence to them. The main street was quiet save for the newsagent, who was seated outside his shop dozing, a newspaper on his lap.

At home, Chris dropped his bag, went into the kitchen and put the kettle on. He sent Georgia a text saying he'd arrived safely. Then, with a coffee and a cheese sandwich beside him, he opened his laptop, picked up the thread of his story and began to type.

When Susan poked her head in, Chris was surprised to find that two hours had evaporated.

'Glad you're back,' said Susan. 'I had book club today. We discussed our book over a very pleasant lunch

407

and a nice glass of wine. Best way to look at literature, I always think.'

He stretched. 'I'm ready for a coffee refill. Is Megan over at Mollie's this afternoon?'

'I assume so. She said that she wants to start learning dressage and that could be beyond old Squire. Mollie said she knew of a good teacher who might take Megan on if she's really serious.'

'Do you think she is? Or will boys and parties and her music start to impinge more on her time?' wondered Chris.

Susan laughed. 'She does have a lot going on. She did say she might drop the debating team but stick with the jazz band, the school orchestra and netball. She has a very full agenda.'

'I could go over to see her later this afternoon. I haven't seen Megs ride for a while.' But before he had the chance, the phone rang. It was Mark.

Susan spoke to him for some time. When she hung up, she looked grave.

'Mark has been talking to his friends in the financial world and they are all shocked by Alan's predicament. It seems that the loans he had taken out in the US for the expansion of his business are not going to be forthcoming. Whatever capital he has in Australia will have to be used to try to salvage his American operation. This means that now he is seriously overextended, and Mark thinks he could even become bankrupt if he can't raise more funds straight away.'

Privately Chris had absolutely no sympathy for Alan at all, but he knew that a lot of people would lose their jobs if International Industries went belly up, and he wondered if any new loans would materialise.

Over the next few weeks, more and more stories appeared in the papers and online, all following the collapse of Alan's business. There were a lot of phone calls between Mark, Evan, David and Susan. Only Mark had any real information. Evan was shocked by what was happening and constantly suggested that things could not be as bad as they seemed. David said that he didn't really care what happened to Alan.

'I did hear that he had to sell his estate in Bali. I bet his waterfront place in Sydney will be the next to go,' David said to Susan, who relayed his comment to Chris.

Chris just nodded.

Now that the physical threats from Alan, if indeed they had been from him, seemed to have evaporated, Chris found that, like David, he was watching the decline of the tycoon's business with only moderate interest.

Chris was delighted when the ABC let him work there on a trial basis and he quickly fitted in. He found that the work was interesting and quite fulfilling, if not as high-powered as in other positions he had held. Working on radio was much harder than he had thought it would be, but he soon mastered the technicalities. He no longer had the luxury of chasing just one or two big stories, instead he had to provide bulletins of reliable and relevant news to critical listeners every hour, but he loved the challenge.

He also enjoyed the chance to write for a couple of hours in the afternoon and soon realised that his new book was much more engaging than his first literary attempt. He knew that writing part-time meant that the book would take quite a while to come to fruition, but he appreciated being able to work under less pressure. Although he scarcely acknowledged it to himself, a small kernel of an idea was forming in the back of his mind for a further book. But he pushed the idea to one side, knowing he had to concentrate and finish this book first, and do it well. Nevertheless, he was comforted that this might not be the only book he had in him.

Chris felt a bit guilty about telling Shaun that he would be leaving the courier business, but his friend had no trouble finding a replacement straight away. There was now even talk of expanding the business, especially as Shaun was becoming less and less enthusiastic about working on the family farm.

When David arrived for a visit two weeks later, Susan announced they were all having a big roast dinner.

'Is this in my honour?' asked David.

'Of course! No, actually it's so we can all catch up. Megan never seems to be around and Chris has his head down all the time these days and I've been pretty busy, too, so it's a big Saturday night feast for us all to enjoy together.'

'Shall I make my best dessert?' offered Megan.

'You bet,' said Chris.

'And what are you up to, Megan?' asked David.

'I've started dressage classes. I love it. My teacher, Judy, says I have a good seat, very straight, and I move well with the horse.' She sat up straight in her chair to demonstrate what she meant.

'On Squire?' asked David. 'From what I saw, he seems to be a bit of an old plodder. Bit like me.'

'Nonsense,' interrupted Susan. 'Plodder you are not.'

'No, I use one of Judy's horses. She's amazing. She breaks in horses and everything. Maybe I'll break horses when I leave school,' said Megan, her voice full of admiration for her new teacher.

'Maybe not,' said Chris. 'I think you'll need to have a lot more experience to do anything like that.'

'I think I should dedicate the rest of my life to horses,' said Megan, dreamily.

'Could you dedicate the next half hour to the dessert?' said Susan, but she had a smile on her face. 'I remember your auntie Kate saying much the same thing about horses when she was your age.'

'Well, I say good for you,' said David, exchanging a wink with Megan.

When they all sat down for a roast with all the trimmings, Chris asked, 'What plans do you two have for tomorrow?'

'We're going up to Applebrook to see Jean Hay,' said Susan.

'It's such a magic old house. Is the land any good for growing the sorts of things you had in mind, David?' asked Chris. 'Pass that roast pumpkin, please, Megs.'

'More than good,' replied David, spooning greens onto his plate. 'There are rich alluvial river flats as well as good grazing land. It's a bit overgrown, but nothing that can't be fixed. Jean's husband really knew how to care for the soil. He didn't go in for putting a lot of chemicals onto his paddocks, but that didn't mean he couldn't make decent money from good fat cattle. Used to grow feed on the flats too, Jean says. So, all in all, I can't tell you how pleased I am that Jean will sell me the property. It's exactly what I've been after.'

As David spoke, Chris saw the expression on his mother's face; her eyes were filled with love.

Megan saw it too. 'I think you should live in Neverend, David,' she said bluntly. 'When you took me up to Mrs Hay's place, I could only see the outside of the house, but I just know it would be perfect for you. Bunny would so like that, wouldn't you, Bunny?'

'Well, Megan, that was very perceptive of you,' said David. 'I can't be an absentee landlord. I need a place where I can be on hand to watch my plants.'

'So, Mum, is Jean going to move into town when David buys her out?' asked Chris.

Susan shook her head. 'No, David knows how much Jean's place means to her and he has no desire to uproot her, especially at her age. As far as he's concerned she can go on living in her house. He just want to use the land.'

'Yes,' said David. 'I might be buying the whole property, but I'm happy for Jean to stay on. So your grandmother is about to reinvent herself as a renovator.'

'David's decided to make the old barn into a proper home,' said Susan, excited to share the news.' It'll be all fresh and white inside with French doors and a patio. I have so many idea,' she added enthusiastically.

'You're so clever, Bunny,' said Megan. 'When can I go up and see Mrs Hay?'

'How about tomorrow?' said David. 'I'll walk around the property with you both and show you what we're thinking of doing.'

'That's wonderful. I think that is a very generous offer. I bet Jean's pleased,' said Chris.

'She was quite overwhelmed when we suggested it and her family seems happy about the arrangement, too,' said Susan. 'Now, who would like some of this crackling?'

*

Next morning, Susan and Megan packed a picnic lunch and they all set off in David's four-wheel drive.

'It's so pretty out here along the river,' said Megan. 'I never come this way.'

'Not a lot of people do. Unless you live out here, there's no reason to drive on this back road,' Susan explained.

'Is this the area called the Promised Land?' asked David.

'No, that's in the opposite direction, out near the waterholes on Neverending Creek, where Chris and Megan swim in the summer,' said Susan. 'I'll take you out there some time, if you like. It's really lovely, too.'

'Hallelujah, I suppose that's where the hippies thought they'd found Nirvana?' joked David.

'Yes, although the cedar cutters and the dairy farmers beat them to it. There is such rich and abundant land all around this valley,' said Susan.

'I'm going to enjoy experimenting with it. Maybe I'll be able to convince some of the local farmers to get involved in trying out some of the ideas I have in mind.'

'David, you could really start something in the district,' said Susan proudly.

Moses, the dog, heard them arrive and came to the front gate, giving a friendly bark. Jean appeared on the front verandah.

'Come in, come in. Kettle's on.'

Megan patted the dog and followed the others into the house. Once inside, Susan and Megan made their way to the kitchen, where the kettle sat on the old fuel stove.

'I made a fritatta; I'll set it on the side of the hob to warm though a little, if you like, Jean,' said Susan.

It was the first time Megan had been in the house and she looked around in astonishment. 'Dad, how old is this place?' she whispered to Chris in the hallway. 'It's like something in a fairytale.'

Overhearing what Megan had said, Jean chuckled softly. 'It's old, older even than me. But it's sturdy. And there are a lot of stories I can tell you about what happened under this roof.'

'It's just so interesting,' said Megan, emphatically. 'I see why Georgia wanted to take photos of it all. I've never seen a house like this. Can I look around, please?'

'Mrs Hay would love to give you a little tour, I'm sure,' said Chris with a smile. 'David, shall we go for a walk before lunch? I'd love to hear your ideas. Want to come, girls?'

'Megan and I might stay and chat to Jean for a while,' replied Susan.

The two men walked through the stand of trees that screened the house from the old barn, with its views across the open paddocks to the river beyond.

'The barn has the best view on the whole property,' said Chris.

'I reckon it was built even before the farmhouse,' said David.

'So, is this place a definite goer for you now?'

David nodded. 'Absolutely. Jean's happy to see something useful happening with the land. And I'm happy for her to go on living here,' he said.

'I think that what you have done for Jean is very generous. Do you plan to live on the property fulltime?' asked Chris.

'Pretty much,' said David. 'Although I still want to travel to Italy each year for a couple of months, and I'm hoping your mother will come with me.'

'I'm sure she'll enjoy that. And she sounds pretty excited about helping to do this place up,' added Chris, gesturing to the house.

'She's a born renovator. She drew up some plans which appear to involve knocking out the odd wall and replacing it with French doors, putting in some recycled windows and installing a couple of bedrooms, and of course I'll get the old timber slab walls lined,' said David.

'It sounds like quite a makeover,' said Chris, cautiously. 'Are you expecting your family to visit?'

'Possibly. They'll have to camp in the lounge room, because I want to use the second bedroom as an office, and your mother also wants to have a sewing room. I thought we could share that space.' David smiled.

Chris stopped walking. 'Wait a minute, why does Mum need a sewing room at Applebrook? I mean . . .' Chris stared at David. 'Is my mother going to live here with you permanently? Or just weekends?'

David paused. 'You talk to her, Chris. I think she should be the one to tell you about our plans.'

There was a shout behind them and both men turned around. Chris could see the two women coming towards them, Megan running ahead of her grandmother, her face filled with excitement.

'This place is totally awesome!' declared Megan, breathlessly. 'It's beautiful.'

'I think so too,' said David, as Megan and Susan caught up to him and Chris. 'Megan, come with me, there's an idea I'd like to run past you.'

Chris and Susan watched Megan walk beside David as they trudged across the paddock in deep discussion, their heads close together.

'It's all pretty special, isn't it? David's going to do wonders with this place,' said Susan.

Chris turned to face Susan. 'And so are you, from what David tells me of this barn renovation. It sounds as though you're planning to design a whole house. But what's in it for you, Mum?'

Susan looked at the river. 'I've been doing quite a bit of thinking lately, especially after David decided to buy this place, but I wanted to be sure that the sale was going through before I said anything definite.' She looked at Chris, a radiant smile on her face. 'In short, I've decided I'd like to move out here with David. I love our home in town, but this is a new phase of my life. I want the space and views and new interests, and David is a wonderful new interest.'

Chris looked at her, his eyebrows raised. 'Mum! I appreciate what you're saying, and I do understand that David's presence has made quite a difference in your life, but moving out here? It's just a bit of a surprise. Does that mean you're going to sell your house? It's got so many memories. Would you be happy doing that?'

Susan shook her head. 'No, of course not. It's your home, Chris, as much as it is mine. Yours and Megan's. Maybe one day, if you move back to the city, I might sell it, but for now, I won't. Besides,' she added mischievously, 'if things don't work out with David, I'll need a place to retreat to, won't I?'

'Mum, if all this makes you happy, then who am I to argue?' Chris said, but he felt very pleased for Susan. 'Have you told Kate about your plans?' he added.

'Not yet, but I will now that I know everything is going ahead,' said Susan.

'I bet she'll be thrilled about your new life with David, especially the idea of your going to Europe every year, and her kids are going to love this place when they visit.'

Susan put her arm around Chris's waist and they hugged. 'Things have worked out pretty well for me,' she said, withdrawing so she could see his face. 'Who knew when I went to that reunion that my life would change so much? I hope that things work out as well for you. Have you any idea where your relationship with Georgia is going, if you don't mind my asking?' They resumed walking across the paddock.

'Not at all, although there's not much to tell, really,' said Chris, tucking his hands in his pockets. 'Now that I have bitten the bullet and decided to stay in Neverend, I thought that Georgie might become less enthusiastic about the two of us. But thankfully that hasn't happened. Maybe she will eventually decide that she can run her agency from here, and move up. I don't know, but it's what I'm hoping.'

'I'll keep my fingers crossed that she makes that decision.'

'But Mum, even if that doesn't work out, I'm happy with what I have, and that's my daughter. Megan has given me so much pleasure this year that I just kick myself about having missed out on so much of her life. Now I know that there is no job, no matter how glamorous or exciting, that is worth not seeing your children grow up.'

Suddenly Susan stopped and looked at Chris with a wistful expression.

'And Chris,' she said, grasping his arm, 'they grow up so quickly and move away, as you and your sister did, so treasure the time you have with her. It will fly by all too quickly.' Chris caught the hint of sadness in his mother's voice. That's what he and his sister had done. No wonder Susan had become lonely after his father had died. Suddenly he realised how unkind he had been when he had initially objected to her relationship with David.

Chris nodded. 'I'm really pleased that you found David,' he said sincerely, and hugged his mother again before she went to join David. They all walked back to the old house together.

*

Jean was pulling the tea-cosy over her large enamel teapot when Chris came into the kitchen to see if he could help. 'There's coffee in the pot on the stove. I know you're a coffee drinker.'

'That's very thoughtful of you, Jean. I hope it's strong.'

'Ah, it is.' She sat at the table and began pouring herself a cup of tea. 'You've heard their plans? I can't tell you how happy they have made me. What generous people they are.'

'Yes, and I'm very pleased about their decision, too.'

'I think your mother is a very kind person who loves you very much, Chris. You raise your children to be independent, self-sufficient and hopefully successful, and of course we all want our children to be happy, but maybe it's more important to know they are also caring and kind individuals,' she added with a smile. 'I'm sure that's how your mother sees you.'

'Thank you, Jean. I hope she's right.'

Jean smiled and raised her eyebrows. 'Your mother has an exciting new interest in life, and she tells me that your daughter is happy and well-adjusted, and although I suspect you never thought you'd return to Neverend, you're at home in a place you love. I've never wanted to leave this place, because I didn't want to lose what I have here, but lots of people do leave. Some of them never come back home and that is their choice, but to find the road back is a great gift.'

Chris put his coffee mug down with a trembling hand. 'You're a wise woman, Jean.'

'No, dear, just old,' she said, laughing.

*

Several weeks flew by. The Carmichael case had dropped from the headlines, but there were still stories about commercial manoeuvrings, legal teams and feverish investigations.

In Neverend, as the longer days heralded the start of spring, there was now a heightened sense of purpose. Susan gathered samples of floor tiles, plumbing fittings, fabric and paint samples; Megan and her jazz band rehearsed endlessly at the end of the verandah for a forth-coming competition, and Chris hammered away in his study on his new laptop, which he'd bought not long after he started working at the radio station.

One afternoon their endeavours were interrupted by a phone call from Jill. She sounded affable, so Chris knew at once that there weren't to be any complaints about Megan.

'How're things, Chris? Megan tells me your mother is moving in with her boyfriend. That's a bit of a turn-up, isn't it?'

'Not quite yet, their place isn't ready.'

'Megan seems to be rather enamoured of the whole idea of this farm. Who is this boyfriend your mother's acquired?'

'David and Mum go way back. She knew him even before she met my father. He's a really nice person, very intelligent and interesting, and I think he and Mum will be very happy together. And how're things with you?' he asked, pointedly, to change the subject.

'Rather good. We are also contemplating a few changes.'

'Are you coming back east?' asked Chris, suddenly worried that Jill would demand Megan's return.

'Not at all. Actually, Trevor's had an offer of a job in Indonesia. It all sounds a bit foreign, but I've been told that the International School we'll send the boys to is quite good, and of course we'll have servants,' she added, trying to sound blasé.

Chris didn't know whether to laugh or be outraged. It struck him then how far apart he and Jill had grown, and how their decision to separate all those years ago, in spite of the heartache it had caused at the time, had definitely turned out to be the right one for both of them.

'Do you think you and Trev will be able to cope with somewhere so foreign? You never wanted to live abroad when we were together.'

'That was different. You would have had to travel, leaving me to look after Megan by myself. Trev is working for a big company and they will look after us. I don't know how much you know about Indonesia . . .'

Chris suppressed a laugh. 'Jill, you'd be surprised. But you're right. I think it will be a marvellous opportunity for you and the boys. I hope they get the chance to learn Bahasa.'

'Oh, the language? I don't think they'll need to; we will be part of the big expatriate community. Everyone will speak English. Now, I assume that you'll have no objections to Megan coming to visit?'

'No, of course not.'

'She could come and live with us, you know. The school up there is apparently quite exceptional and I thought that a couple of years in Indonesia might broaden her horizons.'

Chris froze. He answered carefully, 'Jill, Megan has settled in nicely and is involved in so many things in Neverend, and she's doing so well at school. You can ask her, of course, but I don't think she'll agree.'

'You don't have to be so defensive. You've proved your point, you've turned into a good father. I just thought you might like to have your old life back. Be fancy-free again.'

'Jill, this is about what's best for Megan. And I think she is doing very well and is extremely happy just where she is.'

'But you would agree to her visiting us in Indonesia? I'm sure it will be safe.'

'I think she'd love that,' said Chris. 'Where will you be?'

'In Jakarta.'

'Did you know my mother was in Indonesia in the sixties? I thought of writing a book about her experiences there.'

'No, I had no idea about your mother. And a book! Well, that's all very interesting.' Jill became businesslike, her disinterest in Chris's life very apparent. 'We'll be going there in a little over a month.'

'I hope you enjoy it. I'll get Megan for you and you can tell her the news. And good luck, Jill.'

Chris went to Megan's room and handed her the phone. Then he walked out onto the verandah with mixed feelings. He knew that he didn't want Megan to leave him for a life in Indonesia, but it was hardly fair not to let Megan make up her own mind.

Megan joined him on the verandah a few minutes later. She was taken aback. 'Mum asked me to go and live with her and Trev in Indonesia,' she said somewhat dubiously.

Chris said nothing. He didn't want to sway his daughter's decision, but he certainly didn't want her to go. Megan was quiet for a few moments, her brow furrowed.

'Dad, do you think that Mum would be really disappointed if I didn't go?' she said finally. 'I really have way too many commitments in Neverend. If I went to Indonesia, I would be letting a lot of people down. I shouldn't do that, should I?' Megan spoke in her most rational tone of voice. Chris tried to keep a straight face, but he couldn't hide his joy.

'Megan, the decision to live in Indonesia is yours alone, but I am pleased that you are considering your responsibilities to others as part of that decision,' he said.

'When it comes down to it, I think that going would be very unfair on Squire. I mean, he's old and he's no good for dressage, but I can't just walk away from him. And there's the jazz band. The competition is coming up, and we've worked so hard for it, and if I leave then the others won't be able to take part. Do you think that Mum would be okay if I just go up there over the Christmas holidays? You don't think she'd mind, do you?'

'Darling, I think she would be absolutely delighted, and so would I. Living in Indonesia for even a few weeks would be a wonderful experience.'

*

One afternoon later that week, Chris found Susan watering her sweet pea seedlings.

'Bronwyn just rang,' he said. 'My position has been confirmed and I'm now a permanent staff member. I feel both relieved and pleased. I am enjoying doing something new, and one thing about working locally is that everyone thinks that they own a bit of me. I'm part of their community.'

'I'm pleased to hear that. This is your town and your region, so you should feel a sense of belonging,' said Susan.

'You're right. I am pleased to be working as a journalist in a place I love and now I also have a better salary than I had working for Frenchy. Not that I'm ungrateful for his help,' Chris added quickly.

'You know, Chris, giving up your newspaper career and coming home for Megan's sake might have been a bit of a compromise in the beginning,' said Susan. 'But when your daughter's an adult she'll look back at this time and understand what a magnificent father she has.'

*

A couple of weeks later, Chris arrived home from doing his radio shift to see Carla's motorbike parked in the driveway. Leaving his car in the street, he walked onto the verandah and immediately spotted her boots, leather jacket and helmet dropped on a chair near the front door.

He found Carla and his mother at the kitchen table amidst the remains of tea and homemade biscuits. Carla jumped up and Chris gave her a hug.

'Been ages,' he said. 'How was your gallivanting around the outback?'

'Sensational. What an astonishing country we have.'

'Neverend will do me. Any tea left in the pot, Mum? No, don't make a fresh one, I'll grab a beer.'

He grabbed a cold bottle out of the fridge and took a seat beside his mother.

'Your mother has been telling me all the exciting plans, Chris,' said Carla. 'Congrats on the job.'

'Thanks, Carla,' said Chris.

'And Carla, what's this news you have?' Susan turned to Chris and explained, 'Carla has been waiting for you to get home so she can share her gossip.'

'It's more than gossip. Greg says it's official.' Carla looked at Chris. 'Carmichael's Victorian development is not going ahead. You know that he's in big financial trouble? Well, the plug has been pulled on the shopping centre.'

'Not surprising, I suppose,' said Susan.

'My mate Greg has been keeping an eye on things,' Carla said with relish.

'Is he the chap Chris met in Melbourne?' Susan asked.

Both Chris and Carla nodded.

'Suddenly, Greg says, there have been a few whistle-blowers coming forward to say that the rezoning was not quite as squeaky clean as it should have been. Evidently there were a few doctored reports, especially about the amount of new traffic that would be going through a residential area. It seems that the figures presented to the council were fabricated. If the true figures had been presented, hardly any of the councillors would have agreed to the rezoning,' Carla told them breathlessly.

'Well, I'm pleased that Greg was proved to be right,' said Chris. 'I assume that people were bribed to create reports that would ensure Carmichael's plans went through.'

'You assume correctly.'

'I don't know if you've heard this, Carla,' said Chris. 'But the latest I heard about Carmichael is that in an effort to stave off bankruptcy, he has done a bit of a money shuffle, robbing Peter to pay Paul, that sort of thing, but he still can't get enough funds. He's definitely going under.'

'A good thing too,' said Carla. 'But bankruptcy could be the least of his worries. It's not just the Victorian police that have been making inquiries into his construction operations, there have been interstate investigations as well. Greg has heard that there have been several arrests already and that the police are going to charge Carmichael too. If you ask me, if he was prepared to give out bribes for one development, I'll bet he did it for a lot of others. Once the lid on his activities starts to come off, well, who knows how much of the brown stuff is going to hit the fan?' Carla sat back in her chair with a large and satisfied smile on her face.

'Holy cow!' exclaimed Chris.

'Oh, what a tangled web we weave,' quoted Susan. 'And frankly, I can't feel sorry for him. Do you think he'll go to gaol?'

'I should hope so, Susan. The man's a common criminal. These rich white men all think they can get away with not playing by the rules, but they should be brought to justice,' said Carla indignantly.

'They should be, but that's not to say that he will be,' said Chris. 'Maybe Carmichael will be able to hire enough lawyers to get himself out of this.'

'Let's talk about something else,' said Susan with a wave of her hand. 'I'm sick of Alan Carmichael. He didn't do a lot for my life.'

'Right you are, Mum. How about we go out for dinner tonight? Megan's hanging out for pizza at the Italian place.'

'Sounds good. I'm always up for a plate of pasta,' Carla replied.

'Me too. I've got to go and get the washing in, but you two keep talking,' said Susan as she rose from the table and headed outside.

'So, Chris, what's this book you're working on? I thought that had been dumped?' asked Carla in her usual blunt fashion.

Chris laughed. 'You don't let me get away with much, do you, Carla!'

'Friends are allowed to be nosey. Your mother looks happy, you look contented. Want to walk downtown? We can pop in and book a table at the pasta place and you can tell me all about the book.'

'Okay. I'll bore you with my book ideas.'

'Try me. You know I'll give you a candid opinion.'

'That's for sure,' said Chris with a chuckle.

*

The little barn had been beautifully renovated and extended and was now a pretty cottage. Susan had spent weeks painting and decorating, and there were only a few small jobs still to do before she and David could move in.

'David's due back from Brisbane in a couple of days and then it will be all systems go,' she told Chris one evening after dinner.

'I bet you can't wait. Want to watch the seven o'clock news?'

Like a haunted shadow, Alan Carmichael's drawn face appeared briefly on the TV as he was arraigned on bribery charges. Surrounded by his legal team, he left the court after paying a hefty bail before darting into a dark green Mark 2 Jaguar. As it sped away, the news returned to the studio presenter and Susan turned the sound down.

'Beginning of the end,' she said quietly. 'I wouldn't have recognised him.'

'This case could drag out for quite some time. Those lawyers know how to stall,' said Chris. 'It could go on for years.'

'I'm sure he's guilty. But do you think he can get out of this?'

'Who knows what the lawyers have up their sleeves. Maybe Alan'll find someone to take the fall for him. Get some young manager to come out and say that he was responsible for all this bribery and corruption and did it entirely without Carmichael's knowledge. And the young manager will go to gaol knowing there's a fat reward sitting in a bank somewhere for him when he gets out.'

Susan looked saddened. 'That is so cynical. Alan could do that?'

'It's been done before. The guy at the top is very hard to reach. He just says that there was a bad apple in the company who acted without his knowledge and that everyone else is squeaky clean.'

'It's a cut-throat world out there in corporate land,' said Susan, standing up. 'I'm just going to stick my head in Megan's room to make sure she has everything she needs when she goes down to Port Macquarie tomorrow for that jazz band competition.'

'Thank heavens. I thought it would never come around. They've all practised hard enough. It's a shame that I won't be there to cheer them on.'

*

As he drove into Neverend the next day after work, Chris noticed a fisherman on the river and decided to see if any of his mates wanted to go fishing on the weekend. It had been a while since they'd been out together and now the weather was warming, the idea was appealing.

He turned into View Street and slowed to a stop when he saw a car parked on the grass verge opposite the house. It was a classic dark green Jaguar, the same model he'd seen on TV the night before.

Could it be Alan Carmichael's car? Suddenly fear gripped him. Megan was still at the jazz competition, but Susan was home. He quickly drove up the driveway and raced into the house.

'Mum, are you here?' he shouted.

'Yes, dear, in the kitchen. Whatever is it?'

'Are you all right?'

Susan looked surprised, then concerned at the expression on his face. 'What's wrong?'

'It's him, Alan. I'm sure it's his car out the front of the house.'

'What! Are you sure? Quickly, shut the door.'

Chris raced to the front door. Terrible scenarios started to run through his mind. Why on earth would Alan Carmichael be here in Neverend? What did he want with them? Had he come to harm them?

As Chris approached the front door, he saw through the window a man crossing the road, heading for their house. It was Alan Carmichael.

He was wearing a short bomber-style jacket and not carrying anything. Chris stepped out onto the verandah, closing the door behind him, and walked to the railing. Alan stopped in the driveway as soon as he saw Chris.

'Mr Carmichael? What can I do for you?' asked Chris, calmly.

Alan stopped and stared up at Chris, pointing a finger at him. 'Are you Chris Baxter?' Chris nodded. Alan continued, his voice seething with rage. 'Then I think you've done enough for me already. You and your mother.'

'I've had nothing to do with your current problems,' replied Chris, now very puzzled as to why Carmichael had turned up on their doorstep.

Alan walked to the verandah steps and put one foot onto the bottom tread. Chris didn't move. 'My problems only started when you began nosing around!' he suddenly shouted.

Chris gripped the balustrade. 'I'm not sure how. I have no idea why you tried to stop me writing a book about your success.'

'What I do is my business. I don't want people poking their noses into my affairs.'

'Is that right? Well, it seems that you like to take action against anyone who tries. Me, for example. I think you had someone intimidate me and my family to try to stop me from writing about you.'

'And it worked,' said Alan, nastily. 'Bit sad for me that by the time I got you to stop writing your poxy little book, it was too late. You'd already done the damage.'

'I didn't do anything. I backed off, remember? I sent you a letter from my solicitor to that effect.'

'But that didn't stop you from telling Thomas Anderson about me and what happened to his brother. Isn't that right?'

Chris stared at Carmichael with a perplexed expression.

'How do you know that I spoke to Thomas Fairfax Anderson?' he asked.

'Because he told me. He enjoyed telling me. He said that he'd waited a long time to see that there was justice for his brother.'

'I'm not sure that I fully understand.'

Alan gave a bark of a laugh. 'Oh, I think you do. Once Anderson found out that I was involved in the death of his brother, then I became persona non grata as far as the financing of my projects went. Anderson made sure that no one in the States would lend me money, and without those loans, well, you know the rest. I've lost my homes, my business – years of hard work all gone – because you had to interfere.'

'So you had no idea that Thomas Anderson was Jimmy's brother until he told you?' asked Chris, slowly.

'Of course not. Why on earth would I have connected someone as important and successful as Thomas Fairfax Anderson to that Yank who used to hang around your mother and the rest of us all those years ago? Don't you think that if I had known he was Jimmy's brother, I'd have given him a wide berth? I don't know how you found out, but you're the one who told Anderson what I did in Bogor and ruined everything for me.'

'My son didn't tell Tom Anderson about what really happened to Jimmy. I did.'

Chris spun around to see Susan standing behind him. She walked to the railing of the verandah and looked down at Alan.

'Why are you here, Alan?'

'Just so I can tell you both that you won't get away with what you've done to me. It doesn't matter how long it takes, I will pursue you. I want to see you both come unstuck.'

'Alan, I only wanted Tom to know about his brother. I had no idea Tom was integral to your loans for your US expansion. But I tell you something, Alan, even if I had known, I would still have told him the truth. He deserved that.'

Carmichael put both feet on the bottom step.

'Please don't come any closer. You're not welcome here. Neither my mother nor I want to have anything to do with you,' said Chris angrily.

'You have ruined me and I'm going to make you pay!' Alan yelled, and Susan took a quick step backwards.

'Mum, go inside and call the police. Carmichael, get off our property.' Chris heard the door close as Susan hurried inside.

'Just remember this, Chris Baxter,' Alan said grimly. 'I'm going to beat the charges. There's no way I'm going to gaol, and I want you and your mother to know I'm going to make sure you're haunted every day for the rest of your life. You'll always have to be looking over your shoulder and that includes everyone close to you, including your daughter.'

Chris stared at Alan in horror. Surely Megan wouldn't have to pay as part of this man's revenge? With all the calm he could muster, Chris said, 'The police will be here in a minute or so. I suggest you leave right now, Mr Carmichael.'

'Remember what I said. No matter how long it takes, you'll pay for what you and your mother have done.' With that, Alan hunched his shoulders and, suddenly looking like an old man, turned and stalked back to his car.

Chris watched the Jaguar roar off down the street.

Susan put her head cautiously around the front door. 'Has he gone?'

'Yes, Mum. Are you okay?' Chris reached for his mother, pulling Susan close to him.

'Yes. Except that I can't stop shaking.'

'I think you were very brave. You certainly stood up to him. What did Pete say?'

'I was on the phone to him when I saw Alan leave, so he said that if he turns up again, we are to ring him straight away and he'll come right over.'

Chris nodded and realised he was shaking too. 'I think we need a cuppa,' he said.

They sat inside with mugs of tea and coffee and went over the incident again.

'Are you going to tell David?' Chris asked Susan.

'Of course I am. We don't have any secrets from each other, and I expect that David will be part of the threat, that is if Alan is serious and it's not all bluff and bluster. Will you tell Georgia?'

Chris paused. 'I will, but I'd rather do it face to face. I don't think I can tell her about that vile conversation over the phone. But I want to ring her now, just to hear her voice after that horrible episode.'

Chris settled at his desk to call Georgia.

'Hey, nice surprise. What are you up to?' she asked.

'Nothing much. Just wanted to hear your voice, that's all. Megan is at a jazz comp in Port. Her band is taking part. What have you been up to?'

'A lot. Chasing a young author who sent me a manuscript for a novella that I think has a lot of potential. Been talking to an old actor I heard interviewed on Radio National. I thought it could be turned into a very interesting autobiography. But darling, you do sound a bit funny. Is anything wrong?' asked Georgia.

'I'm just missing you.'

'I miss you too. Shall I come up this weekend? I can juggle appointments.'

'I'll be okay. You're busy, I'm working.'

'And writing?'

'Yes, I love doing this book. It's funny, but now that I've got a good job and the pressure is off, I'm finding it so much easier to write than the first time round. It's my escape and pleasure now, not my whole future hanging on it. The radio position suits me and comes with a few pluses. I've actually had some people stop me and say they enjoy what I'm doing, especially when I do the occasional off-beat story.'

'Chris, I'm very proud of you and have enormous faith in you.'

Chris smiled. 'Thank you, darling. I'm so lucky to have you. I feel better just talking to you.'

'Chris . . . ?'

'Yes, my lovely?'

'It won't always be like this . . . being apart.'

'Nah, we'll work something out.'

'Yes, we will. I love you.'

'Gotta go. Love you.'

A few hours later, Chris heard a car in the driveway and walked outside to see Sergeant Pete Pollard stepping out of his police vehicle. The policeman took off his cap and rubbed his hand through his hair.

'Pete, g'day, thanks so much for your help before. Can I offer you a beer?'

'I'm still on duty, so would you fancy making me a cuppa? Your mother around?'

'Sure thing, but Mum's just popped over the back to see one of the neighbours for a bit of a chat. I think she feels she needs a change of scenery after what happened.'

Pete looked grave. 'I can understand that.'

Chris made the tea and the two men sat together on the verandah in the gathering twilight. There was not a breath of wind, and the remnants of the sunset glinted on top of the hills. In the valleys the temperature was cooling and a light mist began to form.

'It's still nice to have the occasional fire going at night, but you can sniff spring coming over the ridge,' said Pete, as Chris handed him his tea.

'I can never decide which season I like best,' agreed Chris. 'Maybe we could take the boat out for a bit of a fish soon.'

Pete sipped his tea. 'Sounds good. I remember when we used to go out fishing with your dad. We had some good times.'

'Do you take your sons fishing these days? Must be a nice thing to do.'

Pete smiled at him. 'It is, but I also know a bunch of kids who need a father figure in their lives, and I like to take them fishing, too. Maybe you could come out with us some time.'

'I will. I'd like that.'

They sat in silence for a few minutes, then Pete straightened up. 'This isn't just a social visit, Chris. I have some news for you.'

Chris gripped his mug at the tone of Pete's voice.

'That visit you had earlier today . . .' Pete paused. 'I got a phone call a few minutes ago. Carmichael drives a green Mark 2 Jag, right?'

'Yeah. That's the car he came here in,' said Chris.

Pete nodded. 'Well, a car matching that description just drove into a gully on Palmers Road. The driver took a corner too fast, it seems.'

Chris stared at Pete. 'And Carmichael, how is he?'

'He's dead.'

Chris was silent for a minute or so. Initially, all he could feel was relief. All those threats that Carmichael had made were now as nothing. He would never be able to carry them out. Then anger began to stir in him. Carmichael would never be made to face all those charges of corruption. His death meant that he had escaped the justice system.

'You're kidding,' Chris said finally, shaking his head. 'Man, this is a lot to take in. It's some surprise. I'd like Mum's and my involvement with Carmichael kept out of this, Pete. Only you know that he came to the house. It has nothing to do with this accident.'

'I don't suppose it has,' said Pete in a low voice. 'But maybe what happened was no accident. It's early days yet, and the accident unit are still investigating, but I have my doubts. The man was facing not only bankruptcy, but the prospect of spending years in gaol. Big comedown for a man of his standing, and he wasn't young, either.' The sergeant rubbed his chin. 'Maybe he didn't want to have to face any of it. Of course, we'll have to see what the accident guys have to say, and these things are not always conclusive. You might want to break the news to your radio station. It will be everywhere tomorrow morning.' Pete swallowed the last of his tea. 'Give your mum my regards.'

'Thanks for telling me, Pete. I'll let her know.' They shook hands and the sergeant left the house. Chris sat looking at his empty tea cup for a long time, not sure what to make of what he had just heard or how he should feel. Alan was gone and the episode was over, but Chris still felt puzzled. His family was safe, but they

433

would probably never know the whole truth about what happened.

As darkness fell around Neverend, Chris felt the stillness steal over him, comforting him as only home can.

*

As Sergeant Pollard had predicted, Alan's sudden death was a media sensation, and over the next few weeks more evidence came to light about Alan Carmichael's corrupt business practices.

'The tabloids are having a wonderful time trashing Alan's reputation,' said Chris, sitting companionably with Susan in the peaceful garden.

'I've noticed there have been questions as to why Alan had driven so far north,' said Susan. She and David had moved into their little cottage, but Susan usually popped in if she knew that Chris was at home.

'I've thought about things, and I don't know if Alan killed himself or was just so angry that he wasn't paying attention to the road,' continued Susan.

'I suspect we'll never know the answer to that. Why do you think he blamed us?'

'I think that Alan was simply not prepared to accept that the collapse of his business and the charges he faced were the result of anything he had done himself. He wanted to be able to blame someone else for the shambles his life had become, and that was us. Nonsense, of course – he brought it all upon himself – but he was never going to admit that. Threatening us made him feel in control, I suppose.'

'He certainly was in denial. I think men like Alan honestly believe that the law does not apply to them, only to lesser mortals,' said Chris.

Susan nodded. 'I've had a lot of long chats with Evan and Mark on the phone, and I've also had a call from Tom Anderson.'

'Really! What did he have to say?'

'He said it was all very unfortunate, and he was sorry his call to Alan had caused trouble for us. I didn't quiz him about his business dealings with Alan. I don't think that I really want to know all those details. Anyway, what he was really ringing to tell me was that he was going to further the education of some bright young Indonesian kids by setting up scholarships to allow them to attend some of America's leading business schools. The scholarships will be called the James Anderson scholarships. Jimmy would have liked that,' she said with a soft smile.

Chris nodded. 'That's impressive. A great thing to do.'

'I also rang Norma to let her know about everything.'

'What did she say?'

'She mentioned something about karma. She's heading back to Indonesia for a couple of weeks to check on the clinics she helped set up.'

'I would like to get up there myself sometime. I might go when Megan visits Jill at Christmas. Might see if Georgie wants to come with me. I'd like to go to Bogor, to see where you were.'

'I think it'll be very different from the place I remember,' said Susan. She looked across the lawn towards the vegetable garden. 'Now, are you across looking after the garden here? Those tomatoes have well and truly finished. You might want to think about planting some more pretty soon.'

'Yes, Mum.'

Susan chuckled. 'Oh dear, tell me to butt out. You're living here, so you do whatever you want, Chris.'

'It's fine. I'm still adjusting to being man-of-the-house and Megan misses you, but we're getting on very well, just the two of us. She's good company.'

'Yes, well, she's growing up. She'll be fifteen in just a few weeks. She doesn't want to hang out with her grandmother so much anymore. She's a bright, intelligent girl with lots of healthy interests.' Susan rested her hand on his arm. 'Chris,' she said earnestly, 'you're not sorry you came back, are you?'

'How could I be? Maybe it's not what I expected my life to be, maybe it's even better. I've got a good job and a book happening. I've become a solid fulltime father, not a token dad, and I have an amazing daughter. I have a beautiful, loving girlfriend. I've reconnected with the place I love. I've got great mates who are true friends, not just professional acquaintances. I have a mother who is not only very contented, but is actually in love with a very nice and interesting man. I'm living in a paradise. How bloody lucky am I!' He grinned broadly.

Chris walked with his mother to her car and gave her a kiss on the cheek.

'See you both on Sunday? Now the house is finished, David and I will be heading off to Italy in a couple of weeks, even if it is slightly out of season.'

'You'll have a ball, Mum.'

He watched her car turn out of View Street. All was quiet once more.

In the warmth of the sun, Chris closed his eyes, but he could still see in his mind's eye the green paddocks dotted with fat cows, the hills rising like protective green pillows, the river running under the bridge. It was a view he'd seen all his life and was forever imprinted on his heart.